GOTREK & FELIX:
KINSLAYER

The northmen were coming thick and fast from the river, drawn to the ring of steel and the Slayer's bellowed challenges. Felix sliced through a Kurgan's jack, then reversed his grip and sliced his blade back across the northman's throat in a red slash of arterial blood.

'I can't believe I actually missed this madness.'

'What do you... want?' Gotrek wheezed, parrying the stab of a knife, then punching the eye of his axe into its wielder's gut. The man doubled over, head parting company with his shoulders a moment later. 'Another... gold ring?' A hand-axe decorated with evil glyphs clanged off the flat of his blade. Gotrek elbowed the Kurgan in the face, kneecapped another, and sliced his axe through the belly of a third. 'Was Altdorf not exciting enough, manling?'

More Warhammer from Black Library

• THE END TIMES •

SIGMAR'S BLOOD
An End Times prequel by Phil Kelly

THE RETURN OF NAGASH
Josh Reynolds

• GOTREK & FELIX •

By William King
TROLLSLAYER • SKAVENSLAYER • DAEMONSLAYER
DRAGONSLAYER • BEASTSLAYER
VAMPIRESLAYER • GIANTSLAYER

By Nathan Long
ORCSLAYER • MANSLAYER • ELFSLAYER
SHAMANSLAYER • ZOMBIESLAYER
SLAYER'S HONOUR – *a novella*
SLAYER OF THE STORM GOD – *an audio drama*

By Josh Reynolds
ROAD OF SKULLS • THE SERPENT QUEEN
CHARNEL CONGRESS – *a novella*

By David Guymer
CITY OF THE DAMNED • KINSLAYER • SLAYER (2015)
CURSE OF THE EVERLIVING – *an audio drama*

By Jordan Ellinger
THE RECKONING – *a novella*

By Frank Cavallo
INTO THE VALLEY OF DEATH – *a novella*

Visit blacklibrary.com for the full range of Gotrek & Felix novels, novellas, audio dramas and short stories, as well as many other exclusive Black Library products.

WARHAMMER
THE END TIMES

DAVID GUYMER

GOTREK & FELIX

KINSLAYER

BLACK LIBRARY

For Rose

A BLACK LIBRARY PUBLICATION

First published in Great Britain in 2014 by
Black Library,
Games Workshop Ltd.,
Willow Road,
Nottingham, NG7 2WS, UK.

10 9 8 7 6 5 4 3 2 1

Cover by Slawomir Maniak.
Map artwork by Nuala Kinrade.
Additional artwork by Nicolas Delort and Winona Nelson.

© Games Workshop Limited 2014. All rights reserved.

Black Library, the Black Library logo, Warhammer, the Warhammer logo, Time of Legends, the Time of Legends logo, Games Workshop, the Games Workshop logo and all associated brands, names, characters, illustrations and images from the Warhammer universe are either ®, ™ and/or © Games Workshop Ltd 2000-2014, variably registered in the UK and other countries around the world.
All rights reserved.

A CIP record for this book is available from the British Library.

UK ISBN13: 978 1 84970 729 9

US ISBN13: 978 1 84970 730 5

No part of this publication may be reproduced, stored in a retrieval system, or transmitted in any form or by any means, electronic, mechanical, photocopying, recording or otherwise, without the prior permission of the publishers.

This is a work of fiction. All the characters and events portrayed in this book are fictional, and any resemblance to real people or incidents is purely coincidental.

See Black Library on the internet at

blacklibrary.com

Find out more about Games Workshop
and the world of Warhammer at

games-workshop.com

Printed and bound by CPI Group (UK) Ltd, Croydon, CR0 4YY

The world is dying, but it has been so since
the coming of the Chaos Gods.

For years beyond reckoning, the Ruinous Powers have coveted the mortal realm. They have made many attempts to seize it, their anointed champions leading vast hordes into the lands of men, elves and dwarfs. Each time, they have been defeated.

Until now.

In the frozen north, Archaon, a former templar of the warrior-god Sigmar, has been crowned the Everchosen of Chaos. He stands poised to march south and bring ruin to the lands he once fought to protect. Behind him amass all the forces of the Dark Gods, mortal and daemonic. When they come, they will bring with them a storm such as has never been seen. Already, the lands of men are falling into ruin. Archaon's vanguard run riot across Kislev, the once-proud country of Bretonnia has fallen into anarchy and the southern lands have been consumed by a tide of verminous ratmen.

The men of the Empire, the elves of Ulthuan and the dwarfs of the Worlds Edge Mountains fortify their cities and prepare for the inevitable onslaught. They will fight bravely and to the last. But in their hearts, all know that their efforts will be futile. The victory of Chaos is inevitable.

These are the End Times.

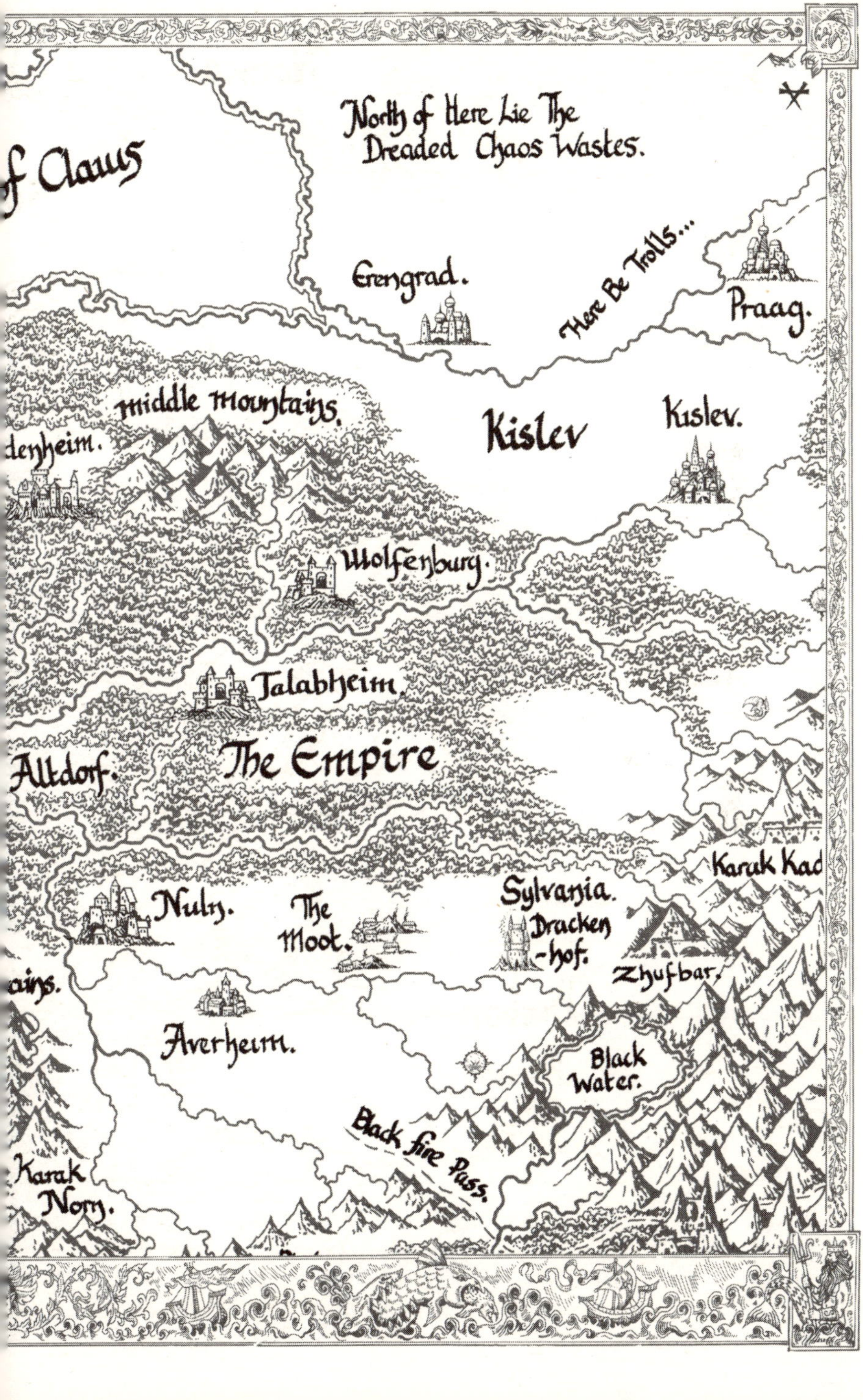

North of Here Lie The Dreaded Chaos Wastes.
f Claus
Here Be Trolls...
Erengrad.
Praag.
middle mountains.
denheim.
Kislev
Kislev.
Wolfenburg.
Talabheim.
Alltdorf.
The Empire
Karak Kad
Sylvania.
Nuln.
The Moot.
Dracken -hof.
Zhufbar.
ains.
Averheim.
Black Water.
Black fire Pass.
Karak Norn.

'Knowing the object of the Slayer's quest as I do, I have never laboured under the illusion that our friendship – if you could call it that – would last forever. Indeed we might both have had cause to bemoan ill fortune that our association had lasted as long as it already had when Gotrek and I finally parted ways.

'Many was the cold night that I had lain awake and dreamed of the day I would be free of his oath, and looking back I cannot blame myself for taking the chance of a settled life for myself and Kat when it was offered. And yet, it is only human to wonder what hurt might have been spared had we all left Karak Kadrin together that day. The truth that I cling to is that our paths have always seemed guided by unseen powers with a great destiny in mind. For how else could a dwarf so determined to seek death ever have survived so much?

'Does this mean that I can forgive him for what we did in Kislev?

'Though I try, I cannot. Perhaps I write this too soon after the event, but the End Times are upon us, and I fear that this grief will not fade in the short time we have left...'

– From *My Travels with Gotrek*, unpublished, by Herr Felix Jaeger

PROLOGUE

Autumn 2524

'It can't be done,' said Gotrek flatly, scooping up his tankard and sitting back, challenging the longbeard to convince him he was wrong.

Borek Forkbeard took a moment to consider his reply. It was not the way of longbeards to be hurried, and particularly not over so important a matter as this. The old dwarf sat quietly, thinking, polishing the lenses of his pince-nez spectacles with one white fork of his beard while the bustle of the inn went on around him. It was rough and dirty and the patrons were no cleaner. The dwarfs here were farmers, herders, and miners of what little lead and tin there was to be found in this part of the Worlds Edge Mountains. The longest faces were worn by a party of prospectors consoling themselves with a last drink before making the short return to Karaz-a-Karak. Through the open doors and windows, the grassy foothills basked in sunshine. Goats and hogs dotted the hillside. The Skull River was a sliver of sparkling light between two hills on the western horizon. Gotrek sipped his Bugman's – Borek was neither poor nor shy with his wealth – content to wait on the longbeard's mind. Snorri Nosebiter, however, had never been so patient.

'Snorri does not know what there is to think about.'

'Snorri wouldn't,' said Gotrek.

'Gotrek and Snorri will both be famous and rich, Snorri thinks.'

'Famous maybe,' said Gotrek. 'The famous fools who thought they could ride into the Chaos Wastes, find a dwarfhold two centuries lost and return with her treasures. Aye, we'll be famous all right.' He took another mouthful of Bugman's, then snorted and turned to Borek. 'And may shame find you, Forkbeard, for putting such ideas into this wazzock's head. He's a miner not a warrior and his mother wouldn't let him even as far as Everpeak for the ore market.'

Borek blinked at the rebuke, then cleared his throat and reset his pince-nez on his nose. 'This expedition is not without peril, you are correct, but it can be done. Every precaution has been taken.'

'These wagons of yours,' said Gotrek, sounding particularly unimpressed. 'Aye, you mentioned.'

'Protected by steel and rune, and driven by the power of steam alone.' The longbeard nodded to Snorri. 'We have plenty of strong arms and stout hearts, but I need good engineers in each wagon to keep the convoy together through the madness of the Wastes.' He removed his glasses again and fixed Gotrek with a stare as if laying down a challenge. 'Snorri tells me that you are one of the best.'

'Snorri tells you…' Gotrek muttered.

'Do it,' urged Snorri. 'It will be just like your adventures with Hamnir. Only with Snorri.'

'It's different now and you know it,' said Gotrek, though from the wistfulness in his tone it was clear that he was not at all as sure of his position as he wanted to be. 'I have a family to consider.'

'Will you at least promise to think about it?' said Borek.

Snorri grinned hopefully.

Gotrek scowled into his beer and drank. 'Fine, I'll think about it.'

* * *

Snorri stared into his empty tankard and let the earnest talk of Khaza Drengi, the Slayer Hall of Karak Kadrin, break upon the huge bulwark of his shoulders. He kneaded his knuckles into his temple and rapped on the bar for the attention of the steward. His memory was coming back.

He was going to need another beer.

PART ONE
OLD FRIENDS

Autumn – Midwinter 2524

ONE

Lost

Snow fell across the oblast in thumb-sized flakes, white-furred reavers of the frozen north. Where exactly these raiders ravaged, Marszałek Stefan Taczak could not say for this was the time of *raspotitsa*, of roadlessness, when hills, rivers, and whole *stanitsas* sank under a flat plain of featureless white. The remnants of the Dushyka *rota* reined in on either side, reduced by the blizzard to little more than mounted shades.

Nine men.

That was what remained of the cavalry *pulk* he had led into the Battle of the Tobol Crossing. Nine men. Beaten men. They rode slumped in the saddle, swathed but for their eyes in bloodstained cloaks and captured Kurgan furs. Their animal layers were flecked with white, like a froth of exhaustion, but a numbness of heart and body meant no man shivered. It was that same fatalism that granted each man a shot of satisfaction, like *koumiss* still warm from the mare's teat, at the fate that winter would soon share with the northmen. Raspotitsa returned the herdsman and the hunter to his *tirsa*, the merchant to his city and the warrior to his hearth, but to an army on the march it was death.

As fiercely as Stefan wished to see the closing of the year in such terms, he could not. There were no victors when Lord Winter marched to war.

'Thirty Kurgan, marszałek. All dead.'

Stefan's *esaul*, a beef and gristle man named Kolya, reined in his steed beside him. The mare, Kasztanka, responded numbly and Kolya clapped vigour into her neck and snow from her mane. He looked to Stefan. Blood flecked his blue eyes. He nodded once to the scene of butchery that had led Stefan to call a halt. In the lee of a rough horseshoe of banked snow, bodies and parts lay scattered around a doused firepit. A thin sheen of ice glimmered from the bodies where their warmth had melted the snow. Now they were cold. The snow slowly covered them, smothering the butcher's ruin as purblindly as it did roads and tirsas and the hideous skull dolmens of the Kurgan. This had happened recently.

They were gaining.

'The same as before,' Stefan murmured. Not a battle but a massacre. This was not war as he understood it. 'What did this?'

Kolya offered a *no matter* shrug. 'As the wise woman would say, marszałek, when the winter is hard the wolf will eat wolf.'

In the privacy of his face-scarf, Stefan smiled. It was easy to forget the huntsman who had used to paint stick-horses on stones to scatter wherever one of the oblast spirits had spooked poor, skittish Kasztanka. They were half-brothers, a blood relation as common as widowed mothers, and it was good to remember that the oblast had not always been this way. The northmen had come many times and always were driven back.

Kislev was the land and the land was Kislev.

Stefan looked up and squinted into the icicle teeth of the blizzard. The snow-swept vista stretched to the ends of his experience and beyond. It had suffered a grievous wound, perhaps more than one, but it still looked like Kislev to him.

Kolya made a clicking sound under his tongue and brought Kasztanka around to the right. She whinnied shyly, jumping into the high snow before settling into a walk as Kolya guided her around the edge of the Kurgan camp. There were more bodies, scattered, a breadcrumb trail leading north. Some of the northmen had tried to flee from whatever it was that had caught up with them. It had not done them any good. They had been beheaded, dismembered, taken apart by a monster so far beyond the abilities of an entire marauder warband that there was no evidence of *it* anywhere. Stefan fixed on a severed hand half buried in the snow. A hand-axe was still gripped in the blueing fingers. He felt a kind of gratitude for that. Many of the northern tribes shared the Norse belief that a warrior's spirit would forever roam unless he died with weapon in hand.

The north wind turned then, skirting the northmen's horsehoe wall and blasting both their faces with snow. It carried the coppery, obscenely sweet odour of recent death. The horses snorted anxiously. Kasztanka stamped her hooves and whinnied until Biegacz, Stefan's mount and a stablemate since birth, nuzzled his old companion and blew reassurance into her ear. Men of the southern cities liked to mock the bond between an oblast man and his horse, but few men loved an animal as Kolya loved Kasztanka. It was her, rather than his own blood brother, that was keeping the bold man Stefan had known alive.

'Marszałek!'

The shout cut through the blizzard with little warning of the horseman who cantered through, then reared to a standstill in a flurry of snow. Boris Makosky was younger than Stefan, had been a trapper making a decent living selling meat and fur to merchants from Praag before the incursion, but defeat had aged him. There was grey in his fringe and something feral never far beneath the surface when he spoke. Even when he did not, it was there in his eyes. If a man was brave enough to look.

'There are tracks that continue north. It is too heavy to be a man, but whatever else it may be it is a beast of two legs.'

'Can you not tell what it is from its tracks?' said Kolya.

'An ogre mercenary that fled the fall of Volksgrad, perhaps? One of the trolls that the Kurgan say now occupy Praag? We have seen worse migrating south.'

'But these tracks head north,' said Stefan. 'They follow the same warband as we do.'

Makosky shrugged angrily. 'What I can tell, I have told. If you want more then speak with Bochenek.'

That stung. The rota's scout was feeding the foxes of the last stanitsa they had found: the price paid for spotting the Kurgan ambush too late. Stefan said nothing. On the oblast, a man learned to conserve warmth any way he could and that included keeping his mouth shut when words were not welcomed. Instead, he glanced again to the ruined corpses, worrying what such a monster might do to the captives those Kurgan had taken with them. The capture of the wise woman, Marzena – who had clearly exhausted her good fortune when Kolya and Bochenek had heard her screams and rescued her from the beastman herd that had invaded her home in the Shirokij Forest – had hurt them all, but Kolya most of all. His brother had always been one to seek out omens in the shapes of clouds, to beseech the spirits before partaking of a spring, and to heed the wisdom of the Ungol hags.

Stefan shook his head grimly. Snow dropped from his brow. What kind of beast, though, would render such carnage and not even pick at the bodies it had left behind? Stefan did not like the inevitable option that that left.

Daemon.

He shuddered, reaching for the *szabla* scabbarded by his left stirrup.

'A man may seem brave when fighting sheep,' said Kolya, quoting another of Marzena's proverbs, 'but be a sheep when faced with brave men.'

Stefan drew himself upright in the saddle to regard his brother fully.

'I speak of the monster, not you,' said Kolya, the memory of a smile haunting his thin lips. 'These men were frost-bitten and half-starved. Their war leader left them behind while the bulk of his host continued north.' He indicated that direction with a nod. 'We ride on?'

'For our lost brothers,' said Stefan, spurring his mount around to face north. 'I would not leave any man in the hands of the Kurgan, and I certainly won't abandon an old woman.'

Kolya nodded, but Makosky's scowl merely darkened. The man seemed to come alive only in the heat of the hunt. The land was wide, with too few beastmen to be found roaming lost and starving on the steppe. Usually they were ridden down with relish.

Other times, they were made to *pay* for what they had wrought on Kislev.

Nothing that Stefan could think of short of a victory, however small, or the remote possibility of reuniting with the Ice Queen's pulk would rally his men's hopes.

'We are gaining,' said Kolya, then raised a hand to sweep over the dead. His manner was grim, barren of hope and glad for it. 'These men will not miss their furs now. When the horses are rested, we will bring the vengeance of Dushyka onto the Kurgan and their pursuer both.'

* * *

'Tell me of your adventures in Praag,' said the black-robed priest of Grimnir, walking barefoot through the soot and steam of Grimnir's foundry, deep within the halls of Karak Kadrin. The air was thick and black. It tickled the throat with the honest taste of coal and cushioned the clangour of hammers upon anvils and the hiss of bellows. Shrouded to their bare arms in the murk, visions of Grimnir himself at his fabled forge, a score of dwarfs worked their anvils with a single-mindedness that bordered on brutal. Their straining muscles crawled with tattoos and coursed with sweat. Not one of them spoke. It was just them, the iron, and the sanctity of the forge.

Snorri Nosebiter said nothing, for it was an old question, and merely watched as the priest padded in a circle behind his back, Snorri twisting in his chair to follow his progress as far as he could. The snap of taut leather arrested him and pulled him back into the chair.

Oh yes. Snorri kept on forgetting that.

He was secured into a high-backed wooden chair and, though it took a lot of leather to strap in a chest as massive as Snorri's, this priest was taking no chances. The stump of his right leg was laid out upon the anvil in front of him. He remembered that his old friend Gotrek Gurnisson had cut it off for him. He grinned in success at having remembered, but then almost immediately frowned.

Was he happy about that? Clearly he was still missing something.

'Snorri,' the priest prodded, circling back round to the front. He wore his black hair long and his beard forked, and walked with his hands clasped behind his back as he spoke. He wielded his voice with an authority as unsubtle as Snorri's hammer. His bare feet slapped the hot floor. 'I asked you a question.'

Snorri maintained his frown. He was here to remember, that much he remembered. Deep thought scrunched up his face. It was unique, even as faces went. It had taken so many beatings that bony regrowths knobbled his jawline and brow and his nose was flattened between his cheeks. One ear was a cauliflowered mess while the other had been torn clean away to leave a pinhole in the side of his head. Sometimes, when things got boring, Snorri could hear air whistle through it.

'What kind of name is Skalf Hammertoes anyway?' said Snorri.

'I was a ranger, and not a very good one. I do not hide from my shame as some might.' He looked askance towards Snorri. 'Praag.'

'Snorri does not remember.'

'I think that you do.'

Snorri watched the priest circle behind him once again. It was making him dizzy. He closed his eyes to think. Praag. He had travelled there with Gotrek and with young Felix on the airship, *Spirit of Grungni*, to fight Chaos. The fighting had been all right but he hadn't enjoyed the journey much. There had been too much time with nothing to do but think.

Snorri did not like thinking. It did not agree with him. It gave him memories.

As he thought now, back past that point, his mind flinched like a dog from an old master who had once been cruel. There was an old wound that was still buried there despite the years he had spent trying to forget. And now he was supposed to remember. Why?

Because he had promised, that was why.

He saw a dwarf woman and her child. He did not remember if the child was his but the regret, the anguish, that knotted in his chest at the memory told him that he had loved these two as if it were. The knot tightened. His heart was a lead weight on his lungs. He had killed them both. Or had he? But their deaths had been his fault. Yes, that was right. He could not remember.

'Interesting,' said Skalf, checking his stride. Snorri opened his eyes, blinking as if he had just had his head submerged in a barrel. The priest's lips twisted in amusement. 'You talk when you think, Snorri Nosebiter. I can only assume it is that thick skull of yours that has seen you through so many of our age's great battles.' Snorri beamed. 'I want you to tell me about the second time you visited that city, when you returned there without Gurnisson and the human. It was around then that your memory began to fail.'

The priest snorted at some private joke and Snorri bristled. This beardling priest was mocking him. By what Grimnir-given right? Something about being asked the question, though, made his mind go there. His skull ached. The three brightly coloured nails that had been hammered into his head in place of the traditional Slayer's crest throbbed. Pain threatened to flush his mind of hard memories, but he grunted and willed himself past it. He had made a promise. He owed Gotrek that much.

'Gotrek and young Felix disappeared into a magic door. When Max could not find them he and Snorri went back to Praag to fight Chaos some more.'

'This is Maximilian Schreiber? Your wizard friend?'

'Max is the wisest human Snorri knows. One time Snorri fell asleep in a bucket of vodka and when he woke up Max made his sore head go away.'

'Then perhaps he is not so wise,' Skalf snapped, 'for a hangover is Grimnir's way of making the last night's fools suffer.' The priest took a deep breath and went on. 'What did you and Max do in Praag?'

'Er...'

Snorri vaguely recalled the following summer as a sequence of disappointing skirmishes with beastmen and marauders with just the one halfway memorable battle with a champion's warband somewhere upriver. But he could not really remember that either. Then there had been that incident with the daemon-possessed violin that, even after he had sobered up, Snorri had thought sounded rather unlikely. Max was not the sort to make that kind of thing up, though. Not at all like that young rascal, Felix. He remembered being sad to have missed it. Then he remembered something that he had not before.

'Ulrika was there too, Snorri thinks.'

'The *zanguzaz*?'

'Oh, she wasn't a vampire then,' said Snorri, then paused to think. 'At least... er...'

'Doubt,' said Skalf with a grim half-smile. He unclasped his hands from behind his back, then laid them flat on the anvil by the stump of Snorri's leg. He leaned forward. His eyes were a hawkish amber. 'Doubt is progress, and progress is good. I think you have always wanted to forget.'

'Snorri thinks this priest is stupider than Snorri.'

'Gotrek and his rememberer were unique individuals,' Skalf pressed. 'They were possessed of a destiny I cannot pretend to understand. Their quests swept you along, Snorri, allowed you to forget your pain. But then one day they were gone, and you were left alone.' Snorri tried to pull away. There was a leathern moan and the strap buckle bit into his massive forearm. Of course, Snorri thought miserably, Snorri forgot. 'Pain is like gold. However deep you try to bury it, someone will always dig it up again.'

'Snorri thinks... Snorri thinks he would like a beer now. Or ten.'

'Of course you would,' said Skalf. He gestured towards someone that Snorri could not see. Snorri smacked his lips. They would probably be bringing beer.

Another Slayer strode through the smoke. He wore his hair in two crests, sharp red horns at the front but shaved down to the scalp at the back. His bare, muscular torso was a web of red and black tattoos. It looked like the musculature of a flayed body. But not a dwarf's though, Snorri realised, as the Slayer's face emerged from the smoke, painted into the snarling visage of a daemon. Snorri grasped instinctively for a weapon, causing his chair to rattle.

Acknowledging neither Snorri nor Skalf, the Daemonslayer dropped a large leather bag onto the anvil. It hit with an iron clank. The bag was open and Snorri glanced inside. In amongst the common hammers and tongs of the smith's craft, there rested an oddly proportioned spiked mace. There were no spikes at the very head of the weapon and there was no grip at all. The end of the handle where it should have been was flat and smooth and skirted with triangular iron flaps that were each punched through with eyelets. But nowhere in amongst it did Snorri see his beer.

'Snorri wants to know what you two are up to.'

The Daemonslayer laid his palm on Snorri's shoulder. Burning, bleeding ligaments and sinews crawled across the well-muscled arm, but the touch was not unkind. 'I owe you a debt, Snorri Nosebiter.'

'Snorri will take your word for it.'

'As you should, for my word is iron,' spoke the Daemonslayer, retrieving his hand so that he could devote both to removing the mace from his bag and laying it reverently upon the anvil. Hammer and nails followed and the Daemonslayer then positioned the smoothed-flat haft of the mace up against the stump of Snorri's leg. It was surprisingly warm and was a suspiciously good fit.

Snorri had a very bad feeling about this. He hoped he was going to get his beer sooner rather than later.

'That worm-eaten peg that the humans gave you to replace your leg is hardly fit for a son of Grungni,' said Skalf, but Snorri was having difficulty focusing on him. His gaze slid to where the Daemonslayer was making a ring of measured little guide nicks around his leg by scoring an iron nail through the meat. 'Surely the shame of it was the reason you refused your old companion, Makaisson, and remained here while he joined King Ironfist's throng for the march to Sylvania. Or could there be some other reason?'

'Snorri… cannot remember.'

Skalf snarled; the wrong answer. 'The von Carsteins rise again, Snorri. All of the blood-suckers. The king aligned himself with elves, *elves*, to fight them.' He looked to the ceiling and presented his open palms in dismay. 'Many Slayers found their dooms there in that mighty defeat. Even Makaisson did not return.'

Skalf nodded to the Daemonslayer, who then picked up a nail and threaded it through one of the eyelets at the junction of the mace-leg. It dug into Snorri's thigh. The Daemonslayer lined up his hammer.

'My name is Durin Drakkvarr,' he muttered. 'I owe you my life, and my death. On the lost halls of home I will see that you find yours.'

'This is going to hurt,' said Skalf.

'Can Snorri not have his beer first?'

Skalf stuffed a rolled up leather belt into Snorri's mouth. 'You have already had too much. That is the problem.'

From the corner of his eye, Snorri saw Durin swing his hammer. He tightened his eyes, bit down on the belt, and grunted as the Daemonslayer took his time striking nails through the eyelets of the mace-leg and into his thigh. The hammering from the nearby Slayers proceeded unabated. As if they did not hear.

When it was done, Durin laid a hand briefly on Snorri's shuddering shoulder, then diligently wiped up the few splatters of blood and put away his tools.

'Tell me of your "Spider Lady",' said Skalf, quietly, pulling the belt from Snorri's mouth as though nothing had just happened.

'Snorri is going to kill you when he gets out of this chair.'

'There is nothing darker than a kinslayer,' said Skalf calmly. 'Even threatening it is enough to earn your name in blood in a clan's book of grudges.' The priest shrugged. 'Lucky for you I have no family. Now answer my question.'

Snorri tried to think of something else, but couldn't stop his mind going where it was bidden.

Woods. Giant spiders in the trees. An old lady screaming.

'Snorri... saved an old lady in the woods. Big spiders... attacking her... Snorri... killed them all.'

'Slow down,' said Skalf. 'Take a breath.'

Snorri did as he was told and found it helped. 'They stung Snorri a lot and when he woke up, the old lady told him that he would not die yet. She said Snorri would have a great doom. Like Gotrek's.'

'And this destiny, is it to be found here within the temple of Grimnir?'

'Maybe,' said Snorri, disfigured brow knotting in concentration.

The old lady in the woods had said more, been more specific than he remembered, but it was gone now. *An old lady standing over him. She is sad. You will have the mightiest doom.* Even though it made his head hurt he tried to remember. He had made a promise. The harder he tried to remember though, the harder it seemed to be, like swatting a fly with a hammer. Thoughts of his supposed destiny always carried him nearer to memories of his shame, as if they were connected somehow. He wondered what Gotrek would do. They had been friends since before either of them had taken the Slayer oath. Perhaps he and Gotrek would both meet their ends together. That would be nice. It would make up for... for... He winced, his crest of nails throbbing in the roof of his brain.

'Snorri can't remember.'

The priest stroked his beard thoughtfully, took a considered breath, then directed a nod to Durin Drakkvarr. Snorri watched as the Daemonslayer produced a massive pair of tongs. Durin studied the straps holding Snorri down.

'These will not hold him for this.'

With a nod, the priest turned and whistled into the smoke. The two nearest Slayers looked up from their anvils, then downed tools and started towards them. Each took one of Snorri's arms and, at a hand gesture from Skalf, one of them put a hand over Snorri's brow to hold steady his head. The iron bite of Durin's tongs approached from behind, followed by a yawning silence, and then a pressure on his skull as the tongs clamped onto the first of Snorri's nails.

'Not those,' Snorri moaned. He strained against the two massive dwarfs, but they had him pinned. All he could move was his eyes. They rolled up to fix the Daemonslayer with a pleading gaze. 'Please.'

'Forgive me,' Durin whispered. 'But I owe you too steep a debt.'

'Grimnir takes sacrifice in the blood of his Slayers,' whispered Skalf. 'Malakai has gone. Gotrek has gone. It has been over a year now, Snorri, and still you cannot or will not recall.'

The priest nodded to the other Slayers to begin.

'And now Grimnir demands his due.'

'It was for your own good,' Durin growled over the low murmur of grim talk that permeated the pipe smoke of the Khaza Drengi. He glared straight down into the iron jug of ale that he circled with his hands. Red ink picked out the tendons and black emphasised the shadow. It was as though a daemon of blood and bone sought to crush that tankard with its bare hands.

The Daemonslayer did not drink and Snorri regarded both him and the dwarf's ale with equal glumness. Tentatively, he ran a hand across his head. His fingers brushed piggish grey bristle, and he winced as they passed over the scabbed-up punctures where his crest had been ripped out. It hurt as though he had jumped prematurely from a gyrocopter and been scalped by the spinning blades.

He glared at Durin, dunking his little finger into the mug of water in front of him and withdrawing it for inspection. His expression soured.

Snorri was not feeling especially forgiving just now.

At low-slung tables all around the hall, Slayers sat hunched, locked in conversation over the great battles being fought all over the Old World and drinking with the determination of those for whom tomorrow was an unasked-for concern. The tables were packed and half a dozen dwarfs stood with beers resting on the bar, trading boasts with the bar-dwarf for the day, a leather-faced old Slayer named Drogun in an ill-fitting white apron. At the other end of the bar, a sullen slab of dwarf called Brock Baldursson dished up meat paste and potatoes from a steaming pot. The hall was busier than Snorri had seen it all year and was filled with unfamiliar faces.

It was a sign of the times that Khaza Drengi was the last hall in Karak Kadrin to house more dwarfs than it had been designed to accommodate.

Two tables over, a pair of dwarfs built like battlements wrestled arms across the table. Snorri recognised one of them. Krakki Ironhame roared merrily, a large pie in one hand, as he nonchalantly inched his opponent's fist towards the tabletop. The Slayer's girth was mammoth, even for a dwarf, and his hair, a natural fiery red, produced a fat, undyed crest. The day the dwarf arrived from Karak Hirn on his way north, Snorri had broken his knuckles on that same 'lucky' table. They seemed to be better now, but Krakki did not appear to have got any nearer to Kislev.

Snorri turned back to Durin. The dwarf had still to touch his drink. It made Snorri angry just thinking about it going to waste.

'If you choose to dislike me, Snorri, I will understand. But I am trying to help you.'

Snorri scowled into his mug. 'Tell Snorri again why he can't have a beer too.'

'Because Skalf would not untie you until you vowed to renounce it, remember?'

Every word from the Daemonslayer's mouth sounded blank, emptiness coloured only by the dimmest grey of regret. It was impossible to hate a dwarf that sounded like that. It would be like trying to hate the dark. Snorri rubbed his head ruefully, and then his throat. He could not remember the last time he had been completely sober, but then that had always been the point. Some dwarfs got philosophical when they drank, others belligerent, but not Snorri. It made him numb and that was how he liked it. He shook his head, scratched the grey boar-bristles across his scalp as if he could scour his thoughts from his mind. Then, into that induced emptiness, popped an unrelated thought. He brightened immediately.

'Snorri remembers a human tavern called the Emperor's Griffon. Human beer doesn't count, does it?'

'It is still beer.'

'So they say,' Snorri grumbled.

The idea of never having another beer made his throat ache like the Arabyan desert, but forever was too big for him to deal with then and there. He wanted a drink *now*. He glared sulkily over the hard-drinking Slayers. If he could not drink then there was always the possibility of getting hit. The world was an ugly and unjust mistress and always looked better after it had knocked Snorri about the head a few times. Cheered by the prospect, he appraised the Khaza Drengi with a fresh eye. Brock Baldursson had the hard look of an old fighter, and Snorri had once seen Krakki punch out a priest of Grimnir with a set of freshly broken knuckles, but the rest were a disappointing bunch of scrawny-looking shortbeards that Snorri would not bet on in a fight with a goblin. He sighed.

'Snorri hopes he finds his doom very soon.'

Durin lowered himself to the table until he dropped into Snorri's eye line. 'I hope that for us both. I have sworn before the Shrine of Grimnir that you will find a worthy end.'

Snorri stared acidly at the other Slayer. He was not getting off that easily, not after he had stolen Snorri's nails and would not even let him have one beer to make up for it. 'Does that make you Snorri's rememberer then? Because Snorri doesn't need a rememberer.'

The Daemonslayer sat back and picked up his tankard as if considering his words with the care of a gemcutter over a rare stone. He took a sip, swallowing as if it might be his last. Snorri watched every twitch as it went down his throat.

'I am not your rememberer, Snorri, though clearly you need one more than most. I am just a dwarf with a debt.'

Intrigued now despite a stubborn will not to be, Snorri waded into the murky stew of his memory. He had journeyed with many fellow Slayers in his time, but most had already beaten him to their ends. Rodi Balkisson, although the details of it were hazy, had been slain by Krell at Castle Reikguard while his other recent companion Agrin Crownforger had fallen in battle with an entire beastman herd. Grudi Halfhand had taken the orc that had shamed him to a worthy end at the bottom of an ale barrel. Further back, memories became sharper and came quicker. Bjorni Bjornisson, the selfish bastard, had been cut down by that Chaos warlord during the siege of Praag, cheating both Gotrek and Snorri of mighty dooms while he was at it. Ulli Ullisson had fallen earlier that day. He thought back further. Grimme had been as sour as this Slayer, but the red tattoos and air of horror that clung to this one were wholly different. In any case, Snorri distinctly recalled Grimme being incinerated by a dragon, just moments before that dragon had gone on to crush another Slayer, Steg. Snorri chuckled. That one had made Snorri laugh.

It had been a good death. They all had. He sighed.

But not for Snorri.

'I am not surprised you do not remember me,' said Durin. 'And not just because of your problem.' For a moment, the dwarf's gaze was distant. His eyes seemed to widen, sinking into the black-inked pits of their sockets. He swirled his ale. 'There were many of us that you and your companions rescued from Karag Dum that day.'

Durin looked up to find Snorri staring intently at his face. The daemon's face he wore twisted into the first smile Snorri had seen on it. It was not, he decided, something he wanted to see again sober.

'The face of the Destroyer,' said Durin. 'Like you, it is difficult for me to remember. Like you, I must make myself if I am to follow my true path. How long before that which befell Karag Dum is the fate of all? The Chaos Wastes expand. Already daemons walk freely across the Troll Country.' Durin's words were growing louder and his face hotter as he continued. Behind him, there was a crashing of bone into oak and a thunderous eruption of laughter. Durin ignored it. 'I am leaving for Kislev, with you or without you. I will not be here when Karak Kadrin is caught by the Wastes. And be assured that it will be. I have lived through that once, and daemons will not hunt me through my own halls a second time!'

Durin was on his feet and panting with emotion. Snorri did not know what to say. He should probably want to punch him for suggesting Karak Kadrin might fall, but even Snorri knew that greater holds than her had fallen before and would fall again. Durin Drakkvarr came from one of them. He shook his head. Tempting as it sounded, he wanted to remember his shame first. He had promised.

Except he did not want that at all. He wanted–

He hung his head.

Valaya's sweet breath, he wanted a beer.

'Snorri!' The shout from the arm-wrestlers' table startled Snorri from his thoughts. Krakki Ironhame thumped on trunk-legs towards them. 'Grimnir's britches!' he laughed. 'Did you lose a wager or did you just walk underneath Malakai's Magnetic Rune? Hah! You look old without your crest. I barely recognised you.' The fat dwarf gave Snorri a mighty smack across the back. Snorri's nose wrinkled. Even at the best of times, Krakki smelled like sweaty pork that had been left the week to marinate in ale. These were not the best of times. 'But I like the leg.'

Snorri's mace-leg thunked into the flagstones as he remembered it was there. 'Snorri is getting used to it.'

Krakki's grin slowly faded as he took in the contents of Snorri's mug. 'What in Gazul's damnation is this?'

Snorri sagged miserably into the table. Whoever said that thing about misery and company had definitely not been a Slayer. 'Snorri made an oath.'

'Then maybe I can piss in that mug for you, Nosebiter,' Krakki laughed, belly rippling with coloured tattoos. 'My water's richer than anything drawn from the wells of Karak Kadrin.'

'An oath is an oath,' said Durin, softly spoken yet deathly serious as though arguing in his sleep. 'It is not to be mocked.'

Krakki jerked his thumb over his shoulder in the direction of the Daemonslayer. 'Friend of yours?'

Snorri pulled a face. 'Snorri would not go that far.'

With a shrug that suggested he had not really cared either way, Krakki helped himself to a chair and deposited his bulk into it. There, he leaned in, as though sharing a secret for Snorri and Durin alone. 'You speak of Kislev,' Krakki boomed and Snorri winced, wondering if the dwarf thought Snorri could not hear properly with one ear. With horror, Snorri wondered how Krakki would sound through two. 'And you are not alone, but first you have to worry about getting there. The Underway north of here is overrun with beastmen. They even drove the goblins out, bless their evil green hearts.'

'We will clear them,' said Durin.

'Good for you,' said Krakki, then mimed a *wazzock* gesture with a finger looping over his temple and returned to Snorri. 'The manlings kindly allowed the Chaos hosts to march right over them and now they've nothing better to do than find and break all the Underway gates they find. A runesmith led an expedition of Ironbreakers and Slayers under the humans' fort at Rackspire to reseal the ways, but he was captured by beastmen and carted off to Praag. Or so the survivors of his throng say.' He glanced at Drogun, fiercely polishing tankards behind the bar.

'Wait,' said Snorri. What Krakki was saying chimed with something that Durin had been trying to tell him before. What was it? He scratched the pinhole where his ear had once been, slowly coming to a conclusion so stupid it could only have come from Snorri's own head. 'Kislev can't have fallen,' he said slowly. 'Kislev men fight almost as well as they drink. Snorri likes them.'

Krakki smacked the table and barked with laughter. 'You have been buried in Khaza Drengi too long! Here, give me that troughwater they're feeding you.' The Slayer took Snorri's mug, and then Durin's too, spreading them apart on the table. With a frown, he bellowed to the bar. 'Drogun! Bring me that old clay tankard, the ghoul-ugly one.' Krakki waited, drumming his sausage-fingers on the table while the leathery old Slayer came grumbling over and stamped the requested vessel onto the table. It was indeed ugly. Gargoyles leered from every side of it and the handle had been shaped to look like bone. Why anyone had ever made such a thing, Snorri could not guess.

'This is Praag,' said Krakki, positioning the gargoyle mug in front of him 'Obviously. It was sacked months ago by a warlord named Aekold Helbrass, only he got pushed out of Praag by some other warlord, leading a horde of trolls so they say, and continued south.' Here, he placed his huge palm over Snorri's mug. 'This one, being piss-weak, can be Kislev city. Their queen tried to catch the Chaos horde as they forded the Lower Tobol.' He shook his head grimly and took his hand back. 'Helbrass crushed them. Their city fell soon after.'

'Sounds bad,' said Snorri. He liked Kislev. He had had some good fights there and liked their vodka. He did not want to think that it could have been destroyed without him even realising the fight had started. And also, he was almost certain that Kislev city had been where Gotrek had been headed. 'Does anyone still fight?'

Krakki sat back, big eyes rolling to indicate the sullen potman behind the bar. The dwarf noticed the attention, but merely grunted and continued to stir his stew. 'Brock Baldursson was on the Tobol Crossing that day with a throng of the Kislevite clans. It takes something to drive a dwarf from his home and Brock won't say much, but it sounds like Helbrass unleashed a special kind of hell that day.' Krakki's eyes lowered, voice dropping to a rumble. 'Of course, he wasn't a Slayer then.'

'And Helbrass?' murmured Durin. 'What became of him?'

'It's not as if he's anywhere to go but south, but there's no one left to tell of it.' Krakki pointed then to Durin's mug. 'Erengrad. She still stands, but has been essentially annexed by the Empire. And she's on the other side of the Auric Bastion.'

'The what?' said Snorri.

'That'd take some explaining,' Krakki laughed. 'What matters is it's keeping the enemy good and hot. They've nowhere to go so there'll be plenty waiting for us once we've cleared the Underway.'

'What is... here,' said Snorri, jabbing his finger into a knot in the table. It fell just to the left between 'Kislev' and 'Praag' and just looking at it made Snorri's head feel funny.

'There's nothing there,' said Krakki, gently. 'That's just the table. Try to pay attention, Snorri.'

Snorri stared at it anyway. *You will have the mightiest doom.* Spindly brown legs split out into the oak from a dark core. *Spiders in the trees.*

'But Helbrass?' Durin pressed again.

'Better question,' said Krakki, leaning back against his chair and grinning like a half moon. 'What threw the conqueror of Kislev out of Praag?'

Praag, thought Snorri, letting the Slayers' talk fade into the whistle through his torn ear. It always seemed to come back to Praag. It was a city full of memories, and despite the certainty of battle and death he found that he was not at all eager to return there.

'Snorri,' Krakki's voice dragged him up by his working, cauliflower ear. 'If I didn't know better, I'd say you looked scared.'

With a sad grin, Snorri went back to staring at the knot in the table. *An old lady standing over him. She is sad. She is… angry.* Snorri shook his head. Scared? He was outright terrified and the fact he was not certain why did not help at all. The image of that dwarf woman and child rose in his thoughts. He could smell burning, feel blood on his hands. He scrunched his eyes and tried to think of something else. There were too many memories and the priest had been right. Snorri did not want any of them.

The thought of those ghosts following him from Khaza Drengi and catching him alone on the wastes of Kislev petrified him far more than dying in shame.

Slowly, Snorri unclasped his fingers from around his mug and dragged them to the lip of the table. There, his fingernails crunched into the ancient wood and he pushed himself until he stood eyeball-to-eyeball with Krakki Ironhame. His new mace-leg thunked against the stone floor. Krakki met Snorri's eyes, his ginger brows lifting questioningly. Snorri wanted a drink. His head ached for the need of it. Without breaking eye contact, Snorri reached for his mug, brought it to his lips and tossed it back. A shock of mountain water struck the back of his throat. Snorri's eyes widened. His throat tightened in protest, but it was too late. Snorri gave a gargling sound as the dregs drained into his belly.

And just like that, Krakki began to laugh.

That's it, thought Snorri. Snorri has had enough.

Muscles bunched through his neck and shoulders, then exploded forward, sending his forehead crashing through Krakki's nose. Blood spattered from the fat Slayer's face and he tipped back, spinning on nerveless toes before smashing full-on through the end of a table of feasting Slayers. The other end of the table swung up, swiping the bowls from under the dwarfs' noses and catapulting gravy and ale across the hall. Leaving the shouting dwarfs and Krakki's poleaxed body to their own devices, Snorri slumped back down into his chair. He wiped a piece of beef gristle from his head.

That had not been nearly as satisfying as he had hoped it would be.

It seemed that there was nothing for it but to go to Praag and die as quickly and as gloriously as was still possible. It was what the old lady had promised, what everyone seemed to want. Everyone except Snorri, of course, but when had that ever mattered? He had always followed others, ever since that first trip into the Chaos Wastes. That had been before he and Gotrek had both become Slayers, before he–

His jaw clenched.

No. He would not remember that.

A proper fight was what he needed. The priest was right about that too. And at least Kislev was where Gotrek and Felix must be. They had a marvellous knack of being where the fighting was fiercest. They were both just lucky that way. He looked up over the wreckage of the table, heart sinking at the sight of Durin picking his way through it to fetch him another mug of water. He let out a long, resigned breath.

The End Times could not come soon enough.

TWO

Jaeger and Sons

The Kurgan marauder stumbled through the shin-high snow and slush that banked the partially frozen river. A white skeleton of frost filled the lines between his armour's leather plates, the pieces haloed in turn by snow-sodden furs. His eyes were bloodshot. His greased face bore the scars of a torturous journey, over the Frozen Sea and across the Worlds Edge Mountains, all for this one chance at the soft lands of the south. The man fell to his knees. His voice raised a bitter scream as Felix Jaeger planted his boot into the Kurgan's chest and wrenched the glittering runesword from his belly.

Felix backed off, sword raised into a guard as the northman tumbled away to the river. The sound of ice water slushing against the rocks drove under the howl of the wind. A collection of burned-out cottages poked out of the snow where the land abutted the water. The snow fell thick and heavy and he blinked around in confusion. He could not seem to recall how he had got here. His confusion faded with the intrusion of battle. It was coming from all around. Felix tightened his two-handed grip around the dragonhead hilt of Karaghul. The Templar blade had never fit so perfectly into his hands.

There was meaning here, even if it did not extend beyond the reach of his blade or the next second of his life.

His eyes were starting to throb, so hard had he been staring into the blizzard, but he dared not blink. Who knew how many northmen were out there? Felix watched the thick flakes fall. He could not keep his eyes trained any longer. He blinked.

'Manling! To your left.'

Felix jerked, shot his gaze left, and swept Karaghul across his body to parry the heavy *berdish* axe that hacked for him through the snow. The two weapons clashed apart, but Felix had been on the receiving end and his knuckles took the worst of the impact. He spun aside as the axeman came on in a storm of white fur and seal-blubber breath. Felix parried, danced back, set his feet and angled his blade for a flawless *nebenhut* guard to catch the overarm slash that the Kurgan's posture screamed was coming next.

But the steppe barbarian was no student of fencing and in truth Felix's own body was no longer as quick as he remembered it being. The northman gave a berserker howl and, rather than slash his axe back, turned his great strength to control the weapon, swing it up and stab the spear-like point on the eye of the blade at Felix's breastbone. Felix cried out in surprise and flung his sword across the path of the blow. It hit flat into the haft of the axe, deflecting it instead onto Felix's face. He ducked and turned aside, then watched the heathen weapon stroke an inch past his eye and impale the flapping red Sudenland wool of his cloak.

Felix dug his heel into the bigger man's foot, then punched him in the throat as he doubled over. The Kurgan staggered back, but held onto his axe and dragged Felix by the cloak along with him. With a guttural curse, the warrior yanked on the haft, throwing Felix sideways before beating at him with the flat of the blade. A tavern brawler's instinct hunched Felix into a foetal position and the blade passed overhead. He gave a muffled cry as the move swept his own cloak over his head and the world turned red.

For an instant, all Felix could feel was panic. His heat pounded, his muscles falling slack as if to ease the passage of the Kurgan's axe, but it could not have lasted more than a second. He could feel the presence of the northman's body tangled up with his, the warrior refusing to let go of his weapon even though it was still caught in Felix's cloak. His side was pressed into Felix's chest. Felix needed no second invitation.

He knifed his knee into the proximate area of the northman's kidneys. The muffled grunt of pain that elicited was sweeter than a harp's strings. The grip on the axe loosened, enough for Felix to bring up his sword and thrust it straight through the taut red wool and into the northman's chest. There was a wet cry and the opposing weight fell away.

Felix shook his cloak back over his shoulders. A fresh blast of freezing air welcomed him back with an icy slap in the face as Felix kicked aside the berdish axe and silenced the northman's gurgling with a swift stab through the throat.

Clearly the Kurgan had never worked Nuln's seedier taverns.

A dozen fur-clad marauders were advancing through the ruins by the river. Felix could hear more battling out of sight, but he tried not to worry too much about those. Chances were he was not going to live to have to deal with them. To his surprise, the thought left him oddly elated, as if there could be nothing finer than dying on this nameless snowfield today.

A brute howl pulled his gaze back from the ruins. There in the snow, a sanguinary blur of starmetal silver and ink-strapped muscle hacked through a score of barbarian northmen. Gotrek Gurnisson fought in a ring of bodies and human debris. Despite wearing nothing above his tattered trews but piercings and spiralling blue tattoos the dwarf gave no care to the cold as, with a roar like a collapsing cliff, he swung an axe that a man would struggle even to lift and severed a northman's leg below the knee. The marauder, meeting the bone-hammer of Gotrek's knuckles, was dead with a snapped neck before his knees were fully bent. Gotrek roared for more and more came. At their head strode a warrior in a ringmail hauberk with a white bear cloak and an antlered helm. The northman's bare arms were heavy with trophy rings. He spun his twinned axes in anticipation as he chanted some guttural gibberish about his deeds and his gods. One blade left a crimson trail of power through the air it cut.

A champion.

Felix had seen Gotrek dismantle such arrogance a hundred times, but as the two warriors joined it became clear that Gotrek was struggling. The dwarf looked as though he had been fighting without relent for days. Somewhere along the road he had lost his eye patch and gore bled from the gaping socket. Cuts and bruises coloured his skin as if they and his tattoos fought a contest to see which could take the greater portion of the Slayer's flesh. A pair of arrows stuck out of his chest. The shafts were thick, garishly fletched in the Kurgan style, and had been fired from their powerful recurved composite bows. Had Felix taken a shot to the heart like that he would have been dead before he knew what hit him, but Gotrek's slab-like chest was tough as tempered steel and sterner protection than Felix's mail vest any day. But still, they slowed him.

Slipping the Slayer's guard, the champion dragged his blade across Gotrek's chest, adding a deep score to the tally and bringing a spurt of blood. The Slayer howled, throwing the Kurgan champion off and driving him back with a storm of blows. His starmetal blade slammed deep into the northman's gut. The not-so-favoured of the Chaos Gods regurgitated blood, choking on that last mouthful as Gotrek flung him from his axe and into those that came roaring in behind.

With a yell, Felix cut down the last Kurgan between him and the Slayer, hurdled the northman's corpse and, turning mid-leap, slammed into Gotrek's back to beat down a northman axe that had been destined for his unguarded shoulders. There was a strange thrill, the feeling like that of wielding one's first practice blade and finding it achingly familiar but not quite as remembered. He parried another attack, feeling Gotrek's massive shoulders grind over his as the dwarf carried on doing what no one did better. Felix ducked a swinging adze, parried a sabre. The northmen were coming thick and fast from the river, drawn to the ring of steel and the Slayer's howls.

Kislev, Felix realised, with the sudden clarity of ice-cold Kurgan steel, and that river was the Lynsk. He had seen it often enough from Praag's Gate of Gargoyles and could not count the times that his dreams had returned him to this spot since. It was as though his subconscious would not believe he had survived that battle, as if he was living on borrowed time. Felix laughed.

He did not know why exactly, but this whole situation was surreal. If he was in Kislev then he must also be behind the Auric Bastion, the magical barrier that had been erected to hold back the Chaos hordes.

And trapped in Kislev with those very same hordes!

No wonder Gotrek looked so awful. The Slayer regarded Felix, laughing as he parried and fought, as if he had gone mad. Talk about pots calling kettles black. His laughter turned melancholy as he sliced through a Kurgan's hide jack, then reversed his grip and sliced his blade back across the northman's throat in a red slash of arterial blood. Well, thought Felix, spitting Kurgan blood from his gums, you have to laugh don't you.

'I can't believe I actually missed this madness.'

'Less... talk,' Gotrek wheezed, parrying the stab of a knife, then punching the eye of his axe into its wielder's gut. The man doubled over, his head parting company with his shoulders a moment later. 'Don't fall for want of a breath and miss my...' A hand-axe decorated with evil glyphs clanged off the flat of his blade. Gotrek elbowed the Kurgan in the face, kneecapped another, and sliced his axe through the belly of a third. '...my doom.'

'Wouldn't miss it for the world,' Felix said. And by Sigmar he really meant it.

'The world's ending, manling. Or hadn't you noticed?'

Felix ceded the point, parrying a sword thrust then offering a counter that left a northman one hand the poorer. The next time someone suggested he spend a winter campaign in the north of Kislev he would know exactly what to tell them. Assuming of course there was going to be a next time for anything. He glanced up at a rumble from within the blizzard. Hoof beats.

'*Gospodarinyi!*'

A single horseman swaddled in sheepskin and hemp galloped from the blizzard, guiding a shaggy Ungol pony by the stirrups as he drew back on a recurved bow. Coloured tassels shivered from the bow's tips as the rider loosed. The feathered shaft zipped through the falling snow, and smacked through the Y-shaped opening of a marauder's bull-horned barbute with a ferocious *clang* as the metal head exited the back of the man's skull and struck the inside back of his warhelm. The marauder spasmed backwards as though his corpse was trying to work out how to run before he was dashed against the breast of the careening pony. A second Kislevite horse-archer chivvied his horse through the shank-high snowdrift, screaming 'Yhah!' at the top of his lungs and drawing back on his own bowstring.

The arrow flew over Gotrek's shoulder and took his assailant through the heart. Gotrek howled pure frustration and beheaded the dying northman. Another centaur-like shadow breezed in false-silence through the blizzard and charged into the disordered northmen. What had seemed a certain massacre became a rout. The Kurgan were running and the Kislevites yipped and urged their steeds on to give chase.

Gotrek growled and sank to one knee. He caught himself on the haft of his axe and pushed himself back up. Felix offered no help. He could not have supported the Slayer's weight even if he thought his aid would be welcomed. The Slayer met his look and nodded grimly, lowering his own axe at last.

'Aye, manling. I thought I had it for a moment there.'

Felix smiled. He doubted there were many men who could understand why a dwarf might be less than thrilled at surviving such a battle, but Felix and Gotrek had shared much that was unusual. They were as near to friends as it was possible for members of two such different races to be. And strangely enough, he had come to share his companion's disappointment. 'There'll be more out there.'

Gotrek's grim look passed and he chuckled, running the pad of his thumb down the edge of his axe until it produced a bead of blood. It was one of the few parts of the Slayer's body that was not already bleeding. 'It is the end of the world, after all.'

'That's the spirit,' said Felix.

Man and dwarf both turned towards the Lynsk as the tramp of hooves and the jingle of tack turned from the pursuit and galloped towards them. Just from the sound of it, Felix could tell that it was a larger beast than the rugged steppes ponies ridden by the horse-archers. The runes of Gotrek's axe painted the falling snow a baleful red as he watched a snow-white Reikland destrier trot into view. It carried the nobility of its breeding with the force and assuredness of an emperor. It deserved a satin caparison, a harness of pure silver, and a knight in shining full plate, but somehow the warrior austerity of its leather saddle and tack was appropriate. And the woman who reined it in and turned towards them was as striking in her own way as any knight of the Reiksguard.

She was almost as tall as Felix and, though unhelmed, garbed in a gleaming haubergeon crafted from lamellar plates of white steel. Knee-high leather riding boots encased her legs. Despite the cold she wore neither hat nor gloves and her pale skin was laced with blue veins. He looked up, already knowing whose face he would see.

This was a dream.

The realisation was as sudden as it was obvious. It hurt like a blow to the ribs.

Of course it was a dream.

The woman looked down from the saddle, chin tilted proudly upwards. Her short hair was blonde as ash and railed against the wintry conditions of her homeland. She had not aged a day. The Slayer hefted his axe warningly.

'What's *she* doing here?'

Felix had no answer. Assuming that this was a dream, then her presence was obviously his doing. Unfortunately it was one thing to recognise that one was dreaming and quite another to act on that knowledge or make sense of it. He had loved her, would always love her, but she had been lost. The pain struck him like new. He had lost so many good friends while he and Gotrek ploughed on, but none still hurt him in the same way that she could.

The woman bared sharp, inhuman teeth. Her smile was colder than the oblast and more feral than any Kurgan. Dream or no dream, Felix felt sure that she, if no one else, still knew how to hurt him.

His surroundings began to slip away. Gotrek's scowl sank into blackness. The horse-archers and the ongoing battle grew distant and dim and even the cold was blunted before it reached his skin. He tried to cling onto it, even the cold, but it was as if there were cracks in his very soul, like some ancient Nehekharan urn that would leak empty as fast as it could be filled.

No, he thought, sensing wakefulness like a remembered dream. No, there is nothing for me there.

'Ulrika!'

'It is all right, Felix,' the vampire smiled. 'I will wait for you.'

Weak autumnal sunlight slanted through the casement window and across the oak desk where Felix's face lay on its side and half buried in parchment. The early strains of arguments and of passing horses intruded from the street beneath his window. The study in his family's Altdorf home was east-facing – the better for Felix to suffer early – and hateful little splinters of light shot off the uneven glass into his eyes. Felix buried his face under his arm with a groan, disturbing his delicate filing system and sending parchments sheeting to the floor. Eyes duly covered, he sank deeper over the desk. It smelled of iron gall ink, tannins from leather bindings and, from a more recent spillage, of sweet apple schnapps.

His dream was a world away, but it remained so vivid he could still feel the snow on his face and the weight of Karaghul in his hands. His thumping skull made him grimace. He certainly ached as if he had just spent the night painting the oblast of Kislev red. This, he concluded, though arguably several hours too late, was what became of men his age drinking themselves to unconsciousness upon their desks.

Grudgingly, he withdrew his arm from his face. The unkind sunlight glanced off the band of dwarf gold on his ring finger. He studied it like a man hypnotised. Angular dwarfish script ran around the outside. With his thumb, he turned the ring around his finger, watching the sun highlight one rune after the next. He never had asked Gotrek what it said.

This is my life now, Felix thought.

He wondered if there was any schnapps left in the bottle.

'Felix?' The voice was the hangover that followed the excesses of his dream. It was a woman's voice, but not at all like Ulrika's. The accent was that of a Drakwald peasant rather than of a boyar's daughter and had not the noblewoman's confidence or strength. 'I know you're awake, Felix. I can see your eye is open.'

Kat.

Felix grunted something that he had intended to be intelligible and levered himself up from the desk and into the back of his chair. The sudden rush of blood to the right side of his face made him wince.

Kat held by the study door. She had been young once, still was really, twenty years Felix's junior, but their battle with Heinrich Kemmler had worn her. Her skin was drawn, her hair brittle like straw. The brown of her eyes seemed to be sinking into the white. The Bretonnian silk chemise she wore had been a sumptuous fit when it had belonged to his brother's wife, Annabella, but on Kat it draped like a robe. That Felix had recovered from the lichemaster's magic while she did not was a mystery that baffled every physician in Altdorf. Even Max Schreiber had been at a loss. She bit her lip, as if there was something she wanted to say, but she would not meet his eye. Instead, her gaze took in the clutter of manuscripts, books, dropped clothes and old plates. Annabella called it his 'hermitage'.

'Is something the matter?' said Felix when she still did not look inclined to move or speak. Irritation took over. Had she woken him from a good dream just to stand there and judge?

'You never talk about Ulrika,' said Kat and as soon as Felix heard that name on her lips, he groaned under his breath and looked to bury his face in his hands. He must have mumbled it in his sleep.

'Just a dream,' Felix muttered into his fingers.

'Do you dream of her often?'

Felix dragged his fingers from his face. Stubble scratched his palms. Sigmar, how long had it been since he had shaved?

It had been years since he had last seen Ulrika, and their involvement, even when he could still call her human, had not ended on the most cordial of terms. He took a deep breath, as if he could still smell the sweat and horse of her from his dream. His heart danced. Yet all it took was one dream.

'I told you that she... died. I couldn't save her. I don't like to talk about it. I can't help my dreams.'

Kat nodded slowly, looking as though she meant to press, before hugging herself around the chest and taking strength from it. Periodically they would have this argument or one like it. Felix had experienced so much, while she had been struck down in her prime. Sometimes Felix forgot that it must hurt her more than it hurt him. Guilty, he turned back to his desk as though nothing was currently more crucial than unscrunching these balls of parchment and ordering them into neat piles.

From behind his turned back, there came a shiver of silk as Kat shifted from the doorway. A sheet of parchment crunched underfoot. An empty bottle fell over and rolled across the carpet. Felix winced, steeling himself for a lecture.

'We missed you at dinner,' said Kat.

'I was busy,' said Felix, indicating the sprawl of papers without looking up. Much as it might have amazed him twenty years ago, Imperial propaganda did not write itself. At the touch of a hand upon his shoulder he softened slightly. He covered it with his own, then drew it to his lips to kiss her fingers. Kat's wrists were so thin he could see where the flesh sank between the radius and ulna bones. Felix sighed. He had spent too much time speaking with Kat's anatomists and physicians.

'You didn't come to bed again.' Kat leaned forward, ran her fingers through his soiled cloak and sniffed his lank blond hair. Her nose wrinkled. Kat seemed peculiarly sensitive to bad odours lately. 'At least put some clean clothes on. You reek like a sewer.'

Taking a deep breath, knowing there were things that Kat hated more than his drinking, Felix nodded towards the chart that had been tacked to the plaster wall behind his desk. To the uninitiated it was nothing but a tangle of blue lines and strange symbols. To the more erudite, however, it would have been apparent that there was an order amongst the scrawl that resembled the layout of Altdorf's main streets. There was Karl Franz Avenue, and there Hans Josef Street, and when looked at through that lens, the gulf that split the diagram roughly into thirds could only be the confluence of the Reik and the Talabec that separated the islands of Altdorf into equivalent portions.

It was the most complete map of a city's sewer system that existed anywhere in the Empire and probably anywhere else but the dwarfholds themselves. Felix had commissioned it himself and had mapped some of it personally. More than he let on in fact, but what Kat didn't know...

'I hope you found something this time?'

Felix sighed and slumped back into his chair. He dragged a sheet of parchment – scribbled with the worst kind of populist bile he had ever seen – from the desk, scrunched it up and idly tossed it at the map. 'Nothing but rats. The sewerjacks Otto hired are either blind or every last skaven has abandoned Altdorf.'

'Or they were never down there.'

'Don't you start,' Felix snarled. 'It's bad enough that Otto still clings to that fantasy. Even after what they did to father.'

'I'm not saying they don't exist,' Kat snapped back. 'I'm just saying that in all my years tracking beastmen, I never saw one of these ratmen.'

'And just how many years was that?' Felix cut in.

'*Maybe*,' said Kat, Felix's acid only making her harder, 'the city you found under Nuln was for a special purpose. Maybe after you and Gotrek defeated them they retreated from the Empire, or–'

'Kat!' said Felix, raising a hand to ward off any more. Kat looked stunned and he realised he had shouted. 'I swore an oath to punish the vermin that murdered my father. It's the *one* thing I still have that I...' Felix caught himself and very deliberately clammed his mouth there. Kat just stared at him, willing him to say what they both knew was on his mind. His frustration was no fault of hers. She was sick. It was the guilt that poisoned him. He felt like a murderer who had cheated another into his noose on some legal technicality. After he had seen Snorri safely to Karak Kadrin, Gotrek had honoured his own promise and released Felix from his oath. Felix had been perfectly entitled to his decision, but no one had forced him to return with Kat to his brother's charity and leave his companion to seek his doom alone.

These were Felix's troubles, not Kat's. He had made an oath to her too, after all. Instead, he took a handful of parchment sheets and shuffled them loudly. 'Sorry, Kat, but I do have real work to do as well. I wouldn't want Otto to throw me out again.'

'Fine,' said Kat. 'But Otto and Annabella have asked after you and I told them you would join us for breakfast. So you'd better.'

'I will,' Felix muttered.

'Fine,' Kat breathed, turning to leave just as Felix's brother, Otto, burst though the study door.

'Felix, I–' Otto's fleshy nose recoiled and he drew back as though personally affronted by the odour. 'You really do live in here, don't you? I had thought that Annabella was merely exaggerating for effect.' He took a breath that set his jowls to shuddering, unaccustomed by the exertion of limping up the two flights of stairs from his study to Felix's. Despite the hour, Otto was fully dressed in robes of velvet and brocade accoutred with folly bells and a glittering satin sash. A gold-topped walking cane wobbled in the grip of one pudgy hand while the other held a clutch of rain-splotched letters. Politely, he bowed to Kat, an excuse to eye the improperly-covered neckline of the younger woman's chemise. Not for the first time Felix wondered whether it was only brotherly love that had behoved Otto to set aside grievances and take them in when they had turned up on his doorstep a year ago. Otto swallowed heavily and returned his attention to Felix. 'Why are you still not dressed?'

'Because I can write as well in yesterday's clothes as in anything else.'

'Yesterday's?' said Otto, as though this was a fallacy too far.

'Is there something you wanted?'

Otto thrust one of the letters he held into Felix's hand. Felix took it and examined the handwriting. It was addressed to him. He masked his surprise well, flipping the letter over and presenting its broken seal to Otto. 'You opened it.'

Otto waved the statement away. 'Do you know how much correspondence this war generates for me, Felix? Of course I opened it. I don't even read the addressee any more. But that's not important. It's come all the way from a village called Alderfen.'

'Is that meant to impress me?'

'Spare me, Felix, I thought you were travelled. Alderfen is in the north of Ostermark, only days from the company offices in Badenhof.'

'Ahh, I see,' said Felix, returning his attention to the letter and reading through narrowed eyes as Kat slid a consoling arm around Otto's elbow and hugged him to her. 'It's from Max,' Felix smiled, temporarily forgetting the both of them. He and the wizard had been romantic rivals, allies, and before the other man's summons to the von Carstein war in Sylvania and then on again to the north they had almost managed to become friends. Memories, it turned out, were as good a foundation for it as any. He checked the date on the letter. Nachgeheim: almost four months ago. Felix hoped the situation had improved since then.

Max and the other magisters of his college had been called to the aid of the Supreme Patriarch himself in maintaining the Auric Bastion. It was an impregnable barrier, Gelt's great miracle that would forever end the threat of Chaos to the Empire. Or that was what the Reiksmarshal would have Felix write for the information of the masses. But Felix was wise enough to recognise a thing that was too good to be true.

Felix skimmed over Max's disquisition on Chamonic principles, leylines, and aethyrial harmonism. It was enough to make Felix want to bury his face in a bowl of water. Sigmar's blood, it was as if the man was right here in the room.

...no one has ever succeeded in holding Chaos at bay, Felix. I do not believe that anyone has ever even thought to try, and for good reason. My colleagues and I will tread water for as long as we can. I do not know if there is safety in the south, even here I hear rumours, but were I in your position I would find somewhere safe and take Kat there. And I hope for your sakes that you both remember how to wield a weapon...

Felix glanced at the glass-doored cabinet on the wall that held Karaghul and folded the letter. 'This is dated months ago,' said Felix. 'Before Gustav even left Altdorf.'

'I know, I know,' said Otto. 'I can read, but it shows that a letter *can* get through.'

Kat patted his hand. 'Your son will be fine.'

'Of course he will,' Otto mumbled stiffly, avoiding everybody's eye. 'He is safe and well in Badenhof and keeping a good eye on those thieves we call distributors. It's just...' He trailed off, then waved despairingly towards the letter in Felix's hand. 'I did more than just open it.'

Felix nodded slowly. It sounded bad.

Ask me. The words jumped unbidden into Felix's head, fierce in sword and mail. *Ask me. I will go north and find my nephew.*

'Anyway,' said Otto, after a calming breath. 'Get yourself dressed. We have to go.'

'Go?'

'The Reiksmarshal is conducting a public rally at Wilhelmplatz this morning. Every guttersnipe in the altstadt knows there's a pfennig in it for anyone who brings word of his appearances. Kurt Helborg can't pass the gates of the castle without me hearing of it.' Otto snatched the letter from Felix's hand and waved it in the air. 'I am going to show him this and *demand* his news of the Kislev Verge.'

Felix sighed. What with Mannfred von Carstein and his brood said to have escaped the blockade of Sylvania, with Chaos on the march and rumours of strife in every human realm but the very heartlands of the Empire, Felix suspected the Reiksmarshal had enough on his plate without caring to concern himself with one missing merchant. He stood up all the same. Family, when it came down to it, was all he had left now. 'I don't know whether he'll be able to tell us much.'

Otto scoffed, his old self again. 'Jaeger and Sons is the main provisioner of wood and cereal to the entire front. If we stopped today then tomorrow there would not be a full belly in Ostermark. Perhaps I will remind the Reiksmarshal of that too when I see him.'

'Am I to stand behind you and look menacing?' said Felix.

'Nothing so terrible, Felix. Have you been working for the Reiksmarshal or not?'

'Not exactly,' said Felix, mindful of the parchments scattered all over the floor. 'No more than every sword, scribe, and battle mage in the Empire. I've never even met him in person.' He shrugged. 'Considering my misspent youth, I think that's for the best.'

'Just get changed,' said Otto, already leading Kat away by the arm. 'And wash yourself, would you? You smell like a sewer.'

The chill in the courtyard was biting. The sky was the colour of washed slate and the wind blew dead leaves over the walls and into the garden of the townhouse. A young girl with boyish blonde hair shivered in a woollen smock as she raked them up from around the feet of the servants that bustled around Otto's best coach. They were women mostly, young and nervous-looking, supervised by a few of Otto's greyer hands. Like so many of Altdorf's young men, the bulk of Otto's household had already gone to war.

The rake's iron teeth rattled across the flagstones.

Not a good day to be abroad, Felix thought, only then to smile sourly at the irony. Just minutes earlier he had been craving the wilds of Kislev. It wasn't exactly Estalia at this time of year. Wondering what was keeping Otto, Felix stamped his feet on the cobbles and wrapped himself deeper into his cloak. It was a deep blue and, though very fine, far too heavy for his own tastes. It felt like walking around with a child perpetually tugging on the back of his shirt. It was warm though, he could not deny, lined with mink, and felt like being embraced by a cushion.

With nothing much else to do while the hostlers applied the final buff to the coach's brass finishings and replaced the horse's nosebags with halter and bridle, Felix watched the girl as she obliviously raked leaves. He tried to conjure in her place an image of the lad that had done this job before her: black hair for blonde, halberd in place of a rake, the rich cream of Reikland instead of drab homespun. His mind rebelled. It was the mental equivalent of imposing a death's head mask over the poor girl's face. How many boys like that had signed up and gone north because of him? And for what? War and plague, the march of the dead, rumours of a man claiming to be the Herald of Sigmar? If Otto heard half of the rumour that Felix had then he would be a lot more worried about young Gustav than he was already pretending not to be.

'No, no, no, that's not good enough. I ordered twenty barrels. For twelve it is not even worth the haulage all the way to Hergig.' Otto limped from the house accompanied by his butler, Fritz, and a gaggle of expensively fripperied young men that seemed to all be competing to jump on Otto's shadow. 'You tell Muller I expect the rest of the consignment by tomorrow morning.' He signed a document that was pushed in front of him without reading it. 'Good. See that the count receives a half-ton more grain on top of that.'

'Charity, Otto?' said Felix.

'Business,' Otto replied, shooing his assistants with an exhausted wave. Over the last twelve months Otto had visited every town west of the Talabec and even when at home he was up at all hours receiving agents, clients, suppliers and the middlemen of the lot. Forget great destinies, mystic leach from artefacts of power and the changing touch of Chaos, to Felix it was abundantly obvious why the penniless rogue remained hale while the merchant grew fat, white-haired and frail. 'There is money in war, but the real profit is in rebuilding. It is crucial that Jaeger and Sons be in the best position to benefit from our patriotism when the war is won.'

'You think it will be?'

'Father built the Ostermark business from the ashes of the last

Chaos incursion, Felix. Every few decades, it seems, they come, and every time they are sent running back. This time will be no different.'

Felix wasn't sure it was that simple, but decided to keep his mouth shut. Nobody liked a doomsayer and he should know, he had argued with enough of them over the years. All he knew was that this time it felt different. Perhaps he'd just got old enough that he had become one of those old men that sat in taverns nursing their favourite stein and complaining that the winters had grown colder.

Taking Felix's silence as agreement and – accepting his knowledge of such things – trusting it, Otto grinned. His teeth were black from too much Lustrian sugar in his wine. One hand gripping his cane, he snapped his fingers until his butler handed him a large roll of parchment. From the plaster dust on the back and the splotches in the corners, it looked as though it had been pulled from a wall. 'I wanted to show this to you before we left. Look.' With Fritz's help, he unfurled it.

Felix's heart sank. It was a poster of the type commonly found nailed to village posts or to the walls at crossroads. As few men in the Empire were able to read, it was dominated by a huge illustration. It showed a gleaming phalanx of halberdiers marching towards a vast wall in the distance. The depiction of the wall was perhaps the most striking thing. It was drawn so as to appear mountainous, with a halo of power around its summit. Artistic licence perhaps, but Felix's own conversations with Max suggested more truth than fiction. The image was surrounded by small print, beneath the bold header: '*Victory in the North*'.

A little premature, Felix thought, but Otto was tapping his finger on the second of two signatures at the bottom; the one that came immediately below Kurt Helborg's. Felix sighed. When Otto had first had Felix's journals published without his knowledge, the last place he would have expected the damned things to end up was in the lap of Reiksmarshal Kurt Helborg. Apparently the name of the Saviour of Nuln carried a helpful romance amongst the pfennig dreadful-reading peasantry.

It said *Felix Jaeger*.

'The servants have been collecting them,' said Otto, blind to Felix's darkening expression. 'Not very civic of them, I realise, but I doubt the city will miss just one.'

'I'd say not,' said Felix sourly. 'I sometimes think that they are using them to buttress the walls in case of a siege.'

'Don't be prickly, Felix. Keeping the young men of Reikland up for the fight is valuable work, and certainly worth more to Jaeger and Sons than the paltry sum they pay you to do it.' He tapped his finger on Felix's signature again, then gave Fritz the nod to furl the poster up and take it away. 'That's the Jaeger name on every street corner and barracks of the Empire. That's what's paying your way in my house, Felix, and maintaining Katerina's donations to the Shallyan hospice.'

Feigning numb toes, Felix stamped his feet and turned his back. He closed his eyes and mumbled his own imprecation to the goddess of peace and mercy. He didn't want another argument about how much money Kat was costing his brother and he certainly didn't want to listen to him enthuse about the number of men that Felix had coaxed to war.

The heavy scuff of ill-worn leather boots made him look up. A pair of big men exited the servant's quarters under the screening maple trees and the tangle of ivy and started across the yard towards the coach. Both men were dressed in long black coats and gloves with cudgels buckled at their hips. The first was a head taller even than Felix, broad shouldered and with a neck like a cannonball. The second man was older, bald-headed and scarred, his muscular upper body counterbalanced by a gut that strained against his gentlemanly waistband. Felix knew professional muscle when he saw it. These were dangerous times for a merchant to be travelling, even within the borders of Reikland which was as yet relatively untouched by war. Why, only recently, rampaging flagellants had put the torch to half of Nuln, the offices of Jaeger and Sons and Otto's own home included. Felix sighed.

That city had no luck.

Schraeder, the senior coachman, directed his companion up to the box as he put on a tall black hat. The man tugged on the rim of his hat and opened the passenger door. Felix was in no way reassured by the show of deference. That hat and coat could not have been more intimidating on a troll.

'Ready to leave when you are, sir.'

THREE

Encounter in Wilhelmplatz

The steam of Felix and Otto's breath filled the closed passenger compartment as the coach clattered over the cobbles of Befehlshaber Avenue. Suppressing a shiver, Felix took a handful of cloak to smear condensation from the glass window.

A mist clung to the ground and there were few people about at this hour except beggars and refugees from the south, homeless and frozen and with nowhere else to go. Face to the cold glass, Felix watched a black coach pull out and follow them a way before disappearing into the fog. Felix shifted his attention to the colourful rank of daub and wattle shopfronts and town houses that dragged by. Behind them lay Karl Franz Park, and the bordering trees raked the rooftop shingles. Autumn had burnished their leaves a dazzling copper. Each one shone in the low sun like a ritual blade as the wind willed them again and again to cut. Their cultist-robe rustle drowned out the dire portents of the street-corner doom-mongers and the weeping of the foreign vagrants that clung like mould to the roadside. Despair was on the air, and whether native Altdorfer or amongst the influx fleeing the wars in Tilea, Estalia, and

Bretonnia, the taste of it was the same

Already, men were calling these the End Times.

It was going to be a hard winter. Felix's natural cynicism reminded him that the priests of Ulric and Taal and Manann made similar pronouncements every year in the hope of extorting a few more pfennigs from those praying for a short snap and a warmer spring. This time though, Felix believed them. The ratcatchers were up to their ankles in vermin, the geese had fled the Reik early for their southern roosts, and the chill had come early. The signs were clear, but only the most dyed in the wool curmudgeons were complaining about it. Felix had firsthand experience of how powerful an ally the Kislevite winter could be, but somehow Felix doubted that this one would bring anything more than a respite.

If the rumours were to be believed, that Praag and even the proud Gospodar capital, Kislev City itself, had already fallen, then the northmen had all the shelter they needed to gather their strength until spring. Felix could not help a shiver of dread, some premonition of horror. Even the terrible Asavar Kul himself, in the great incursion two centuries past, had failed to broach the city of Kislev. That it had fallen now without most men of the Empire even realising that it had come under attack was deeply disturbing. Doubly so as it had been achieved without a single substantiated report of Archaon, Asavar Kul's infernal heir apparent, taking to the field. Recalling the many ill-fated attempts he had made to confront the so-called Everchosen of Chaos during his career as Gotrek's henchman surprised him with a smile. Then he sighed, shook his head, and resumed to staring out the window. The rattling of the coach over the cobbles bumped his head against the glass. He was an idiot.

There really was nothing to commend those days.

Nothing at all.

'Pfennig for your thoughts,' said Otto. His heavy cheeks were flushed with cold and every so often he stamped his feet on the boards and rubbed his arms with mittened hands.

Both men swayed to the right as the coach took a left turn.

'Uncharacteristically generous of you,' Felix replied drily.

A dull roar from the direction of Wilhelmplatz rose slowly over the dry whisper of the trees. It sounded like the cries of the beast-man hordes at the walls of Praag and seemed oddly fitting to his memories. Felix watched his breath re-steam the window. Then his eyes narrowed. Using the hem of his cloak, he again wiped it clear and looked back the way they had travelled.

The black coach was still with them, about a dozen lengths behind. The two horses pulling were winter white and long-haired, trotting through mist up to their shaggy fetlocks. A pair of pennons fluttered from the rear. They depicted a white bear on a frozen field. The motif was itchingly familiar, but Felix could not quite place it. His hand moved to his lap, but the reassuring touch of Karaghul was not there.

Merchant gentlemen, he had learned, do not carry swords.

He was about to mention the coach to Otto, but his brother had reclined into the leather-backed seat and closed his eyes. Felix could not tell whether or not he was asleep: his lips were moving, but he might equally have been preparing his speech for the Reiksmarshal as dreaming.

Felix looked back. But the coach was gone.

The Wilhelmplatz rocked to the roar of the hundreds of peasants crowded in between the gates of the Imperial palace and the surrounding tenements. Women in wool dresses and winter shawls screamed curses. Old men hoisted orphaned grandchildren onto their shoulders that they might share the vitriol being directed towards the mutants being paraded before them. Upon a raised wooden platform surrounded by a double rank of halberdiers, a pack of mutants closed in on a single knight of the Reiksguard. His full silver-white plate shimmered with cold. The scarlet jupon that overlay it ruffled in rhythm to his footwork, the rampant griffon of the house of Wilhelm rending the air with claws of gold thread. The man had on an open bascinet, his face tanned, and wore a trimmed black beard and a broad smile. The pitch of the mob grew fevered as the knight danced from a mutant's clutches, swung his sword in a bravura flourish, and rounded on a second with a cry.

'Not exactly von Diehl, is it?' Felix yelled, citing the great playwright as the halberdiers ushered another trio of 'mutants' onto the stage, stuffed limbs swinging from bloated costumes as they walked. There was a gathered hiss as one flailing limb forced the knight to duck, then a roar when he came up grinning, saluted the crowd and set about the poor actor with the flat of his blade. The crowd jeered as the mutant stepped on the oversized foot of its own costume and crashed onto the stage. The knight planted one foot on the body, raising one clenched fist in triumph. On cue, the square erupted with laughter and mocking cheers, the high stone walls of the Imperial palace providing a thunderous acoustic return.

All eyes were on the tableau being enacted on stage, but Felix felt certain he was being watched and it was making him nervous. Bowmen liveried in the red and blue of Altdorf kept watch from the palace's sprawling ramparts while swordsmen in feathered sallets and padded hauberks patrolled the perimeter of the heaving square. The approaches were blocked by units of halberdiers, large weapons gleaming, as the soldiers searched carriages and held up foot traffic. Spilling out of the White Lady tavern just out of the square along Downfeather Alley, a group of drunken adolescents hurled abuse at the picket of halberdiers. The soldiers ignored it, but Felix saw the bowmen in the nearby windows shifting their aim and he did not doubt that there would be plain-clothes Kaiserjaeger following those boys home after the rally, probably with conscription papers handily pre-signed by the Reiksmarshal himself.

'You realise I'm still technically a wanted felon,' said Felix, eyeing the nearest unit of swordsmen warily.

'Nobody cares, Felix,' Otto replied, yelling directly into Felix's ear.

Felix gave a tight smile. He did often wonder if his current employers had the faintest idea that he had been dodging Imperial justice for the past two decades following his role in the Window Tax riots. Probably not. Most of the officers in Wilhelmplatz today, up to and including the Reiksguard on the stage, looked like they would not even have been born when Felix had been breaking windows and generally making a nuisance of himself. Simpler times, he thought, suddenly feeling very old indeed. There was a reason that nobody remembered the Window Tax riots any more.

Like Felix himself, they were simply not that important.

'Pay attention now, Felix.' Otto's voice was water thin under the oceanic roar of the crowd. Schraeder and the even larger coachman stood either side of him, and the peasants wisely gave them a wide berth. 'I'm going to catch the Reiksmarshal before he takes the stage himself. You stay here and keep an eye out.'

'For what?' Felix called back, but Otto and his men were already off. Felix swore, the prickling scrutiny on the nape of his neck growing ever so slightly more urgent now that they were gone.

A tumultuous cheer filled the square and Felix's attention was drawn along with everyone else's to the stage. The knight had just tripped one of the mutants and pushed him into his companion, causing them both to roll off the stage and land on top of each other in a heap. Only the surrounding box of halberdiers held the baying mob back. They beat at their breasts and screamed slogans into the soldiers' faces. With a sick realisation, Felix recognised the ones that he had written himself. Some kind of collective madness had them. Surely even the dimmest villein knew that those mutants were just players in padded costumes.

Felix scanned the crowd. Something about it all made his skin crawl, reminding him of the summers spent at the family logging camps in the Drakwald. He had used to watch the forest from the house as he watched these men now, convinced utterly that something hidden lurked there.

From the Kaisergarden entrance, just to the left of the road that he and Otto had taken, the picket of halberdiers waved through a black coach. A chill passed through him. No, not just any black coach. It was the exact same black coach that he had seen before. The white bear pennons fluttered in the storm of noise like topgallants in a gale. Feeling a nervous itch crawling up from his chest, Felix watched the coach pull into a roped-off enclosure. Dozens of other coaches were parked there, worthies attended by Altdorfer soldiery and by gruff-looking heavies in an array of heraldic surcoats. The horses nuzzled each other and whickered their own reassurances against the commotion. Felix recognised the heraldries of Nuln, Stirland and Ostermark – mainly because of the amount of time he had spent in and around the guardhouses and gaols of those states over the years – but most he did not recognise.

The driver jumped down from the box to open the passenger door, but Felix could not see who emerged for all of the rippling banneroles and halberds in the way. He cursed, then shuddered, that feeling again, and crossed his arms under his cloak.

An animal scream from behind made him start.

Felix turned, shivering off his unease, to find a gang of young bravos had clambered onto Otto's wagon. They shook it and screamed like Arabyan monkeys. One of them danced with bottle in hand from the box. They all wore the red and blue ribbons of the newly enlisted around their sleeves and, doubtless encouraged by the free spirits of a grateful city's innkeepers, were all uproariously drunk. While Felix felt no great enchantment towards Otto's property, the men were clearly spooking the horses. The farther of the two threw its mane as it fought against the tracer in a vain bid to back into the chassis of the coach. The nearer horse merely trembled, wide-eyed and staring, as if it had just smelled a wolf. Out of habit, Felix swept his cloak over his left shoulder to free his sword arm. Even after all this time, Karaghul's absence just felt wrong. He shook his head ruefully. There was nothing like a sword to de-cloud sotted minds, but he doubted this situation called for it. He started forward.

At least he had meant to.

The crowd roared, oblivious to the revelation that his feet were rooted to the ground as though glued to the cobbles. Felix gasped as he tried again and failed. Grabbing one leg in both hands by the knee, he tried to pull but it did not move an inch. He was sweating now despite the cold, yet absurdly grateful that his arms at least had done as he had asked. He had felt them as they touched his thigh. His legs were fine.

They simply would not move.

A piercing laugh made him look up. One of the young men had tripped over his own ankles and fallen off the top of the coach, to the great mirth of his comrades. Felix grit his teeth and tried to push himself through whatever was preventing him. It was not so much that he failed as that his legs refused to try. Shaking the muscle of his thigh under one hand, he fought down a rising panic. It could not be that gang of drunks. What in Sigmar's name was going on!

'Forget wagon, Jaeger,' came a guttural, but deliberately precise voice from the crowd behind him, right where the poor horse directed its terror. 'Only give yourself nose-bleed. And maybe attract soldiers. Not want attract soldiers, *yhah?*'

Unconsciously, Felix's gaze found the troop of state swordsmen that had unnerved him so just moments before. 'Do I not?'

'No,' said the hidden man. 'I not come all this way to harm, Empire man.'

For some unfathomable reason, Felix laughed. Why did he find that so difficult to believe? Bracing himself for the effort of turning, he was surprised to find it easy. He barely even had to think about it before his feet were shuffling him around to greet a short man in brightly coloured fleece breeches and coat and a hemp cloak. His eyes were narrowed, his skin walnut-hard and of a hue that looked mildly jaundiced but for the absence of any other obvious symptoms. His bowed gait indicated a man more accustomed to riding than to walking. Now Felix placed the odd accent; as plainly Kislevite as the drooping moustache on the man's face and the mink-flapped *chapka* on his head. He was one of the Ungol nomads that subsisted on the northern oblast and the Troll Country.

Had subsisted.

Felix tried to raise a hand in greeting, found he could not. He grimaced. 'Do I know you?'

'You are Jaeger, yhah? You are – how you say in Empire – friend of my friend.'

Some friend, Felix thought, struggling increasingly desperately to move an arm, a leg, anything; but all he seemed capable of controlling was his eyes and his mouth. Only the certain knowledge that he was utterly under this strange man's power kept his tone civil as he asked, 'Who?'

'My lady, you remember?' The Ungol smiled, teeth starkly white against his tan skin. Something was coming. Felix could sense the darkness of it spread through the subliminal unease of the crowd. Behind him, the horse whinnied in terror. It was a wiser beast than the fools around it gave credit for. A sense of recognition thrilled through the will that bound Felix's body, like dogs with prey and excited by the approach of their master. What was worse, Felix thought he recognised it too. He stopped fighting, surrendering to that itch that had crept from his chest and now hid like a spider at the back of his mind.

It could not be...

The Ungol stepped aside and dropped to one knee. 'I present my lady: the Boyarina Magdova Straghov.'

The crowd seemed to fade, the brightly clothed Ungol receding into it, and Felix was dreaming again. At least that was his best explanation for it.

She looked exactly as Felix remembered her, a sleeveless jerkin worn over a white linen shirt, leather britches cinched at the waist with a studded belt, long legs encased to the knee within fur-edged riding boots. A long cavalry sabre was sheathed in a leather scabbard at her hip. The only incongruity was the black widow's veil and long leather gloves that she wore to shade her skin from the sun, but despite the layers between them, Felix could still make out the pale skin, the high cheekbones, and those wide, almond eyes.

'You are not going to scream, are you, Felix?' said Ulrika, breaking the spell. 'It would not be very attractive.' She glided nearer, then brushed back his overlong fringe with the back of her hand as if to see him better. Felix's skin tingled at her touch. Belatedly, the thought arose that he should tell her to stop, but then her fingers nipped something in his hair. He felt a pinch. Then she yanked sharply back.

'Ow!'

Ulrika presented the pale strand tweezered between forefinger and thumb. Her eyes sparkled with amusement. 'A grey hair, Felix?'

'Keep it,' said Felix. 'I've plenty more.' He rubbed the sore spot on his head, realising only then that he was free to move again. He held his hand out, gave the fingers an experimental flex. The last time he had seen Ulrika had been in Nuln over two years ago, before his and Kat's paths had crossed.

If she had had this kind of power then, she had kept it to herself.

'I apologise for the entrance,' she said, setting her hands on her hips and angling her jaw proudly upwards. Without meaning to, Felix smiled. He had seen that posture all too often when they fought – and Sigmar had they fought – with Ulrika acting every inch the spoiled boyar's daughter who could think no wrong. 'But you were the one about to fight six men half his age.'

'Half *our* age,' Felix corrected. 'And I could still have taken them, thank you very much.'

'I don't doubt it.'

Felix watched her for a moment, trying to determine if she was teasing him, sorely tempted to remind her who had ended up with their backside on the floor more often than not when the two of them had sparred. He looked again at his hand and tested the fingers once more. Of course, that had been then. He shook his head with a sigh.

'It's good to see you, Ulrika. Truly. But you could have just called for me at my house like a normal person.'

'I wanted to speak with you alone,' said Ulrika, indicating the screaming crowds packed in all around them, the drunkards still jeering at those below from atop Otto's coach. 'I thought a public place would be best, and–' her husky voice took on a nasal quality '–every guttersnipe in the altstadt knows there's a pfennig for anyone bringing word of Helborg's appearances.'

Felix chuckled at the surprisingly passable imitation of his brother. Then an odd chill stole it away. Ulrika had never met Otto... at least not to his knowledge.

With a smile, Ulrika tucked a copper coin into Felix's cloak where it was creased at the collar and laid her hand on his chest. His heart kicked. 'I need you to stop looking at me like you have just seen a vampire in the middle of Wilhemplatz.' She moved in, nodding to his left and to his right and breathing kisses on his cheeks in the Bretonnian manner. 'People see a war widow and her lover, and I have learned that it pays to keep up appearances.'

Felix swallowed. The gauze of her veil brushed his unshaven chin. He barely dared breathe lest he smell her. Glancing over his shoulders as she indicated, he saw a wall of bodies, a blur of blind noise. No one was paying either of them the slightest attention that Felix could make out, but then he hadn't a vampire's senses. Or their paranoia.

While his head was turned, Ulrika came the rest of the way, leaning her body into his and wrapping her arms around his neck. Felix's pulse quickened but to his impotent shame he did nothing to resist her. It had been a long time. She was colder than she had been, harder, and eerily still where a heart had once beat, and yet her body's every contour and curve was as he remembered. Even the scent of her hair was familiar.

'Marriage has made you prudish, Felix.' Ulrika took his hand in a grip that was – in every way – irresistible and clasped it to her hip. Felix smiled nervously, apologetically, though he wasn't sure for what. A tremor took up in his hands. Desire? Guilt? He tried not to look at the wedding ring that nuzzled against Ulrika's hip. He looked away, closed his eyes, cupped his other hand behind Ulrika's shoulder and told himself that it was all just an act.

'There,' Ulrika whispered. 'That was not so bad now, was it?'

'What do you want?' said Felix, eyes still closed, trying not to think about the lips separated from his by nothing but a thin layer of fabric. He tried to think of the fangs those lips hid, but it didn't help. 'Please tell me that your dropping by during the largest Chaos incursion since Magnus's time is just a coincidence.'

'Try the largest since Snorri Whitebeard's time,' said Ulrika, clutching him as though to impress upon him something of deadly import. 'It is already far worse in the north than you can conceive.'

Felix nodded, found himself stroking her veiled head without realising it. 'I heard what became of Kislev. I'm so sorry. What with Sylvania, it all just happened so quickly–'

Ulrika waved away his platitudes with a shake of the head. 'It does not matter, as my father would have said were he alive.' She pushed him back just slightly, enough only to encourage Felix to open his eyes and look into hers. 'I have come about Max.'

'Max?'

'Yes.' Ulrika dropped her gaze. 'The Auric Bastion is still weak at Alderfen, and despite the best efforts of Max and his brethren it is under constant attack. It took me two weeks to get here, Felix. That is how long it has been since Max fell.'

Felix felt the bottom fall out of his chest. Max could not be dead. There were certain people in this world that Felix had, without quite realising it, come to believe were invulnerable. Gotrek was one, and Max was another. The idea of him falling in some dismal corner of Ostermark while Felix drank himself stupid and dreamt that he was there just twisted the knife.

'He fell, yes, to a mounted raid, along with every other priest and wizard the marauders could lay their hands on before being driven back into Kislev, but he is not dead. Don't ask me how I know that, but I am convinced he was taken alive for a reason. It is difficult even for me to get news from north of the Auric Bastion, but a new warlord establishes himself in Praag and has been scouring Kislev of sorcerers for months. He calls himself the Troll King. That, I believe, is where Max and his fellows have been taken, and I want you to help me get him back.'

Felix had to keep his mouth shut to avoid saying 'yes' right away. She was offering him everything he had been yearning for, everything that had been missing since he and Gotrek had gone their separate ways. His ever-reliable inner cynic told him that, of course, Ulrika would know that. He would not be surprised if she could recite the contents of every fabricated war report he had ever written for the criers and knew the name of every sewerjack with whom he relived his glory days and where to find the taverns in which he would blast his mind with cheap schnapps afterwards. Max and Gotrek were the heroes. Felix was just a failed poet with a magic sword. He wasn't the same man who had left his life at the drop of a drunken pledge to a Trollslayer and spent the next two decades gallivanting through horrors that most men would prefer to pretend could not exist. He had responsibilities now, and aches in places that *he* would prefer to pretend could not exist. Otto would not take him back again if he ran off now, and Kat...

The autumn light that reflected off the ring on his second finger struck him like a bucket of cold water.

'I can't go with you.'

'Max risked his life to save mine from the plague, do you remember? And after that he raced across half of the Old World to rescue me from Adolphus Krieger.'

'As did I,' said Felix, defensively.

'As did you,' Ulrika echoed. 'Do you value Max's life that much less than mine?'

The words stung as they had been meant to. Felix felt a flickering ember of resentment amongst the confusion of passions. Had the choice been solely his he would have left Altdorf with Max from the outset. Had it been up to him he would probably be dead in a field somewhere in Ostermark by now. For some reason that thought did not trouble him. In his heart of hearts, he knew that he was never meant for any other kind of end.

'If your positions were reversed I would tell him the same.'

'Is it your work?' Her face was a mask, but her voice sneered. 'Do you know how pathetic your odes to the green fields of Reikland and the goodness of Emperor Karl Franz look in Hergig or Bechafen? Do you know the lengths they must go to to maintain an army that can still fight, the bargains they have been forced to make? Even I now have the field rank of general in the state of Ostermark. Do you think they care what I am as much as what I can bring to the field? Do you think they even want to know?'

When Felix did not react, she went on. 'Is it your hunt for the rat that killed your father, then?'

Felix did tighten his grip on her shoulder at that. An image of his father brutalised and killed in his bed flashed through his mind. Part of him had been glad when the flagellants had burned that house down.

'You will find nothing. The skaven have abandoned their northern holdings for some ploy in the south. I do not know what or where, so don't ask.' Her mocking tone became gentle. 'You're meant for better things than skulking around sewers and trying to hide the stink from your wife. Help me. Help *Max*.'

'I told you, I can't. And not for those reasons.'

'Ah yes, the lovely Katerina Jaeger. You're a living cliché, you know, taking a girl young enough to be your daughter.'

'Young enough to be *our* daughter,' Felix cut in reflexively, and immediately winced at how those words sounded out loud.

Ulrika looked away coyly, but Felix could see that she was smiling.

'The world does not work like one of those dreadful Detlef Sierck plays you used to recite for me. The damsel does not recover simply because she has her prince.' She shook her head and slowly peeled herself from his embrace. 'You will not find a physician in Altdorf wise enough in forbidden lore to undo Kemmler's necromancy, but I...'

Felix's entire ribcage constricted and froze. She could cure Kat! Or was she just offering him what he wanted to hear?

'Are you promising me something?'

'Find me in the Black Rose on Leopold Avenue tonight,' said Ulrika, signalling to her man that she was ready to go. Felix blinked, as though tricked by some cunning sleight of hand, as the Ungol and his brightly coloured fleece coat reappeared in his vision. 'And it must be tonight. I will be gone by dawn. I am already two weeks behind Max's captors and it is a long road back to Badenhof.'

Felix looked to the ground and smiled. In other circumstances he might even have laughed. Ulrika had thought of everything that might sway him, boxed it neatly for him and tied it off with a sweet little bow. He sighed. Fine, he'd take a peek.

'Badenhof?'

The Ungol drew a sealed letter from his coat. He displayed the wax Jaeger and Sons seal for a moment, and then slid it back into the fleece pocket.

'It appears that your nephew, Gustav, has been having difficulties with the local lord and requests the experience of his knavish uncle in resolving them. Join me tonight, Felix, and I will ensure that Otto receives this letter. And the message that you departed at once to help him. Neither he nor Katerina will suspect.'

'I... I still don't know. I'd have to be sure that Kat is looked after.'

Ulrika closed her eyes and was still. It might have been a sigh, but of course Ulrika's lungs had not expelled air in over twenty years. 'And if she could be made strong again, so she could look after herself?'

'What are you suggesting?'

Ulrika smiled and made to withdraw. 'Max saved her life as well, Felix. I am suggesting that she might want her own say in this decision.'

Ulrika strode through the crowd, bodies sighing from her path like grass before a night wind.

Until only recently, she would have been able to move amongst the flock as one of them, but now her passage was marked by goose bumps and shudders, hammers stutteringly drawn across chests to ward against the evil eye. Chaos was waxing, Shyish, the Wind of Death, was in flux, and Ulrika's own powers continued to grow. Even the simple townsfolk around her could sense the presence of the *other* in their midst. Until only recently, that growing disconnect between her and her remembered humanity would have troubled her. Now, her own senses could pierce the beating hearts of every one of these people. She saw the warmth that fled their veins and turned their fingers blue and, though they had only the dimmest perception of her presence amongst them, she could smell the fear on their breath.

Damir, the Ungol warrior who served her in exchange for the base pleasure of doing so and the dim prospect of one day joining her in immortality, waited for her by the coach. Her mortal family's bear rampant flew from the four corners. The thrall pulled open the door. 'To the Black Rose, my lady?'

'No,' said Ulrika, accepting Damir's hand and allowing him to help a lady into her carriage. He closed the door on her, and then climbed to the box.

Ulrika pulled thick black curtains over the raucous scenes without, then unhooked her widow's veil and smiled a good shepherdess's smile.

A human would not know what was truly in their heart if she was to open it up and show it to them. She leaned forward to knock on the front quarter partition.

'I think it is time that I met this Kat.'

FOUR

A Proposal

Could Ulrika really make Kat whole again? Was that what she had been offering? The idea troubled him, perhaps more than such an apparent kindness should, and not just because Ulrika's appearance in Kat's life was going to lead to a lot of awkward questions. Felix wasn't quite that selfish. He knew there were individuals in the world with the power to reverse what Heinrich Kemmler had done. Perhaps Ulrika was now one of them. Her display in Wilhelmplatz had certainly been impressive and maybe that had been the point, a demonstration. He would give almost anything to see Kat whole again, but few such powers gave without demanding a commensurate cost. His mind conjured images of secret covens, rituals conducted on darkest Geheimnisnacht, pacts with daemons, and vile blood magic. It was the varied and terrible possibilities excluded by that *almost* that had Felix abandoning Otto's coach to the drunks that had claimed it and pushing through the screaming crowds towards the guard picket at the east entrance on Black Castle Alley.

The soldiers, however, were too overwhelmed holding back the tide of people trying to catch a glimpse of their regent, the Reiksmarshal, to care about one more trying to get out. Felix hurried by them and into the boisterous crowds around the Kaisergarden. Seeing the grinding foot and horse-drawn traffic ahead of him, Felix drove through the press of urchins and vagrants to pass into Hubert Alley on the opposite side of the Kaisergarden, knocking a bowl from a beggar's hand in his haste.

The tall buildings of the altstadt meant the sun rarely landed here. It was dark and reeked of stale urine. Families huddled amidst refuse from which the eyes of rats glittered. Men, women, and children followed him with dead eyes that saw naught now but nightmares, mumbling in the languages of Tilea, Estalia and Araby. Felix understood only a little and tried to ignore even that much.

'The rats, signore. The rats...'

Felix squeezed past the Tilean and his children and into the sudden light of Sigmarplatz. Red leaves blustered across the perfectly square flagstones like the heralds of war. The square before the temple's severe marble frontage was packed with worshippers come for the midday rituals. A unit of halberdiers in slashed doublets and faded red and blue livery warmed their hands over a brazier on the temple's steps and watched the faithful and the hopeless file past. Felix quickened his pace until their prayers were behind him and he was on Befehlshaber Avenue.

Stately, three-storey structures of dwarf-cut stone rose above the poorer surrounds of the altstadt, hoarding the high ground like a profiteer. Each residence sought to outdo the next in the beauty of their finials, the mullioned quality of their windows, or the quantity of their chimneys. As well as the homes of the merchant classes, there were banks, jewellers, dealers in exotic luxuries. In one lungful Felix had the bitterness of Arabyan coffee, the sickly tang of New World sugar, and the spices of Ind; a collective pomander to the noses of the affluent against the desperate reek of the dispossessed. It made Felix feel sick.

He broke into a jog. His heart raced, his vision funnelled, but it was not due to the exertion as, despite age and Otto's best efforts, Felix remained a fit man. It was the need to see Kat again, to purge his skin of Ulrika's memory in his arms, that pushed him through the well-heeled gentry and their servants. He started to run. It did not feel nearly fast enough. It never was, no matter how fast he ran. He had been too late to save his father.

He had been too late to save Ulrika.

With that thought burning a hole in his brain, Felix slammed into the heavy iron gate that was set into the brick wall surrounding Otto's property and shook the bars. It was locked. In frustration, he beat against the bars and yelled the name of every servant he could recall. Of course, most of those names were already in the Reiksmarshal's war ledger for the march north, but Felix shouted them anyway, to no avail. He rattled the gate until the dead leaves impaled on its crowning spikes shook loose, but there was no answer from the house. He could see the old building, across the coach yard and behind a screen of bronze-leafed maples. To the right of the yard was a herb garden, the stables and, obscured by a creeping tangle of vines, the servants' quarters. There was no one there either. Curse this war! Felix took the gate in both hands as if he might tear it loose and shook it.

'Someone open this gate! Kat!'

He loved Kat.

The reminder took him in a bear hug and crushed the air from his lungs. They had always planned to leave Altdorf once Kat was well again, hunt the beastmen she had once sworn to eradicate, live village to village. On the nights that Felix actually made it home and was sober enough to find their bed they still talked of the life they would have. As if it might one day happen. Felix blinked away the threat of a tear. He didn't need Ulrika to tell him that Kat was getting no better. Felix wondered when he would ever grow up enough to talk about these things with the woman he loved rather than bottle them up and take them to the nearest tavern.

Did he love her as intensely as he had Ulrika? Or Kirsten, for that matter? He didn't know. Sickness and circumstance had tramped mud through feelings that had once been so clear. As Sigmar was his witness though, he loved her.

Felix shoved himself back from the gate and looked up to its spiked summit. He realised he was attracting stares from the passing gentry, but he didn't care. At least so long as none of them considered him so curious as to warrant summoning the watch. He took three steps back and then charged the damned gate, planting his boot into the iron frame just before he ran into it and kicking himself off and up, just high enough to grapnel his fingertips over the top of the gate. The bevelled iron bit into the pads of his fingers and he grunted in pain as blood welled under his grip. From the street behind him, people were pointing, shouting, but no one went so far as to try and stop him from pulling up his legs and dragging himself up and over.

And why should they? It wasn't their house.

He landed on the other side, his heavy blue cloak almost throttling him for his troubles after its over-embroidered hem got snagged on the barbs and swung him by the neck like a noose. Choking and swearing, he tore off the clasp and shrugged it off, letting it fall over the gate behind him like some rich woollen modesty screen as he ran under the line of trees to the house.

The door was unlocked and he burst through, sprinting for the staircase up to the first floor. The balusters bore ornate intaglio in the Tilean style. The walls were panelled in dense oak. Felix pounded up the carpeted steps and almost charged right through Fritz as Otto's butler emerged from one of the guest suites bearing a stack of linen over the crook of one arm and a silver carafe of red wine in the other. Felix grabbed a hold of the handrail to keep from colliding with the man as Fritz turned his body to shield the carafe and breathed a sigh of relief at his livery's near miss.

'Kat,' Felix demanded. 'Where is she?'

'She is not here,' said Fritz, straightening to deliver that missive in a tone of irritated dignity.

'Damn it, Fritz,' said Felix, taking the butler by the collar and making him squawk. 'Where is she, then?'

'Frauchen Annabella has visited the Bretonnian embassy every day since their war began. For word of her family,' he added, then swallowed as Felix tightened his grip and hurried on. 'Frauchen Katerina rides with her as far as the Shallyan temple.'

Felix let the man drop. *Every day?* How could he not have known that? The question though was whether Ulrika knew. With a curse, Felix barged past the still-spluttering butler and raced up the second flight of steps. Could he even doubt it?

On making the second floor, Felix spun, both hands clutching the handrail, and shot back down, 'Fetch me a new cloak and my mail. Right now.'

'But, Herr Felix–'

Felix couldn't care less what the butler had to say. He had the key to his study door in his coat, but he was too agitated to be fiddling about with pockets and simply kicked the lock to splinters, then flung the door aside. His entrance sent half-written speeches and pamphlets flying, but he ignored them, striding through the clutter to the glass-fronted cabinet on the back wall.

Karaghul glittered in the noonday sun that shone through the window. Sealed against the dust that hung across the air, it looked serene, a king lying in state, but Felix didn't need to test its edge to know that the enchanted blade would be as sharp as the day he had found it in a troll's hoard under the lost dwarfhold of Karak Eight Peaks. He took a deep breath and opened the glass door, then reached inside to lift the sword from its silver hooks. Unconsciously, he smiled. A thrill shot down his arm. The feel of that dragonhead hilt was as familiar to him as his own name.

An image of Kat fled through his mind and the moment left him.

He squeezed his swordbelt over his stomach and slid Karaghul into its sheath. He just hoped he wouldn't have to use it.

Not against Ulrika.

The warm colours cast over the great hall of the Temple of Shallya by its stained glass windows could not detract from the cold. A chill wind blew through the open doors, but on straw mats throughout the cavernous space men threw off their blankets, doused in sweat as they raved of sorcerers, monsters and dead men walking. Judging from their livery and the accent of their rantings they were Altdorfers returned from the north. They looked weary, broken, and glassy-eyed. Their hacking coughs echoed from the vaulted ceiling. The air they breathed was sickly sweet with the odour of putrefaction. Priestesses in soiled white robes hurried amongst the men with mops and muslins and bowls of lukewarm vegetable broth. Lumps of dried vomit crusted the joins between the flagstones.

Perched on a bench at the short end of the hall in the camphor-scented warmth of a candle shrine and the pastel glow of stained glass, Kat watched the sisters in their work. Theirs was a perilous and largely thankless calling, but Kat envied them. She missed having that kind of purpose.

Stiffly, she pulled her knees up onto the bench and drew herself into the corner between back and armrest. Her eyelids felt warm and heavy, like baked honey. Even the short ride from the house had proven tiring. Annabella could be exhausting company, though Kat supposed that she would probably be anxious too if her country were ravaged by war and her family unaccounted for. With a feeling of heartache, her thoughts turned to Felix. She embraced the pain of him, let it fill her.

He had given her all the family she had now.

More and more since the lichemaster had... *touched* her, she found her thoughts centred on him, or more specifically that night in Flensburg when she had been a girl. It was all she dreamed of. She always recognised the dream when it came. There was the forest that she could walk in her sleep, the glare of the fire, the screams. But each time it was different, as terrifying as it had been when she had first witnessed it as a child, as though fate were showing her the infinite ways in which weakness or inaction might have yielded the death of the man she loved. She had been the one to slay the Chaos warrior, Justine. She had saved both Felix and Gotrek that night. But what if she hadn't? Opening her eyes, she raised her left hand to reassure herself that the heavy gold ring she wore was still there. The thick angular band had been pushed over the thumb up to the knuckle. Her fingers were too thin: a reminder that she was not as strong even as that girl in Flensburg.

Would she be able to save Felix now?

She knew that she wouldn't, but that didn't mean she would stop fighting for him. She was his wife and she was a fighter. Today she might draw a bowstring twelve inches. Tomorrow it would be twelve and one eighth. It would not have the beasts of the Drakwald fleeing for their herdstones, it might not even draw Felix's attention from his charts and his cups, but it was proof that she was getting stronger every day, even if nobody saw it but her.

Time stretched on while she waited her turn with the sisters and her stomach began to growl. The priestesses were busy, she understood that and didn't mind. It was preferable to being cooped up all day in the house, and sometimes a woman needed a sister's care. It was her own fault anyway for scrimping on breakfast, but it was too easy when it was only herself and Annabella, and these mornings her stomach threatened outright upheaval at the merest scent of vollkornbrot or liverwurst. It clenched now, a pre-emptive warning.

It was normal, the sisters had assured her, and would soon pass.

The breeze blowing through the open door sent a shiver through her bones and she burrowed deeper into the hardwood corner of her bench. It was too cold for autumn. In fact she'd not been touched in such a way since that Nachhexen night in Castle Reikguard when Heinrich Kemmler's necromancy had sucked the warmth from her veins. She shuddered at the memory.

'You appear unwell, sister.'

The unexpected voice from behind gave her a start. It was a woman's voice, but deep as midwinter snow and layered over an accent that harked at lands far beyond Kat's travels.

Wearily, her head ever so heavy on her withered neck, Kat tilted her face back across the clamshell arrangement of benches that surrounded the candle shrine and towards the door. The woman who had spoken was seated on the bench behind her but one, leaning forwards with her arms crossed over the back of the one in front. Even seated and slouching, it was clear that the woman was tall, and shapely in a way that Kat had never been. Her slender body was neatly clad in tough leathers that Kat could appreciate. A black widow's veil masked her face. A passing glance would have shown a war-widow in mourning, but Kat never trusted first impressions. There was something about the woman that suggested grief was as alien a feeling to her as love. Just looking at her gave her unseasonal chills.

And Kat knew the feel of death when it sat eight feet behind her.

'Finding an ill woman in Shallya's house is no great feat,' said Kat. Felix wasn't the only one to find solace in sarcasm.

The woman smiled as if reading her thoughts, her own impossible to make out for the black veil that covered her eyes. She appeared to consider her words for a moment before speaking again, leaning forwards over her crossed hands. 'What if you were shown a way to become strong again? You and Felix could travel as you were meant to. You could again be the terror of the beasts you so despise. More than you ever were before.'

Kat's grip on the back of her bench tensed. Unbidden, her other hand moved to cover her belly like a shield. 'Do you know me?'

With a wooden growl that echoed through the hall, the woman pushed back her bench and stood. She was even taller than Kat had initially thought, as tall as Felix. Almost certainly a noble. No one else could be fed so well. The woman moved out from the formation of benches and stalked towards her. Stalked was the right word. Her footsteps were soft and silent, like a hunter. A sword swung at her hip. Looking at it made Kat's fingers curl around the phantom yew of her bow.

The woman held her position just beyond the blue-green wash thrown by the large stained glass window. Almost as if the light, its sanctity, or both repelled her. Kat shuffled further along the bench and deeper into the light.

'I once feared as you fear, Katerina.' The woman's use of her name caught Kat like a fish on a barb. The woman prowled the edge of the light. Kat tried to make out her features, but her weak eyes felt like they were being cooked with a turquoise glow. 'Even after this gift was given to me I would have rejected it.' With a laugh as hollow as the ring of moon chimes, the woman stepped into the light, painting her riding leathers in greens and eerie corpse-browns as she knelt and cupped a hand under Kat's jaw with a supple creak of leather. She brushed aside the single white lock that lay over Kat's left eye. 'Now I realise that it does not matter where this strength came from or who gave it. It is mine now and he is gone. And I am more powerful than he ever was.'

'What do you want?'

The woman seemed almost to purr as her big blue eyes filled Kat's world. Her mouth opened to reveal the long fangs of a fiend.

'To do a good deed for an old friend.'

Felix staggered into the great hall of the Shallyan temple with the bandy-legged gait of a sailor, having sprinted across half of the altstadt from Otto's house to get there. He took in the bare stone walls and columns, the coloured windows, the stink of sickness in one breathless second as he collared a young, white-robed priestess.

'Kat Jaeger. Where is she?'

The woman pointed through a series of arches to where a half-circle of benches had been arranged before a large stained glass window depicting doves in a clear blue sky and what appeared to be a candlelit shrine. He saw two figures there, one seated while the other knelt, and his heart lurched. The seated figure was clearly Kat, but the other...

Sigmar, he prayed, don't let me be too late.

'Please, if I could just take your sw–'

Felix pushed past the priestess, weaving around, and on one occasion jumping over, the bodies of sleeping men that were scattered like dead leaves over the hall until he stumbled, spent, into the backmost of the wooden benches. The thing gave a cacophonous snarl as it scraped over the flagstones, but Kat didn't react. Her eyes were glazed as if she'd been drugged. Ulrika however glanced up and smiled a welcome. She was on one knee, as though in the act of proposing. Her body shimmered in the colours cast onto her back by Shallya's stained glass.

'The old outfit suits you, Felix. You look yourself again.'

Felix spread his hands in a gesture of surrender. His tatty and oft-mended cloak of red Sudenland wool – all that Fritz could find at short notice – fell from his arms. 'Just let Kat go. Leave her be and I'll go with you gladly.'

Ulrika snorted angrily. 'She is not a hostage, you idiot. I am trying to help you.'

Slowly, Felix edged around the benches that separated him from the two women. Ulrika followed him with her eyes, a lioness guarding her kill from some scruffy scavenger. Felix resisted the impulse to draw his sword. Ulrika had one too, and the last thing he needed was an armed confrontation with a vampire in the house of the Bleeding Heart. He remembered how utterly she had been able to dominate him in the Wilhelmplatz and forced his hands flat against his thighs. If Ulrika chose to do something to Kat then Felix knew there was precious little he would be able to do about it.

Besides appeal to her better nature, and whatever she had become, she was still Ulrika.

'She wouldn't thank you for it, and neither would I. You were changed against your will. Don't you remember how that felt?'

Ulrika's lips parted into a scowl. 'I tried to destroy myself many times. Did you know that? But how hard did I really try when all I needed to do was step out into the light?' Her scowl narrowed into a sneer as she returned her attention to Kat. 'My mistress tried to tell me that I would adapt and – guess what? – she was right. So will Katerina.'

'No!'

Felix rounded the row of benches and hurried forwards, then stopped in his tracks as though physically tackled. As if one more step into that blue pool of watery light would cause the woman he still knew as Ulrika to go under and be replaced with the monster that could do this thing she offered. 'Please, Ulrika. I know you're trying to be kind, but don't. Don't try to help her like this.'

'Ul... rika?'

Drowsily, Kat came to, syllables spilling from her mouth like a drunk's. Her head lolled from Ulrika to Felix and back. She blinked, confused. 'But she's dead?'

Ulrika laughed as if they were three old friends at a feast. 'My dear Felix! You lied to your wife about me.'

Felix groaned and looked up into the faces of the doves depicted in the window. What little he had got away with telling Kat about Ulrika had not strictly been a lie, but right now it felt like the axe of betrayal in his hands. Kat fixed her unsteady gaze on Ulrika. She didn't need to say anything. Ulrika was the daughter of a March Boyar, looked it in every proud line of her face, whereas Kat was a peasant who had never even known her father. Kat's face was scarred, still pretty, but pewter next to platinum when compared to the cold, callous beauty of the Kislevite noblewoman. Ulrika's pale skin glowed with the perfection of immortality, the undimmed memory of days forever tinted rose.

There was no comparison.

'You want me to say that I still think of you sometimes?' Felix hissed. 'Fine. I'll admit to that. You think I miss running around with Gotrek?' He shook his head and laughed. 'I miss a lot of things, but do you think I could have kept up with Gotrek forever? Look at me.' Felix spread his arms and did a turn, showing off his scars and wear and the grey growing through his long blond hair.

He sighed, feeling suddenly ancient. Ulrika, despite her years, would be young forever. Kat had been aged far beyond her youth. Only Felix, it seemed to him, could look and feel *exactly* as old as he was. He knelt and took Kat's hand. It was thin and parchment dry, like that of a mummy. 'Ulrika came to ask for my help. Max is in trouble.'

The slap caught him entirely unprepared.

Kat's left palm struck him a stinging blow across the jaw. She was as frail as an old woman, but it was the shock of it that hurt. That and a ring of twenty-four-carat dwarf gold that left a dent in his cheek. 'Max? What of me?' Felix clutched his jaw. The dwarf gold on Kat's thumb glinted jealously. 'You wouldn't break your oath to Gotrek for me, and yet you would break ours for–' her voice caught, and she glared at Ulrika. 'For whatever *she* is?'

'Try to understand,' said Felix. His cheek stung, his heart felt like it had started pumping air, and he was arguing Ulrika's side. Why was he doing that? That wasn't why he had burst a lung trying to get here. 'He's saved my life more times than I can mention. He saved Ulrika's. He saved yours.'

'That's cheap, Felix.'

'Don't you think you are being a little selfish?' said Ulrika. 'Would you not want to go if you could?'

'He's my husband,' Kat spat. 'I'll be selfish if I want.'

'I told her I didn't want to go,' Felix hastened to add, afraid for a moment that Kat was going to swing for Ulrika too and not at all sure how the vampiress would react. 'Because of you.'

Kat laughed blackly. 'So you send your dead lover to add me to your vampire harem?'

'What?' Felix spluttered, goaded into anger. This wasn't about Kat at all, and it certainly wasn't some kind of competition between her and Ulrika. No one was asking him to choose between them.

'We are *married*, Felix. Do those vows mean nothing to you?'

'Married?' Now it was Felix's turn to laugh, twelve months of pent-up energy and frustration shaking out of his chest. He remembered the day. He was quite famous in dwarfish circles, the human who had wielded the Hammer of Fate, and that and the novelty of a human couple being wed in Grimnir's shrine had brought quite the crowd. It had been cold. He remembered shivering through the entire arduous ceremony because Snorri had pointed out that his cloak was too shabby for the occasion. He remembered the smell of incense, the gruff whispers of dwarfs trying to be respectful. Then Gotrek had presented Kat to him. Their rings had been his parting gift. He glanced at the band on his own finger. A squat dwarfish rune winked in the coloured light. 'We were married in Karak Kadrin by a priest of the Slayer cult. How did either of us think that was going to end well?'

Kat stared at him. She was shaking with weakness and anger. 'Are you saying you regret it?'

I don't know, Felix thought.

'That's not what I said.'

'Hah! Go then if that's the best you can do.'

'Kat–'

'Don't argue, just go. We all know it's what you want.' She glanced at Ulrika. There was fear in her expression, but not for herself. 'But promise me you won't trust her. She's not who you remember.'

'I know what she is,' Felix began, but Kat cut him off with an impatient shake of the head.

'Just promise me. Promise me that when you find Max you'll both come home.' To Felix's surprise, Kat's eyes began to moisten. She took Felix's hand in hers and pressed it to her belly. Felix didn't understand. 'Come back for *us*, Felix.'

And suddenly there it was: the loss of appetite, the annoying sensitivity to the scent of his unwashed body. His mouth hung open. His heart beat for three. Was she saying what he thought she was saying? Was she? *Could* she even?

'How? When did we last...?' Felix caught himself in the middle of a ridiculous mime, then extricated his hand to bury his face in. There had been far too many nights – days for that matter – where his memory ended somewhere between his third pint and the long walk home. Kat smiled sadly and almost broke Felix's heart.

A pit seemed to be opening up around him.

He couldn't be a father. He'd hated his father. And since siring Gustav, Otto had turned out to be just like the old man. What hope then for a feckless wanderer like Felix?

The prospect of going to war had never sounded so appealing.

Ulrika nodded, smiled, then rose as Felix swallowed the butterflies that were flapping up his throat and retook Kat's hand. His fingers were shaking.

'I'll be back. I promise.'

Night was closing in on the borders of the day as the black coach rumbled off the barge and onto the militarised bustle of Pilgrim's Harbour. Longshoremen and day-labourers waded waist-deep into the Reik, men-at-arms barking orders from the bank as the men hauled their goods ashore and loaded them onto waiting wagons. Arquebusiers in long black tunics and leather baldrics that gleamed with brass cartridges stood with firearms half-cocked upon the deck of a long barge recently arrived from Nuln. She lay heavy in the water, longshoremen crawling over her and bearing away bags of blackpowder while, on the shore, a windlass was manoeuvred into position to winch a pair of Helblasters from the vessel's hold. More boats jostled prow to stern to get into the harbour before dusk. Their lanterns twinkled across the water. At every mooring, wool from Solland, lowing livestock and grain from Averland, timber from the forests of the Stir, and armaments from the great foundries of Reikland poured from the river and on towards Pilgrim's

Gate, then down into the great funnel of war.

Felix was the son of a merchant and an Altdorfer. He was no stranger to commercial wharfs and market towns. Trade was in his blood whether he approved of it or not. And yet even he was amazed by the sheer industry that was going into the business of war. It felt as if the productivity of half of the Empire was being channelled through this harbour, as if by organisation, endeavour, and the staggering volume of men and materiel being carted north they might hold the hordes of Chaos at bay.

If only it could ever be that simple.

From the darkened glass of Ulrika's coach, Felix watched the soldiers patrol the shoreline. They were out in force. Swordsmen in padded britches and steel breastplates moved amongst the longshoremen, opening up containers, challenging drivers and searching their wagons. This was war, after all, and the Reiksmarshal was right to be wary of the enemy within. The coach slowed to a halt, taking its place in a queue of carts and carriages that were being held at a checkpoint before being allowed to leave the harbour. Felix pressed his face against the window and looked down the line.

Doors hung open, merchants and drivers remonstrating with bored-looking halberdiers while sergeants checked their manifests against the wagoners' documents, then double-checked both against the contents of the carts. It was clear they had orders to be thorough. No one moved until the officers were satisfied. Felix had a bad feeling about this. He was only a commissioned member of Helborg's staff, after all, and it wasn't as if he was doing anything more treasonable than deserting north in the company of a vampire.

What had he been thinking? Most sensible people were trying to get *away* from Ostermark. To no great surprise, he found that his palms were sweating. What a fabulous way to remind himself what life had been like before he and Kat had got married. He glanced past Ulrika and through her window to the ruddy band of the western horizon.

What had it been, two hours?

'Relax,' said Ulrika. 'I can hear your heart race from here.' With the onset of twilight, she had removed her veil and her face seemed to give off its own pearlescent lustre, like an earthbound vision of Mannslieb itself. A slender scar ran from the corner of her left eye to her temple, but despite that, the likeness to the woman he had loved was aching.

'Not being dragged from this coach in irons in the next ten minutes will calm me immeasurably.'

Ulrika patted his knee indulgently. 'You were always such a worrier.'

'We live in worrying times.'

'I wish you would stop it. It's distracting.' With a smile that gave Felix palpitations, she drew out the top laces of her jerkin. 'I will deal with the soldiers.'

Leaning salaciously over Felix's lap, she dropped the door handle and pushed open the door. A six-foot-tall officer in blue and red livery, breastplate, and a feather-plumed sallet held the door open while, behind him, the sight of a smiling noblewomen spilling from her carriage brought redoubled attitudes of attention from a previously taxed pair of halberdiers. Felix, rather late in the day, realised that he was not cut out for this sort of thing. The innocuous problem of where to put his hands suddenly seemed of terrific import. Even pressing against Ulrika's chest through the simple, mechanical sin of breathing in felt like an inappropriate level of contact.

'Good evening,' said Ulrika, in the most syrupy Kislevite accent Felix had ever heard. 'How we help brave men of Empire this day?'

'Orders, my lady,' stated the officer, simply, and to Felix's eternal gratitude.

'Of course,' said Ulrika, her smile lingering on the man as though she was admiring herself in the mirrored shine on his breastplate. Felix took pains to look anywhere else. Was he really the only one to notice her complete *absence* of a reflection in that surface? Ulrika leaned a little further, twisted towards the front of the coach and snapped her fingers. 'Damir. Dokumenty.'

The swarthy Ungol stooped down from the box and handed over a roll of parchment with an illiterate grin. The officer unrolled it. His eyes widened as he read.

'This is the seal of the Reiskmarshal. My apologies...' he re-read the foreign name on the document '...my apologies, General Straghov. You should have said.'

'Is of no matter,' said Ulrika with a nonchalant roll of the hand.

The man saluted. 'Honour and glory to you in the north, general. And to you, Herr Jaeger. Please allow my men to escort you on to Pilgrim's Gate. I'll not have the generals of Commandant Roch held up on my watch.'

The officer and his men set about clearing traffic as Ulrika closed the door. Her demeanour was smug. Only after the soldiers had been allowed a good ten seconds to be about their business did Felix trust himself to speak. '*You* have papers?'

'You think I seduce everyone?' said Ulrika in mock horror. 'Do I look like I have the energy for that?'

'I'm just surprised, that's all. Those things aren't easy to forge. Trust me, Otto's asked. And how did that officer know my name?'

'Because,' Ulrika began patiently, 'these are the legitimate orders of Kurt Helborg, for the dispatch of the Hero of Praag – that's you, Felix, in case you've forgotten – to the command of Commandant Roch. They both agree that a tour of the front would be a boon for morale.' She produced a sarcastic smile. 'Messengers have already ridden ahead with arrangements for speaking dates across Hochland and Ostermark.'

Felix shook his head, disgusted. 'All of that, in Wilhelmplatz and with Kat, and I never actually had a choice at all.'

'I wanted you to want to come with me.'

'Why?'

Ulrika didn't answer.

'Is there even a Commandant Roch?'

'Of course,' Ulrika murmured, mind still elsewhere. 'He has command of the Auric Bastion's entire eastern flank. From his fortress of Rackspire it is even still possible to see over it and into Kislev.' She paused for a moment as she collected herself, considering her next words before she spoke them. 'This quest of ours is done with his knowledge and blessing. He is the one I call master now.'

'I thought you had a mistress.'

'This is a war that my Lahmian sisters have proven themselves many times to be unsuited for. Archaon will not be moved by a hitched skirt or a beguiling smile. This is not about who we pretend to call master for the next hundred years. This is existential. Roch knows how to utilise my talents best. He has Gospodar blood in him.'

'High praise.'

'The very highest.'

Felix could think of nothing to add to that and so retreated into contemplative silence, watching through the darkened glass as wagoners less fortunate in their patrons slid behind them. Despite the nearness of Ulrika, his thoughts kept returning to Kat. Was he doing the right thing by leaving? Somehow, knowing that he had not in reality had a choice did not seem to justify his decision. He couldn't decide if Ulrika had been trying to be kind or had actually rather enjoyed tying his emotions in knots. But all of that was just a distraction from what he really didn't want to think about.

Kat was pregnant!

The prospect of fatherhood found him no more certain of himself than it had in the Temple of Shallya, but part of him – that small, helplessly romantic part that had once composed poems for Ulrika – thrilled at the thought of returning home to see Kat carrying a little son or daughter of his own. Of *his* own.

'She was lying to you, you know.'

Felix didn't answer, didn't want to.

'I can hear the beat of an unborn's heart, and I can feel the tension in a liar's voice.'

'Stop it,' said Felix, though there was no strength in it. His heart had been pushed through too much today. 'Why would she lie?'

'To make you change your mind and stay? To make you risk failure by hurrying home? It would have gone easier on you both if you had just let me turn her.'

Felix just shook his head and went back to staring out the window. 'Why me? You want Gotrek for this sort of thing, not his henchman.'

'You should prepare yourself for the likelihood that Gotrek is dead. He was already in Kislev before the Auric Bastion was summoned.' Ulrika turned in her seat, then took Felix's hand in hers. She looked into his eyes. Her empathy was beguilingly genuine. 'He was in the capital when it fell to the warlord, Aekold Helbrass. I doubt even he could have survived the aftermath of that battle.'

Felix sighed.

'And this is the place you would have us go.'

FIVE

The Mightiest Doom

'Are we nearly in the Chaos Wastes yet?' said Snorri, staring glumly out the porthole as the steam-wagon clattered and huffed across the vast, featureless expanse of Kislev's northern oblast.

Gotrek looked over and swore under his breath. His face, beard and arms were black from shovelling coal, everything except his eyes that reflected the heat of the furnace. He slid its iron cover shut, then set his shovel blade-down and crossed his arms over the handle.

'If you ask me that once more before we reach Ivan Petrovich's place, then I swear the next time I pick up the shovel it's going between your ears.'

'Snorri hears his wife is a looker.'

'Don't be disgusting, Snorri. You need to stop listening to what those wattocks say about human women.'

With a sigh, Snorri returned his attention to the porthole. The sky was too wide, like a great blue lens above their heads. And the ground was too flat. Staring at it day in day out, all day, every day, gave Snorri the impression of a pit mine that had been fully exploited and then padded back down to confuse any following

prospectors. The view hadn't changed, but then it hadn't changed in days so it probably wasn't about to.
  He hoped Ivan Petrovich had beer.
  'Snorri hates Kislev...'

'The air grows cold,' murmured Durin Drakkvarr. The Daemonslayer stood at a fork in the tunnel, deep eyes distant, running the tattooed claws of his fingers down the damp, uneven wall. The flickering lantern carried by Krakki Ironhame was the sole source of light. It made the moist ceiling glisten and sent the shadows of a dozen Slayers, a priest of Grimnir's cult and an apprentice runesmith weaving over the walls. The air smelled dank. Durin's blackened nose chased a scent over the wall's rough stone. 'I smell taint on these stones.'

'Bully for you,' Krakki grumbled, voice squeezing low and flat through his cracked nose. The fat dwarf kept to the rear of the company, guarding their beer from the skaven, goblins, and faeries that still mysteriously managed to snaffle their share despite his vigilance.

'This is Kislev,' Snorri sighed, thinking about beer, then rubbed his eyes tiredly. The lantern light was making them sting. He had been avoiding sleep – and dreams – for the five days that their journey through the Underway from Karak Kadrin had taken. But even a dwarf as damaged as Snorri always knew where he had been.

And Snorri had been this way before.

'Well done, Snorri,' said Skalf Hammertoes, with a smile as proud and probing as a crowbar. The priest stood from where he had been crouching in the tunnel's westward branch. His bare feet were half-submerged in a puddle, ripples riding out with the movement of his toes. 'They've already started calling it North Ostermark, but aye.' He twiddled his toes in the puddle and looked up to the wet ceiling. 'We've passed under the Upper Talabec.'

'What were you doing on the floor?' Snorri asked.

'Beastman spoor.' Skalf pointed to the tufts of hair that floated in the puddle, then to the scrapes in the ceiling that might have been cut by horns. 'They've been this way, but not in numbers. I say we carry on north for now, seal the way only when we can go no further.'

The Slayers nodded agreement and made ready to move on to the northward tunnel. The old bar-steward, Drogun, his stiff muscular frame squeezed into a leather jack, stuck to the runesmith like rust to human metalwork. Krakki – big mouth that he was – had explained how the last expedition had failed when Drogun had gone chasing his doom rather than defend his charge. The new runesmith was called Gorlin and, in Snorri's opinion, too young by at least a century and a half to be a proper runesmith. His beard was rust-brown and came only to his waist. His armour was a mix of steel plates and leather joints. At his belt were buckled a brace of pistols and he walked with a hammer-headed staff inscribed with a rune that resembled a lightning bolt. He wore a rain-proofed leather backpack on a single strap over the opposite shoulder.

The runesmith eyed Krakki's torch warily, turning his pack away from the flame and giving the Slayer a wide berth. Krakki teased him into a skipping run with a jab of his torch, then laughed and hauled a leather harness containing four kilderkins of Ekrund Brown over his shoulders.

Snorri wondered how long had it been since he had had a drink.

His temples throbbed. And his skin had shrunk, he was sure of it. One beer surely couldn't hurt. It was less than he needed, which had to satisfy his oath to Skalf. Just one beer and he could sleep again.

To try and keep his mind off his dry mouth and itching head, he checked his own pack. The leather was worn and had a rune sewn into it. It was the name of a town, but not one he recognised any longer. *His mother wouldn't let him even as far as Everpeak for the ore market...* He shook his head before the memory of fire and screams could return. He did not think it was of a place that existed any longer.

'Few Slayers carry keepsakes,' said Durin, appearing like a shadow at his side. 'I do not recall you carrying it in Karag Dum.'

Snorri shook his head slowly. 'Skalf said Snorri had it with him when he came to swear his oath. But Snorri doesn't remember.'

'What is inside?'

With a shrug, Snorri unbuckled the bag and opened it. He gave it a hopeful shake in case some beer might have magically appeared between now and the last time he'd double-checked. For the most part it was just old clothes. They were stained with blood and still reeked of smoke.

'What is this?' whispered Durin, reaching in to withdraw a necklace. He spooled the thick gold chain through his fingers, examined the runes engraved into the outside edge of each of the links. 'It is engineering code. Strange, on a woman's chain.'

'What does it say?' said Snorri.

'I was a smith, not an engineer.' Durin dropped the necklace back into the bag as though it had never interested him. 'And even if I could read it, I would be honour-bound to the secrets of my guild.'

'Snorri thinks his rememberer could share some little secrets.'

The Daemonslayer turned his face to the ceiling and for an instant looked as if he might be about to experience an emotion. 'For the final time, Snorri–'

'Come, Slayers,' announced Skalf Hammertoes, padding silently towards Durin and Snorri. He acknowledged the Daemonslayer with a nod, but his eyes never parted from Snorri. 'There will be battle ahead. Tomorrow? Perhaps. The day after? For certain.' His eyes probed Snorri, as if suspicious of water in their beer. 'Have you remembered any more of your promised doom?'

Woods. Needles in his back as he lies flat, can't move.

Snorri crunched his eyes shut.

Giant spiders, everywhere, dead. An old lady stood over him. 'You should have died today, Snorri, but I will not allow it.

'You will have the mightiest doom.'

He shuddered and opened his eyes to the guttering light, the intent stare of Skalf and the blank one of Durin. Why was it that the more he remembered of that prophecy, the more it sounded like a curse?

'Snorri can't remember.'

For almost an hour, Stefan Taczak and the Dushyka rota followed the monster's tracks north. Makosky was adamant that a creature of its apparent size, and in this depth of snow, could not have been more than half an hour ahead of them, but no matter.

They had surely found it now.

A small herder's tirsa lay in the snow like a camouflaged hunter. The dark timber walls of two dozen small structures were banked with snow, sloping roofs hidden under a foot of the stuff except for a few where stub-nosed slate chimneys poked through glittering, refrozen ice. The settlement was too small for a wall, but there was evidence of a ditch, lighter packed snow in a ring around the tirsa and a stockade of wooden stakes and hanging skins inside of that.

But this hunter's hide had been stumbled upon by another. A mass of furs and dusted snow, war cries rumbling through the blizzard, the assaulting force of Kurgan resembled a giant bear, aroused early from its winter slumber and angry for it. The blizzard made it difficult to make an accurate count, but Stefan estimated three hundred men, maybe four, and nearly half as many horses.

Their foot soldiers were running at the ditch from the south, coming in a sweeping crescent that enveloped the tirsa from west to east. They would be probing for a fording point for the cavalry. Stefan saw the Kurgan horsemen holding back with a handful of reserves and a clutch of snow-blinkered war banners. Stefan nodded snow from his brow and returned his attention to the tirsa. The first Kurgan charge had flailed into the deep snow of the ditch. Arrows took off from the stockade, silent black dots in the distance like a flight of starlings.

'Teeth of the bear,' Kolya breathed, for once seeing the steppe exactly as Stefan saw it. 'You were right. Someone does still live.'

He had been right!

Vengeance was good, it was *kvass* in a man's belly to warm him through a winter's night; but even the most boisterous kossar could only drink so much. Hope was better. Unable to hold down a triumphant shout, Stefan gave the order to dress for battle.

The rota did so in the saddle quickly, for there were no hiding places on the oblast. If you could see, then you could be seen. In the span of a few minutes the fur-clad rabble that had looked little better than the marauders they pursued became once again the gleaming pride of Dushyka.

Steel winked dully in the snow, like misted mirrors, beautifully ornate three-quarter armour accoutred with amber and jet. Capes cut from the pelts of predatory beasts were clasped at each man's collar and worn over the left arm. Kolya had downed most of those beasts himself, and Kasztanka looked justly proud under the pelt of a chimera. Like all traditions of the oblast this one was steeped in pragmatism, for a horse accustomed to the scent of wolf would not panic in the face of goblin raiders. The riders' magnificent 'wings' snapped in the wind, curved wooden poles fixed to the cuirass and feathered with the plumage of eagle, falcon, ostrich, peacock, and swan. Every man unique. Every life precious.

Through the heart-shaped opening between the cheek-guards of his tall, fur-edged helm, Stefan watched his brother tie coloured ribbons through Kasztanka's bridle. They would ward off the spirits that might spook her in battle. Each was a different colour and intended for its own malicious spirit.

The rota were still ordering themselves when a guttural roar rumbled through the blizzard. Kasztanka shied from it, wrecking the formation, coloured ribbons flailing from her harness as Kolya hushed soothing words into her ear. The call growled out for what felt like minutes, snowflake to snowflake, too long for any human's lungs.

It came not from the assaulting warriors but from the encampment at their rear.

'The daemon strikes for the Kurgan's heart,' observed Makosky.

Stefan threw a longing glance towards the tirsa's embattled stockade, then wheeled Biegacz about and spurred him straight into a gallop without waiting for the rota to question what he was doing. There was no need for a speech. Every man could hear what he heard, see what he saw. This tirsa was beyond the help of nine men, but there would be others. Stefan was more certain of that than ever.

They could still rescue the wise woman, Marzena, and the traditions of Kislev that she carried with her.

If the Dushyka rota could spare her from the daemon first.

The roar of the siege became tinny and distant, the snow falling so densely all of a sudden that it was as if the lancers bore it with them. Snow and horses, the last two things on the oblast that were constant and true. So heavily was it coming down, so numbing in its blankness, that Stefan failed to spot the Kurgan horseman charging in the opposite direction until they were almost on top of each other.

And thanks to months of aching cold and hunger, Stefan was the slower to react.

The horseman reined in so hard that his muscular black mount reared, forehooves flailing as the northerner bawled orders to the other riders now emerging from the blizzard in loose formation behind him. Man and beast, they were bigger than their Kislevite counterparts. The steeds were draped in heavy hide caparisons that slapped wetly against their flanks. The men themselves wore thick furs over plates of hide armour that still bristled with hairs and leather helms adorned with antlers and horns.

Stefan had hoped that the cover of Lord Winter would allow them some element of surprise, but the marauders rode ready for battle, either fleeing the daemon in their midst or riding to bring back their warriors to fight it. At their chieftain's shout, they hefted javelins and spears and drew back on powerful recurved bows.

'Gospodarinyi!' Stefan roared.

At the same instant, that point-blank volley was unleashed.

Granted power by two sets of rapidly closing horsemen, arrowheads punched through steel plate and barding like pegs through frozen earth. Men screamed, muscle memory alone keeping them in the saddle. A javelin struck a horse in the chest. The animal shrieked, twisted as it fell and crushed its rider beneath it. Stefan screamed into the storm of shafts. An explosive pain flared in his left shoulder. In the heat of the moment though it was bearable and he channelled the pain into guiding Biegacz as the horse rammed the chieftain's mount in its flank as it tried to turn. The Kurgan horse was stronger, heavier, but today the momentum lay with Kislev.

The marauder chieftain shouted curses and grabbed in vain for

Biegacz's tack as his own mount went over, those curses turning into screams for the leg broken under the massive horse's shoulder. The northman's efforts to escape grew spasmodic as the panicked animal sought to right itself, sawing over the Kurgan's legs and abdomen and reducing the chieftain to a paste of blood and guts that seeped out of his armour into the snow.

Six more Kurgan riders went down as the Kislevite charge drove through their loose formation. Stefan heard a whir and flinched instinctively as a lariat flew at him. The rope noose hit his wings and bounced off, then raced over the snow after the departing rider.

Stefan twisted in the saddle to ensure that they were not returning for another attack, then gasped in suddenly excruciating pain. It was his shoulder.

The gardbrace plate was smashed and painted with blood. The bloodied shaft and fletching of a Kurgan arrow stuck out. Stefan put his hand to it and shuddered at the agony that contact brought him. It nearly blacked him out, but he bit into the pain to keep his hand where it was. After a few seconds the agony faded enough to become manageable.

Kolya regarded him sombrely. It was bad and they both knew it. The arrow had punched right through the bone. Even with rest and good care and the blessings of Salyak, it was doubtful he would ever have use of the arm again.

Stefan groaned, but not with pain. It was the knowledge that his fight was done. He reasserted his grip on his szabla. It could have been worse.

It could have been the right arm.

'You can go no further,' said Kolya. 'I will leave one man with you and take the rest ahead.'

The clangour of steel on steel drifted through the falling snow with the rumour of battle, a promise from the next world. Stefan's shoulder was turning cold, icicles of pain etching deeper into the muscle of his arm and back. Marszałek Stefan Taczak had fought his last battle, but he was not dead. The return of Marzena, of her wisdom and lore, would be his last great victory for Kislev.

Grunting in pain, Stefan nudged Biegacz around with his knees. He looked from Kolya to Makosky to the other two riders still in the saddle.

Five men. All that remained of the two thousand he had commanded at the Tobol Crossing. It hadn't been enough then and it still wasn't.

'I will ride ahead and find where Marzena is being held, draw them away as best I can. I will call out so you can avoid the enemy and rescue the wise woman.'

'With respect, brother,' said Kolya with a gristle-thin smile, 'that is a terrible plan.'

'I am injured,' Stefan insisted, turning his shoulder to show them. 'I am most expendable.'

'We are all expendable. We were all dead and mourned for the day we rode south from Dushyka. *I* will go ahead. If you wish the Kurgan distracted long enough to rescue the wise woman then it should be me.'

For a moment, Stefan intended to argue. He was Marszałek, and the decision was supposedly his, but Kolya was right. Stefan slumped back into the saddle. 'Very well. If you can draw the daemon from Marzena then do it, but in Ursun's name don't try and fight it. Leave it to the Kurgan with my blessing.'

'I will go with you,' said Makosky suddenly.

'The plan requires only one,' said Stefan.

With a feral grin, the rider shook gore from his *nadziak* and directed his horse into position alongside Kasztanka. 'As your esaul reminded you, it was a terrible plan.'

* * *

In Dushyka, when the morning dew became morning frosts, the animals of the stanitsa too old, too young, or too weak to endure the winter would be butchered in a day-long ritual of kvass, bloodletting and revelry. Those were the sounds that Kolya heard now as he listened to the screams that rang through the falling snow. Not a battle, but a slaughter, a cull of those too old, too young, or too weak. The smell, however, was beyond anything he had experienced before.

Even warriors of Chaos, it seemed, spilled their bowels when death came for them.

The horses placed their hooves between the bits of Kurgan warrior that littered the ground. Their eyes were wide, ears rigid, every scream and bellow causing them to freeze until their riders encouraged them on. Fallen weapons, trophy rings and knotted ropes of entrails lay everywhere. Blood stained the snow, as if some giant bear had taken a bite out of the ground. Kolya felt more pity for the Kurgan horses, butchered right alongside their masters, than for the men themselves. It was they who had unleashed such horrors upon Kislev. He smiled grimly.

And to the victor, the spoils.

The mounds of bodies grew higher and closer together as Kolya and Makosky rode on. The savagery of their slaying seemed to increase correspondingly. These Kurgan had seen the brutality of death before it found them, and not all of them were dead. There were at least two men writhing about that Kolya could see, viscera-soaked and wailing like newborns. Makosky spat on a dying northman's forehead. Kolya shuddered, clutching at Kasztanka's mane.

Chaos had come to the oblast. Not its armies, they had been and passed, but Chaos itself. The essence of it. The Time of Changes. Kolya could feel it in his bowels, and somewhere in that clangour of combat the Blood God was laughing.

'Enough, Boris,' Kolya murmured.

Through the blizzard, he could just make out the battle ahead. Grey figures both mounted and on foot swirled through the snow. Horses brayed. Screams disconnected to any obvious living thing were birthed, beaten bloody, and then buried under shadowplay swipes of wood and steel.

The business of calming Kasztanka's nerves left Kolya no room to notice his own. He had been resigned to this fate since before the Tobol Crossing. Kislev was the land, and the land was beaten. His family in Dushyka had mourned him when he had ridden out with the rota, but he had not thought to mourn for them and had likely outlived them all.

But now that his moment was here he found that this headless chicken was not yet ready to stop running.

He didn't bother to pray. When a fool prayed to Ursun it was his own arm that got bitten. Instead, he filled his lungs and issued the war cry of Dushyka. Stefan would know what it meant.

'*Dzień dobry,*' said Makosky with a wild smile.

It meant *goodbye*. Or alternatively, *die well*.

Kolya supposed that it did not matter.

Both men noted the crest of orange hair that emerged from the grey of the melee, though neither gave it any mind as they kicked in their spurs and charged.

'Pull it. Do it fast.'

Stefan Taczak gripped the pommel of his saddle, the kvass still hot in his mouth, as the lancer tightened his grip around the brush of fletching sticking out of his shoulder. Stefan tensed against the pain but didn't cry out. That had come earlier, when the two men had removed pauldron, bevor and rerebrace and wielded knives to his leather aketon and furs to expose the wound to the cold. Worse was coming. The shaft was lodged in his gardbrace, but the head had not gone far enough through the bone to penetrate the back of the piece.

There was no way to remove the plate. The arrow would to have to come out the same way it had gone in.

The lancer teased the shaft to unfasten it from the bone. Stefan's chest heaved and he pulled back, but the second man had his horse beside him, an arm tight around his waist. A wooden cup appeared at his lips and kvass spilled down his chin. His shoulder felt as if it were being levered from his neck. He screamed through his teeth.

'Faster than that, damn it!'

With a spurt of blood and a shredding pain, the shaft came free. Stefan slumped against Biegacz's neck and there, he shuddered. Again that wooden cup appeared before him, but this time he found the strength to turn it away. There was a battle still to be fought, and he had already drunk more than his share.

With trembling fingers he picked at the strappings of his gardbrace and let the piece fall. After the pain he felt hollow, as if this was a dream or he had just been woken from one. With a hiss, he hoisted his left arm so it lay across the saddle and his hand could grip the pommel. The lancer with bloodied fingers, a short man with a snow-leopard pelt over his shoulder, took Biegacz's reins, but Stefan warned him off, then sat up and handed the lancer his szabla so he could handle his own reins.

'I am a marszałek of Kislev. I will not have my own horse led for me.'

Meanwhile the second lancer, an older rider in cunningly filigreed but painfully dented three-quarter plate, swung down from the saddle and set about recovering the discarded pieces of Stefan's armour. The sight of it, the pride, wealth, and beauty of Dushyka just lying there, turned his stomach and made his shoulder throb anew. He said nothing though, merely grunted gratitude as the man secured it amongst Biegacz's saddlebags. As long as her rota wore it with courage, then Kislev lived.

'Did you hear that, marszałek?'

A shrill cry carried through the snow and the dulled murmur of distant battle. The cry of a chimera. Stefan mouthed a prayer for his brother. And for Kislev.

Kolya and Makosky charged into the hated Kurgan. There was no cohesion to the Kurgan's ranks, and the two lancers punched through, men falling under their hooves like so many matryoshka dolls. Their wings wailed like dying men. Kolya belted out his war cry as he lashed out with his *pallascz*. The huge blade was for stabbing rather than slicing. It had no cutting edge and without the power of a charge was essentially a six-foot steel mallet. A northman with a bearskin cloak and a flail staggered into range, dazed, blood streaming down his face from the backswing of Makosky's nadziak. Kolya hacked his pallascz across the man's skull, then parried a groin-stab from an adze. He jawed the marauder with a booted stirrup and, with a shift of weight and a yell, bade Kasztanka to side-step into the man, trampling him and throwing down those beside him. He was getting bogged down, but through sheer force of will and ferocity, Makosky had driven himself a horse-length ahead.

'Back,' Kolya yelled. They were too lightly armoured to survive a melee, and their weapons were not designed for that style of attritional combat. He slid his weight back across the saddle and drew on the reins. Kasztanka whinnied in fright, trailing coloured ribbons like a prize mare to market, as she tried to turn through the raging crush of northmen. 'Withdraw and charge again.'

But Makosky was not listening. His nadziak tore a fistful of blood from a Kurgan's face and cast it over the melee. His horse managed another step.

'The blood of Kislev returns for you, daemon!'

The press before the former trapper thinned. The Kurgan fought with a demented savagery, like rats fleeing a burning tirsa, but Makosky forced his horse in and through them. And then Kolya saw it, the killer that passed raspotitsa on its own road of blood and looked in no mood to be halted now. Its look was one of stony-faced barbarity, so accustomed to slaughter and pain that it felt neither the dead that piled around its feet nor the blades that found their way past its enormous axe. The glowing light of viscera-red runes only made the weapon look even more hellish than it already was. The fighter slammed the flat of that axe into the legs of the marauder beside him. Both knees shattered, the man's face becoming a rictus roar as a cannonball fist crushed his groin, doubling him over and hurling him back. Its hard face was crossed with brutal tattoos. One eye was covered with a patch. Its orange crest of hair was torn, its bare torso covered in cuts old and new.

It was a dwarf!

Kolya's mind whirled, the dwarf's axe moving so fast it defied the injunction to be in one place at one time. Kolya might have thought it some runic illusion but for the death it reaped. A northman in blue-painted leather armour raised his twin swords in warding as the dwarf's aura of steel came upon him. The man fell apart like butcher's cuts. The dwarf's one eye was a cut gem of fury. It no longer recognised friend from foe.

'Boris! Stop!'

Too late.

The dwarf ducked the swing of Makosky's nadziak and the charge of his horse and, with such casualness that he seemed to be fighting through something thinner than air while all around him laboured, swung back with his axe to tear out the lancer's entire right side between hip and ribs. Blood fanned from the wound. The horse charged on until Makosky went down like a felled tree.

'Gospodar,' Kolya roared, thumping his breastplate for emphasis as the dwarf came on.

It was still too tight for Kasztanka to turn. In panic, he had her side-step away. The dwarf's axe cut through a spear-armed marauder, then wove around his falling body to strike at Kolya. Kasztanka reared, spooked by the blood reek of him, and the dwarf's axe clove through her fetlock instead of Kolya's knee-joint. Screaming, she made a three-legged jerk backwards, thrashing her bleeding stump until, unbalanced and terrified, she fell chin-forward into the snow.

Holding her to the end when he might have jumped clear, Kolya went down with her. His cuisse buckled around his thigh, but did not break. His feathered harness snapped and jackknifed over him as the side of his helm hit the back of a fallen Kurgan's adze. He felt none of it, but his heart cried with hurt as he drew his leg out from beneath the struggling horse. She kicked once more, and then she whom he had loved since she was a foal, she who had so often been brave when tormented by wicked spirits, was at peace.

Weeping tears of rage, Kolya swept up the adze that he had landed on. It was an unfamiliar weapon, a long wooden haft with a curved blade at the top. It could have been a rock and he would have blessed Ursun for its delivery. Hatred filled him, made him so hot that his skull buzzed with it. All that he had persevered for through devastation and damnation had been taken away. His stinging eyes found the dwarf.

Let every spirit that had ever plagued Kasztanka know.

He would have blood for this.

* * *

'What is this?'

Stefan Taczak stared around the Kurgan camp in disbelief. Surrounding a firepit, and the bodies of the handful of guards the northmen had thought sufficient to defend it from an impassable and already-conquered steppe, was a half-ring of wagons. There were five of them in all, open rear sections turned into unroofed cages by hammering long spears point-down into the boards. Furs had been draped over the outer side of the cages to protect the occupants from the worst of the wind and snow. That in itself was reason for confusion. The Kurgan would not treat even their own wounded with such consideration. But it was those occupants that dragged open his jaw.

A boy in the torn vestments of an initiate of the cult of Dazh lay apparently sleeping in the corner of one, beside the hooded and trembling figure of what appeared to be a cave-goblin shaman. There was an ogre firebelly, sitting alone in a wagon filled with the chewed bones of what might once have been five or six other men. There was another goblin, a beastman bray-shaman, a mutant sorcerer, college men from the south with foul-smelling robes and haggard beards. Stefan mumbled an oath to Ursun. The Shirokij wise woman had been but one of many. This warband had been pillaging sorcerers and scholars from all over Kislev, even stealing from their own and carrying them north.

Why? What awaited them there?

'The King of Praag, marszałek.'

A hunchbacked old crone with ice-white hair pinned with a glittering jet spider brooch crouched by the bars of the wagon that she shared with the cave-goblin and the initiate of Dazh. It stank of excrement, but the filth did not seem to touch her. Her layered skirts were of black silk. The curve of her spine gave her the appearance of a hunting insect, an impression compounded by the glittering, almost faceted eyes that peered out from their ancient web of lines. The way those eyes pierced him was a reminder of why even the Ungol shunned and revered their wise women in equal measure. Theirs was the power to perceive taint in all its hidden forms. Small wonder then that Kolya and Makosky had been so keen to put themselves out of sight and out of mind.

'Marzena,' Stefan murmured, averting his eyes from the hag's stare. He had the itching sense that judgements were being passed on his soul. 'Forgive me, wise woman, that I do not show greater respect. I fear that if I dismount, I will not be able to climb back up.'

The wise woman cackled. 'Do I look like a tzarina to you, Stefan Taczak? Is the weakness of your body all you can think of? Has it been so long that you have forgotten to heed the words of your wise woman?'

'No,' said Stefan, quickly signalling to his two lancers to find a way to get the hag out. There was no obvious gate in the wall of spears. The goblin shifted to the far side as one of them picked up a fallen battleaxe and tested its edge. 'Forgive me again, Marzena, but Praag does not have a king.'

'You could once both wield a blade and guide a horse. This is the Time of Changes. Does denying it let you raise your arm again?'

Stefan shook his head.

'Hurry then and free me. It is not you that the spirits showed to me.'

'We have pursued you all the way from Uvetsyn.'

Marzena gave a delphic smile of daggered teeth. 'Did you think you were the only one?'

Kolya pushed through the press of northmen, just one more screaming warrior in the churn, and swung his stolen adze for the dwarf's head. The dwarf smashed an axeman's shin with a single kick, rolled from the stab of a horseman's spear, and met Kolya's adze mid-stroke. On colliding with the dwarf's rune-axe, his primitive weapon simply shattered. Bits of iron flew from the useless haft of wood before Kolya could throw it down and stagger back, his buckled cuisse refusing to bend properly at the knee. A Kurgan berserker saved his life, charging into the dwarf's path with a short spear. His life ended with a tearing of meat and a bone shudder. Kolya ducked behind the man, and bent to take the axe from the warrior with the broken shin just as the dwarf ripped his rune-axe from his enemy's gut and kicked the dead man aside.

Kolya dragged a northman between them and shoved him into the dwarf's path. The man practically fell onto the dwarf's rune-axe and Kolya swung for the dwarf's temple while it was stuck in the marauder's belly. The dwarf was quick though, too quick for one so huge. He tilted back his thick trunk of a neck, Kolya's axe shaving the bloodstains from his beard, merely grazing his temple and instead slicing through the thong that secured his eye patch. The scale of black leather flapped to the ground to be trod into the mire by a Kurgan warrior who was mercilessly hacked open.

The dwarf clapped his hand to his gaping socket and roared like a bull.

Kolya chuckled blackly, spinning his axe until it hummed. He favoured the axe no more than the adze, but in his wanderings he had been forced to defend himself against worse with less.

'I have fought your kind on the plains of Zharr, dwarf. I do not fear you.'

Muscles flowing like plates of molten rock, the dwarf charged.

The rune-axe struck Kolya's blade like a boulder from a catapult and threw him a foot through the air with a titanic *clang* of metal. He stumbled, ears and fingers ringing in tune, holding onto his wits only just enough to dodge the follow-up that would have severed his elbow had he been a second slower. Kolya ducked and spun low, sweeping for the dwarf's ankles. The dwarf jumped the blade, landed his lagging foot on the axe, then kicked Kolya hard enough across the jaw to shatter half the teeth on that side. For a second it felt as though his neck was going to tear away from his shoulders, but then the rest of his body screwed into the air and he was sent piling into a group of Kurgan warriors.

That seemed to be enough for the northmen. They had just seen one dwarf demolish their warband and a rota of Kislevite lancers *at the same time* and they did not like it one bit. One by one, they began to break and run.

Kolya pulled off his helm and spat out teeth, searching through the blood and guts for another weapon. By the stinking remains of a Kurgan horse, he found a bow and, after rolling over it to put its bulk between him and the dwarf, a quiver. The fletches were globbed with blood, but they would not have to fly far.

Retreating, he nocked a shaft to the bow and drew back. It was a horse-archer's bow, a composite recurve of maple, horn, and sinew, designed to pack maximum power into something that could be fired from horseback. It was still less powerful than a proper longbow or crossbow, but more than enough to drop a dwarf at ten paces.

The dwarf jumped onto the horse's flank and Kolya loosed.

The arrow punched the dwarf's chest, the force pushing the dwarf's shoulder around to the left, but did no more obvious damage than that. Cursing, Kolya nocked a fresh arrow, drew, and fired again. Again, the arrowhead thumped into the iron of the dwarf's pectoral muscle. The dwarf's bruised lip curled into a sneer as he jumped down from the horse.

Snarling, blinded to the fur-clad men in full flight all around by his hunger for vengeance, Kolya prepared a third arrow. This one he aimed right between the dwarf's eyes. He drew back until the recurved ends groaned and his fingers shook with the strain.

Shrug this off, you murderous dastard.

'Kolya, you will hold!'

The sound of his name on a harsh, woman's croak made him flinch. His fingertips trembled on the bowstring. He didn't release it, but nor did he lower it. The dwarf leered, but he too did not move, as if Kolya's arrow had him pinned. Instead, he ran his thumb down the blade of his axe until it bled. Kolya met the dwarf's stare, fire on rock. Acid burned inside his arm. His fingers were numb. He would do it. He would do it now.

'Do as you are told, child,' spat the hag again.

'Please, brother.' Stefan's voice. 'It is Marzena. Do as she says. Can you not see it is a dwarf?'

'This is not a dwarf,' Kolya growled. 'It is a fiend from the frozen depths of the Wastes.'

With his one baleful eye the dwarf glared. Blood trickled from the gaping socket of the other. And suddenly, Kolya could match it no longer. With a distraught cry, he let his arm drop and loosed his shot into the ground. The dwarf just grunted.

Snorting in disgust, Biegacz picked his way through the snow and into the ring of corpses. Stefan guided him with one hand on the reins. Behind him, the old crone Marzena rode side-saddle in a nest of black skirts and spiderweb hair. Kolya emptied the remainder of his quiver and dropped his bow. He had never disobeyed a wise woman since he had been a boy. The dwarf shifted his stance so that his axe could cover the three of them equally and growled like a beast.

Stefan eyed that axe warily. As well he might. It had taken more lives in the last few weeks than Kolya's brother had in a lifetime fighting greenskins and *kyazak*. 'I am Stefan Taczak,' he said. 'Marszałek of Kislev.'

The dwarf grimaced as though something had landed in his mouth and tasted foul. His axe angled indecisively between the two men. He ground his teeth until a giant blue vein bulged from his temple. Kolya wondered when the dwarf had last opened his mouth to do anything more wholesome than scream his battle cry and feast on the spoils of the slain.

'I was there the day the Ice Palace burned,' spoke the dwarf at last in twenty-four-carat Reikspiel. Then he spat on the ground. 'So pull the other one. There is no Kislev.'

'What is your name, friend?'

Again, the effort of dredging speech. 'My name is meaningless to you, manling. If you are Kislevite then be on your way. If you are not...' He cracked a smile full of broken and yellowed teeth and what hint of hurt there had been in his voice was gone. He hefted his axe meaningfully. 'Then my axe still thirsts.'

'You are lost, Slayer,' said Marzena. She silenced Stefan with a hand on the lancer's shoulder. Her words prickled the spine like prophecy, like a spider running down one's neck. The dwarf glowered, but said nothing. 'As Kislev is lost. Your story is that of the Old World itself. With its ending comes your own, or perhaps it is the reverse? Prophecy is ever treacherous. The world cries out for a hero, for the Magnus of this age. And yet you are here. Surely you are lost.'

The dwarf grunted, then shrugged. 'Breaks my heart.'

To Kolya's consternation and surprise, the crone smiled as though amused. 'You have a destiny, Slayer, one that is known even to the spirits of my land. It was they who guided you to me. They speak to me in one voice, and of nothing but doom.'

Interest glittered in the dwarf's one eye. Kolya felt his guts knot, as if they were all stood on some precipice awaiting the slightest twist of fate, a gust of wind, to push them all into blackness.

'If you will not go south, then go north.' Using Stefan's unwounded shoulder as a support, Marzena pointed across him, north and west. 'The King of Praag gathers an army the like of which has never been seen, a host to whet the blood of any Trollslayer. And I see death there. One for you, and one for your companion.'

The dwarf's glower knotted tight. 'I have no companion.'

'Perhaps that is as you see it,' murmured Marzena, but the dwarf was not listening. He planted the shoulder of his axe to his own and turned to look north.

'Then just what is the King of Praag?'

'A favourite of the Dark Gods. He calls himself the Troll King, but I see no more clearly than that: he is jealous of his gifts and resentful of the spirits that would spy on him. What I know is what these dead men knew.' She waved dismissively over the fallen Kurgan. 'He seeks wizards of every race and kind and will trade them for a winter in his city. That is why warbands scour the oblast while their kin besiege the Auric Bastion.'

'Why does he want wizards?' said Gotrek. Marzena shrugged to indicate that she did not know.

'Wise woman,' Stefan cut in while the dwarf glared thoughtfully at the crone. 'This dwarf is a champion sent by Tor himself. With his aid we can hold this tirsa until spring. Easily.' He turned to Kolya, extended his unwounded hand, beseeching. 'Tell her, brother.'

Lips pursed, Kolya bent to pick up his stolen bow. His hands had left bloody prints on it. It was Kasztanka's blood, and already cold. 'Kislev is done. All that remains is to decide how the last of us will die.'

'Kolya–'

'Is dead. Mourned by a family that is dead.' His gaze fixed on the dwarf. The dwarf glared back. 'At least this way, I will get to see the dwarf die.'

For some reason, the dwarf seemed pleased.

'Then it is settled,' said Marzena, silencing Stefan's protest before he could utter it. Her eyes glittered like spiders in ice. '*Dzień dobry*, Gotrek son of Gurni.

'You will have the mightiest doom.'

PART TWO
WAR IN THE NORTH

Midwinter 2524 – Late Winter 2525

SIX

Let there be Life

Three weeks of lengthening nights and worsening weather saw Felix, Ulrika, and Damir arrive at Bechafen.

The state capital of Ostermark cut an impoverished picture; a mezzotint of grey stone walls and millet skies. Smoke sputtered from chimneys in gasping fits, the rooftops layered with white powder, seeded with the promise of Kislev's fate by the clouds that rolled over the Auric Bastion to the north. Through the snow, across the Upper Talabec, the great barrier was just the glim-ghost of a shimmer. But it was enough to take Felix's breath. Even from afar its power was palpable.

The three of them stayed just the one day, an arranged stop during which Felix was introduced to a succession of captains and counts – all of them half his age and as bemused by the purpose of his visit as Felix was – and whisked away to speak about his own war-time experiences at various garrison posts and inns throughout the city.

He had spoken hesitantly at first, the grim stares of men who slept in the same billet as death like lead weights on his tongue. He was a writer not an orator, and it was painfully apparent that if any of these men had seen one of his books they would have burned it for warmth. After a few fumbling anecdotes about his time in Praag he grew into the role, and actually started to enjoy the experience of recounting the tales of his adventuring days to rooms full of strangers who had never heard them and whose own lives more closely paralleled his own than anyone he could meet in Otto's circles in Altdorf. Here a rousing tale of battles against mutants and fiends on the streets of Mordheim, always a crowd-pleaser in Ostermark, there a bawdy reminiscence of his time touring the brothels of Araby hunting the so-called 'Lurking Horror', and come the evening, voice hoarse, Felix had the warm feeling that he might inadvertently have done some good here after all. The Ostermarkers were a hardbitten lot, underfed and underslept, faces blighted by battle and pox. They had earned what brief smiles Felix's tales could grant them.

No sooner had Felix pulled up a stool in his final venue, a tavern called the Hog's Head, and summoned the barmaid for an ale to soothe his throat than Ulrika reappeared and they were moving again. They beat the closure of the city's gates by minutes.

Three weeks from Altdorf to Bechafen.

With that knowledge and a map of the Empire, a man might then con himself into believing the last few dozen miles up the course of the Upper Talabec, the Empire's boundary with Kislev, would be a journey of days, but arrival in Ostermark marked the drawing out of their journey rather than its drawing in.

The roads in the north had suffered the war as gracelessly as the men and even beforehand had been poor relations to those that bore the wealthy and the powerful across the fields of Reikland and Averland. Brambles scratched at the undercarriage as if pleading to be taken away. The ruts left in the muddy track by every other preceding cart had been frozen in for the winter to make every turn of the wheels a gambit of axle-shattering courage. More than once they found the track blocked by a fallen tree, the sort of thing one expected for the dense tangle of the Gryphon Wood at this time of year, but on one occasion the smashed remnants of a wagon train indicated an ambush. There were no bodies left behind, but enough hoof-prints to suggest beastmen. Felix watched the tree-line warily, knowing the herd that he and Kat had destroyed on the Barren Hills had been just one dead leaf in a forest, but nothing attacked. Nothing even moved.

Felix wondered how much of that was due to Ulrika. It didn't matter who your gods were: seeing a woman move a felled oak with her bare hands would make any would-be ambusher think twice. How armies of mere mortals could be moved under these conditions was a mystery.

It took another week to travel the Upper Talabec to its source in the foothills of the Worlds Edge Mountains, where the famed hot baths of Badenhof had once entertained nobles and royals.

Time enough for a Kislevite winter to welcome Felix to the north.

Felix tapped his ring on the pommel of his sword and watched the black coach rattle down Badenhof's swampy main street towards the Breden Bridge and the looming rock talon on the eastern skyline that was Castle Rackspire. He had not been exactly heartbroken when Ulrika had suggested that she go on and announce them to Commandant Roch without him. Being alone with her in a carriage for the last month had been disconcerting. Not unpleasant, definitely not that, but confusing, as if he couldn't quite remember who or what he had been before Ulrika had come back into his life and didn't really want to either.

He was curious though. What kind of a man – *being* – was this mysterious Roch? And why would a man with a hundred miles of battle line, the mustered strength of at least three provinces, and the service of the likes of Ulrika care about the fate of one kidnapped wizard? He chuckled sourly. These were thoughts above the station of washed-up former adventurers and war-poets. Right then he was simply grateful for a few hours of peace in his own head. The chill helped. Sleet blustered into the town down that east-west thoroughfare and contributed to dousing the hot-coal warmth that Ulrika's nearness seemed to bring out from under his skin. He shivered, longing, and wrapped himself into his cloak.

On balance he was happy to squelch into Badenhof in ignorance.

The town's old stone prosperity was braced into the confluence of two rivers, an unpaved and provincial-looking market square squeezed on two sides by the torrent of water where the brash waters of the Breden foamed into the shoulder of the Upper Talabec. A bridge of native grey stone straddled each river. The square itself was buried in sleet and snow, tracked through with footprints from Empire soldiers and displaced kossars hardy enough to brave the cold. What light made it through the sky's grave-dust pallor was supplemented by seepage from the shuttered windows of inns and late-closing shops. Stone-fronted and half-timbered, they closed on the other two sides of the square as if hoping to push it into the river. The weathered stone mass of Badenhof's famous bathhouse brooded amongst them, evocative, made somehow cruel by past glories.

Huddled out of the sleet under the bathhouse's projecting second storey, a group of miserable-looking men in the burgundy and gold of Ostermark shared the slim warmth of a pipe. They looked like the retinue of some lord or other, left to guard the pair of monstrous destriers tethered by the entrance beside them. The horses snorted wetly, occasionally flicking their tails through the sleet. Suppressing a shudder that he couldn't explain, Felix turned from the bathhouse towards the row of tall properties that stood against the more resigned waters of the Upper Talabec. After a few minutes trying to peer through boarded windows marked with the black cross of plague or the old guardian magicks of hawthorn sprigs and garlic, he found what he was looking for.

The wet sign that creaked above the front gate announced it as *Jaegers of Altdorf.* Felix smiled. The provincial branches of Jaeger and Sons frequently traded under that name, the allusion to the Emperor's seat carrying profitable weight in faded, out of the way backwaters like Badenhof. There was no sign of a black cross. He let out a sigh of relief. That was something.

Mopping his fringe from his eyes, Felix swept his cloak free of his sword arm and used his foot to nudge open the little wooden gate. It creaked inwards and he walked to the front door. It was boarded, as were the windows. Felix tilted his head back and squinted up into the sleet. The upper storey too. He ran his hand over the boards that had been hammered over the door frame, then put his ear against it and listened.

Nothing but the white rush of the Breden.

He thought about knocking but then quietly chided himself for being an idiot. The thing was nailed down. Nobody was about to open it, were they?

'Gustav?'

No answer. The whole building was dead.

If only Ulrika had been able to give him more details about the difficulties his nephew had managed to get himself into. It had been nearly two months now since Ulrika had carried Gustav's letter to Altdorf and who knew what could have happened between now and then. For a moment, Felix wondered if Gustav could have abandoned the office altogether, perhaps relocated to the marginally safer and more salubrious company branches in Osterwald or Bechafen, but rejected the thought out of hand. Felix knew that for a certainty because *he* wouldn't have left. Gustav had inherited his grandmother's stubbornness, had confidence enough to land just the right side of arrogant and, not unlike his old fool of an uncle, would beat his head against whatever obstacle this town could present him with until it killed him.

Backing up to take a more measured look at the building, he noticed a side gate leading around the back to the riverside. He tried the latch, but it too was locked. He looked up to the top of the gate and sighed. Typical.

He was getting too old to be climbing fences.

'Do you ever wonder what it is they do up there?' said General Matthias Wilhelm von Karlsdorf, studying the hazed ring of figures within the standing stones upon the adjoining hill. Sleet pattered across his view as he scrolled his eyeglass across the stones. Men old enough to be even *his* grandfather stood under the rain and snow, their rich raiment of gold and pearl now sodden wet. He focused the lens on their faces. The weather had flattened their beards to their chests. Their mouths shaped a chant that the secular magic of the eyeglass made silent. Even without the words, he could feel the hairs on the insides of his ears prickle.

Lowering the glass, he turned to the man beside him, giving himself as long as was politick for a brother-in-law of Ostermark's Elector and a distant cousin of the house of Wilhelm to remember the fellow's name. 'Well, do you, gunnery sergeant?'

Sheltered under a rippling canvas roof, the artilleryman leaned back against the muzzle of his mortar and shrugged. The weapon was a thirty-inch calibre monster made possible by the latest casting techniques of the Engineering School. Her carriage was muddy from its slow subsidence into the hilltop. The barrel glistened with moisture. From the black feather in the man's cap and the gold trim to his overalls, the sergeant was one of the hundreds on permanent attachment from the Nuln regiments. From his nonchalant mien and pox-scarred features, he was a veteran of his fair helping of human misery and failed to share his general's enthusiasm for more.

'Sigmar, may it continue,' he stated simply, voice roughened by powder inhalation and the general moral lassitude of the common-born.

General von Karlsdorf chose not to respond. It was, he thought, rather chivalrous of him.

Matthias Wilhelm was a hawkish man, fleshy in the face, and with a congenital bend to his hips that gave him a stoop and a painful awkwardness in the saddle. A burgundy greatcoat fringed with gold hung off his shoulders and a damp fur colback was pulled down over his ears. A brace of pistols were holstered at his hip and a Hochland longrifle with a carved walnut stock was bound within a leather sash across his back. For this was how a modern gentleman waged war.

At range.

The open veldt of the new North Ostermark was a patchwork of dykes, drystone walls, and the tents and regimental standards of the citizen levies, all in the foothills of a series of massive and wholly artificial earthworks that were a true marvel of the age. Between them they boasted enough firepower to face down a dragon charge. Together with the mortars here on the hill, the arquebusiers, crossbowmen, and archers camped under the walls and farmsteads, and the almost four thousand infantrymen picketed on the veldt that had survived the beastmen raids and plague, von Karlsdorf doubted that Archaon Everchosen himself could make it past him to the Empire in one piece.

And if the Auric Bastion were to come down anywhere between Rackspire and Bechafen then General von Karlsdorf was well prepared for the Chaos forces' inevitable first target.

The standing stones.

The locals called them Trzy Siostry, or the Three Sisters, for the weather-pitting of the three sandstone blocks on its summit did render them vaguely feminine. So not much of a stone 'circle' then on any erudite consideration, but then that was Kislev all over – numerically inferior, semi-barbaric, and womenfolk barely distinct from their men. Well, now Kislev was dead.

Long live North Ostermark.

The hill on which von Karlsdorf had embedded his prized field pieces and carved out his own command post from the dozen-or-so other generals that answered to Commandant Roch didn't have a local name, being little more than a shoulder of Trzy Siostry raised in a characteristically defeatist shrug. Amongst its Imperial occupiers it had come to be known as Wilhelmshügel. General von Karlsdorf took that as testament to the popularity of his command. He returned his attention to the Three Sisters, wiping condensation from the viewing lens of his eyeglass and then peering through.

'Is it me or are they fewer than usual?'

'Conclave with Commandant Roch,' supplied the gunnery sergeant.

'Arch-Hierophant Sollenbuer is gone,' von Karlsdorf mumbled to himself, sweeping the eyeglass along the hill's rugged crown and counting at least a dozen magisters that he could not see. 'Can they carry on with so few?'

The gunnery sergeant did not know, so he did not try to answer. He sucked on his teeth and watched the snow fall.

'General!'

Von Karlsdorf turned as a youngish man in a burgundy-bright

travelling cloak led his horse through the natural rock barricade and scree that would make Wilhelmshügel such a daunting prospect for an attacker. Breathless from his climb, he passed his reins to an aide before stepping under the thin canvas shelter and shivering sleet-water from his doublet.

'Missive from Badenhof, general.'

'Has Roch found where those beastmen are coming from? Just yesterday I lost an entire volley gun crew in Kurzycko.'

The general scowled at the memory. The Kislevite village was square in the middle of the Imperial formations. It was the centrepiece of the defence between the Auric Bastion and the Three Sisters and had been heavily refortified around the solid stone hub of the old attaman's manor. The building had been converted into the most northerly temple of Sigmar in the Empire and a redoubt bristling with small-calibre demi-cannon. Its extensive wine cellars now stored blackpowder and grain. Some of the more febrile flagellants camped in Kurzycko even claimed they were connected to a branch of the dwarf Underway, but twelve months of idling had not uncovered a hidden entrance, so von Karlsdorf was content to scotch that rumour as hearsay. So how a band of beastmen had managed to get in and kill five men there without any of the garrison spotting their approach remained a mystery.

'Not that I know, general. I bring word that General Straghov has returned from Altdorf.'

'Anything else? Did she bring reinforcements with her or any word of when we can expect them? I don't care about the Bretonnian border, or the Sylvanian front for that matter. The summer's plague took nearly a quarter of my men.'

With a shake of the head, he nodded towards the great mass of infantry camped nearest to the Auric Bastion, beyond the range of all but the largest of the earthworks' great cannon. Campfires winked between the layered curtains of sleet, but otherwise they were as still as freshly turned earth. They were Roch's men, an amalgam of soldiers in the colours of Ostermark, Ostland, and the southern oblast, and brought by far the greatest contingent of troops to the field. Although none of von Karlsdorf's superior ordnance.

'One day I hope to hear Roch's secret.'

'Forgive me, general, but no. She travels with a Herr Felix Jaeger whom we were told to expect.'

'One man? I lose a thousand without once getting the enemy in range and Helborg sends me one man.'

'Some kind of hero, apparently. Slew a giant in Nuln, or something like that, all very inspiring. He wrote a book about it.'

'Just what we need,' muttered von Karlsdorf, taking up his eyeglass and dismissing the messenger from his sight before he uttered something uncouth. 'A damned writer.'

The yard behind Jaegers of Altdorf was dark. The building was sufficiently large that it blocked out the few mean sources of illumination from the square, and the few structures on the opposite bank of the Upper Talabec looked long abandoned. The air tasted damp and raw and the only sound was the urgent rush of running water, the river tormenting the pilings of a jetty with white foam and freezing spray. An unladen riverboat bobbed on a bed of seething bubbles and pulled on its moorings.

On the bank by the jetty the unsecured corner of a canvas sheet flapped wetly, revealing sack upon sack of grain. From the bitter odour the weather had soaked through and caused it to spoil. Set back from the water, what looked almost like a rampart of sturdy wooden crates had been thrown up between the river and the back of the house. On the side of the yard nearest the side gate was a stable occupied by ten slightly malnourished horses.

Something still lived here.

Muzzles poked inquisitively from the stalls and snorted hot mist as Felix passed. Without thinking about it, he caught one of the friendly snouts and stroked the horse's chin. It nosed his palm for food and, finding none, pushed it away with a disgruntled snort.

This part of the house would have been where tradesmen and servants had come and gone, where Gustav would have taken and stored shipments from Altdorf and elsewhere before sending them on. He turned back to the stables.

The horse could have been for transporting goods or for running messages, or perhaps even for mercenaries on the company's books. Felix didn't really know how to tell the difference. There was one thing however that he was growing increasingly sure of.

Gustav was here somewhere.

It was then that he registered a light: a tiny chink of it streamed through the cracks in a back door. It was what he was currently seeing by. A wooden hammer had been nailed into the door frame and a sprig of hawthorn looped around the handle. Felix frowned. It seemed a little peculiar for his modernist nephew Gustav. This door was not barred.

He knocked, bringing a drizzle of fine slush from the narrow portico above his head. He hugged himself deeper into his cloak, hunched his shoulders and shivered against the chill. He waited, counting heartbeats under his breath as the echoes of the knock faded from his mind. No response.

'I know you're in there, Gustav,' Felix murmured to himself.

The constant rush of water was starting to get on his nerves. An old adventurer's instinct. Anyone could sneak up behind him here and he'd never hear it over the river. Uneasy, he glanced over his shoulder. Sleet pattered against canvas sheets, the edges rippling in the wind. He forced himself to take a deep breath. He was getting himself worked up over nothing.

Turning back to the door, he saw something. The slice of light that shone through the door wavered, just once, as though someone had just passed between the door and their light. Holding his breath, Felix drew an inch of steel from his scabbard and stepped back. His breath clung to his beard as he carefully watched nothing happen. He was beginning to think he'd imagined it, a trick played by his moving head: a stray strand of fringe or a blink at the wrong time.

Then it happened again, followed by the iron moan of a withdrawing latch and the slow gape of the door as the wind nudged it open. Light spilled out on a breath of warm, sweaty air. Felix grunted as the light hit his dark-adjusted eyes, watching through narrowed lids as the half-open door swayed back and forth.

'Gustav?' he said, easing Karaghul quietly from its sheath as, blade leading, he shouldered open the door and edged into the house.

The floorboards creaked underfoot. The room smelled lived in, of breath and sweat and salted meats. The warmth of a fire brought a shiver. His eyes were still adapting to the brightness, but he had a sense of space, of plastered walls stacked with more goods and, to his right, a suite of armchairs surrounding a low table. The floorboards gave another groan.

Felix froze. He hadn't moved. It had come from his left, just beside the door.

Instinct flung him back into the door frame as a golden blur struck for his chest. His sword rose to meet it, catching it with a *clang* and driving it up into the lintel. A cultured voice swore lightly and Felix slid from under the door frame and backed into the room, trying to put the light behind him. He raised his sword to guard. His eyes throbbed, but he forced them to stay open, his attacker a painful outline around a red glow that pulled his sword from the lintel beam and came again.

Felix twisted and parried. He couldn't see, but he could do this one-handed in his sleep. A *hengetort* guard caught his opponent's blade like a man catching a thrown egg, then the slightest shift of balance and a push sent the swordsman across his body, and into the unchivalrous elbow waiting on the other side.

The man – from his strength and the tenor of his voice, it was a man – screamed as Felix's elbow cracked his cheekbone, and then lashed out with a frenzy of thrusts, slashes and lunging stabs that had Felix falling back. His eyes had recovered enough to glimpse a tall, blond man in light mail and a blue cloak. The other man might have lacked some of Felix's skill, but he was stronger and quicker. His blade too was considerably lighter than Karaghul and made sharp, incisive lunges over or under Felix's guard, and it was taking everything he had to keep up.

Felix gave ground, too busy to notice the table behind him until his calves were up against it and his counter to a belly slash sent him crashing into it.

Shot glasses shattered underneath him and went tumbling, Felix's sword whipping athwart his chest to intercept a downward stroke. Felix grunted as the swordsman turned his height advantage into weight against the two blades. Inch-by-inch Karaghul sank until it was at Felix's throat.

He had always thought his end would have more... *meaning*.

With a snarl, he kicked out, making a satisfyingly meaty contact with his attacker's groin, and then rolled off the table as the downward pressure on his sword relented. He hit the floorboards in a crunch of shattered glass fragments, clothes sticking to their alcohol glaze as he rolled under it, sword still in hand, to rise on the far side already en garde.

His assailant, however, had not got up. The young man lay groaning, slumped up against one of the armchairs with his head on the seat cushion and a rapier loose on the ground a few feet away.

The resemblance to a certain roguish ne'er-do-well in his early twenties was striking: the long blond hair, the sharp blue eyes and hard jaw. All he was missing was the scars. Felix lowered his sword.

'Sigmar's blood, Gustav!'

'Felix?' said his nephew, one hand cupping his groin while the other nursed a bruised jaw. 'I was expecting... someone else. What are you doing here?'

'You called for me, you dolt,' said Felix, sheathing his sword and trying very hard not to shout.

'Months ago. I thought you weren't coming.' With a piteous moan, Gustav manoeuvred himself up off the floor and into the armchair. Wincing, he fingered his cut cheek.

'Don't be such a child,' said Felix, collapsing into a chair of his own. 'Women love a scar.'

'Is that right?'

'Wasn't it Hölderlin who gave the classics their first imperfect hero?'

'I wouldn't know,' said Gustav snidely, but his fingers treated the scratch Felix had given him with new respect. 'I never read that jingoistic rubbish.'

Shaking his head in exasperation – and though he tried to mask it, exhaustion – Felix looked over the room. It looked like an overspill warehouse and smelled like an ale den. Crates had been stacked high and pushed up against the walls. Some made secondary tables, cluttered with weapons and yet more drinking glasses. A few had been wrenched open to spill packing straw and reveal the greenish glimmer of unopened bottles. A fireplace glowed dully in the wall nearest the chairs and a lantern turned to its fullest illumination blazed from the mantel. The two windows were both boarded. By the door, cloaks and weapon belts hung from a row of pegs, enough for eleven or twelve men. Pinned to the neighbouring wall between four knives was a poster that Felix was starting to think would follow him all the way to Kislev.

Victory in the North.

Someone had scribbled something terribly witty regarding Felix's manhood over the illustration of the Auric Bastion and some of the text had been charred around a puncture that looked suspiciously like a bullet-hole.

'That was the staff, not me,' said Gustav. 'Some of them are remarkably literate for Ostermarkers.'

'They don't approve?'

Gustav shrugged, then winced, his expression souring further. 'I suppose some people just don't like being foisted paper heroes.'

Felix raised an eyebrow, then shook his head. Sometimes he almost got the impression that Gustav didn't care much for his uncle. Things must have been serious indeed for him to call on Felix for help.

'Just tell me what's going on. I might have killed you.'

'Or I might have killed you,' Gustav retorted. 'I've been practising since father sent me north. It's not as if there's much else to do.'

'Anything's possible, I suppose,' said Felix, dropping a pause and inviting Gustav to fill it.

His nephew duly obliged.

'Roch wants me dead,' he said simply, glancing at the open door before rising gingerly to go and close it. He peeked out one last time before resetting the latch and hobbling back to his chair. 'I noticed things were off as soon as I arrived. The whole eastern front is supplied through this office, but almost nothing we ship out goes where it's supposed to. I had one of our own supply wains followed and found that it's all just piling up inside Castle Rackspire.' Gustav gesticulated to the crate-blocked north wall. 'There's forty thousand men across the river, uncle. Or at least there's meant to be, but what are they eating? How are they keeping warm?'

Felix regarded his nephew sceptically. He supposed he should be flattered to find his own example of clueless agitation being so well followed by the next generation of Jaegers. 'Other suppliers, perhaps?'

Gustav gave a mocking laugh that he wasn't nearly old enough to have earned. 'Jaeger and Sons *owns* this part of the Empire. Grandfather saw to that after the last war.'

'Stockpiles? Loot from the enemy? Or maybe Commandant Roch simply likes to control his own supply chain.'

'No, no, and no,' Gustav snarled. 'I'm being watched, Felix, and I can't leave this house without being followed.'

'So you stay in the house?'

Gustav indicated the pile of gear by the door. 'After the first few visits from Roch's goons, and particularly after they promised to string me up outside the bathhouse with the beastmen, I decided to hire some mercenaries. They're upstairs.'

Felix glanced up at the ceiling. 'They're not exactly rushing to your defence.'

As though annoyed by the observation, Gustav ignored it. 'Father did ask me to show willing, be patriotic. I thought raising my own free company would kill two birds with one stone.' As an unwelcome afterthought he added. 'I'm sure I'll not actually have to do any fighting with them. You've not seen the Auric Bastion. Trust me. *Nothing's* coming through that.'

'Forget the Auric Bastion,' Felix cut in. 'I can't believe that this Roch could be, what exactly, running down his own army? Ulrika speaks highly of him.'

'You know General Straghov?' asked Gustav, then smiled like a moonstruck young swain. The look on his face irritated Felix more than it should.

'Old friends.'

'She's all right, I suppose.' Gustav gave a ribald chuckle. 'More woman than I'd expect from a horse-loving Kislevite.'

'She's at least twenty years too old for you,' Felix replied sharply.

'That kind of "friend", is she? How very bohemian of you.'

Felix gave his nephew a withering glare, but his wedding ring felt suddenly very tight around his finger.

She was lying to you, you know.

'She came for help, that's all,' Felix explained, pushing the memory aside. 'A friend of ours was captured when the Chaos forces broke through at Alderfen.'

'Another friend?' said Gustav, sarcastically. 'How many you seem to have collected.'

Felix took a deep breath. 'What can you tell me about Alderfen?'

'Not much, so few of the men sent downriver to oppose them came back. I'll tell you this though: I hope that friend of yours likes snow, because he's not coming back.' He laughed like a condemned man who'd just seen the man ahead trip on his way to the gallows. 'You don't just *walk across* the Auric Bastion. It's not some glittering portcullis in the sky that a kindly wizard will raise for you if you ask nicely. It's so high that even the enemy's winged monsters can't cross it.' He signed the hammer across his chest, then knocked superstitiously on the tabletop. 'Praise Sigmar.'

'Perhaps I should go and see it,' Felix mused.

'Don't be so brazenly heroic, uncle. I've just eaten.'

Levering himself from the clutches of Gustav's armchair, Felix stood and flexed the stiffness from his muscles. They weren't used to the exertion. Perhaps he should thank Gustav for the warm-up.

Smiling at the thought of how well that conversation would go down, he walked to one of the broken crates and took a couple of bottles.

The glass was a seaweed green and unlabelled but judging from the smell that still clung to his cloak after falling in a tableful of the stuff, it was some local variety of pear schnapps. He snuck the two bottles under his arm as he opened the door. He doubted Commandant Roch would miss them, and he'd not been able to enjoy a proper drink since his last night in Altdorf. He sighed.

Perhaps it was the young man's resemblance to how Felix still pictured himself. Or maybe it was the thought of Kat, her lie, that he would not have a child to raise in his own likeness. Whatever the reason, he held the door open and turned back.

'Are you coming?'

Ulrika's black coach followed the rising trail as it wound into the Worlds Edge Mountains. The iron-shod wheels broke ruts into brown slush and sent scree scrambling down the scarp to the canopy of spruce that clung to the foothills far, far below. Ulrika listened to the echoes of their fall, and to the assurances that Damir muttered like a mantra to the horses. The sky was grey enough that she could travel unveiled and with her curtains drawn, albeit in some discomfort. She could feel the sun behind the clouds, as one would feel a pyre through a blindfold.

But it was worth it for the view, which was nothing short of spectacular.

The grand might of Ostermark lay before her, a flood of burgundy and gold. She could pick out the stitching of every epaulette and cockade amongst those tens of thousands, but the glorious colour of it all was something she could now only infer from memory and from the dim hues that her inhuman eyes perceived. The army was camped in a rough battle formation around a series of fortified earthworks and the pre-existing creases of the drystone walls that criss-crossed the veldt of Kislev's southern hinterlands. There were hundreds of regiments down there. Dozens of generals flew their colours over the sleet and mud. Like any honest Kislevite, she had used to joke at the virility of Sigmar's Empire, but had someone suggested to her then that the Emperor's poorest province could deploy such a force she would have laughed twice as hard.

At the heart of the aggregated formations was a knoll topped by an ancient-looking henge that her people had called Trzy Siostry. The standing stones were cloaked in black soot from the mortars dug into the surrounding hills. The engulfment of the old by the new. Wizards in the robes of the Gold and the Light Colleges held alternate positions within the henge, a circle of men within that circle of stones, hazed by incense and aethyric power. Around them, warrior priests and their acolytes chanted in unison with the mages.

Like her maker, Adolphus Krieger, Ulrika was master of only the bare rudiments of sorcery. Her new master however had encouraged the development of those talents and through the eyes of her aethyric self she *saw* the magic drawn from the henge like water from a well. The power of the Light brought it from the earth. The alchemy of the Gold transformed it, melded it with the incantations of the clergy to turn it into something holy, and sent the product flooding north.

To the Auric Bastion.

Less a wall than a mountain dragged out of the very earth, it was invincible. Even the winds of magic themselves were blocked. The ground before it was bare of snow and the banners of the Ostermarkers flaccid for want of a breeze from the north. It could not be breached, could not be overflown, and such was its scale that it would have taken a spell of truly apocalyptic proportions to make so much as a crack. It exuded a very real, visceral kind of holiness and, in spite of the enchantments woven around her coach, Ulrika felt as if she were in the presence of Ghal Maraz itself. Ever since Nagash's defeat to Sigmar, and the curse that the Great Necromancer then laid upon all vampire-kind for refusing to aid him, the Heldenhammer's power over the Arisen had been strong. The repulsion from that barrier of force blocked even her master's attempts at scrying.

And yet Ulrika knew that Max was alive.

They had a connection that she could trace all the way back to Praag when his magic had purged her then mortal body of plague. A part of him had remained with her ever since. It had outlived death, endured even as her perception of colour, her internal organs, and all other affections had withered. Perhaps it was the nature of the magic for the Light was, of course, always anathema to the dark.

She thought she loved him.

Her master might have had only a passing interest in Max's welfare, but to Ulrika the wizard was almost as important as their other goals. Nothing less than saving the world. Or at least preserving it.

The rising trail turned in towards the Worlds Edge Mountains, robbing Ulrika of her view and pushing her into her seat as the ascent steepened.

Ahead rose Rackspire. It was a black talon of volcanic rock that jutted from the Worlds Edge Mountains like a vestigial claw. Its battlements studded the flanks of the mountains themselves. From casemates of hewn stone stub-nosed cannon were angled onto the trail and scarlet banners fluttered from the turrets, but there were no guards that Ulrika could perceive. At least none with a beating heart.

The trail terminated at a stark, granite gatehouse. The gates were open and the portcullis raised, but the edifice was far from welcoming. The iron spikes at the base of the portcullis resembled a vampire's fangs. The horses responded to Damir's goading to draw the coach into the barbican's cold throat. Ulrika felt the nocturnal flutter of nervous butterflies. An acceptance of one's power came with the acute realisation of one's place in the scale of such powers.

And Ulrika was but an infant compared to the dark majesty that now masqueraded as the late Commandant Roch.

'My doom is at hand,' whispered Durin Drakkvarr, eyes closed as if in prayer. His face had taken a second layering of muck from the maltreated portion of the Underway they now travelled. He ran his fingers over his face to re-expose the ligament-like lines of his daemon tattoos. 'By the face of the Destroyer, by the coming End Times, grant this dwarf a swift and bloody doom.'

'Not so keen at the front there,' Krakki grumbled from the rear of the column. The way his torchlight deepened the shadows of Durin's face made the Daemonslayer look like a dwarf buried within another dwarf. Krakki cleared his throat, suddenly nervous. 'You'll make the rest of us look bad.'

Durin returned the laughter with a hollow stare. He flexed his fingers and stared at his hands as though marvelling at them. 'Can you not feel it? The end is nigh.'

'Beastmen,' said Skalf with a short nod, then pointed forward. 'Ahead.'

'Snorri thinks we should all stop talking about it then,' Snorri snapped, trying and failing to forget about the beer strapped to Krakki's back.

'Heedless or measured, Snorri, these are the End Times,' said Skalf. 'A doom will find us all however we seek it.'

'Aye,' Krakki murmured without confidence before taking a deep breath and turning to Durin. 'So chuff off about yours.'

Drawing his axe, Durin smiled coldly, then said nothing and walked away.

'I don't like him,' said Krakki, pulling a face

'That's Snorri's rememberer you're talking about,' said Snorri.

'I do not like anyone,' said Skalf. 'And they, in their wisdom, do not like me. You are Slayers and all that matters is your oaths to Grimnir, to me, and to Gorlin.' He nodded at the young runesmith as he passed, burdened by his heavy pack and walking with the aid of his staff. The thin old Slayer, Drogun, and a posse of shortbeards stuck to him like rust. Big Brock Baldursson marched with a graven scowl, axe berthed against his shoulder and eyes fixed forward as though determined to ignore the dripping walls that evidenced dwarfish decline in their own former domain. 'Guard the runesmith with your lives and the rest will follow as dirt follows digging.'

Krakki drew a noisy breath and pulled on a fistspike. A mail sheaf fell down his forearm to his bicep. After jigging it until the mail was free of kinks and comfortable, he adjusted his shoulders into his beer harness. Snorri smacked his lips. He had to force himself to swallow and work some saliva onto his tongue before he could speak.

'That looks heavy.'

A sorry grin parted Krakki's beard. 'I should've known you weren't sticking around at the back for my company.'

'Just a little. Snorri only wants one mouthful, he promises.'

Krakki sighed, shoulders slumping under their load. 'I think Skalf pulled a cruel one on you, Snorri, I do, but an oath is an oath.' The dwarf looked hurt, despite his grin, and suddenly Snorri didn't feel so thirsty any more.

He had hurt enough friends. He remembered that much.

'I suggest you stand by Durin rather than me,' Krakki went on. 'He seems intent on a fast doom for you both.'

* * *

The black coach clattered through the long grey tunnel of the barbican and out onto a cobbled bailey. Ahead, encircled by a natural chasm, was the rugged keep of Rackspire itself. It was built high onto a knuckle of rock, towering high enough over its mountainous fortifications to grant a view over the Auric Bastion itself and into the heartlands of home. On a clear day, her master could see all the way to Kislev City. Ulrika looked inside of herself, expecting to be moved by the thought of home, but there was nothing, just a vague emptiness that she felt that she should fill.

The coach continued over the uneven cobbles towards the chasm-spanning drawbridge that led on to the keep.

Ulrika sensed the granite integrity of the outer walls enclose her. They were massive, almost dwarfish in the ruggedness of their construction, and struck from mountainside to mountainside in a rough diamond around the keep.

The bright colours of Ostermark fluttered through the sleeting rain, interspersed with banners bearing a heraldry that a man of this province would have to study far indeed to recognise. The motif was unusual and chilling: a snarling, inhuman skull, winged like a bat and displayed upon a field of blood-red cloth. Beneath their banners, shadowed figures were slumped on the parapet. Ulrika's dark-piercing vision picked out halberds and crossbows, but not a breath of movement, not a glimmer of warmth. They were meat wrapped in Ostermark livery.

Besides Damir and his horses, not a single heart beat.

The prevailing sense of emptiness only served to emphasise a sense of what she could only describe as *omniscience* as it closed around the coach. Ulrika felt her hairs rise.

'*Welcome back, Ulrika.*'

The urbane voice spoke directly into her thoughts, words rushing through the blood vessels of her brain. It was cultured to the point of antiquity, the ancient roots of an accent discernible only to a fellow child of the steppe who knew where to look. The casual display of power was astonishing. Ulrika had last imbibed her master's blood before she had left for Altdorf, and it remained strong.

The recollection made her mouth ache. This was how Damir felt when she went too long without bleeding him. The monster within her bared its fangs and announced its hunger. This was what Krieger had felt when he had been trapped in Praag the last time Chaos waxed.

'The lifebringer marches on the Auric Bastion as we speak. Everything is prepared for him. For us.'

Ulrika peered through the window of her coach, studying Rackspire's distant pinnacle. One thing Felix had thus far failed to realise was that to get into Kislev, the Auric Bastion would first have to come down. She considered the countless thousands of currently living Ostermarkers in the path of the Chaos horde on the veldt below.

And still she felt nothing.

Kislev was alive, and it had become a land of surpassing beauty. Gone were the fields of grain and barley, their monotony of colour and form. Gone too were the men that had grown them, the livestock they had fed, the vermin they had harboured.

In their place had come *life*.

Mile upon infinitely diverse mile of beastmen, marauders and Chaos warriors clamoured under the falling snow. Armour of every type. Flesh of every hue. Horns. Hooves. Tentacles. Claws. Every twisted possibility of creation was here and here for battle. The roar from so many divergent varieties of throat was all consumptive, a thunderous outpouring of adulation to their champions and their gods. The sound of one name rose above all others. He was the conqueror of Kislev.

'Helbrass!'

Where the bare opal-coloured flesh of his feet fell, the snow melted and birthed flowers. The very air around him crackled with an aurora of changeling energy. It fizzed and popped, spontaneous generation summoning iridescent dragonflies that hummed ahead of his path like evangelists to a new order. His plate armour met the colour-shift of the Auric Bastion with a rainbow iridescence of possibilities. Through the eye slits of his helm he studied the edifice's artificial wrongness. It was a barrier, and life suffered no barrier. Life would dig, it would bore, it would learn how to fly. And however distant its bars, Aekold Helbrass would not exist within a cage.

He had broken free of the Troll King. He would break this.

Watching the legions crushed against the Bastion's base was like watching ants at work. From the mutated giants battering it with massive uprooted trees, through the sorcerers beseeching the aid of the infernal, to the harpies that screeched their frustrations from the clouds it was individually chaotic, but collectively driven. A staccato string of concussive screams resounded over the plain as the daemon-possessed hellcannon of a Chaos Dwarf contingent blasted the barrier. From the forest to the west, beastmen locked horns and fought for the right to enter the ancient dwarf tunnelway they had uncovered there. Perhaps the tunnels even led somewhere? Helbrass was not omniscient. There was no purpose beyond the effort alone.

One amongst the legion sorcerers paused in her incantations as Helbrass approached. Beneath a long, decorative silk robe she wore plate mail the colour of roses with mouldings edged in gold, each piece stylised into the form of androgynous figures that seemed to writhe in orgiastic embrace. She was flanked by an honour guard of fleshy pink trolls accoutred in stylised Chaos armour and with fixed expressions of existential wonder.

The colours of Helbrass's armour blurred into red as he ground his bare hands into fists.

He hated trolls with a passion.

'Helbrass,' moaned the sorceress as if pleasured by the mere sound of her voice. 'I have claimed this part of the wall for my own. When it falls it shall be the name of Porphyry the Unchaste that they sing: conqueror of the Palace of Flesh, survivor of the Trial of Twelve Pleasures, defiler of the flower of Kislev.' Extending a hand, she planted it flat against the sheer stone of the Auric Bastion and produced a smile that could have corrupted a dead man.

'I stand corrected,' Helbrass bowed. 'It is yours.'

Porphyry laughed, then suddenly cried out as a spasmodic wave wracked her body. The life-giving power of Change crackled through her. Her thighs bulged and pushed her feet into the earth. Knots formed in her perfect flesh as it hardened, cracked, and birthed new life in the form of buds and flowers. Her mouth opened to scream, but rather than a human voice there emerged a green shoot that, as if drawn by some sustenance other than sunlight, whipped into the Auric Bastion with a great splintering of stone. Porphyry the Unchaste gave one last moan as the last plates of Chaos armour were pushed aside and more questing shoots forced their way through.

Life was emergent. The humblest fungus would tunnel through the mightiest wall. For food, for shelter, and often for the simple imperative of expansion.

It was better to blossom as the flower of Chaos than to toil in the cages of Praag. He could not defeat the Troll King, but he had escaped him, smashed the Ice Queen, torn down her Ogham stones, and gifted every magician that his former captor craved an invigorative new form.

The Unchaste gave a zoetic pulse, a *push* of labour that thrust squirming hyphae into the wall. Rock groaned, and then the Auric Bastion began to split.

Helbrass drew his weapon, the two-handed broadsword named Windblade. The cracks rose higher and so did the pitch of his laughter.

'Let there be life.'

SEVEN

The Battle of Trzy Siostry

'Heldenhammer help us now,' breathed Gustav Jaeger, his wiry mare spraying to a halt on the black slush road north of the Talabec Bridge crossing.

Everyone knew that Sigmar would return for the final battle. The 'now' was to beseech his aid early and, on current evidence, appeared to Felix completely superfluous.

Across the low, battlement-crusted hills of the Empire's northern front, men climbed from their tents, lowered their weapons, and stared upwards in disbelief. The Auric Bastion was a mountain. It had stood inviolate for a year. And it was coming down.

The creak of wild roots and splitting stone resounded over the plain. It was louder than thunder, as though the earth had been turned downside up and then wrenched asunder. A clutch of gargantuan vines ripped through the surface of the stone. Thorns like dragons' teeth bit into the wall as the Chaos vines strove higher, throwing out waxy leaves with the span of galleons' sails to bat boulder-sized debris out over the dumbstruck Imperial lines.

Horns began to sound off as boulders hammered down on the

forward positions like meteors. Men were crushed and wagons smashed to smithereens, stretches of drystone wall as old as the borders of the Empire were reduced to flying rubble under the sheer tonnage of rock. Into the screams of confusion and pain came the harpies.

Like a cloud of bees released from the nether reaches of hell, they swarmed through the Auric Bastion's breach, cackling and gambolling between the pulsing vines towards the artillery batteries on the surrounding hills. At once feminine and monstrous, they swept down on those men forced from cover by the preceding barrage to hoist them screaming into the air. A sputter of handgun fire peppered the cloud, a futile gesture of defiance compared to the shrieking of the harpies and the continual gut-rumble of fissuring rock, but the wall of musket-shot was enough to drive the flock from the batteries. Shrieking into the blackpowder thunder, the swarm spiralled into dozens of splinter flocks that tore across the Imperial lines. Men cried out, ducked, those that didn't snatched up by clawed hands and dropped from a great height. Matchlocks crackled, the spark of ignitions rippling back across the battle lines.

And then came the rest.

Felix had seen and done too much to fully share in his nephew's horror, but even he found himself shaping the hammer across his chest and mouthing a prayer for Morr to welcome his soul to the garden of the dead. As he watched, a giant so muscular and oiled that he gleamed kicked his way through the vine-choked rubble of the Auric Bastion like a living battering ram. Horsemen in thick furs waved stub spears above their heads and yapped like wild dogs, pushing their mounts past the striding giant until they foamed at the mouth. Beautiful daemon-women with pincer claws kept pace on loping, two-legged steeds while strange stingray-like creatures soared overhead, wings rippling on the invisible currents of magic through which they swam.

Like a man coming around to find the reality of waking infinitely worse than his nightmares, the first cannon roared, then another, the artillery *crump* shouting down the rattle of halberds, spears, a hundred banners, and the cries of forty thousand Ostermark soldiers. Felix's heart lifted to see men of his Empire respond to the hell of the End Times with such stubbornness and courage. He wished Gotrek was here to see the mettle of men.

The Slayer would have loved this.

'Gustav. Ride back to Badenhof, and quickly.'

'You'll get no argument from me,' Gustav returned. He had one of a brace of pistols drawn and tracked the swooping of the nearest harpies anxiously. 'But what are you going to do?'

Felix smiled wryly as he drew Karaghul. Sigmar, but that felt good. Even the knot of pre-battle jitters in his belly felt as familiar as an old pair of shoes or a poem that he had written as a child and thought forgotten. Bretonnia burned, Kislev was gone, the End Times were here and damn it if it was prideful but Felix Jaeger had played some part or other in every major conflict of the last twenty years and he wasn't about to start sitting out now. 'What I came to.'

'You realise how ridiculous you sound. This is what comes of reading von Diehl.'

A vast wedge of Chaos infantry and monsters had emerged from the ruins of the Auric Bastion and was charging after the giant towards the fortified but clearly doomed village between them and the main Imperial positions. Ulrika had called it Kurzycko.

From the shape of the battle lines and the contours of the various gun emplacements and earthworks, it was clear that this was – if it could be called that – some kind of idealised scenario. The Empire's commanders had anticipated, and correctly, that the first objective of the Chaos host would be to take the standing stones from which their wizards summoned the Auric Bastion. The enemy marched under a withering enfilade of crossbow and handgun fire, buying every foot with a hundred lives. Mortar shells whistled overhead to detonate in plumes of dirt and fire. As Felix watched, a Helblaster volley gun sited within a drystone bastion on a hillock to the side of the advance unleashed all nine barrels in a cyclone of ash and thunder. One thing was clear from the explosions and the screams.

It was not enough.

For a second, Felix wanted to send Gustav off with a message for Kat. Nothing complicated, just that he loved her and had been thinking about her at the end. For some reason though, he didn't, instead spurring the horse Gustav had lent him on towards Kurzycko.

Because he still wasn't sure that either was entirely true.

Gunner Heiss of the Nuln artillerymen detachment drew aside the straw gabion that blocked the embrasure of the drystone bastion and yelled range and distance, resorting to miming 'up' and 'down' and indicating yardage on his fingers. The Chaos horde made such a din it was as if the bastion had been flooded with screams. By comparison, the ringing report of the Helblaster with which their own great cannon shared a berth was as homely as songs on Sigmarstag.

Through the narrow slits in the walls, both crews tracked the monstrous pink-skinned giant striding towards Kurzycko. Its bald head rose almost level with the bastion on its hill, inducing handgun fire to snap across from the stake-lined picket below it.

'Range, ninety feet. Wind speed, eighteen knots. Two degrees down.' No one could hear him, but Heiss screamed directions anyway out of habit, then yanked down his fist and threw himself flat against the wall.

'Fire!'

* * *

Ulrika watched from the back of a galloping white stallion as a terrific explosion blasted the giant's head from its shoulders. Blood spouted from flaps of flesh that moments before had been part of a neck and the monster yawed over, crushing dozens and sending a shock wave through the ground that sent hundreds more flying.

'*Gospodarinyi!*'

The Ungol warriors cheered to see the monster fall. Forget for a moment that there were a score worse horrors in its wake: nock another arrow, have another drink, for today it did not matter. Damir hollered with them, standing in the stirrups and riding with no hands like a circus performer as he pumped his fists to encourage them to shout louder.

And a hundred horse-archers from the northern oblast of Kislev – all that she and her master had been able to save before the Auric Bastion had been conjured – could make one hell of a din.

Ulrika wished she could appreciate it more.

The Ungols were warriors born, and commanding them in such a battle should have been a singular thrill. Everything was as she craved it: enemies to fight, a fine horse beneath her and the soil of Kislev beneath him. She was one of the Arisen, reborn to war. She could feel the winds of magic where they flowed, could track the path of daemons by the sour taste, and could foretell the ebb of fortune by the wavering of men's hearts.

In her pearl-white half-plate armour she felt invincible. It was heavier than a mortal knight could wear and still function, and had been specially strengthened around the heart and the throat with the vulnerabilities of a vampiric warrior forefront in the artificer's thinking. She would have slept in it if she could. The old leathers she had travelled in from Altdorf had been for Felix's benefit and now, with battle looming, he had managed to wander off.

Had she not explained often enough that she *needed* him?

Her great white charger thundered through the sleet, droplets lashing Ulrika's face as she cast her nose side to side in search of Felix's scent. She knew his body inside and out. She had just spent the last four weeks alone in a carriage with him. All she needed was a trace and she could track him across mountains and oceans.

There!

Ulrika reined with a curse, wheeling the braying stallion around to face Kurzycko.

'Felix, you idiot! Do you do these things on purpose?'

'*Where are you going, Ulrika?*' The voice rushed through her mind. '*My forces await you to the east. All I lose here today will be for nothing if you do not make it to Praag.*'

Ulrika snarled, but she had no power to deny her master access to her mind. 'I will never make it back without Felix. You know that.'

The howls of the Chaos horde and the boom of the Empire's guns filled the air. Ulrika felt the tingle of their collective roar upon her skin, like the remembered sense of walking in from the cold and standing too close to the fire. The enemy were so numerous that they looked more like some metallic oil that had risen from the hills than an assemblage of independent men and beasts. They were a tidal wave. They could only be mitigated, not reasoned with and certainly not stopped. They were a force of nature that she and her master had permitted to be unleashed.

As she watched, Roch's tattered regiments redeployed to oppose them. No, not to oppose. Their ranks mustered to the flanks of Kurzycko, as if to channel the Chaos legions right down onto it and away from other parts of the field. Such as the east.

'*You cannot prevail against what is coming.*'

'Damir,' she called. Her thrall sank into the saddle and reined in beside her, a wide grin on his wizened chestnut face. Ulrika pointed to the far east of the battle line where a battalion some two thousand strong of heavy infantry and demilancer companies waited out the fighting with an inhuman detachment. The crimson banners of Commandant Roch fluttered in the wind. 'Carry on as planned. I will join you shortly.'

'Don't ask me to leave you,' said Damir. In spite of his rough features and colourful steppe-warrior garb he looked as lost as a puppy.

Ulrika was reminded why she had always resisted the keeping of thralls. Baring her fangs, she drew a long, slightly curved sabre from its saddle sheath.

'Don't make *me* ask you again.'

The fury of the End Times bore down on the walls of Kurzycko. Its battlements flared with handgun fire. A trained arquebusier could make two shots in a minute, three if he was particularly skilled, and the two hundred soldiers with their thick burgundy hauberks, slashed sleeves, and bandoliers stuffed with munitions were the best left in Ostermark. Iron pellets punched through bone, steel, and Chaos plate, and brick by bleeding brick assembled a wall of corpses five feet high. Kurgan berserkers clambered over it. Mutated ogres smashed it down before they too were riddled with shot. Mortar rounds blasted whole sections to pieces.

Whether it was the frustrations of being held behind the Auric Bastion for so long being unleashed or some madness that came with the worship of Chaos, they pushed on, undaunted.

Cannon and handgun fire blistered the emplacements of the surrounding hills and earthworks.

'Reload,' roared Gunner Heiss over the ringing in the cannon crew's ears, waving his hand in a circle above his head. *Turn it around. Quickly. Quickly.*

The great cannon was hauled back on its tracks until the chains on its carriage yanked taut. A crewman rammed a sponge down the muzzle to clean the inside of the barrel while a second fetched powder. The sponge was removed, powder poured inside followed by wadding and then a third man tipped in the cannonball. It hit the wadding with a dull *thunk* and the fourth and final crewmen rammed it tight. Then all four men put their shoulders to the wheels and heaved it back into firing position. Heiss withdrew the gabion from the embrasure, then screamed as a torrent of flame jetted through the slit and immolated the top half of his body.

Harpies shrieked overhead as the Chaos dragon, Kalybross, thumped into the hillock, warbled like a strangled child, and then demolished the entire bastion with a swipe of its claws. Men and their machines scattered down the hillside. Kalybross beat its wings for lift before washing a parting gout of dirty red flame over the terrified arquebusiers on the hill. Armour melted and flesh burned, powder cartridges ignited like bones popping in a fire.

Praag had been too small, and the Troll King too patient in the gathering of his monstrous host. Kalybross craved conquest and with Helbrass he would have it.

A sibilant chuckle rippled along the dragon's long neck as it launched its bulk into the air and swooped on Kurzycko.

Crael of the Blue Wolf sprinted ahead of his warband. Sleet beat off his bare chest. Arrows and solid-shot rained from the front and from both sides, delivering death with the distant hand of gods. The Zar of the Blue Wolves drove himself through the storm with a roar and launched himself onto the ragged block of stinking, blood-soaked halberdiers like the wolf into which the Changer had remade him.

They didn't react, or did so too slowly, halberds jerking about like bad clockwork toys as Crael's axes went to work, tearing out jugulars, splitting bellies and severing limbs. There was little blood.

Even their guts flowed sluggishly. They stank of emptied bowels and rot. A warrior whose weapon arm Crael had just severed stumbled around after him, moaned, and then lunged to take a bite out of his neck.

The walking dead. The southmen were desperate indeed.

With a scissoring motion of his axes, the Zar beheaded the dead thing.

'Helbraaaaassss!' he howled, crying to the Chaos moon, as the fastest of his warband caught up and ploughed into the halberdiers.

'Archaon!' came the return. 'Tchar!'

No man could stand against the onslaught of the Blue Wolves, but the dead fought on even as they were torn limb from limb and with hearts impaled on blood-soaked adzes. The charge slowed, bogged down in a stew of entrails and cold bodies. Clammy, rot-softened soldiers pressed him from all sides.

With a snarl of animal rage, Crael drove forward: the Wolf of Tchar would rip himself a path in the dank blood of the dead! A heavy blade swung for him. He ducked and smashed the corpse's head from its shoulders. The grave held no fears for one of the gods' immortals. He pounced on another, splitting its skull and spilling its cold brains over the snow. He gave a triumphant howl that his warband picked up.

The plains to the east of the southman village lay open. Only a handful of zombies and a single woman still stood in his way. She was slender, in the way of southern women, and pale as bone carved from the earth by a winter storm. She was garbed in a dress so white it was almost translucent and seemed to sink away *through* the earth at her feet.

Crael bared his teeth and advanced.

The woman smiled back, spreading her arms as if to welcome him. As she did so, she floated an inch from the ground, the hem of her dress falling past her feet. Her hair billowed around her like the moon's halo, skin seeming to wither and retreat into a cruel mask that had been blackened as if by a witch's curse.

Eye sockets blazed diamond blue as, still smiling, the banshee took a deep breath.

The banshee's scream turned hair white and sent shivers through men's hearts as far away as Wilhelmshügel.

'Sigmar's blood,' breathed General von Karlsdorf as the malignant pulse shocked through the flanks of the Chaos charge.

After a moment's hesitation, pride trumped fear and he raised his eyeglass. The motive blur focused onto a pale figure, ethereal as starlight, and surrounded by wizened and lifeless corpses. Only their furs and barbarian trophy rings identified them as Kurgan. He watched in horror as some of them began to twitch, atrophied muscles struggling to grasp dead men's weapons and rise again. With trembling fingers, he lowered the glass.

Ostermark had her share of horrors, but never would he have expected to see the living and the dead side-by-side this side of the Sylvanian border.

The alliances we must make, he thought, wondering, not for the first time, who Roch had sold his soul to. Reaching into his burgundy greatcoat he pulled out a silver hip flask filled with a liquor the natives called *gorilka*. He swirled its contents without the slightest intention of opening it.

Dimly, his hearing virtually obliterated by the pound of mortars, he became aware that the guns had stopped. The gunnery sergeant in charge turned to him with smoky, bloodshot eyes.

'What should we fire at, general?'

Von Karlsdorf stared at the Reiklander as though he had been replaced by a village imbecile.

'They're in Empire colours, aren't they? So fire at the blasted northmen.'

Felix screamed as the banshee wail pierced his mind and stripped years from his body. He felt the lines in his face deepen while new ones were etched into his skin. His hair whitened, the world beginning to turn grey until he scrunched his eyes shut to block it out. The hands clamped over his ears began to shake as muscles withered and joints swelled. The horse beneath him faltered and ribs started to poke through against his knees.

This was it. This was how Kat had felt under the touch of the lichemaster.

Felix clung to the saddle pommel with fingers that already felt like they belonged to a skeleton and drew a rattling breath as, after what felt like a hundred years off his life, the scream faded into the blessed background roar of battle. Stutteringly, his grip strengthened and his horse recovered its stride, though neither felt quite as sure as they had been and Felix feared the effects would prove permanent. If his stomach had felt any less feeble he was sure that he would have thrown up.

A banshee: the restless shade of an evil witch.

What had the lords of Ostermark aligned themselves with to stand strong against Chaos? And how exactly did that differ anyway from his journeying alongside Ulrika? Watching as the shambling line of halberdiers – and now marauders too – groaned and hacked at the tide of Chaos, Felix prayed they might all live long enough to regret their choice of friends. This at least explained why Commandant Roch hadn't needed Gustav's wares.

He smiled. One less thing to worry about.

With a shriek, a harpy swept overhead. Felix clung to his horse's neck as it raced by, swinging blindly back to ward off the flock that followed. There was a rustle of leather, the grave-stink of rotten flesh, and claws stitched across the back of his mail. He cried out and struck back for the harpy that was savaging his cloak, missing by a yard as the winged beast veered aside and caught an updraft.

Felix cursed as it tucked its wings and dived back in, wondering how anyone managed to fight and ride at the same time. The harpy swooped down, claws outstretched, just as the galloping horse leapt a drystone wall, slamming Felix's face into its neck and his back into the harpy. The creature squawked in surprise and began to flap away, but Felix too reacted on instinct, slashing the tip of Karaghul across the membranous underside of its wing and sending it on a wailing spiral to the ground. The remaining harpies seemed content to streak overhead onto Kurzycko and Felix let out a relieved breath.

Handgun and bow fire tracked them, but they were too nimble, swooping around the ornate onion dome of the attaman's manor and harrying the defenders that were still trying to target the Chaos infantry. Soldiers ran through the streets with spears, accompanied by charging horsemen wreathed in smoke from their discharging pistols. Felix tried to think of something he could do to help, but it was hopeless. He was one man in the face of a hundred thousand.

The horse galloped on, and despite his continuing conviction that they were all finished, he felt warmth spread from his hand where it touched the dragonhead hilt of his sword, up his arm and into his body. It was too hot to be comfortable but didn't burn, more like a hot pack to reinvigorate a sore muscle. New strength and a strange courage washed though him. He was still doomed, but it didn't seem to trouble him nearly so much. Karaghul became so hot that it scorched his hand, but rather than make him flinch his fingers tightened.

The sleet was no longer falling on his head and he looked up just as a heavy shadow fell across him. Felix gawped at the Chaos dragon that swept overhead, blood oozing from the red scales of its titanic frame. A droplet splotched Felix's mail and the downwash from its flight ruffled his hair. Its shadow stretched on; neck, wings, body, finally moving on with a spatter of sleet and a muscular whip of the monster's tail. He saw the terror that gripped the defenders of Kurzycko at the monster bearing down on them from above. But Felix didn't share it. All he felt was a desire that made his earlier pleasure at holding the sword again seem shallow, an anger that the dragon was heading towards the village and not towards him.

The rational part of him knew that that was a foolish thing to be annoyed about whilst one was surrounded by the forces of Chaos, but it was coming from the blade not from him. The Templar blade was intended for a certain life, as Felix was becoming increasingly convinced that he was. It was forged to be the bane of dragons. Felix still didn't know what he was meant for, but right then and there, with the semi-sentient will of Karaghul saturating him with its power, that didn't seem important.

The dragon banked as it approached the village, long tail whipping a chunk from the battlements of the attaman's manor and sending a pair of crossbowmen screaming to their deaths. Flame licked over its fangs and then erupted in a raging torrent of fire that seared down a Kurzycko street and reduced a score of spearmen and a unit of pistoliers to ash. Survivors screamed, stumbling into sidestreets and rolling through slush to douse burning livery as, around them, wood and thatch began to flicker. The dragon beat its wings and circled the manor for another pass. A loose volley of gunfire chased it, but it was so vast they were little more than pinpricks. It would take a direct hit from a great cannon to make it blink.

The smell of smouldering timbers filled Felix's nose as the dragon glided lazily around the manor's onion dome roof and unleashed another jet of blood-tinged flame onto the streets. Felix waved his sword above his head and shouted abuse. The blade seemed to glow as if it had been plated with gold as the monster swelled in Felix's vision. He felt excitement rise, but retained just enough good sense to dismount and shove his horse back on its way.

He was one man, but the Chaos dragon seemed to regard him as something more. It was probably just the sword, he thought. With a crunch of masonry, the dragon landed on the roof of one of the fortified buildings at the edge of the village. Its massive wings beat to steady itself, the power behind them snatching at Felix's cloak and threatening to throw him over. From somewhere he found the strength to stand up to it, angled his glowing sword into what must have seemed a pointless guard, and continued to yell challenges and threats that would have turned his stomach had he been thinking clearly. Its neck snaked high above its beating wings. Felix could see the blue tint in the dragon's eyes and smell the sulphur of its breath. Liquid fire dribbled from its jaw.

'What are you waiting for?' Felix shouted. 'I've slain bigger than you.'

The dragon's neck rippled and it emitted a barrage of breathy barks. Felix strongly suspected it was laughing at him. He tightened his grip on his sword, willing it to come, but then the monster's head swung back towards the village as if startled. Felix glanced that way too, just in time to see the sturdy oak doors of the attaman's manor explode outwards in a blast of timber before the battering ram shape of a monstrously-armoured minotaur.

A handful of broken Empire swordsmen were flung out onto the street before it. The creature lowered its head and bellowed, scraping its cloven feet through the road and smashing the butt-end of a monstrous warhammer into the ground. A mass of beastmen spilled after it. Their coarse fur was thick with mud as if they'd been travelling underground. Embers caught burning reflections in their dull cow eyes as their senses adjusted to the fire and cries of the outside world. Where in damnation had they come from? Felix watched them clutch axes and wicked-looking glaives and charge into the smoke that was filling Kurzycko's streets.

A lot of them were running towards Felix.

Perfect, he thought, turning his body and angling Karaghul to receive the charge. He kept one eye on the dragon, which watched from its perch as though amused.

Absolutely perfect.

'Where did Snorri's one go?' bellowed Snorri Nosebiter, searching about for the armour-plated juggernaut that had been looming over the horned heads of the beastmen packing the tunnel with their braying and dung stink just seconds before.

'Damn it, Snorri. Just hold the gate, will you?'

An arc of lightning jagged around the runesmith's staff and blasted a ram-headed gor into sizzling meat that painted the ceiling and made Snorri hungry. Gorlin pointed his still-crackling staff down the tunnel to a stone dolmen engraved with runes that surrounded what had once been a rune-sealed entrance to a set of stairs to an old watchtower or a mine. Snorri grinned.

'That's where it went.'

'Get in line, Snorri.'

Krakki punched his foot-long fistspike down a beastman's throat, then hoisted the creature off its feet, bludgeoned it against the ceiling and tossed it like a set of caltrops under the hooves of its brethren. His paunch was splattered with gore and he was sweating hard under the torch he held in one hand.

Smoke at the end of the valley.

Snorri shook off the unwelcome memory, took off a beastman's snout with his hatchet and then shattered its chest with his hammer. The bull-headed thing went down with a piteous mewl and Snorri gleefully kicked it in the head with his mace-leg until its shoulders were glued to the floor by the sticky paste that had been its neck.

Dead dwarfs with arrows in them floated face-down in the river.

Torchlight flickered across the tunnel, alighting on beastmen and Slayers seemingly at random.

The beastmen filled the tunnel, horns and herd totems scraping the ceiling and crushed six abreast between the walls. Brock Baldursson bellowed the names of the lost Kislevite clans as he went down under a mass of spears. Lucky. Drogun and Durin led the majority of the dwarfs in a more measured but no less resolute advance, shielding the runesmith and forcing the beastmen onto a wall of death-hungry Slayers. Gorlin shouted a command that caused the bound magic in one of his staff's many runes to flare and send a chain of lighting searing through the cramped beastmen.

The sweet smell of well roasted meat filled the air. It disturbed the ale sloshing in his otherwise empty belly and he threw up over the bloodstained flagstones.

Snorri blinked away the strobing after-images of skeletons contorted by a weird dance of agony, ducked a beastman's swing then tackled it to the ground and hammered the butts of both his weapons into its eyes. Krakki gutted another that Snorri finished off with an axe across the throat. The fat Slayer cursed Snorri's selfishness with every oath he knew and then some, but Snorri was already moving on. The smell of ozone and burned hair clung to them all. His mace-leg tripped a beastman twice his height. His hammer shattered the kneecap of another. Snorri's axe then splintered the haft of its halberd as it attempted to brain him, and he finished it off with a headbutt to its dog-like snout.

'That one almost had me,' Krakki roared indignantly, but Snorri was no longer listening.

He wanted to laugh, but couldn't. It wasn't fun any more. He beat at his bare skull and howled in the goat face of the beastman that was swinging a hammer for his face. Before it could hit, a crossbow bolt zipped by Snorri's ear and took the beastman through the heart. It grunted in surprise and dropped its hammer, then fell itself.

Skalf Hammertoes calmly slotted another quarrel into the track and manually heaved back the draw as Snorri glared at him. His fists clenched around his weapons until the wooden hafts groaned. That could have been it done.

No more memories.

'No doom for you yet, Snorri,' said the black-robed priest. 'There are other oaths yet to be fulfilled today.'

'Where is Snorri's rememberer?' Snorri growled.

'I am not your damned rememberer,' Durin shot back angrily. Snorri realised he had never seen the Daemonslayer angry before, or anything but blank, as if he came alive only when he fought. A tuft of bloody fur was stuck to the eye of his axe and his fell tattoos were wet with blood. He pointed to the dolmen. 'Just take the gate and we can all die in peace.'

Krakki let out a great huff of breath and wearily beat his bulk another foot in that direction.

Die in peace.

That sounded nice.

With a full-throated battle cry, Snorri charged after the other Slayer.

* * *

The first beastman out of the village was foaming at the mouth and on fire, and easy prey for Felix's fiercely glowing runesword. It practically impaled itself with its own head-down charge. Felix withdrew the blade, turning outside the dead beastman's collapse and lashing behind it to open the chest of the horse-headed beast following. The beastman stumbled, pressing on its exposed ribs, but the hulking bestigor behind it drove its ram horns into the beastman's back and hurled it bodily through Felix's guard.

Felix cried out, dipping his sword out of the way as the beastman hit him like a side of beef in the ribs and twice Felix had the air driven from his lungs; first as his back hit the frozen earth, and then again as the beastman landed on top of him. Wheezing, he took a grotty handful of its chest hair in a bid to hold it off him while with the other he maintained his grip on Karaghul. The longsword was not exactly of much use when one's horse-headed foe was snorting its foul breath into your face, but he could still feel the strength it was pushing into him. Felix was still even-headed enough to realise that, pound-for-pound, he had no earthly right to be wrestling with a beastman without it. He almost smiled.

The Chaos dragon was still enjoying the show.

Praise Sigmar for small mercies.

The beastman that straddled him squirted blood from its gashed chest and Felix felt his grip loosen. With a gasp of desperation, Felix whacked it in the side of the head with the flat of his blade. Karaghul took a chip from its curling horns and startled it enough for Felix to get strength behind the knee he stabbed into its groin. It brayed in sudden paroxysms and Felix was able to free a foot to shove the beastman back.

The massive bestigor loomed into his vision in its place. It was swinging a morningstar and, insofar as was possible with its warped goat features, looked to be smiling. Felix drew up onto one knee and raised his sword to parry as the spiked ball swung down on its chain. He had time for one wild thought before his brains were smashed out of his skull.

He *really* wished Gotrek could have been here for this.

He thrust up his sword, closed his eyes, and felt blood rain over his arm and face. It was his own, it surely had to be his own, but there was no pain except from where his back had hit the ground and his grip on Karaghul had lost none of its preternatural power as might be expected if his forearm had just been pulped by a morningstar. He opened his eyes and glanced over his rock steady guard to see the bestigor choking on a cavalry sabre that had been rammed so far down its throat that the hilt had cracked its back teeth.

Stupidly, his first thought was that Gotrek had saved him. It had become an instinctual response to having his bacon hauled out of the fire, and the strength required to drive the heavy, slashing blade two feet through a beastman's neck was staggering.

But of course, it wasn't the Slayer.

Ulrika ripped her sword free, taking most of the bestigor's face with it, spun for power and split a beastman from shoulder to sternum with a two-handed slash. Blood sprayed her pearl-white plate armour. She was an angel of the steppe, an avatar of cold-handed destruction.

Another charged in, horns down. Ulrika sidestepped behind it as though the beast was weighed down by chains and neatly severed its spinal cord with a slash of her own claws. As it toppled, she reclaimed her sword from the bisected beastman with a crack like a butcher splitting spare ribs.

In a numb kind of horror, Felix watched the vampiress blur from point to point. He never saw her move. It was like watching static images that were projected onto one place and then shifted when a beastman fell apart into an eviscerated ruin. At one point he was certain he saw two of her. Felix tried to tell himself he was foolish to be so shocked. It was still Ulrika; but that line of rationalisation was starting to stretch a little thin even for him, so he tried another.

Gotrek too had been terrifying at times. Was this really so different?

One of the beastmen swung a cleaver for where Ulrika stood, but the apparition was merely an illusion of her speed. Its cleaver hacked through snow and air and a split second later Ulrika fell on it from behind, lifting it from the ground and sinking her fangs into its neck. Its panicked heart fired a spurt of blood that ricocheted from the inside of Ulrika's cheek and painted her inhuman beauty with crimson splatters. She took one mouthful and then snapped the beastman's neck with such force that its body spun three times before impacting on the ground with a snap of bone. Another charged in, swinging an axe before it like a drunkard trying to strike a wasp. Ulrika twisted like a snake, landing a rib-shattering kick that threw the mewling creature through the smouldering drystone wall of the nearest building. The breach coughed flame and the beastman screamed as it burned.

The surviving beastmen bleated in disbelief.

And something else gave its volcanic rumble of disapproval.

Felix turned as the Chaos dragon opened its mouth. A fire hot enough to burn damned souls rose from its throat. Some undeniable imperative threw Felix in front of Ulrika just as the dragon exhaled. Felix swallowed the desire to scream as a ball of fire struck down towards him and he brought Karaghul up as if to parry a blow.

The runes on the weapon blazed brighter than the blade itself and the dragonbreath struck a shell of energy. Fire raged across an invisible barrier as a blast of pressure drove him down onto one knee. Felix felt the downward force intensify, could almost visualise the dragon dredging every last scrap of breath from its monstrous lungs. With a roar of effort, he pushed back. There was no way he should have been able to stand, much less take a forward step, but somehow he managed both and more. He felt like a champion. Karaghul pulsed in anticipation of blood. He struck, piercing his own sphere of protection and slicing through the meat of the dragon's forelimb.

The dragon roared in unexpected pain, smoke roiling from its throat in bursts as it retreated from the pathetic human that had somehow managed to hurt it. With an exultant laugh that was all Karaghul, Felix ran after it, only for the beat of the dragon's wings to force him back. The flesh of his cheeks rippled under the downwash as the dragon turned its awesome strength into lift. The dragon climbed and Felix set himself for another attack. The monster's blue eyes glittered with a madness and hate beyond human reckoning. The foul smoke issuing from its mouth again became fire. Felix met its stare and willed it to bring it on.

Then the dragon hissed, threw down another blast of copper-tainted wind to climb higher still and then turned away towards the standing stones that Ulrika had called Trzy Siostry. Felix hurled insults after it, but there was absolutely nothing he could do to bring it down from here. As if to taunt him, the dragon sent a fiery wave searing across a line of bowmen. The drystone wall they were cowering behind flew apart as though it had been detonated from underneath to leave a blackened crater strewn with bodies.

Felix wavered, returning the power he had been loaned as the distance between Karaghul and the dragon increased, then slumped back down to one knee.

Strong hands hoisted him back onto his feet. Cold hands. Felix shivered. Ulrika's face was slick with gore, the horror of the familiar juxtaposed with something from a nightmare. He couldn't shake the image of the moment she had torn that beastman's throat out from his mind. She wasn't even breathing hard. But then of course she wouldn't: she didn't breathe.

'What's the matter?' asked Ulrika, swaying a little, no doubt in shock. A well-intentioned smile made her look only more macabre. 'You've fought a dragon before.'

Breathless, Felix nodded towards the dead beastmen. 'It's a lot for just one day.'

Ulrika rubbed her chin as though just realising there might be something there, then shook her head angrily as if to clear it. She pointed east.

The roof of a two-storey building collapsed in flames. Felix wondered why nobody was trying to put the fires out, but then realised that they were probably too busy on the walls. On reasoned reflection, the only thing to wonder was why nobody was running away. The sound of a hymn rose over the flames, its vocals interweaving with the hellish instruments of handgun fire and screams. Smoke was beginning to sting his eyes, but Felix looked where Ulrika directed. The undead regiments fighting on the open veldt were being ground down under wave after wave of berserker assaults.

'My master waits for us on the other side of the line, beyond the Ostermarkers' positions.' She nodded to the zombies as she wiped her sabre clean and sheathed it. 'His soldiers can buy us time, but nothing more. When they fall this entire plain is going to be overrun. My master has planned accordingly, but we have to take this one chance to get through into Kislev.'

Felix shook his head fiercely, and pulled away from her. The heat on his back was intense. For the defenders still in Kurzycko it must've been appalling. But they were going to die for the Empire.

'These people are going to die,' said Felix. 'There must be something we can do to help them.'

'There isn't,' said Ulrika, so cold. 'Even Gotrek would see that and take his doom where it could do some good.' She grasped him by the shoulder, crushing any thoughts of escape. Felix realised that she could pick him up and drag him any time she chose, or dazzle him as she had in Altdorf, and yet she opted to try reason. Felix wasn't sure whether that reassured him or not. 'You just saved my life, Felix. Now let me save yours. For Max's sake if not your own. We'll take my horse.'

Putting her fingers in her mouth, she emitted a high-pitched whistle that made Felix wince.

A sense of foreboding turned Felix back towards the village. Whatever it was, it knotted in his gut. The ground appeared to be trembling, not in fear, but more in anticipation, as if it was possessed of something miraculous *in potentia*.

His gaze fixed on Kurzycko's north wall, a well-engineered construct of limestone blocks reinforced with iron rods and thick oak beams. Specks of blackpowder jigged along the parapet. Banners jerked an odd dance as their poles were shaken from beneath. The Ostermarkers themselves noticed the instability of the battlement but had precious little enough time between reloading and firing to give it any notice. None of them were able to see the hungry white mould spreading through the stonework beneath their feet, mortar crumbling into excremental dust wherever it touched.

Felix watched on, aghast, as the strange plague spread.

The beastman's blood fizzed like some euphoric poison through Ulrika's veins. The village of Kurzycko was a jumble of heat and sounds, but she could not dissociate one from the other. It was not unlike the feeling of being drunk. There was a queasiness deep within her chest, but with it a licence to do and be exactly as her body craved. The beast that dwelled within all Arisen licked its fangs, tested at the bars of its cage. The blood in her mouth was beginning to harden. She was parched. She felt hungry.

Her grip on Felix's shoulder tightened until he gasped. She needed him now. He was a reminder of how it felt to live without a beast. With a growl, she tried to retract her fangs, but couldn't.

How had she been so stupid as to feed off a creature of Chaos? In the moment it had just seemed so right, so natural. Almost worse than the desire to do so was the fact that she had been able to sate it. In the early nights of her unlife she had tried to feed off a northman only for the taint in his blood to force her to throw it back up. Something had changed, either with the world itself as the End Times approached or with her.

She did not know which was worse.

Blood roared through her brain like the Goromadny Falls after the summer melt. Someone was speaking to her. Was it Felix? The braying of the herd and the howls of the beast within its cage blocked it out. She focused on the feel of Felix's arm beneath her hand and tried to concentrate on the words. They were distant, an urgent shout for a comrade lost in a storm.

'*Get out of there, Ulrika. Get out now.*'

Aekold Helbrass strode through the embattled ranks of the Chaos horde. He was one in a vast shoal but where he walked, men and beasts were healed and the risen dead reduced to rose-choked cairns of composted earth. A mighty phalanx of zombies and their immortal puppet lords, tall warriors in archaic plate and chill blades, blocked his path. Kurgan berserkers hacked at rotting flesh. Chaos warriors crackling with the accumulated blessing of their gods fought toe to toe with kings long departed when Sigmar had walked the Empire.

Helbrass flourished the Windblade, and the broadsword was life's scythe. Skeletons collapsed rather than near its edge. Zombies dissolved into glorious bounties of maggots and flies at a glance.

A wight lord proclaiming himself Ætheltan of the Teutogens cut down the Chaos warrior that opposed him and, voice as the gasp of air from a tomb unsealed, challenged Helbrass to single combat. The shade was old and angry, and strong enough in his own will to raise his sword before decay and rebirth caused his body to shrivel, his armour to corrode, and his blade to bleed iron dust. Helbrass trod on the ancient's funerary shroud and strode on, white flowers bursting from the wight's remains to complete the cycle of life.

There was nothing special about death. The simplest primordial slime that eked an existence from the ocean's bottom could die. A rock or a gust of wind could take a life. That event most beautiful to the Changer was thus the transition from dead matter into life.

Already Helbrass could picture the Troll King's wrath, and his laughter was a hammer that smote zombies and ghouls into ash to line his path.

He fixed his gaze on the sorcerers upon the Three Sisters. Only the Kislevite village stood in his path, but that would not hold him for long.

He would bring life to a dead land.

There was nothing here that could stop him.

The clouds above Wilhelmshügel turned black, a creeping grave rot spreading north through the sky. On the darkening ground beneath, messengers rushed from banner to banner with news, hearsay, and orders from a dozen generals. None of it made good listening but then, with a sweeping view of the entire plain from Rackspire to Fortenhaf in the west to Kurzycko in the north, General von Karlsdorf could see that for himself.

Roch's regiments were being ground down. The enemy's monsters had done for most of the forward artillery batteries. Chaos warriors were on the walls of Kurzycko. Beastmen were slaughtering men in their trenches. Everywhere the general looked he saw men running.

Even as he listened to the gabbled report of a mud-smeared rider, the Chaos dragon that had almost single-handedly dismantled a year's worth of preparations banked to follow the course of a drystone wall. Von Karlsdorf looked away, a sick feeling in his gut, as the dragon overflew an earth and timber redoubt and introduced the arquebusiers garrisoned there prematurely to the fires of hell.

Damn it! He wanted to tear off his hat and rip it up with his teeth. How in Sigmar's name was a man supposed to fight something like that? He interrupted the messenger's stream of gibberish with a snarl.

'Ride to General Szardenings and ask... no, *tell* him to send out his demigryph knights against that thing. And the rest of you!' He raised his voice to carry over the ceaseless bombardment to the gunnery crews. 'Keep firing. One hit would be something.'

The rider bowed and then ran off.

Alone amongst the chaos, General von Karlsdorf did up the buttons of his greatcoat and shivered. He shot a glance towards the wizards still upon the Three Sisters. Despite the havoc being wrought around them, there was no change in their ritual that he could discern. Was this strange darkness their doing, some magic to confound the enemy? Impossible to guess. It was so dark as to be almost night, and filled him with a chill the way a good fire might spread warmth. Feigning a desire for a better view of the battlefield, he stamped to the low drystone barricade at the lip of the hill and saw what some visceral intuition of the kind he had always dismissed told him was the source of his disquiet.

A company of knights in armour as black as smoke were galloping across the veldt, charging under the wake of the dark skies towards

Kurzycko. The crimson swallowtails of Commandant Roch's personal colours tore from the vexillary's standard. Von Karlsdorf prided himself on being a reasonable man, but something about the sight made him shudder. It was surely just a trick of low light and powder smoke that made it look as if the entire formation had just charged *through* a defensive wall.

He summoned one of his aides.

'Round up what cavalry we have and dispatch them to help Roch.'

'It's only free companies left, general. Some of them have already tried to run away once.'

'Give the order,' said von Karlsdorf, lifting his eyeglass to study the flame-lit walls of Kurzycko. 'Before it's too late.'

In a thunderous shriek of hooves and steel and bone, the wedge of black Templars with Commandant Roch at their tip smashed open the anarchic Chaos formation like a nut under a hammer. Men and their allied beasts went down under hooves at once ethereal and iron hard. A gratifying number broke, and Roch paid them no further mind. He did not chance his own unlife for a few hundred marauders from the enemy's vanguard. He bared his fangs as he surveyed the effacing flood of Change between him and Kurzycko.

This is why we fight, he thought. As if the reminder were required.

Roch had drained ten strong men in preparation for this encounter. His most learned necromancers had warded his armour with magicks of binding and unlife. There would not be enough left of Aekold Helbrass to burn on the plague pyres of Bechafen.

Ulrika covered her ears against the sudden tumult of screams as the battlements of Kurzycko ceased to be a wall and became instead an unsupported collation of stone blocks and tendrilous fungal growths. It was a futile effort for one who could measure the pulse of the harpies gliding high overhead. The mycelial tendrils lashed out from the stonework, tossing men aside in convulsions of hunger before shrinking back and then, in the grossly accelerated culmination of their life cycle, exploding in a mushroom cloud of puffy white spores. Soldiers wailed, clinging on suddenly to nothing at all as the entire length of wall came apart underneath them and dropped them into the choking cloud.

Felix covered his nose and mouth with his cloak, the spores irritating his throat even from the other side of the village. Ulrika was glad that she no longer needed to breathe. It seemed strange and a little grotesque that she had once been so wedded to it. Skin tingling, claws extruded, she watched as a single armoured man stepped through the cloud.

She would have known him had she been staked through the heart and left for the sunrise with a silver blindfold. Aekold Helbrass, the conqueror of Kislev and Praag. Apart from his hands and feet that were as green as new shoots, he was clad in a suit of plate armour that shifted constantly in colour like oil on water. Nothing in his physical stature shouted 'Champion'. He was neither especially tall, nor powerful in appearance, but looking at him was like staring too long at the sun. Feeling her cheeks beginning to moisten, Ulrika blinked, looked away, and wiped red tears from her eyes.

Helbrass was life: violent, explosive, untempered life, and just looking upon him made her eyes bleed.

Blind to the fires burning all around, she started towards him. She wanted to rend him apart for what he had done to her homeland, and she wished to test just how far Felix would go to protect her, but really her need surpassed and transcended all logical considerations.

She was a moth to the flame.

She had pulled away from Felix and drawn her sabre when she

heard a rumble of hoofbeats and an armoured knight on a ghostly white charger burst through the cloud. He wore heavy black armour, moulded plates accoutred with rubies and bronze-fretted embossings of snarling bats. A jewelled broadsword was in his beringed hand and it had clearly tasted blood in getting its bearer here. His skin carried an unearthly pallor and a white stream of hair ran out in his wake. Blood called to blood.

It was her master!

Aekold Helbrass turned and readied his blade, but made no move to step out of the way. There was something mocking in the shift of patterns across his helm. Roch shouted at Ulrika to run.

Then he struck Helbrass's life-giving aura, the power of an ancient bloodline meeting the vigorous, carefree exuberance of Change. The wards upon the commandant's armour blazed aethyric black, smoke venting from the joins as his skin sizzled. Calling on the restorative power of his blood, he howled fresh agony as burned flesh was healed and then incinerated anew. With willpower alone, he lifted his sword and urged his horse on, but the magic that bound the undead beast did not have the power of the ancient curse that bestowed unlife upon its rider. Like vapour from a blacksmith's cooling bucket, the horse evaporated, hurling Roch's armoured bulk to the ground.

'*You* would challenge *me?*'

It was the first time Ulrika had heard Helbrass speak, and his voice was like the light that lanced through a cloudy sky. She reeled from it, but stronger, older, Roch rose and smashed his sword against Helbrass's. The champion parried, countered. Roch received and returned. The champion was quick, but the vampire lord was quicker, unleashing a storm of blows that even Ulrika did not believe she could match for speed or steel-rending power. Helbrass defended himself with almost equal speed and no little skill, but Roch left no opening for an attack.

Until he started to slow down.

The effect was so slight at first that Ulrika did not even notice, but then Roch coughed, splattering blood over Helbrass's visor and dropping to his knees with his hand upon his heart. Ulrika watched with mounting fury as her master's pectoral plate buckled and gave before his swelling chest. The Arisen crossed his arms over his breast and roared defiance. A nauseating ripple passed out from his brow as Helbrass placed a hand upon his head. Flames flicked across his gums, his chest continued to heave, and just as it looked as though his body could stretch no further, he emitted a scream and burst apart into a screeching cloud of bats.

Chuckling, the champion of Chaos strode through their flapping wings and levelled his sword.

Ulrika unconsciously took a backward step, but then checked herself and brought up her own blade to match. She felt the roar of her beast as the bars of its cage grew brittle. There was no escape from here even if she wished it.

And she did not.

This was something that she and Felix would have to face together.

EIGHT

Lifebringer

'Ulrika, what are you doing? Get back!'

Acting without thought and purely on instinct, Felix put himself between Ulrika and the Chaos champion. He had seen for himself what this warrior had done to that vampiric knight and, for all Ulrika's strength, Felix knew this was not a foe that she could confront and survive. He shook his head ruefully and raised his sword.

And did he think that he could?

'I am life,' said the champion, without break in his stride, his voice the roar of the fire that would scorch away the forest so that life might flourish anew. 'She is death. Is this the side you choose?'

A flash of silvered blue was all that Felix saw of the champion's blade as it clove towards him. In that brief second, Felix acknowledged that he was probably as good as dead, but an impulse sent his sword darting into the path of the stroke. The clash of steel threw the two blades apart. Felix winced at the pain in his fingers. Against the dragon he had felt invincible, but now he felt as stiff as a tree with one too many rings under its trunk. Muscle memory spun him away from the champion's counterstroke, then shaped him to slash back-handed under the champion's throat just as a hissing black shape bombed into his peripheral vision.

He swung around to parry, but the winged ferocity of a bat flew into his face and flapped madly around his head. It was one of those that had been birthed in the other vampire's demise. Felix turned his face to try and shrug the creature off, but it stuck with him. A mad laugh sounded over the leathery snap of wings and the growl of burning thatch and Felix parried a groin thrust that he caught a fraction too late. He swore as it nicked his thigh, and stumbled back.

The heat pouring from the burning buildings was intense. The flames conjured a strange tableau whereby the horned silhouettes of beastmen fought a deadly game with zombies and other, stranger, creatures of crazed if undeniably intelligent design. Blue-finned daemons shrieked overhead while from all around reverberated the muffled thunder of distant cannon. It was as if Felix had been swallowed by some hellish daemon and was listening to its heartbeat. Even the smell of burned meat seemed apt to the scenario.

Through the fluttering lashes of beating bat-wings, Felix caught a glimpse of Ulrika. Her eyes were red as those plucked from a dead man, crimson tears streaming down her cheeks. With one clawed hand shielding her face as if just looking at the champion was painful, she and her sabre cut in. She looked almost bestial as with raw strength alone she beat aside the champion's sword and lunged for the join between helm and gorget.

The champion parried and Ulrika came again with a growl and a flurry of blows, the Chaos warrior cackling as each came a little slower and lighter than the last. The sickly smell of sizzling fat rose from her armour.

She threw one more attack before she could endure no more and fell back with a shriek and smoke streaming from her hands. 'A curse on you, Helbrass!'

The patterning of the champion's armour implied amusement, if not outright mockery. 'That is not within your power to bestow, stagnant one.'

Taking the opportunity, Felix swatted aside the blasted bat and hauled Ulrika to her feet.

She recoiled from his touch as though his mortal warmth was enough to burn her. The smell of her alone was enough to make him want to be sick, but her appearance was worse. Her flesh had liquefied and run, congealing as it cooled into malformed shapes that didn't always fully sheathe cracked and blackened bone. The white scales of her armour were charred at the edges. She wouldn't lower her hands from her face.

'Run. You can't fight this.'

'And you can?' Ulrika snarled through still-smoking fingers.

Felix angled his sword into a guard, turned his attention to Helbrass and backed slowly away. The vague idea of falling back to the attaman's fortified manor was somewhere in there amongst his thoughts. He gave a wry smile, surprised to find he was actually enjoying himself a little bit. Change was overrated.

'I said I could fight. I didn't say I could win.'

'I will enjoy this,' said Helbrass. 'It is always a precious gift to face a man with a destiny.' The champion threw a decapitating stroke. Felix watched its edge come.

Some destiny.

Parrying for his life, Felix retreated with Ulrika behind him. Attacks fell thick and fast, and Felix's sword danced without any conscious input from him, but he could only wish that the gulf between him and his foe was a simple matter of swordsmanship. Vines burst from the ground to turn defensive stances into stumbling retreats. The earth hatched sinuous insects that crawled up his legs and into his armour. The very sleet falling from the sky became buzzing, stinging things, a droning mob of fat yellow-back flies that for all Felix's efforts clung to his head as though it had been basted in honey. And through it all came the changeling armour of Aekold Helbrass.

It dawned on him fully then that Helbrass was not an opponent against whom an ordinary man should fight. He had routed the Ice Queen from her own land, sacked a city that had never been conquered, one where Gotrek Gurnisson was said to have faced his final doom.

The utter certainty that he had no chance at all was strangely liberating.

He risked a sideways glance. Ulrika was black and hunched, but somehow with her sword in hand. Steam rose off her where snow fell.

'What are you still doing here? Go. I'll hold him here.'

Ulrika lowered her hand from her face. It was burned almost beyond recognition. Even her eyes were shot through with crimson, suspended by some blood curse within an unblinkered socket. A string of white teeth including two unmistakable vampiric fangs gaped where lips and gums had been burned down to the enamel. 'You would do that for me?'

Felix parried a numbing blow and spat out a wasp. Somewhere on the outskirts of his vision a skeletal knight galloped through the flames. He'd almost forgotten there was still a battle raging out there. 'Of course I would. Go!'

Ulrika's skin cracked as she smiled. It was horrifying, but she seemed to stand a little straighter and her eyes became marginally less wild, as if drawing conviction from the – frankly shocking – revelation that he still cared.

'I am not leaving. This is Kislev whatever Empire men try to call it. It is *mine*.'

In other circumstances, Felix might have laughed. He did know how to pick them. Gotrek had craved death more than anything, and Ulrika couldn't die, at least not with any kind of finality. For all their differences they were as bad as each other.

'Stop arguing,' he spat, his ears beginning to go numb from the relentless clangour of beaten steel. He had lost sensation in his fingers some minutes ago. 'You can't even stand within reach of him.'

'I do not need to.'

Ulrika spread her claws, scything them through a sequence of gestures as a rivulet of bloody syllables coursed from her lips. A dark wind from the forced gates of Morr's garden fanned her hair. Felix shivered at its touch. It was one thing to know that she was capable of these arts, but quite another again to witness their use. The cloud of insects shrivelled and dropped dead from the air.

Helbrass spun back and lowered his sword. The impression of something loathsome left its colour trail upon his armour. 'A sorceress? Count your stars that I am here to save you from yourself.'

Helbrass clenched both fists and roared as his entire body erupted into a pyre of incandescent flame. The howl of it filled Felix's ears, but the sound was that of a gale rather than of a fire. It pulled back on his cloak. He raised an arm to shield his eyes. He could see things, flickering things, places between the tongues of multicoloured flame. Those places were real. With some visceral comprehension of the power of the Prince of Lies, he knew that.

Ulrika's claws continued to carve the air into frayed and bloody sigils, but Felix could no longer hear the words she screamed.

'You can thank me,' shouted Helbrass, 'when the Troll King does not take you.'

Runesmith Gorlin dumped his satchel under the ancient stone arch of the gateway up to the surface and dropped to his knees to start tugging out the straps. He flinched as Snorri's hammer crushed a beastman against one of the squat stone struts, smashing it in so hard that the creature stuck there, still twitching after Snorri turned back to the horde.

The runesmith mouthed his thanks and returned to work.

'Snorri doesn't see why we don't just kill all the beastmen. Then we can fix the door.'

'Seconded,' wheezed Krakki, tattooed paunch glistening by firelight.

'*Grobkaz*,' the runesmith swore, running his hands over the dolmen runes. 'The gate is irreparable. It cannot be resealed.'

'Does that mean we can try Snorri's plan now?' said Snorri, breaking a beastman's spear on his forehead and then shattering its shin with a blow from his mace-leg.

'It means that all of Chaos has a shortcut into the manlings' Empire,' Gorlin shot back.

'And that's...' Snorri's face screwed up in thought. 'Bad?'

'I came prepared,' said Gorlin, almost proudly, returning his hands to his pack and shaking out a number of tubular containers with long tapers at one end. They smelled of saltpetre.

'Snorri doesn't mind getting blown up,' said Snorri conversationally, pinning his own satchel to his side and ducking a swinging axe.

'Don't be a wattock,' said Krakki. 'You'd only light the wrong end.'

'Would not,' Snorri returned, and Krakki gutted a charging beastman on his fistspike with the biggest grin he could still muster.

'Have you been carrying the torch all the way from Karak Kadrin?'

'Enough, both of you.' Skalf Hammertoes clutched his crossbow stock in fingers like talons and regarded them both. 'These are the End Times and there is no need to bicker over every possible doom.' He grunted, unearthing a decision and finding it poorer than he'd hoped. 'Krakki, light the fuses. The rest of you...' He grinned, swung up his crossbow, and started towards the wall of beastmen that blocked the Kislev-bound tunnel. 'Run as fast as you can.'

Aekold Helbrass extended a green shoot of a hand, sapphire flames spiralling down the raised arm as though burning along a trail of spirits and then geysering from his open palm. Arresting her own incantation, Ulrika screamed a word of power and threw up a barrier that ran with the horrified faces of the battle's dead. They cried out in one voice as Helbrass's blue fire disintegrated against the glassine shell. Dazzling motes of change cascaded from the impact like willow blossom. Spirits shaken loose went whimpering back to their battlefield limbo. It was as if the most pessimistic of street agitators cried.

The old gods turned their faces even from the dead.

Fire coiled around Helbrass's armour like a living thing. His stance was easy, utterly in control and yet free. It reminded Felix of the snake charmers that he and Gotrek had encountered in Ind. They had given their bodies to creatures that could, and perhaps should, have destroyed them, but emerged stronger for the union. It was not a reassuring comparison to draw.

Spitting at the snow, Helbrass's serpents of energy darted forwards. Two of them this time, blue and gold, they smashed against Ulrika's barrier in a welter of sparks and banished spirits. Ulrika shuddered and pushed back. Maws of multicoloured flame slid and slathered across her shield like sea-dragons over the bottom of a boat.

Felix didn't fool himself that he knew much more about magic than any man not of the colleges, but he knew a fighter on the back foot when he saw one.

'Fight back,' he cried over the screams of the dead as they burned in the Changer's fires. 'Give him something to worry about.'

Ulrika groaned, arms spread-eagled as though she personally held up the weight of the sky. The pyrotechnic display washed her charred flesh. 'I know how to fight, Felix. I can beat him. I just need...'

'What?'

Swift as a knife in the back, Ulrika took a handful of Felix's collar and bared her fangs.

'Blood.'

Felix screamed as the vampiress dragged him towards her and then several things happened at once.

The barrier emitted a final death scream and Felix and Ulrika were momentarily encased within a shell of golden-blue flame. With her weight entirely beneath Felix, she gave a hungry snarl and hurled him wide, using the counterforce to duck back as the forked tongue of fire licked between them.

Felix flailed and then crashed into a wattle and daub wall on the other side of the street. His cry was driven out of him and he hit the ground under a patter of chalk dust and lime aggregates from the daub.

With a groan, he pushed himself up, watching as Ulrika sped away. She was moving so fast that her passing not only parted the smoke but dragged it on behind her. A stream of blue fire shot after her, but somehow she outpaced it and the jet flickered and faded back to Helbrass's fingertips.

The champion followed at a walk, patient as an oak. Blue and yellow fire crackled over his left and right shoulder, blending over his helm into a perfect halo of infernal, life-giving green. Almost as an afterthought, he turned his head in passing and thrust an open palm towards Felix.

Felix hit the ground just as the pillar of blue fire *whooshed* over the spot and struck the building behind him. The impact punched through the wall and blew out the window shutters. Felix covered his head under his arms as bits of wattle and thatch hailed down. He tried not to look at them. Each was burned but also subtly changed, each one a mirror onto a scene of past triumph or future tragedy. Coughing, he pulled himself out of the debris and staggered onto his feet. Then he found Karaghul, wiped his fringe from his eyes, coughed again, and cast about for a sign of Helbrass.

The champion was striding after Ulrika. Where the vampiress had carved the smoke like a fish through water, around Helbrass it twinkled and fell again as fresh spring rain that nourished the virgin shoots at his feet.

Felix shot a quick glance the other way. He could pick out a few northmen through the smoke and fire fighting in the breached wall, but it seemed that Roch's army and the Kurzycko garrison still held the line.

Covering his mouth and hunching underneath the thickest smoke, Felix chased after the Chaos champion. So long as it remained two-on-one then they had a chance.

He really should've known better.

The smoke cleared sufficiently around the incombustible stone solidity of the attaman's manor for Felix to see more than a few feet without his eyes stinging. Its high walls had been buttressed with a pine stockade, the red stone balconies blocked up with ramparts of Ostermark lime from which the occasional matchlock flared to send bullets winging through the melee in the courtyard before its splintered gates.

A herd of about twenty beastmen filled the square with the clash of their weapons and their braying battle cries. The flagstones had been pulled up long before to construct the curtain wall and reinforce the structures deemed defensible, and the ground had been churned to a filthy slush under their hooves. As he watched,

Ulrika fended off five one-handed, keeping the manor's wall to her back as a sixth lowed ecstatically in her embrace. Blood spilled down her chin and over her breastplate. Black flesh softened and turned milky even as he watched. Only the scar above the left eye remained.

Felix tasted bile and had to cover his mouth for fear that he was going to be sick. With every beat of the foul creature's heart that pumped blood onto her lips, her eyes grew fiercer. Her grip hardened. Even over the noise of the beastmen, Felix thought he heard ribs snap. He shook his head and swallowed his disgust. She did only what she had to in order to survive. They both had more important concerns right now than Felix's civilised mores.

Slush became good soil and sprouted wildflowers as Helbrass walked onto the courtyard. Blue and yellow flames became indigo and capered from his fingertips.

Felix opened his mouth to shout a warning just as a beastman blundered out from one of the burning cottages and barrelled towards him. Felix swore and brought up his sword to parry aside its axe. He pedalled back for space and adopted a guard. Either Helbrass had numbed his hands more than he'd realised or the beastman's strike had been unusually weak.

The muscular, goat-headed gor stamped its hooves and brayed a challenge. It was a foot taller than Felix and half again as thick around its chest. Felix could hear its lungs scraping for breath. It drew a huge breath of thick smoke, swung a blow that fell a foot to Felix's left, and then collapsed to its knees with spittle on its wispy goat-beard. Felix didn't even bother finishing it off. His own lungs were burning too, though he was smart enough to cover his mouth and measure his breathing. He staggered away from the beastman's drowned-fish gasps, watching helplessly as Helbrass flung his indigo fire through the herd towards Ulrika.

Whether it was sense or the survival instinct of a beast, Ulrika withdrew her dripping mouth from her meal's neck and flung the beastman underarm into the fire.

Indigo flame bloomed around the beastman and it brayed in pain, seizing as if the mutagenising beam was triggering every nerve in its body to fire. Flesh rippled beneath its fur. Its muzzle opened but, rather than a bleat of agony, produced a slimy proboscis that stretched out from the gor's terror-stricken throat. The beastman jerked in the grip of the beam, choking as the worm-like creature filled its mouth, swelling until it pushed out its cheeks and dislocated its jaw with a horrific *snap*. Felix stared in horror as the newborn thing hissed at him and then lashed back to sink fangs into the beastman's eye. Blood and clear fluids spattered down its muzzle. The beastman convulsed, but Felix wasn't sure the creature felt it any more. More of those tendrilous horrors burst from its snout and armpits and from under its nails and slithered through their own birthing gore to join the feast. What remained of the beastman simply came apart. The stained rags it had been wearing split to spew a dozen blood-soaked worms that screeched as they tore into each other for the last scraps of meat on the creature's bones.

Felix watched it collapse, wide-eyed and open-mouthed, as if the experience had hollowed him inside and out. Death was one thing, but that? For some selfish reason, the yearning wish that he and Kat had found the time to have a child filled his mind. Even Gotrek had understood the power of immortality.

But that was wrong. It wasn't immortality. It was continuance.

Ulrika snarled, poleaxed a beastman with a hypnotic stare, grabbed it with both hands and positioned it between her and Helbrass like a shield.

'Do you know what happens to those like us in Praag?' said

Helbrass. 'Would you not rather die than live forever in a cage?' Laughing, he extended an emerald claw. 'Or do I seek understanding from the cursed?'

'You were a prisoner?' said Felix, unable to believe it. What kind of a monster could hold *this* captive?

'I and others. More than I could kill before I escaped.'

'What of Max?' Ulrika spat suddenly. Her voice was slurred as if she was drunk and her fangs had become engorged to interfere with her tongue. 'A Light wizard of the Empire called Max Schrieber. He was taken after the battle at Alderfen.'

Helbrass spread his hands in what might have been a shrug. Flame flicked along the edges of his armour. 'All life is connected. All life is one. Even the Troll King understands this in his heart.'

'Understands what?' said Felix.

'Death or life,' Helbrass roared, those flickering embers igniting into a pyre of incandescent madness. Felix covered his eyes. The surviving beastmen lowered their weapons and bleated in confusion. The Ostermarkers stopped firing. Everyone had stopped to watch the Chaos champion burn. And his eyes were solely on Ulrika. 'Stasis or change. Stagnation or expansion. Since before the age of the Old Ones that has been the only choice that matters.'

The multicoloured flames turned grey, roaring higher until the champion's entire body was consumed by them. And then the inferno flickered back down. Felix stared. Helbrass was gone.

'Ulrika–'

Before he could finish, Helbrass reappeared inside the manor gate in a thunderclap of shadow-grey flame that sent cracks splintering up through the lintel stone and threw Ulrika and her beastman hostage flat on their faces. Felix ran to protect her. Despite what he had witnessed, she was still the Ulrika he had known. He readied his blade as if it could be of any use whatsoever as the very air beneath the arch was distorted, excited to the point of ignition by the energy of change.

'Stasis or change?' Helbrass yelled. 'Those are the choices.'

'Men don't change,' Felix returned.

Helbrass emitted a shrill laugh. 'Allow me to open your eyes to how wrong you are.'

The champion stabbed his sword into the ground and then clenched his fists over the pommel as though straining to draw it back. Flames spat from his armour, like tightening muscles, shifting from grey to orange. Looking at them was like staring into a prism, but rather than colours it was reality that they split, spraying out all its component possibilities.

'Witness your destiny! Experience the manifold possibilities of destruction before one claims you.'

Felix couldn't close his eyes fast enough to keep from looking.

He saw Kislev.

Cries of despair rose from every quarter of the city as the besieging army poured in through the warped and still-living gate. He charged down the Goromadny Prospekt. If there was to be a last stand, if there was anyone else left, then it would be at the Ice Palace. He looked over his shoulder, hearing the cries of the Kurgan gaining ground, and saw the chariot racing up the prospekt. Its painted blue hull was wrapped with chains and pulled by three black horses, a pair of marauders in the car. One pointed him out with his spear. With a curse, Felix ducked against a wall and swung his sword around to face them. It was hopeless anyway, now that Gotrek had fallen...

Alderfen.

Covering his nose and mouth to keep from vomiting, Felix matched blades with the hideous plaguebearer of Nurgle. Pus drooled from its hanging jaw, its cyclopean eye staring blankly as if with fever, but despite its famine-wasted form it was hideously strong. With a blast of purifying light, Max Schreiber reduced a score of them to a foul smell on the aethyr. Not enough. The battle was already lost. There was time only for regret – that neither man would leave the other behind...

Altdorf.

Too weak to lift his own head, Kat raised him under her arm and spooned something he could no longer taste into his mouth. It was pointless. Kat should have fled Altdorf with their child like everyone else, but now they would both die like Otto and Annabella. Because of him. Through the window, he could see what men had once called Karl Franz Park, and the putrescent daemon lord that had made it its home...

The Everpeak.

The last and greatest army of the dwarfs stood arrayed in gromril and gold before the skaven horde. They were doomed, and fought only to spare themselves the sight of Karaz-a-Karak in flames. In the front rank of a legion of Slayers, he and Gotrek stood shoulder to shoulder. Gotrek pointed to a figure amongst the hordes, but it was unnecessary. Felix had marked that card long ago. Thanquol! From his throne atop a great horned bell the Grey Seer commanded his minions forward, and in a chittering mass a million strong they obeyed...

Kurzycko.

He saw...

'Sigmar's blood!'

He had seen enough. Without waiting for the vision to finish, he grabbed Ulrika by the hand and dragged her back from the attaman's manor.

* * *

Snorri didn't think he'd ever felt so many beastmen crammed so close. The tunnel stank of blood, guts, and panic – and the sulphurous spark of a lit taper.

With axe, hammer, and mace, Snorri bludgeoned a path through the beastmen. Durin Drakkvarr followed with an ice-cold ferocity, eyes set like ball bearings in a daemon mask. Drogun, Skalf and the other surviving Slayers followed in behind. Snorri bared his teeth, barely even looking at what he was killing any more.

This was it. The end. He could almost taste it.

Snorri Nosebiter would sup ale in the Ancestors' Hall tonight!

'Aren't you forgetting something?'

Durin's voice was typically cold. Between blows, he picked Snorri's satchel off the ground and tossed it over. Snorri dropped his hammer and caught it. The strap had been sliced through. Pity, thought Snorri, the blade must have missed him by a hair's breadth.

'You have borne it thus far. It would be a shame now to meet your doom without it.'

Snorri tried to hang the severed strap over his shoulder. It dropped twice more before he showed it to Durin. 'You'll have to tie it. Snorri... Snorri's not very good at knots.'

Durin did so without fuss. 'Let us race to Praag, Snorri, and the first one to the Ancestors' Hall will have the beers ready.'

With a grin, Snorri picked up his hammer and threw himself back into the fight. He felt good, better than he had in days. This was surely the mighty doom he had been promised.

You will have the mightiest doom.

Blown apart and entombed with a horde of beastmen seemed mighty enough to Snorri and the likes of Durin and Krakki and Drogun were good dwarfs with whom to share it. He didn't even mind overly when Durin tackled the beastman that had been about to bury its axe in his skull, and then screamed something in Snorri's ear as he pushed him ahead into the press.

There was a moment's pause, as if Snorri's crossed stars held their breath.

And then the bombs went off.

The explosion rippled through the reinforced stone walls of the manor like a wave. Felix threw himself on top of Ulrika as Helbrass caught a glimpse of his own future and bellowed. A shock wave from somewhere deep within the structure pummelled his armour and shredded his bare hands with shrapnel. The champion's hand snapped through a new incantation, summoning back his grey fire, but too late. Always too late.

The cracked lintel above his head finally split and the champion looked up, witnessing just one of manifold possibilities realised as the supporting structure gave and three storeys' worth of masonry piled onto his shoulders.

There was a subterranean *crump* as one of the munitions stores in the manor's cellars went off. The walls shook, but that one hadn't been nearly as fierce. Mingled cries of triumph and dismay drifted down from the shell-shocked men on the ramparts.

Dizzied and slightly deaf, Felix picked himself up off of Ulrika. Rubble drizzled from his hair. He winced as his numerous aches and pains let him know where they were. The air tasted burned, and it tingled as if it had felt too much violence on its way to his throat. The sky rumbled with the roar of cannon.

Helbrass's own fires must have ignited one of the blackpowder rooms. That was the only explanation.

Ulrika groaned beneath him and shifted. Felix felt an inappropriately timed pang of desire at the sight of her; tousled, spent, a little groggy from too much drink. He pushed the thought aside. There would be time enough to explore it later if they could just get out of here alive.

'What happened?' Ulrika murmured. 'Did you kill him?'

'After a fashion, I think.'

'How? He was the conqueror of Kislev. And you are–'

'A has-been former henchman?'

'Something like that.' Ulrika smiled and held up a hand for Felix to pull her up. He did and she fell into his arms before she could steady herself. Her body was oddly warm after having drunk. Her white hair was clotted with blood and smelled of smoke. She looked at Helbrass's buried remains, and then at Felix, lips parted in an expression of awe as if he had just done something astounding.

'It's not quite what you think.'

A low growl disturbed the sprinkling rock dust. Ulrika looked up and Felix turned to see the big bull minotaur that had first broken through the manor's doors return to look for its raiding party. Its horned head drew level with the eaves of the row of houses behind it, even hunched under the weight of its armour and the massive warhammer in its hands. It surveyed the wreckage and snorted a great plume of hot air. Felix drew up his sword wearily.

What god did I offend today, he thought?

'*Starovye!*'

Felix had heard that word before, had in context assumed it meant 'drink', but as he twisted around he saw Damir and his stubborn little Ungol pony bolt through the breach in the village's northern wall with his bow nocked and two-score stridently garbed horsemen thundering in his train. With a shiver of forty-plus recurve bows, the minotaur sprouted arrows.

Hollering fury, the monster swung its warhammer across a high, sweeping arc. Damir pressed himself down against his pony's neck as the hammer whistled overhead, then smoothly nocked another arrow, shot it point blank into the bull's neck, and kicked his pony out of reach. The Ungol rode to Ulrika and offered his hand. Ulrika took it, planted her boot into the pony's flank and swung herself up behind Damir into the saddle.

The minotaur bellowed, goring a pony through the shoulder and flipping it and its rider through the air. Ulrika flourished her sabre.

'Let us finish this and be away.'

'*Nyeh,*' said the Ungol, sucking in his teeth and nodding back the way he had just ridden.

More horsemen were following in through the breach, riding hard as if pursued not just by the forces of hell but by hell itself. Felix caught glimpses of Imperial colours within the coloured wools and hemp coats of the Ungol horse-archers. A smattering of pistol shots peppered the minotaur's armour before one, fired from close range, blew out the back of its pot-helm. The beast crashed forwards and riders yipped or else just continued to gallop past.

Felix saw the pistolier cough and wave a hand through the pistol discharge. He was a shade too tall to sit comfortably on a horse the size of the wiry mare he rode. Long blond hair lay over blood-spattered mail. A blue cloak hung over one shoulder. With shaking fingers, he inexpertly refilled the chamber of his pistol from the horn tied to his saddle. His efforts seemed to spill more powder over his fingers than into his weapon. He noticed Felix and gave a fraught half-smile.

'If ever I see a Detlef Sierck or a von Diehl or any of those "just war" poets, then I'm going to kill them.'

'Gustav?' said Felix in disbelief. 'What are you doing here?'

The young man scowled, closing the powder chamber and shaking spilt powder from the gun barrel. Then he holstered it. 'My men are club-footed sots and the guards von Karlsdorf placed on the Bechafen road have patriotism to fill their pockets.'

More horsemen were piling through the breach, firing over their shoulders as they came.

'You can talk later,' said Ulrika. 'We have to ride east. My master's soldiers wait for us there to escort us across the Auric Bastion.'

Felix gestured to the men still clinging on to the battlements of the subsiding manor-fort. 'These men–'

'Will serve Roch and the Emperor long after this, I assure you.'

'At least let me see Gustav to Badenhof. I owe my brother that much.'

'No time!' Ulrika snarled, angered by something Felix had said. The *crack* of pistol shots was growing sharper and more frequent. 'He can risk the ride back to the Empire or he can come with us.'

Felix turned to his nephew; nervous, scared, slightly exalted, face painted by the back-splatter of a monster few would ever see and that he had still to realise that he had just slain. He was family. And Ulrika was essentially asking him to choose the time and manner of his death.

Life or death? Here in Kurzycko or sometime later in Kislev?

He ground his teeth and relented. It wasn't really much of a choice, and at least this way Felix could keep an eye on him.

'Stick by me, Gustav. I'll see you through this.'

Felix was reminded of another promise he had made back in the Shallyan temple in Altdorf, another promise he'd known he wouldn't be able to keep.

'You've got to be joking. I am *not* going to Kislev with you.'

Felix waved his protests down. His nephew's opinion was moot now anyway. He looked around for a horse of his own to ride as a wedge of heavily armoured knights in moulded black plate and riding muscularly caparisoned destriers came through the north breach at a hard canter. A rearguard of pistoliers followed in a skirmish line, loosing a fusillade of solid shot into the pursuing northmen.

The knights reined in by Felix and Ulrika while the pistoliers and the Ungols rallied into a formation to hold the northmen at bay. A standard bearer bore a swallowtailed red banner that fluttered loosely in the heat eddies from the village's burning. Their black plate was shaped into effigies of snarling faces, decorated with unusual variants of holy iconography and strung with tattered scraps of scripture. The wargear was stained and dented, but the marble-hard men within were pristine exemplars of beauty and strength.

To Felix's mind, they could have equally just had 'vampire' emblazoned on the banderoles fluting from their lanceheads.

He could almost picture the recruitment poster right then: a phalanx of rotting zombies marching on the Auric Bastion under the heraldic bat of the vampire counts of Sylvania. Somehow, he couldn't see it passing the Reiksmarshal's approval. He gave a world-weary sigh. Why should the dead not bear their own weight?

'I presume one of you lords has a horse for me?'

'You may ride with me, Herr Jaeger.'

The knights' commander drew in the reins of his chilling, ghost-white charger. His eyes were pupil-less, as clear and compelling as pearls, and just standing under their gaze without bending the knee felt like an act of treason against the natural order. His high cheekbones reminded him a little of Ulrika, telling perhaps of a shared Gospodar heritage. He wore the same black full plate as his command, only much more elaborate and with a faint magical aura perceptible even to Felix.

It was clearly none other than Commandant Roch himself.

'I saw you die,' Felix murmured.

'Life and death are seldom such straightforward affairs.' The vampire lord produced a smile more predatory than anything ever worn by a dire wolf or a Southlands alligator and extended a hand. Felix noted the ring that glittered from his translucent finger. He was reminded of his own. 'If you knew me, then you would know I have returned from worse.'

'Fire! Fire! Fire!' screamed General von Karlsdorf until spittle was flying from his mouth.

The Chaos hordes were streaming out from the chokepoint at Kurzycko. Everywhere he looked now, provincial banners were being tramped under the iron heel of the advancing legions as men were cut down or broke. The stamp of so many feet was loud enough to sound even over the burst and whine of mortar fire from Wilhelmshügel.

Roch had abandoned them. It was over.

Matthias Wilhelm dropped his eyeglass and stared numbly over the coming wave.

'Fire,' he murmured. 'Somebody?'

The words dried up as the corner of his eye caught a flash of red and he turned to see the wizards of the Three Sisters immolated in dragonfire. Harpies and daemons shot through the flames, followed by the imperious glide of the Chaos dragon.

All around, men abandoned their guns in terror, but Matthias Wilhelm stood frozen. He whimpered as the cloud of harpies poured down, claws outstretched for the kill.

Ulrika hardened her heart to the screams as she gave her white stallion its head to run. It was unsurprisingly easy. Men were dying, but it was not as if they were going anywhere. Her master would still need an army to reclaim Trzy Siostry and push the Chaos host back through the Auric Bastion.

She closed her eyes and let her mount gallop, allowing the rhythm of its stride to perfuse the muscles of her thighs. The horse had found its way back to its stablemates after the fight in Kurzycko and she had been pleased, in a detached sort of way, to be reunited for this final leg of their journey. The infamous cold of the oblast wind ran though her hair, but of course, she did not feel it. She did not know what she had been expecting to feel on her return home.

But not nothing.

In Praag perhaps, it would be different. Yes, the true Ungol steppe. That was her home, not this rolling southern country that in all but language and the names of its villages was not dissimilar from the Empire across the river. Burned-out farmsteads dotted the snowscape. The snow-coated firs of the Shirokij Forest prickled the hills to her left while mountains climbed through the clouds to her right. This was not home.

At the approach of familiar heartbeats, she turned in the saddle to watch Felix, Gustav and Damir leading a sizeable force of horse-archers, free company pistoliers, and demilancers out from the Auric Bastion.

Damir of course could ride all day and sleep in the saddle by night. He had done so before and would doubtless be called on to do so again. He was loyal beyond mortal scope and a fierce warrior. She had no concerns about him or the men he led.

For all his griping about aches and pains, Felix compared favourably with his younger counterpart. His greying hair and battle scars lent him an air of experience that men he had never even met seemed to want to follow. Ulrika suspected that there was some block in Felix's head that did not permit him to see – and he would doubtless resent it if he did – that he was a twenty-year veteran and looked it. Men respected that, particularly on the oblast where a man without children at twenty risked both his life and his line.

On turning to Gustav she sighed. The young man was such a mirror to a younger Felix that it almost hurt. Almost.

She had long ago forgotten how it felt to bathe in running water, to feel the breath of the sun upon her skin. Had she finally also forgotten how to feel?

'You are troubled, Ulrika.'

'Not by anything that matters,' she replied, turning to the proud prince of the undead who rode alongside her. Despite her master's ornate wargear and the horse's heavy black barding, his spectral charger kept pace without even appearing to breathe.

'There is a blood bond between us, and I know when you lie. The wizard, Schreiber, is as important to me as he is to you. Balthasar Gelt speaks most highly of him, both as a scholar of Chaos and a man of sound reason. I will need such allies.'

'Yes, lord.'

'But do not forget your true purpose. Even we cannot wage this war alone. Serve me as well as Adolphus Krieger once served my own wayward child and I will see you rewarded in kind. There are nine seats in Nagash's court, Ulrika, and the fate of Walach Harkon at Alderfen leaves at least one open for you.' There was a snarl, a slip of the mask. He stared dead ahead, as though he too yearned for the oblast to give him something to feel. 'Others will fall before this war is decided, and when we prevail then you will rule Kislev for eternity.'

Ulrika grit her teeth and said nothing. Talk about a poisoned chalice. It was easy to speak of the lesser of two evils. Too easy. Especially when the evils in play were both so great.

Stasis or Chaos?

She was a Kislevite. Her instinct was to rebel, to bend the knee to no lord, and particularly not one from a millennia-dead desert kingdom so far removed from the frozen oblast that there were plenty of men even in the mercantile quarters of Erengrad and Volksgrad that had never heard of it. But the middle ground had crumbled into the abyss the day that Archaon claimed the crown of the Everchosen and Nagash arose to oppose him. Now was the time to make a choice, pick a side, and accept that the world was beyond the power of her own stubbornness to mould. She wished that she could explain this to Felix but, as he and Katerina had both proven in refusing Ulrika's gift, the mortals were not yet ready for that choice.

The Great Necromancer or the Great Powers?

'We will be the good shepherds, Ulrika. It is the only way.'

'Yes, lord,' Ulrika whispered. 'It will be done.'

'There is no need for subterfuge here, Ulrika. You are home. You may call me by my name.'

Ulrika turned to regard him properly. He looked back, long white hair thrashing in the wind, white wolf smile gleaming. The compulsion in his gaze was powerful, even to another of the Arisen. How different history might have been had the Vampire Wars ended with the Emperor's crown on the head of this immortal potentate. Would the world be in the crisis it now was with Vlad von Carstein on the throne of its most powerful nation?

'Yes, Lord von Carstein.'

Vlad nodded. His expression was still as the surface of the moon, but a deep hurt glittered in his milk-white eyes. 'I would have made this journey myself. Beloved Isabella once spent the season in Praag, and would you believe that I have never even seen the opera house, the Grande Parade, the Square of Kisses, those sights that delighted her mortal life?' He shook his head. 'It is too late for me. My ties to humanity were broken long ago.' He blinked, an oddly manual gesture that had nothing to do with moistening eyes harder than most men's blades. He turned to regard Felix and the other mortals. 'For almost as long as my own unlife, Praag has been a tainted city. Now it is firmly in Chaos hands. Recall how its influence almost maddened Krieger and think what its power will do to you now.'

'I do, lord. I understand that all too well.'

With a grimace which might have concealed a droplet of affection, Vlad turned his steed about and summoned the Drakenhof Templars to escort him back to Rackspire. He nodded towards Felix.

'Then cherish him, Ulrika, because you will need him before the end.'

Kolya knelt into the snow to wrench his arrow from the beastman's back. The shaft came loose in a tearing of muscle and a small spurt of blood. He did not have the spares to throw away and, as the wise woman had used to say, what falls from the horse on the oblast is as good as gone. He wiped it clean on the back of his mitts and slid it into the quiver he had fashioned from a gor chieftain's drinking horn that hung from his waist.

Looping his bow over his shoulder, he looked across the field of mangled, snow-furred corpses to where the dwarf, Gurnisson, stomped away. The witchlights of the corrupted northern sky paraded purple and green above their destination.

Praag.

Kolya looked down at the crystal beauty of the troll that lay dismembered upon the ground where the dwarf had slain it. It was an ice troll of the Goromadny, that Kolya had thought existed only in old dwarf sagas and the boasts of mountain rangers. A red gleam of alien intelligence had lit its eyes before it had died. It was nothing Kolya had ever witnessed in the eyes of a troll before now.

With a shiver, Kolya rolled the troll's severed head under his boot until it was face down in the snow. Even before the Battle of the Tobol Crossing there had been rumours amongst the Kurgan: talk of trolls that waged war like men, of an army of beasts that had made its stronghold in Praag. The barracks of the city's kossars now lowed with beastmen. Trolls and giants defended its great walls.

Hydra and gorgons guarded its gates. The legion wings of harpies shrouded its towers and blacked the warp storms that raged across its skies.

Or so rumour claimed.

Throwing the slowly regenerating troll one final look, Kolya crunched after his sullen companion. As hard as he tried to think of other things, of how he would witness the dwarf's death and then follow him on Kasztanka's back to the next world, he kept thinking of one of Marzena's many sayings.

A man afraid of spiders should stay out of the forest.

And Kolya was surprised to discover that, for all his resignation to his fate, the thought of facing the monstrous legions of the Troll King had left him very afraid indeed.

Crisped and blackened bodies littered the forest floor, lying where the explosion from the old dwarf shaft had thrown them. They hung in the branches of trees, spines broken over exposed roots, furry bodies steaming slightly under a light covering of snow. A fox picked through the cooked meat as if disbelieving its nose. With a ruffle of wings and a drizzle of snow from the canopy, another coal black carrion crow jostled for space on an already crowded branch. Their harsh calls sounded over the broken rune-gate.

Then one of the bodies coughed.

For an instant the forest fell silent, then an explosion of wings and panicked caws brought more shaken snow down to the forest floor and onto Snorri Nosebiter's head. Coughing up burned fur and blackpowder smoke, Snorri dug his way out of the snow pile and gasped for air. The snow burned his blackened flesh like vinegar. His beard was singed down to the roots, filling his squashed nose with the reek of roasted hair.

Every part of his body stung, all except for one little patch between his shoulders. His chest creaked and cracked as he reached around to try and feel it. He winced, but couldn't lay a finger on it. It was in that annoying spot that was always just out of reach of both hands.

The shape of it felt like a hand print.

The last thing he remembered was Durin pushing him away from the blast and into the mass of beastmen. Why had the Daemonslayer done that? That could have been a great doom. It would have been good enough for Snorri anyway.

Snorri shook his head to silence the organ guns going off inside. When that failed, he smacked his good ear until it stopped, then shovelled up a fistful of snow and stuffed it into his mouth.

'Hhhnnngg.'

Oath of Grimnir, Snorri wanted a beer!

Using a fresh clump of snow, Snorri wiped the char from around his eyes. It was only his back that had been truly burned. His face and chest were just coated with ash and whatever it was that beastmen gave off when they caught fire. Black water running from his face like a clown's smudged make-up, Snorri looked over the forest where he now found himself.

It looked strangely familiar.

Woods. Giant spiders in the trees.

Snorri shut out the emerging memory and turned his head back to take in the rune gate, an angular dolmen of limestone blocks carved with runes. It angled down into the earth. Snorri was no expert, but Underway gates were generally better hidden than that. The entrance still stood, but the tunnel more than a few feet in had collapsed, burying Durin Drakkvarr, Krakki Ironhame, and a few hundred lucky beastmen. Smoke hazed lazily through gaps in the rubble, like pipe-smoke through a longbeard's grin. Snorri sighed.

They had been good deaths. But Snorri was cursed to need a great one.

He looked to the bodies of the beastmen and *lowered his axe and hammer.*

The bodies of spiders lay amongst the boles of the trees, upturned with their legs curled over their bellies. Snorri swayed on his feet and chuckled. He felt drunker than if he had downed two whole buckets of vodka. The trees were jigging back and forth. Snorri threw his hammer at one, but somehow he wound up on his backside. The hammer went somewhere behind him. He looked at his hammer hand and giggled. It was covered in great red bite marks. Strange. He didn't feel a thing.

Dizzily, he became aware of a hunchbacked old human lady coming towards him. Her hair was scruffy white like a ball of spiders' webs. She wore long, layered skirts of black silk decorated with coloured shards of chitin and faceted beads that looked like the eyes of giant spiders.

'You may reward Snorri with beer,' Snorri tried to say, lips smacking open and shut while a trickle of drool ran down his chin.

The old lady crouched beside him in a rustle of skirts, like a winged insect coming in to land, and put her hand around Snorri's throat. Snorri gave a protesting dribble. This was human gratitude right enough! Snorri grunted furiously as the lady felt out his pulse. She stared at Snorri with a strange intensity as she counted under her breath. Her expression, far too furious for someone whose life Snorri had just saved from all of these spiders that infested her home, grew a sneer. She removed her hand from his neck and took his hand instead. Snorri tried to pull it away from her, but the message got drunk and passed out somewhere on the way.

The lady turned his big, calloused hand palm-up and ran claw-like nails along the lines.

Snorri giggled stupidly. That tickled.

'Snorri Nosebiter,' she murmured. Her voice was sing-song, trancelike, and Snorri found himself drifting into a stupor. 'You should have died today, Snorri, but I will not allow it. You slaughtered my guardians, you intruded on my seclusion. You imperil my very soul should my master find what you have done.' She hissed, a strange kind of smile on her lips as a nail dug into a branching line on his palm and drew a bead of blood. An arc of something magical flared from the droplet and crackled over her knuckles. 'The doom you seek shall elude you until the day that I decree. It will not come for many years, long enough for you to suffer. And when you are whole again, when those you most love surround you again, then you shall have a death that brings you nothing but pain. This is your curse,' she sneered. 'A gift worthy of a Slayer.'

The crone cackled as the aura of energy scalded Snorri's hand, redrawing the palm lines in blood. Snorri moaned softly.

'You will have the mightiest doom.'

Snorri smoothed a dollop of snow into his forehead. He moaned softly at the sudden, wonderful rush of cold. Still dizzy, he grabbed his leather bag where it lay rune-side up in the snow. Then he swayed to his feet and made his first tottering steps into the Shirokij Forest.

He wasn't sure how he remembered the place's name, but it was all starting to come back. Snorri had long suspected that the old lady in the forest had cursed him and now he knew why.

The old lady had cursed him!

She had done far more than prophesy a great destiny for him; she had twisted his fate with her own hands to make it so. Snorri felt poisoned. This was worse than Skalf tricking him into giving up drinking or Durin taking his nails.

Could anyone pull a meaner trick on a Slayer than this?

Snorri's mace-leg sank into the snow as he limped miserably on into the trees. The old lady had made it so he couldn't die until the time and place she'd set.

He had to find that place, that time, and then he could find his doom.

When you are whole again, when those you most love surround you again.

Snorri shrugged, paying no thought to the direction in which he trudged. What did it matter anyway? He had a destiny.

Snorri Nosebiter would find the mightiest doom.

NINE

The Crossroads of the World

A chimera circled the haunted citadel of Praag.

Its leonine fur writhed like penitent souls in the crosswinds that cut through the mountain passes to north and east. The beast swooped low over the Square of Heroes, startling the cloud of harpies that picked at the fresh bones hung from the statue of Tzar Alexis in the middle of the square. The hero of the Great War and contemporary of Magnus the Pious had been twisted by the touch of Chaos. Each day, the horns that now protruded from his forehead grew a little longer and whenever the skies blackened and the air crackled with a building warp storm, the graven statue wept tears of blood. It did so now.

With a sonorous wingbeat, the chimera regained altitude, scattering the screeching harpies as it sailed over the old town wall.

Max Schreiber pressed his face to the barred window of his cell. The backwash of its passing ruffled his tangled beard and he moaned for the brief bliss of the sensation of wind on his face. The rolling bellow of a lion echoed across the snow-troubled rooftops of the Starograd. The chimera dipped its right wing, dropping into a turn that carried it over the Mountain Gate and the besieging hordes that froze out there on the oblast. Max angled himself to watch. There were thin screams, a torrent of flame, and then one more contemptuous wingbeat as the updraft of the chimera's own fiery breath lifted it into a glide once again.

Max watched from his high tower as northmen and beasts charged through the flames like ants whose nest had been set ablaze. Drums beat furiously. Horns called by the thousand. Ladders rose out of the smoke and steam and clattered against the walls. On the ramparts, trolls smashed the siege ladders to kindling, beating down the assaulting forces or eating them. It was slaughter unparalleled and this battle had been raging for days. Around one such monster there glowered a faint red nimbus of power. Max recognised the ritual magic by which his captor's bray-shamans imposed their king's will on his minions. Strong as he was however, the Troll King was but one. Amongst the trolls, scrawny, half-beast ungor overseers stabbed down with spears and prodded the trolls to life whenever one became confused or threatened to fall into a stupor.

More beastmen were running through streets that had already been reduced to rubble by the passage of monsters. By the golden onion dome of a temple of Dazh, a red-bearded giant tore a gargoyle from the roof and hurled it over the wall. Max saw it roll through a crush of Chaos warriors carrying a battering ram. Harpies cackled overhead, picking off the pieces.

Max knew that the same scenes were being played out each day and night at the East Gate and the Gate of Gargoyles. He could hear it even when he tried to sleep.

Praag was the crossroads of the world.

To the north, Black Blood Pass and the legions of Archaon.

To the east, High Pass: the Kurgan and the Chaos Dwarfs

To the south, the Auric Bastion, and every warrior that had

returned in frustration only to find the city held against them by one of their own.

Max watched magic flash erratically from the walls. Such eruptions were, Max noted, always directed outwards. It had been a long time since a wizard had dared stand openly before the walls of Praag.

At last the cold metal bars became too much to bear and Max pulled back. Just far enough that they were no longer touching his face: he still wanted the feel of the cold, of the snow that drifted in through the bars with the light. It numbed the bruises and dulled even the hairline fracture in his jaw. His bones ached. He felt light-headed with hunger. Broken sleep made his vision bleary. It was a miracle of endurance that he still stood.

'You have the power to heal yourself,' came a growl from behind, less a voice than an expulsion of words, like gas from a fissure. 'Why do you not?'

Max shut his eyes, a conditioned response to the certain onset of pain, and lowered his forehead to the bars. The cold burned. He no longer cared. 'You would only break them again.'

That brought laughter, the low groan of earth before a quake. 'There are two hundred and six bones in the human body, Max. How many do you think I have already broken?'

'I don't know,' Max whispered.

'Tell me how many and perhaps I will not break another today.'

'I can't remember.'

'*Tell* me.'

'I-I-' Max's fingers tightened over the cold stone of the window slit. A dull pain throbbed in his hand. His fractured elbow ground mercilessly. And his hip... 'Nine. You have broken nine.'

A chuckle, the escape of pressure before an eruption, a volcanic pledge.

'I have another riddle for you, Max.' Something heavy shifted behind him. The bars of his cell groaned and bent under the weight being applied to them. When Max did not reply, the voice went on. 'I am your best friend and your worst enemy, I am privy to your darkest secrets and yet still they surprise me, I know every man you know, but not one of them knows me.' A pause, a weighted challenge. 'Who am I?'

'You are me,' said Max softly and without thinking.

Silence for a moment but for the tinny wail of distant armies, and then the laugh returned, dissonant and deliberate.

'You are the prize pigeon in my coop, Max. It will grieve me to scatter your bones for the harpies.'

There it was, the threat. His bowels tightened. Even after all he had suffered, all he had witnessed from his eyrie here, Max did not welcome an end to it. And he was close, so very close. 'I have been trying,' said Max, breath steaming through the open bars. 'What you want will take time. There will be trial and error involved. Some of your followers will die.'

'Look out of the window,' came the voice. 'Witness the ignorant legions of the Four. See how they crawl out of the north like worms to the rain. Do you know how I captured Aekold Helbrass?'

'No, I was...' Max hesitated. He wanted to say, *was not here*, but couldn't. It was easier to forget his old life than to hope.

'I crushed him because he was stupid. He had neither the will nor the wit to change his stars. Now look again.' Max gazed pliantly from the window as a griffon plunged down into the Square of Heroes and crushed one of the injured harpies under its talons. It was huge, with the mangy hindquarters of a snow cat and the fierce beak and mottled plumage of a bald eagle. It shrieked at the scattered harpies, then tore into the creature pinned beneath it. Max looked away. They were creatures of Chaos, but they felt pain like any other. 'I do not care for the loss of one or of a hundred. I do not need an army. I have the mightiest ever assembled. I need a general. I need an equal.'

'What was done to you was the work of the gods,' said Max. 'It is a... fascinating problem, but I am not a Teclis or a Nagash.'

'This is an age of marvels, Max, and you are the most powerful mage I have crossed who has not had that power gifted to him. If Nagash can rip the Wind of Shyish from the aethyr and confront the ancestor goddess of the dwarfs and triumph, then you can do this thing for me. And if not–'

The voice paused, time enough for Max's gaze to take in the citadel's other towers, the other windows. How many wizards had the king of Praag brought here? Hundreds. Each one was a shortening fuse that promised death to every other. If Max chose not to cooperate then he knew that there was a night goblin or a necromancer who would. His host was clearly no friend to Archaon, so why should Max be the one to die?

And he could not say that his curiosity was not intrigued by the conundrum he had been set.

Max half turned from the window slit to regard the huge, granite-like troll that had been bolted to the wall. It was twice Max's height, but it was the sheer mass of it that was most arresting, as if its scale was such that it drew substance off of everything around it, making itself loom ever heavier while all around it grew small. On an intellectual level Max understood that its rocky physiognomy was an adaptation to this troll's particular habitat, but the mountainous bulk of it still left him feeling the frailty of his bruised flesh and aching bones. It smelled of bare rock. Its chest heaved up and down with a slow regularity. The stare it gave him was utterly vacant. It was more the vague awareness of a plant for the position of the sun than a predator for its next meal.

And there was the conundrum: how to bestow intelligence upon a troll?

Despite himself, Max was gripped. Could it even be done? He knew that it could. Could *he* do it? He *knew* that he could! A part of him, the part that still remembered Ulrika and Felix and Claudia and a life without bars, posed the question as to whether this was the same hubris that had brought the downfall of men like Helsnicht and van Horstmann. A hunger for power could masquerade in the quest for betterment, he knew. But who was to say an intelligent troll was inherently an evil thing? Was evil in their nature, or were they brutal only because they did not understand? No serious scholar would agree that ogres were evil, and perhaps a troll with a mind would prove that evil was not innate except in the Dark Gods' own creations. It would be the proof that the world was not doomed, that it was worth saving. This was good work he did.

Yes, he *could* do it.

Max glanced up from his specimen and through the bars that separated his cage from the dozens of others on this level of the tower. It had been called the Ice Tower, for the late Duke Enrik had sponsored the work of ice witches here and magical apparatus and tomes were scattered between the cells. Within each a troll was bound, dull yellow eyes gazing listlessly through the most horrific of tortures. In the cell nearest, a ratman warlock hunched over the body of a troll that had its brainpan sliced open. As Max watched, the warlock took previously biopsied and regenerated tissue and methodically grafted it back onto the troll's brain. Beyond, mages of every race Max could name muttered and raved, working on trolls without arms, without eyes, or with carcinoid second heads, trolls branded with arcane sigils that steamed in the cold air. And beyond it, through the forest of bars and bodies and the mist of breath and pain, was the door.

The door.

Max shuddered. He had never seen it opened, it was just there, locked, varnished red wood panelling with a brass strip top and bottom. Mysterious. What had started as curiosity had grown and grown into a nagging need to know what lay behind it. What was a door for, after all, if not for partitioning one set of *things* from another set of *things*? Max had watched men drive themselves slowly insane just staring at it trying to glean its meaning, gibbering and screaming and pushing gaunt faces to the bars as if just one inch nearer would put them in position to stare into the warped mind of god.

'Look at me,' came the voice, and Max looked.

The fervid, jealously intelligent visage of a troll leered between the bars of Max's cage. Crystalline shards of warpstone grew from his brow, running down his neck and shoulders like a mane of hair and following the contours of his arms to produce a pair of harshly glowing club-like tumours around each wrist. Upon that gnarled, mineral-encrusted head, above eyes that shone with a god-given intellect, sat a crown engraved with the eight-pointed star of Chaos. The silver circlet of Duke Enrik had been forced over one wrist like a Kurgan trophy ring, and sealed into place by the creep of that living mineral. It was not a face ever intended to speak.

His name was Throgg, favourite of Chaos, the Troll King of Praag.

'What the gods gifted to me can be gifted to another. I will not be the one mind in a race of blunt, witless animals.' Throgg closed his hard grey fists around the bars until they groaned. For all his intellect and strength, the Troll King was bitterly alone.

'I believe in you, Max. I hope it will be you that does not fail.'

TEN

Alone

Kislev was flat and it was open. The wind cut down from the big mountain range in the north, getting stronger and bloody colder as it stormed over the plains unchecked and battered Snorri Nosebiter's face. Snorri closed his eyes and waded into the waist-deep snow. His eyelids rippled as if under attack by tiny blows. His beard thrashed. The force being driven against his broad shoulders was enough to uproot a tree. But Snorri wasn't a tree. As tough as trees looked they were soft in the middle and Snorri wasn't soft anywhere, except perhaps in the head, but if he had to be soft anywhere then that was probably where he would have chosen. With a determined growl, Snorri dug himself out another foot and swung his mace-leg into it. Snorri spat snow from his lips, but his beard was full of the stuff. It was a cold and constantly wet weight on his chin, like he had just been pulled from a river. Snorri hated water. It tasted horrible.

And Snorri hated trees. They were where old human ladies with nothing better to do than surround themselves with giant spiders and curse innocent Slayers lived.

Snorri plunged his massive hands into the snow in front of him and shovelled it aside. Foot-by-foot, that was the dwarf way. His stupid destiny could be a mile away or a thousand and over the mountains, but one step at a time would get him there in the end. He just hoped it would be sooner rather than later. Driving his body into the opening he had cut, he turned, sheltered his eyes under his hand and looked back down the trench he had gouged.

Snow flicked his numb fingers, and he watched for a minute as it filled the trench behind him and patted it down as though burying a body. The only evidence that Snorri had passed that way was that Snorri was right here. It would be so easy to just give up, sit down, and let the snow cover him too. He was tempted. An eternity as a dishonoured revenant denied Grimnir's hall didn't seem so terrible when compared to Kislev. It would be worth it just for the look on that mean seeress's face – take your doom and choke on it! – but Snorri knew he couldn't do that.

Snorri shook the snow from his hand and rubbed his eyes. He had made a promise to Gotrek. The thought of his old friend loosened more than just snow, but he tried not to think about it. It was hard though in this place. The steppe was like Snorri's mind, big and empty and just waiting to be filled. The steppe had its snow and its wind. Snorri had his thoughts.

Was Gotrek involved in his doom somehow?

Did he have something to do with Snorri's shame?

Unable to keep himself from thinking, he tried to think about something else instead. About how many days he had been walking like this perhaps? Snorri grinned wearily. That was too easy. He had absolutely no idea.

What else could he think about?

Thinking hard on that occupied his mind long enough for him to turn back to the snowface. Snorri hated snow. He had come to this understanding only over the last several days, but he held it with a vehemence that most reserved for goblins or elves.

He kicked the hated stuff with his mace-leg, and again, imagining it was goblins. He saw their ugly, pointy faces in its layered folds, their glinty eyes in the flakes as they fell. What did goblins have to do with anything? Furious now without knowing why, he kicked harder. The mace crunched through the snowface and wedged there. Snorri shook it ferociously, so intent on pulling it loose that he didn't even notice his standing leg sliding under him until he was starting to topple. With a frustrated cry, Snorri flailed his arms and crashed back into the snow.

'Get up, Snorri. Get up.'

Borek Forkbeard hooked his arms under Snorri's shoulders and dragged him back from the wreckage of the steam wagon. Smoke was billowing from the portholes in its squat, armour-plated chassis and rolling like cooling magma from the open rear hatch. Two dwarfs lay dead on the barren, oily rock beside it. Aside from a coating of ash, there wasn't an obvious mark on them. The smoke had killed them.

Snorri gave a hacking cough. 'Not another accident. Snorri thinks that's plain unlucky.'

Borek answered with a vigorous shake of the head.

The longbeard had soot and blood down one side of his face and the lens of his pince-nez was cracked. He was loading a big, wide-muzzled blunderbuss. Snorri cast about for his own axe and found it on the ground where he had dropped it after staggering from the steam wagon. He picked it up. Warbling cries sounded through the roar of smoke and fire, and all around Snorri could see ape-like, not entirely solid creatures scrambling on all fours over the twisted terrain of the Chaos Wastes.

It was an attack. And they were surrounded.

Swathed in fumes from the wrecked wagon, Gotrek fought off a pack of the cackling, rubber-limbed horrors, wielding a coal shovel two-handed. The engineer swung wildly, almost accidentally catching one of the daemons over the side of the head and cracking open its skull. The daemon gibbered and flailed, the wound in its temple widening as though pulled apart by something within. It continued to cackle though, even as its flesh was rendered down to an elastic pink gloop. Two meaner, gnarlier daemons shook their parent's remains from their blue hides, bared their fangs and leapt into the attack.

'Valaya be merciful,' Borek muttered, swinging up his blunderbuss to cover the scrum around Gotrek and, before Snorri could even think about what was about to happen, pulling the trigger.

There was a detonation, as if a mining charge had just gone off in Snorri's ear, and then a storm of nails and iron trimmings tore through the pack of horrors. Some were thrown back by the impact. Others jigged on the spot as though tickled by those sharp metal shards. Somehow, protected by the height and the number of them, Gotrek remained unscathed. He clocked one of the few standing pink horrors with his shovel.

'Kill the blue ones,' Borek yelled, reloading his blunderbuss. 'They won't come back.'

With a grateful snarl, Gotrek thrust the blade of his coal shovel through a blue horror's throat, then swung backhanded to spill another's weird, semi-sentient guts. A spitting horror launched itself at the engineer's back, but dropped short with an axe in its spine. Snorri ripped his axe free, using his bulk to shield Gotrek as Borek shouted a warning and sent another withering blast of shrapnel through the weakened daemons.

When their ears had stopped ringing, Gotrek lowered his shoulders and put his hand on Snorri's shoulder. He gave it an approving pat.

'I owe you one, Snorri. Don't ever let me forget.'

Snorri beamed. He didn't much care about fighting daemons or rediscovering lost Karag Dum, but his friend's respect he had always craved.

'Back to the last wagon,' said Borek. He shouldered his blunderbuss and hustled the two dwarfs around. 'It's crowded, but we can still make it.'

'If that's a joke then I've heard better,' said Gotrek. 'I told you the Wastes were impassable. Turn that box around while it has wheels that turn.'

'Never,' Borek screamed back. 'We're so close. Think of the glory. Think of the gold.'

Only half listening over the surrounding din, Snorri lifted his axe to point out the weird, willowy daemon-thing that was drifting through the smoke of the gutted wagon and was heading towards Borek's. Its body twisted into gnashing faces and long, floating limbs that flickered with flame in place of hands. Snorri felt the heat of it, felt it somewhere deep inside his soul.

'Snorri thinks–'

There was a whumf of magical energy, flames racing along the daemon's arms until its whole body was an inferno, and then two jets of blistering heat shot towards the dwarfs' last wagon. The fire struck the angle of its front armour, driving the wagon's nose into the ground, before it punched through and hit the engine. For a split second it groaned, like a dwarf with indigestion, then a many-tentacled eruption of coloured fire ripped it apart from the inside out. The roof rocketed high into the air while bits of wood and armour plate were hurled wide.

'No!' Borek roared, the absolute destruction of his dreams hellishly reflected in the broken lens of his pince-nez. He made to run to the wagon as if he could save it, but Gotrek held him back, just as a string of secondary explosions wracked its remains.

'We're done,' Gotrek growled. He was changed, even Snorri could see it.

The Wastes had changed him. It had changed them all.

Snorri levelled his axe to the flamers and horrors that came gambolling towards them. His heel hit a hammer amongst the debris of the wagon's explosion and he took that too, roaring into the gibbering pack.

'Leave Snorri alone!'

He clutched his head, as if his fingers could bore into the pockmarks left by his old crest of nails and dig these memories from his brain. Borek's first expedition to the Wastes had been doomed from the outset, dogged by accident and disaster long before that final attack. And it had been Snorri that talked Gotrek into going. It was Snorri's fault. All of it. There was more. There was...

Digging his chewed nails deep into his scalp, he groaned, pushed his face into the wall of the snow trench and used it to push himself up. Snow swirled in to greet his suddenly exposed head. Snorri rubbed a stream of snot onto his forearm and suppressed a sob. Then he kicked at the snowface and started moving again. He had a doom, a destiny, places to be. He had no time to remember. But he owed it to Gotrek.

To Gotrek.

Snorri punched his fist deep into the snow and howled *into the warp storm.*

Black clouds rolled over a sky that just moments before had been a string web of colour, the charge of daemonic cavalry, lances of purple lightning jagging frenziedly down, up, and in every direction across the sky. Thunder never stopped rumbling. Pebbles bounced under Snorri's boots. His beard bushed, repulsing itself with charge.

'Gotrek!' *he yelled, but the wind smothered his voice and forced it* back down his throat. If the wind was the strong arm of the Wastes then its claws were pure warpstone. The air glittered with it and Snorri could feel the corruption scratch down his throat with every breath. He squinted back the way they had come, into the wind-beaten warpscape of twisted rock shapes and its gyrating skyline. Gotrek was gone.

'Gotrek!'

Snorri turned, intending to go back for him, but the rope tied around his waist that tethered him to Borek pulled taut and held him in his tracks. The thick knot dug into his belly. It had been the old scholar's idea to keep the three of them together through the Wastes. His hand closed over it, felt one where there should have been two.

'Oh no.'

'Where is he?' said Borek, taking a grip on his own rope as if Snorri's incompetence might dissolve it even at a distance. 'And how in the name of Grungni did you lose him in the first place?'

'It's not Snorri's fault. He said he's no good at knots.'

'You idiot, Snorri!'

'It's not Snorri's fault,' Snorri said again, shouting as if to make it truer, to make it heard over the storm. 'Gotrek checked it. He said Snorri did them good.'

'Well they weren't good, were they?' Borek spat.

Snorri had never seen the longbeard so furious, not even after the daemons had destroyed the wagons. Helplessness and guilt welled up inside him and he spun around to wail into the storm once more.

'Gotrek!'

His friend could not be gone. Gotrek was invincible.

'We will return to Karak Kadrin,' said Borek firmly, seemingly in no doubt that they would return. 'I expect there is an oath there that you will wish to make.'

Snorri hung his head. Stupid Snorri. Gotrek's impenetrable over-and-under arrangements held like iron rivets. Who couldn't tie a knot? Then he nodded. It wasn't as if he was much good for anything else. Perhaps a half-decent doom as a Slayer was what he had always been destined for.

'After,' said Snorri, sadly. 'After Snorri tells Gotrek's family what he did.'

Snorri's mace-leg dragged after him through the snow behind. He wasn't even bothering to attack the snowface any more, just ploughed into it face first. His eyes were limned with frozen tears. His insides felt cold. He still had no idea how long he'd been walking. But he'd remembered. That was his shame! It had been Snorri's fault that Gotrek had got lost in the Wastes. Shaking his head he trudged on. He'd been expecting something more, a great weight off his shoulders or something like that. Instead he felt worse than ever, like someone had just punched a bruise. There was only one explanation.

That wasn't his shame.

It would have been bad enough, but there was more. After all, Gotrek had survived. Snorri hadn't known that of course when he'd taken the oath, but there would have been no need to bury the memory so deep. Something had happened later, something to do with that dwarf woman and child.

'No more!' Snorri yelled it into the wind and snow.

Memories sloshed around in his mind as if the holes in his skull had caused it to leak. Taking a handful of snow, he smothered it over his scalp like a protective cap and roared with grief. This was that priest, Skalf's, fault. And Durin too. They had taken his nails, taken his beer, had saved his life when he might have died and cheated that old lady's curse.

Fists flailing as though everyone who had ever done him wrong were right there hiding in the snow, he lost his balance again and slipped, this time whacking his chin on a lump of packed snow. With a groan, he pushed himself up. The flutter of snow on the top of his head cooled his overheated thoughts somewhat and he relaxed. Glumly, he crossed his arms tight over his enormous chest and stared back the way he had come. Into the past.

It wasn't fair. Snorri didn't want to remember.

All Snorri wanted was...

'Beer.'

'You heard him, Craddi,' said the ranger crouched over him, peeling open Snorri's bloodshot eye with thumb and forefinger. He was grey-haired, gruff-bearded, and grizzled from a century of daylight and mountain winds. A second dwarf, Craddi presumably, appeared at his shoulder. He was younger, dressed in a waterproof cloak painted with what looked like greenskin tribal glyphs, and had a bone grobi-whistle still in his mouth. 'Get this dwarf a beer, he's dead on his feet.'

'Snorri would love a beer,' he drooled. 'He's not had one since the Chaos Wastes.'

'Must be delirious,' said Craddi. 'And who do you think this Snorri is?'

'Snorri is thirsty,' Snorri answered.

'Got by the goblins most likely, same as everyone else,' said the old ranger. 'Stop yapping and give him his mouthful. We haven't time to sit here all day.'

'Aye, Fulgriff.'

The neck of an ale skin appeared at Snorri's lips and its honey-sweetened ambrosia washed the pain of his journey from his mouth and down his throat. Many were the legends told of the fortifying power of dwarf beer, of the drunken clanner who fought off a goblin army with a spear in his belly and a tankard in his hand, of the embittered old greybeard who died mere yards from completing his pilgrimage to Bugman's brewery only to be revived for one final pint by the mere whiff of Josef Bugman's famous hops. This was a far inferior brew, ranger's rations, but to Snorri it felt like something the Ancestor Goddess herself would use to clean wounds and salve broken hearts. Snorri felt a comforting buzz, the promise of numbness and a future without pain. For the first time since losing Gotrek, Snorri imagined that he could face the world again. His parchment-dry lids flickered open and he leaned forwards to try and steepen the flow into his mouth. Infuriatingly, Craddi chose that moment to pull it away from him.

'We are trying to run ahead of a goblin warband,' said Fulgriff. He was crouched down beside Snorri. His cloak smelled of wax and hung stiff in the breeze. Eyes open now, Snorri studied him and his rangers more closely. Including Fulgriff there were six of them, all of them dressed in thick waterproofs painted with greenskin markings and leather caps that bristled with pebbles, bird droppings, and bits of moss. 'Was it they who attacked you?' Fulgriff pressed. 'Was it near here?'

'No,' said Snorri. He shook his head. He had left Borek behind at Karak Kadrin to fulfil his promise to Gotrek, but he didn't know the way. Miserably, he looked at the rune sewn into his pack. 'Where is this?'

Thinking that Snorri was answering his question, Fulgriff answered quickly. 'A week out from Karaz-a-Karak, if you don't rest.' Then the ranger pulled aside, and pointed away down a dramatic gorge that was flanked by wintry, but majestic-looking peaks. Snorri was lying in the shade cast by the mountains on the southern side of the valley, being pointed down to a slender ribbon of water that ran in darkness along the bottom. 'The Skull River. We're following it all the way to the Badlands, warning every watchpost and town of the danger coming their way. Those chuffing grobi have already sacked two mines on Karag Khatûl.' The other rangers grumbled curses, but Fulgriff shrugged. 'Lucky in a way. They got carried away. Gave us time to get ahead of them.'

Snorri had stopped listening some time ago. His home was in a valley, picturesque like this one, on the borders of the Badlands halfway between Karaz-a-Karak and Barak Varr. He smiled weakly. He'd found it after all. Snorri Nosebiter had done something right.

'Are you listening to me?'

'What?' said Snorri. There had been something about goblins, something about warning towns. His gaze slid back to the shortbeard, Craddi, and he smacked his lips. Had they been saying something about beer?

'Blow to the head, I reckon,' said Craddi. 'I vote we leave him. We're only a half day from the Badlands and who knows how close that warband is behind us. We can pick him up on the way back.'

'Can Snorri have more beer?'

'No,' said Craddi and Fulgriff together.

Snorri's look of contentment went rigid. Why were they not letting him have beer? What had Snorri done to them? He made a grab for Craddi's ale skin, but the ranger was young and trained to be nimble and skipped away. That just stoked Snorri's temper even more. Half-falling, half-flailing, Snorri went for the shortbeard, catching the ranger's ankle as he fell on his face and yanking the other dwarf from his feet. Craddi's back hit bare stone, and he gave an unwitting blart on the grobi-whistle still in mouth.

The rangers froze as the slightly wooden goblin war cry resounded over the valley. Time enough for Snorri to get onto his knees, pull off Craddi's belt, and upend the ranger's ale skin in one fell swoop. He sighed in pleasure, then Craddi kicked him in the jaw and he dropped the empty skin.

'What's the werit doing?' The voice came from somewhere behind him, followed by, 'He's after the beer. Get him!'

The flat butt of an axe struck him on the top of the head and Snorri dropped to all fours, his vision temporarily blackening. Another boot in the face snapped him out of it and he caught Craddi's leg in both hands, hands that the Wastes had made strong, and wrenched the leg out of the knee socket.

Craddi howled and grasped his knee as another blow struck down on the back of Snorri's neck. The impact flung Snorri's shoulders down as if he was about to be sick. The rangers closed in. There was one each side of him, raising their axes with the butts facing down to club him down like a tavern drunk. Snorri moved quicker than even he thought he could. The dwarf on the left went down with a wheeze of pain to a punch in the groin, while the one to the right got the full rolling-boulder force of Snorri's shoulder across the knees. They buckled, it sounded like one snapped, and Snorri rose, slightly unsteadily, in time for his teeth to welcome a punch in the face.

Snorri staggered back, accidentally spat a tooth in his attacker's eyes and then grabbed him by the throat when he flapped. Snorri's muscles bulged and the ranger's eyes popped up like bubbles rising from the bottom of a stream. He had always been big. He had worked the mines since he first had stubble on his chin. You didn't need a brain to pull a mine cart – as his mother had told the rather sceptical lodewarden – but his experiences had toughened him. He had fought daemons and survived the Chaos Wastes, and when he tensed his grip and lifted, the ranger's feet parted easily from the ground. With a drunken roar, Snorri flung him into his companion and the two dwarfs went rolling downhill.

That left Fulgriff.

The veteran ranger threw down a half-loaded crossbow and drew a pair of hand hatchets. He wasn't just showing the flat sides. Snorri didn't think that was very sporting. He took his eye off him to bend *down and scoop up another ale skin. The dwarf with the bruised dongliz pawed gamely at Snorri's fumbling fingers before Snorri laid him out with a punch between the eyes, and then uncapped the skin. He chuckled happily as the smell wafted up, catching the gleam of steel as it sliced towards his head. He pulled aside, but too slow to save his ear. He roared in pain as Fulgriff's hatchet sheared it from the side of his head. Blood spurted from the stump. Oddly, Snorri could sort of still hear a rhythmic* whump-whump *under his skull, but everything else had gone dim like his head was wrapped in cotton.*

Soaked to his undershirt in his own blood, Snorri ducked between the ranger's two axes and elbowed him in the collar. The longbeard choked, but was made of sterner stuff than his unit. He tried to strike back with his second axe, but Snorri gripped him in a bear hug, pinning both axes to his sides and hoisting him off the ground. Then Snorri slammed a headbutt into the bridge of his nose and the dwarf went limp in his arms.

Snorri let the body drop, then slumped down onto his backside beside it. Injured dwarfs groaning and whimpering all around, he took a sip from his ale skin. Absently, he rubbed at his severed ear, making it bleed some more. He looked up, gaze flitting from ridgeline to ridgeline down the stark relief of the Skull Valley.

He could have sworn he'd heard a goblin war cry echoing between the peaks.

He clapped his hand over the cartilage stump a few times, then shrugged. He took another sip of beer and smiled in big-hearted concentration.

Now what had that ranger been trying to say about towns and goblins?

Snorri hugged himself and shivered, but it could not shake the certainty that he had done something terrible. But what?

A little shakily, he stood and turned back to the snowface, and then cried out in horror at what he saw. There were two figures in the distance. The blizzard made them formless, genderless, just shadows wreathed in snow. Their darkness made him think of burned-out houses and charred bodies and he covered his mouth with his hand to stifle a moan.

The dwarf woman and her child had found him at last!

He peered into the falling snow, his memory seeming to add details to the empty silhouettes. The child held her mother's hand in a firm grip. She had bright, intense eyes, a quarrelsome frown on a face that, allied to a deep seriousness, struck Snorri as intensely familiar. The mother on the other hand wore her long silver-blonde hair in plaits over her broad shoulders. Her buxom girth was pragmatically attired in goatskin and leather and ornamented with gold, including – Snorri's breath caught – including the chain that Snorri carried in his bag.

Snorri blinked and the snow swept the visions down to the distant apparitions they were. Remembering what the old lady had said to him, he gave a determined growl and limped after them.

Only when he was whole again would he find his doom.

He had already remembered so much, suffered so much.

What was the worst that he could have done?

Felix sat with his back to the warmth of the firepit and gazed out into the gathering dusk that layered the oblast with deepening strokes of indigo, violet, and then black. Watching the snow fall was restful and strangely hypnotic, not at all dissimilar from watching the sky and making shapes from the clouds. A swirl of snow could be a city, a troll on an icy throne, a lover's face. He sighed. Kislev was cold, her people brusque, their culture as strange to him at times as that of the dwarfs, but it was impossible to gaze into its emptiness and not feel a flicker of sentiment. On these lands he had fallen in love, fought a war, almost died at least twice, lost friends, and then fallen out of love again. Love and loss, the great events that had fascinated the poets since Sigmar's day, and Felix had witnessed them firsthand right here.

And now it was gone.

The wind moaned with the birth tremors of daemons, eddies pulling the snow from Felix's reminiscences and shaping them into something darker. Things with horns, tentacles, and bleeding skin. That was the problem with this game. A man could see whatever he imagined, and Felix had seen too much to imagine a happy ending. The borders of the Chaos Wastes were extending south. The old treatises told that such things had happened before, that each time the Dark Powers waxed the Wastes expanded a little further and retreated a little less. The borderlands of the gods had not yet swallowed Kislev, but it was coming. Like an old soldier who foretold the arrival of winter by the ache in his wrists, Felix could feel it, not in his bones but in his soul. A blackness hung over the steppe that had nothing to do with nightfall.

From one of the neighbouring firepits, under a tatty awning emblazoned with the heraldry of some forgotten Border Princeling, Gustav and his free company were playing the same black game. Beer seemed to be involved and thus they were playing it louder. Everyone knew they rode to do battle with the so-called King of Trolls – the monster that stood apart from the champions of Chaos and alone defied them in their heartlands.

Felix shook his head at a raucous cry from the tent. Perhaps he was getting old, but if a man was going to bare his soul to the elements then he should do it alone.

'You fight in Praag before, yhah?'

Damir was sitting beside him, also facing outwards from the fire.

Shadows ebbed and rolled over his patched hemp cloak like the wax and wane of Chaos. The Ungol nomad offered up the liquor he was drinking. It smelled of turps and Felix waved it away.

'Gorilka good for soul.' Damir thumped his chest lightly and then waved it vaguely before him as though scattering seeds. 'Made from same grain as feed horses. Only best.' He grinned and offered it again. 'Yhah?'

With a sigh, Felix took the offering, swallowing just enough to be polite and immediately coughing it back into his hand.

Chuckling, Damir clapped him on the back. 'Yhah.'

Felix too found himself smiling. 'Yes, I fought in the last battle of Praag. I was there when Arek Daemonclaw died.'

'*Doskonale*, Empire man!'

The man looked pleased, so Felix assumed that this was good. Kislevarin was one of the most complicated human languages that Felix had ever come across, with a ludicrous and – to Felix's view – arbitrary gender system. And the fact that Ulrika and her father had spoken Reikspiel perfectly well had also removed any incentive of his own to learn it. 'Where did you fight?'

Damir grinned. 'Before I born, Felix Jaeger. But father and grandfather? They ride in pulk of Tzarina with Boyar Straghov.'

'You make me feel old.'

Raising his gorilka high, Damir saluted. 'To growing old.'

'To growing old,' Felix agreed and joined the Ungol in a shot of the searing Troll Country spirit. This time he kept it down, and Damir's grin deepened until his whole face seemed drawn by it. 'Your fathers served Ivan Petrovich,' Felix observed once the stinging sensation in his throat had sunk deeper into his chest. 'Is that why you ride with Ulrika now, despite...' He trailed off, then shrugged and stared instead into the snow.

He had seen for himself how the common folk of Sylvania

remained servile to their masters in undeath as they had done in life. Deference was bred into the backbone of the Empire and its people weren't about to rise up just because their rightful lord had stopped breathing. There was something to be said for constancy, Felix supposed, but he had expected something better somehow from the famous independent spirit of Kislev.

'Nyeh,' said Damir, failing to disappoint. 'In south maybe that matters, but not on steppe. On oblast, loyalty earned. Not fall after from mother like *popłodu*.'

'And Ulrika earned it?'

Damir gave a noncommittal shrug, then chuckled and elbowed Felix slyly in the ribs. 'But she fine piece of horsemeat, yhah?'

Felix prickled at the Ungol's coarseness, but nevertheless produced a guilty smile and acceded to another hit of gorilka.

She certainly was that.

'Are my ears burning?'

Snow crunched under knee-high leather riding boots as Ulrika strode from the other firepits towards them. With her cropped, ash-blonde hair, and garbed in virginal white plate that fell halfway past her thighs, she looked like a warrior goddess of the steppe. Felix's heart seemed to beat just a little faster. Damir gazed on her as if she was made of gold.

'Tend to your horses, Damir,' said Ulrika. 'We ride as soon as it is full dusk.' The Ungol nodded and departed, and only when he was away amongst the horses did Ulrika cross her arms over her chest and smile. 'Honestly, Felix, men never change. In a way, it is reassuring. Here you are, hours from the battle of your lives, and I find you talking about women.'

'I was just thinking.'

'Just?' Ulrika tapped the lamellar plate that girded her heart. It was thicker than any other part of her armour, barring the bevor that protected her throat, and heavier than any mortal knight could have carried to battle. Clearly the suit's maker had known the vulnerabilities of his work's recipient well. 'You forget what I can hear.'

She sat down next to him, but facing the other way, into the fire, as if their meeting here was in some way illicit. It felt uncomfortably intimate.

'You shouldn't face into the fire,' Felix murmured.

'I think that I know that,' said Ulrika. The firelight caused her eyes to sparkle.

'It'll spoil your night vision,' Felix went on.

'Vampires do not have night vision, Felix. My eyes do not work as yours do. I do not see colour as such. For me it is always night.' Her smile, when she found it, was a little sad. 'It is all just vision to me.'

Felix nodded as if the minutiae of the vampiric condition fascinated him profoundly. The snow swirled, adopting libidinous new shapes.

'What were you thinking about?'

'Hmm?'

'It is an Ungol tradition to share a secret before battle, so it will not die with you.'

Felix shrugged with his eyebrows and gazed into the snow. It sounded sufficiently morbid to be true. He wished he could say he had been thinking of the Troll King of Praag and the thousand images – none of them good – that that title conjured. He had tried. Mulling on the coming battle was preferable to trying to unpick the emotional tangle of his feelings for Kat and Ulrika. He looked past Ulrika into the snow.

Perhaps it was this place. The memories of a lost time tugged on his heart.

'Back in Kurzycko,' he said, turning to regard Ulrika fully. There was no longer any evidence of Helbrass's burns. The scar by her left eye remained, but clearly she had fed and fed well. The idea repulsed him. And it left him more than a little jealous. 'When you needed blood, why did you drink from the beastmen? I was nearer. Why didn't you take mine?'

Ulrika shifted a little closer until their legs touched. The fire divided her face into light and dark. 'Do you wish I had?'

'That's not what I asked.'

Ulrika reached out, slowly, and brushed his neck with ungloved fingers. Despite being girded to the cold, he shivered. 'I could drink from you and it would be ecstasy as you have never experienced, but you would not be *you* any more.' She nodded to where Damir readied his horse and his men. 'I could command you to do anything, but I have thralls enough. I want you to want to be here with me.'

'You said that before,' said Felix. It troubled him to hear her speak of men as though they were less than servants, animals, but seemingly of its own volition, Felix's hand caught Ulrika's fingers and squeezed them to his shoulder. 'Why?'

'Chaos waxes, and for better or for worse I am a creature born of Chaos. You, though...' She drew nearer until their bodies touched. She turned her hand so her fingers entwined with his. Her voice became husky. 'When I'm with you I remember what it felt like to feel.'

'I–'

Whatever he had been meaning to say was fervently forgotten as Ulrika leaned forwards and kissed him.

A shock pulsed through his lips, down his neck, and made his entire body tingle. Her lips were cold, her body incomparably strong, but in every way that mattered she was the same Ulrika he had known twenty years ago. His free hand explored her neck, her ear, her hair. Exactly the same. He inhaled the familiar scent of horsehair, wood fire and vodka that he, an Altdorfer in a foreign land, had found so irresistible and exotic. That tingle became a glow, a warmth of desire that smoothed away any lingering stain of guilt, and he relaxed into her.

Too soon, she pushed him back. Arousal had brought her fangs from beneath her lips. He could see the blood throbbing to them. Her eyes were wide and burned with promises. All he had to do was give himself willingly. Felix's smile shuddered into being, heart warring with his head, and when he opened his mouth he had no idea what he wanted to say. No, that wasn't entirely true.

He knew what he *wanted* to say.

His grin hung indecisively for a moment, long enough for him to become cogent to the squat, ox-like figure that had just tramped out of nowhere from the snow and into the circle of firelight behind Ulrika's back. Felix blinked.

It took another moment to put together what he was seeing. Partly because the figure's appearance had changed so much over the past year, but mainly because his presence was so utterly, astronomically, impossible. Ulrika twisted around and made a short, breathless gasp of surprise.

The thickset and slightly singed dwarf limped over on a metal leg and prodded Ulrika none-too-gently in the shoulder. She resisted the push with a scowl and the dwarf turned to Felix.

'Is she a vampire yet? Snorri's starting to get confused.'

Felix didn't know whether to laugh, smile, or just cry out. His lips still thrilled with Ulrika's taste. His chest felt sore with guilt, but also relieved in a strange way, as if Snorri had just pulled him back from a precipice. His tongue seemed to knot itself up between the options as he scrambled to his feet and beat snow from his breeches.

Sigmar's blood, it was Snorri Nosebiter!

The Slayer looked older without his crest of nails. The hair coming through on his head was thin and grey. Felix brushed his hand through his own hair and smiled ruefully. Snorri wasn't the only one.

'Damir,' he yelled. 'Bring back that gorilka. We're going to need it.'

Snorri winced, as if Felix had just trodden on something bruised and painful, but almost as soon as the expression appeared it lapsed into something more like the dwarf's well-worn idiot grin.

'Thank you, young Felix. Snorri thinks he could use a drink about now.'

PART THREE
OATHS

Late Winter 2525

ELEVEN

Where the Beasts Dwell

'How much has he had to drink?' Gustav Jaeger whispered in Felix's ear.

The two men sat side-by-side in the saddle, watching as a fine if slightly neglected bay gelding of Ostermark stock ploughed a bemused circle into the snow with Snorri Nosebiter hanging one-armed from the bridle. In the other hand he clutched a clay mug that he held above his head. The Slayer's mace-leg waved threateningly and more of the gorilka sloshed from the cup and down his arm. The free company mercenary who had foolishly tried to help the dwarf up lay in a heap in the snow, trying to staunch the flow from his broken nose. His comrades, meanwhile, were content to tend their own horses and laugh at this uncommon display of dwarfish horsemanship.

'Not nearly this much,' Felix replied. Snorri had only had two cups. Full cups mind, enough to put Felix in the ground, but this was Snorri Nosebiter, a dwarf who would sooner outdrink a horse than saddle one. Watching Snorri throw his arm over the horse's neck and dry heave into its mane, it was difficult to believe him the same dwarf.

'Give him a hand, would you?'

Gustav cocked an eyebrow. 'I like my hand, uncle. It's one of my favourites.' He waved towards the struggling Trollslayer. 'Besides, he is another of your idiot friends.'

Cursing under his breath, Felix guided his mount alongside Snorri's to block its movement. Then he claimed Snorri's reins and coiled them up with his own.

'Snorri has it now,' said Snorri, dragging himself inelegantly onto the horse's back. The bay whickered its discomfiture. Its forelegs bent as if about to buckle, but just about managed to adjust to the dwarf's incredible mass. Snorri grinned proudly. 'Now, how does Snorri make it go?'

'And some people wonder how the dwarfs managed to lose their empire,' said Gustav with a sneer. Clicking his tongue, the former merchant wheeled his horse about to rejoin his men.

The circus now over, shelters were being disassembled, bedrolls and cookpots stowed in saddlebags, and torches lit in firepits before the fires were doused with snow and buried. Accustomed to travelling light and moving fast, Damir's riders were already mounted and ready. Their growing impatience came out in occasional catcalls and 'helpful' suggestions regarding where in the stirrups a man should put his feet and how it might all be done faster if it were just left to the horses. Luckily for everyone, Felix was not the only one who found Kislevarin a swine of a language, and Gustav had just enough authority amongst his own men to keep the otherwise obvious mockery from fraying tempers too far.

Despite himself, Felix was actually rather impressed. A little more uncharitably, he wondered how much of it his nephew was putting on for Ulrika's benefit.

The vampiress rode amongst her men, reassuring them with her presence. They knew she was worth twenty fighting men and even the Ostermarkers had been quick to accept what she brought to their chances of getting home. Felix couldn't help but wonder what Sigmar or Magnus would have done, and what their earthly representatives in Altdorf would make of this conversion to pragmatism. As Felix watched, Ulrika drew her mount alongside Gustav's. The two conferred in hurried whispers with Damir joining soon after.

'He looks familiar,' said Snorri, also with an eye on Gustav.

'Doesn't he just,' said Felix with a sigh that he felt in his bones.

'Oh,' said Snorri slowly, then took another swallow of gorilka and grinned. 'Snorri sees. Felix is jealous.'

'Jealous? Of what?'

Snorri pointed towards Ulrika.

For a moment, Felix just watched her, enjoying again the memory of her lips against his. Then he scowled and brushed the thought aside, thrusting his ring finger under Snorri's flat red nose. 'I'm a married man,' he said angrily, though at whom that anger was directed he wasn't sure. 'To Kat, remember?'

With a suggestive elbow in the ribs, Snorri chuckled. 'Snorri remembers.'

In an attempt at changing the subject, Felix turned his mount so he could no longer watch Ulrika and the two men. He looked at Snorri. The dwarf had cheered up no end since getting a drink inside him, but there was still a sadness in his eyes that Felix couldn't remember seeing before. He fidgeted in the saddle. A satchel with a strange rune and a knot in the strap hung over his left shoulder. His axe and hammer were stuffed down his breeches.

'Do you remember the rest, Snorri?'

'The rest of what?'

Felix froze. Had Snorri somehow escaped Karak Kadrin without remembering his shame? But then Snorri's face split into an old pugilist's grin.

'Snorri told a joke.' The old dwarf chuckled and took another drink. Then he looked around before focusing on Felix. His smile wavered. 'Why is no one laughing but Snorri?'

Felix shook his head and tried to mask a grin. 'It's good to see you yourself again. Like old times.'

With a shrug, Snorri upended his cup over his mouth. Nothing came out. He stared at it glumly. 'Snorri said he wanted a bucket.'

'It's probably the last cup in all of Kislev,' said Felix with genuine sadness.

Snorri stuck his thumb in to chase down the dregs and then licked it clean.

Before Felix could say anything more, the haunting whine of an Ungol horn brought him around. He saw Gustav and Damir riding to rejoin their respective companies. Ulrika regarded them all haughtily from atop her snow-white charger. Slowly, the assorted men fell silent.

'Tonight we will ride on Praag. For some of you,' she nodded to the Ungols, 'this was home. It is not home. Perhaps you feel the same emptiness when you look on her as do I.' Lightly, she rapped the steel band above her heart. 'An army the size of which you cannot conceive lies between us and the city.' Ulrika shook her head disdainfully. 'Do not concern yourself with them. They are cold and hungry. They do not know we are coming and would not care enough to stop us if they did.

'Praag is the fortress of the Troll King. A greater and more cunning foe you have not faced and at his command is an army of monsters that would darken a daemon's nightmares.' She fell silent, snow falling soundlessly around her, watching to gauge the men's reactions.

Damir was inscrutable. Gustav was anxious but strangely eager, as though he had something to prove. Snorri belched loudly, earning a glare before the vampiress continued. Felix didn't know what

Ulrika could possibly have against Snorri, but she had been cold ever since his return.

'But you have me to lead you. I am General Ulrika Magdova Straghov. I bring to you the best of the Troll Country and of ancient Lahmia. We will attack at night when my own powers will be at their peak.' With a squeeze of her thighs that brought a knot to Felix's throat, she wheeled her horse northward. 'You do not know the purpose of our quest here, but know that the fate of the world will ride home with us on our success.'

Felix wondered what she meant by that. The free company gave a muted cheer and a rattle of weapons. The Ungols merely nodded, clapped each other's shoulders in mute farewells, and brought their own horses about.

'Snorri feels like he's missed something,' said Snorri, a stage hiss directed towards Felix's ear. 'What is a troll king?'

Felix however was watching Ulrika depart. Then he looked across to Gustav who was doing the same thing. He recognised the same longing in his young doppelganger's eyes and felt a stab of possessiveness for his own former life.

Really, Felix thought, trying to get a hold of himself. You're going to do this now?

'We'd be better off with me leading that free company,' said Felix.

'Snorri would be better off on a bigger horse,' Snorri returned, eyeing Felix's mare hopefully.

'I'm serious. I've led men before. A company of Greatswords too, not some band of drunks, ex-mercenaries, and draft dodgers.'

'Snorri doesn't think that sounds very likely.'

'Snorri was there,' Felix returned, more harshly than he'd intended.

The Slayer shrugged, the sudden shift in weight causing his gelding to skitter sideways in protest. 'Snorri still doesn't think that sounds very likely.'

'Are you sure you have your memory back?'

Snorri blew a raspberry. 'Are you a priest of Grimnir now?'

Felix shrugged, then shook his head.

Looking pleased, Snorri tried to jig his horse into moving forward. 'Snorri thought not.'

Ulrika led the column of horsemen – and one horse*dwarf*, she reminded herself through gritted teeth – inexorably northward. The snow fell thickly enough to blind even her to anything more than a few feet beyond the nose of her horse, but she had other senses that more than compensated. She had told Felix that she was a creature of Chaos and that was not untrue. Its power made up the very bindings of her being and she could orient herself towards the great polar vortex purely by the extent to which the animal that all Arisen kept locked within strained at its cage. She could no longer blame its rage on the beastmen she had drained in Kurzycko, for she had drunk heavily from Gustav's men to cleanse herself of that particular taint. With a concentration of will, she shackled the monster.

It growled and retreated.

For now.

It grew stronger as she grew stronger, and would only test her more savagely the nearer they got to Praag.

Curse that idiot dwarf. She had been this close!

Felix had been right to marvel at the chances of Snorri finding them in the time of raspotitsa and she wondered which power exactly she had to thank for this confluence of fates. What next? Was Malakai Makaisson about to show up in a shiny new airship to deposit Gotrek, Katerina, and everyone else Felix had ever met onto their heads? She snorted derisively, but nevertheless found herself glancing upwards as though she had just hexed herself by thinking it.

Snowflakes landed in her eyes and she had to physically brush them off. There was no longer warmth in her body to melt them.

She didn't think she could cope with the volume of former lovers that Felix had accrued. And they could not all be as insipid as Katerina.

'General Straghov, might I ride with you a moment?'

Ulrika glanced up, irked that she could be so caught up in herself as to be taken by surprise as Gustav Jaeger rode alongside at a hard canter, then matched his horse's gait to hers. He had supplemented his royal blue cloak and riding leathers with Ungol furs and bore a lantern in one hand. The glass was charred, and wet on the outside from snow melt. He rode surrounded in a cloud of mist from the breath of himself and his horse.

'You are on the oblast now, Gustav. A man rides where he has earned the right to.'

The young Jaeger smiled tightly, uncertain if that was a welcome or a rebuttal, but when she did not demand he take himself and his horse elsewhere, his expression lightened. She could read the thoughts in his face as clearly as the lust song of his blood whenever he looked at her, perhaps picturing himself as some romantic lord of the steppe in the manner of the robber barons of 'North Ostermark', so quick to stab their flagpole into Kislev's grave. His cheeks were flushed with near-surface blood. The hand that held the lantern rattled with nervous energy.

'Yes, general,' he murmured. 'Damir's scouts say that something has been this way before us. Two men on foot, one of them heavy like a...' He swallowed and peered into the blizzard. 'Perhaps like a Chaos warrior.'

'That is not surprising,' said Ulrika. 'Even beastmen fear Kislev's winter. Praag would mean shelter, if the Troll King will share it.'

Gustav nodded, gaze shooting sideways and hand going to

his pistol holster as a long lingering cry like that of a wolf shivered through the falling snow. The young man shuddered. Ulrika watched him, captivated by the change in blood flow that caused his eyes to dilate and his cheeks to redden.

A warp storm was brewing. Ulrika could feel it in the ache of her hunger.

Gustav relaxed slightly, his shivers owing more to cold than to fear. Ulrika smiled coyly. He was the same age as Felix had been when they had first met and the resemblance was uncanny. Like his uncle, he was intelligent, handsome, and often unwittingly condescending. He lacked a certain *edge*, however, and seemed to compensate with a corresponding dose of arrogance.

'If there is something more you wish to say, I would do it now. That is something else a Kislevite learns at a young age.'

Gustav coughed nervously, trying to look unafraid. Amongst his own kind he might have succeeded, but there was no masking the fluttering of his heart from an Arisen.

'You say Praag is besieged by an army to make Helbrass's look small. That it's defended by all the beasts of Chaos. How are we to make it inside?'

'You are going to help me,' Ulrika smiled.

Gustav blushed into his collar. 'Free companies haven't the most heroic reputation, general, but whatever you ask of us we won't let you down.'

As though this were news to her, Ulrika glanced down the line of horses to where the diversely armed freemen in their patched greatcoats, ill-fitting iron cuirasses, and criminally distempered horses took up the rear.

Her feeding from them had been about more than mere healing, more even than the power to punch a hole into the aethyr and transport an army across the walls of Praag.

Gustav turned to follow her gaze, showing the partially healed puncture marks on the side of his neck. The memory of his pulse in her mouth inflamed her, poked a sharp goad through the bars that contained the beast. Again she forced the animal into submission. But each time it pushed, each time the bars were bent a little further, it became that much harder to force back. Gustav was not the touchstone to her humanity that she needed if she was to win this battle, but he was not without uses.

If she remembered correctly, a little jealousy had never hurt Felix's affections.

Seeking out the elder Jaeger amongst the rabble at the column's rear, she heard the wolf howl again. It was similar but different, this time from the other side of the column. With a frown, she scanned the steppe, snow-washed and black with the emptiness of the oblast night. She thought she saw movement and focused on it, but for all her preternatural abilities it was one of Damir's outriders that saw the flying shape first and screamed.

'Ambush!'

Felix heard the cry at the same moment he saw the arrow split the scout's face cheek to cheek and spin him from his mount. The Ungol's foot snagged in the stirrup and his skull cracked on the ground as his pony reared and the steppe erupted with whoops and barks. Big hunting hounds bounded from the darkness, lantern light glinting from teeth and eyes, and were followed in by horsemen in white furs; so intangible against the snow that even as they drew on bows and hefted spears, they resembled horses ridden by the dead.

Arrows punched riders from the saddle and horses, particularly those of the Ostermarkers, whinnied in panic. Felix felt one shaft whistle past his ear and strike the rider behind. The arrow pierced his leather hauberk under the collar and the man dropped the pistol he'd been trying to put a match to with a scream. Another shaft droned across the opposite cheek and over Snorri's head.

The Slayer bellowed, propelling his weapons overhead as if the horse's motion worked on the same principle as a jittery gyrocopter. The poor gelding merely circled in confusion, causing Snorri to shout even louder as his back was turned to the fighting.

All around, men were struggling with matchlocks and screaming. More than anything he wanted to be able to tell the men around him what to do, but although he had led men in a pinch he didn't consider himself a commander and he certainly didn't know the first thing about cavalry tactics.

Was it best to form up or to stay loose? When on the defensive should they hold a position or keep mobile? And what was the best way for one unit of light cavalry to balance its advantages and overcome another?

Cursing his ill-informed educational choices, Felix drew his sword and sought desperately to remain calm enough to remember the correct application of reins and stirrups to wheel his horse into the face of the attack.

'Hold and fire!' Felix yelled.

Any command was probably better than none at all, and to his surprise the nearest men appeared to lose a measure of their panic as soon as the words left his mouth. Matchcords were lit and pistols aimed and blackpowder flashes crackled across the rear of the column. A hound went down with a whimper. An iron ball punched through a marauder's chest and blasted his shoulder blade from his back.

By the light of the muzzle flashes that were spreading through the column like a flame along a taper, Felix saw the enemy charge in. They had already got too close in the dark. The pistoliers' weapons were too complicated to reload and fire again. Damir's horse-archers each got two or three more shots away, but it was still too little too late.

Felix saw an emaciated wolf-beast take an arrow in the hip and keep running. It had spines running along its back and a tail as sharp and metallic as the tip of an elven spear. The Chaos hound loped through the snow, ropes of drool hanging between its teeth and the spikes of its collar like a spider's web.

It was heading straight for Ulrika.

Felix screamed a warning. Another arrow buried itself in the hound's flank, but it did not seem to feel it as it bunched its hindquarters and launched itself forward with a terrific snarl. Ulrika bared her fangs as she saw it, barely a second before its flying lunge punched her from the saddle.

The vampiress hit the ground in a thump of snow with the mutant hound landing on top of her a moment later, clawing at the bands of her breastpiece and sinking its fangs into the thick steel guard around her throat. Ulrika growled back, face slathered in drool, and locked one daemon grip under the pit of its foreleg and another around its neck.

For so very many reasons, the ambushers had picked the wrong target.

Ungols and Imperials that had previously been wavering suddenly cried out in wrath. Pistols sputtered inchoate fury as men drew swords and axes and charged to their general's defence. Horses slammed together, barged each other aside, tangled tacks and stirrups and trapped their riders side-by-side to hack at each other with blades. The Kurgan had the edge in size and armament, but now they were in close they were working like slavers with the flats of their weapons and seemed taken aback by their foes' zeal.

In the snow meanwhile, Ulrika had driven the hound's jaw back from her throat until it snapped impotently a few inches from her face. Then, with every outward symptom of great pleasure, she squeezed down on its neck. The dog mewled, pawed at her breastpiece. Its eyes turned blood red and its hindlegs went soft and deposited its blade-tail on the ground. Freed of its weight, Ulrika rose, then clenched the final distance until the hound gave one final whine and then twitched with the sudden snap of its spine.

A shout from Snorri pulled Felix away from Ulrika's show of force. The dwarf had managed to chivvy his horse into the right direction and get it moving. The bay gelding cantered uncertainly through the baying tangle of Kurgan marauders and their hounds while Snorri swung his weapons wildly to left and right without ever coming within a yard of striking another rider.

Dwarfs just didn't have the reach for horseback fighting. Felix would have thought that even Snorri would have had the common sense to dismount, but clearly he was being generous with his assumptions. Could Snorri *still* be drunk? Was that even possible for a dwarf that had once emptied a bucket of Ivan Petrovich's double-distilled Goromadny vodka and then trounced all of his household lancers and their wives in a drinking contest?

Felix swore as Snorri's attempt to lean back and kick a hound with his mace-leg resulted in him windmilling for balance and hugging his horse's neck to keep from falling off.

It was a miracle they had got the Slayer into the saddle in the first place.

Felix looked from Snorri to Ulrika. The vampiress was back on her horse now. A nimbus of energy coalesced into a gauntlet of shadow that she punched towards a charging horseman. A lance of Dark Magic powered through his chest. Ulrika hissed, widening that dark lance into a blade and yanking her hand sideways to bring it scything through the Kurgan that surrounded her.

At her side fought Damir and Gustav and a tight formation of furious-looking horsemen. A part of Felix wished he could be there too. The need to protect her came from somewhere deep inside, and it took a great effort to resist it and turn back to Snorri. The Slayer was disappearing into the night but for the sounds of dwarfish insults and the occasional clangour of an axe and a hammer being accidentally mashed together.

Ulrika had all the protection she could need, and from what he had seen of her she needed none.

'A curse on all Slayers,' Felix swore with feeling, spurring after the departed dwarf.

A Kurgan warrior with a thick snow-salted black beard and a snow lion pelt riddled with icons of the Dark Gods swung at Ulrika with an axe. His heart hammered in her head. His breath was sour with gorilka and the self-digestive stink of starvation. She could hear the grind of bone on ligament, muscle on bone. He was an animal, a filthy degraded animal that soiled her homeland with his gods and his smell.

The axe glimmered closer.

The man did not fear death. Ulrika snarled. That never lasted.

Sharp as a sudden chill, her hand snapped up and caught the axe blade in her palm. The Kurgan roared and pulled back against her. Even in his prime his strength would have been no match for Ulrika's. Now, half wasted and bitten by frost, the Kurgan could do little more than roar the impeachment of his dark masters. Ulrika tightened her grip, coruscating arcs of atrophying magic causing the axe blade to brown and its wooden haft to crumble.

Suddenly pulling on nothing, the northman seesawed back in the saddle. Ulrika caught him by the collar of his cloak before he fell. His pulse quickened under her grip. Horses and men battled all around her, but this was all she cared now to hear. She had fed just hours before, but like a raw neophyte she ached for a taste. It was Praag, she knew. It was Chaos. She didn't care.

'Fool,' she lisped, tongue engorged by desire. With a snarl, she surrendered to the beast's bellow of approval and dragged the marauder off his horse until he lay across her lap like a human sacrifice upon an altar. She licked her fangs. 'Do you even realise what you face?'

The rhythm of his heartbeat fell out of time. She laughed. There was the fear.

The Kurgan screamed and beat ineffectually at her breastplate. Ulrika held him nonchalantly down. Dark power flickered into a gauntlet around her hand as she raised a fist and then punched through the man's chest. Ribs parted with a crunch. The man jerked, spat blood. Then Ulrika tore out his heart. Mouth open wide, she held the still-beating organ above her face and drank. Blood ran across her cheeks and down her throat.

The beast wrapped its talons around the bars of its cage and strained.

With an effort of will over instinct, she blinked blood from her eyes and looked up. This should not be happening. Not so soon.

That was why she had brought Felix.

A pistol shot shattered her thoughts and she glared up hungrily, scanning the melee of mounted men and snarling hounds. She wanted to bleed them all. With the helpless terror of madness, Ulrika realised that Felix had abandoned her.

Her tether to humanity had been broken.

Then she bared her fangs and turned back to the Kurgan.

They would learn what it meant to defy one of the Arisen.

The snowfall thickened as Felix turned a hard canter into a gallop. He'd never ridden so fast in his life. The rapid pound of the horse's hooves seemed to set a pace for his heart to match. The impact on hard snow rang through his bones and made his mail shake. Even flying hadn't been this terrifying. There was something about seeing the ground flashing beneath him and seeing the animal's legs blur that granted a considerable immediacy to his peril.

'Snorri!' he shouted, mouth filling with snow at speed the moment he opened it.

Flakes of bristly cold piled into his eyes faster than he could blink them away. He dared not take his one hand off the reins to wipe them.

Ragged-looking northmen on starving steeds flashed by in the dark. A scattering of moonlight on a chainmail shirt. A glint of lantern light from a silver ring. There were thousands of them out there, he knew. He could hear the howls of their dogs, but more than that he could feel their existence in his gut. It was as if their presence alone was a knot that weighed down the air around him.

Winding his hand once more through frost-stiffened leather reins, Felix shook his face clear and tried to focus on where he was going. Ahead came the sound of ice water slushing against rocks, guiding him through the numbing howl in his ears.

The Lynsk.

Mentally, he oriented himself. Assuming Praag was nearby then the Gate of Gargoyles would be somewhere *there* to the north-east. It was useful to know, but it wasn't going to help Snorri.

A warning shout in a harsh barbarian tongue snapped his eyes back to his path. A Kurgan marauder on foot rose out of the darkness before him. The man's fur cloak swiped out behind him as he turned, leather plate armour so stiffly frozen that ice shavings drizzled from the joints. His eyes were bloodshot. His greased face was gaunt from malnourishment and cracked by frostbite.

Felix cast about once more for Snorri, then swore his surrender to the snow and darkness. He drew in the reins and swung from the saddle, bringing Karaghul into a guard just as the northman barrelled through the snow with a harsh yell.

Felix could just about ride a horse, but the day he tried to fight from one was the day the electors nominated him their Emperor.

A tickling déjà vu came over him as the marauder stumbled through the shin-high snow and slush that banked the partially frozen Lynsk.

The snow, the river, the Kurgan: it was the scene from his dream. He had *seen* this. He knew exactly what was going to happen.

Shifting his stance appropriately to the attack he knew the northman was about to make, Felix sidestepped the marauder's lunge and slid Karaghul between the sinewy lacings that connected backplate to breastplate as if it belonged there. Blood lanced across the snow and up Felix's arm.

Felix grimaced as he shifted his grip, and kicked the man behind the kneecap to drop him into position for Felix to plant his boot on the warrior's shoulder and wrench the glittering runeblade clear. Not exactly as he had dreamt it, but surely too similar to be a coincidence.

Felix recalled how he had always dismissed Max's speculations that he and Gotrek were in some way guided by a greater power than themselves. Perhaps the wizard had been onto something after all.

The northman tumbled away towards the river and its collective of wrecked cottages and Felix backed off warily, sword raised into a guard. The snow swept around him like a weapon of the Great Powers to blind and to frustrate.

'Snorri! Where are you, can you hear me?'

Felix tightened his two-handed grip around the dragonhead hilt of Karaghul. His eyes were starting to throb, so hard had he been staring into the blizzard, but he dared not blink. The sound of battle was coming from all around and who knew how many Kurgan the dead man's alarum had stirred up. Felix watched the thick flakes fall. He could not keep his eyes trained any longer. He blinked.

'Manling! To your left.'

At the sound of that familiar, guttural shout, Felix almost failed to react as he knew he had to. His heart soared like a caged bird set free. He wanted to turn right, to see with his own eyes, but at the last instant he jerked left and swept Karaghul across his body to parry the hefty berdish axe that hacked for him through the snow.

Just as he remembered.

The two weapons clashed apart heavily and then, inspired by foreknowledge, his fighter's reflex took over. He dodged back, spinning away from the overarm slash that he saw in his mind's eye even before the Kurgan had committed himself to deliver it. Felix turned his evasive spin into a slash across the northman's hamstrings, then kicked the screaming man face-down into the snow.

Felix shook his head dizzily. Useful as it was proving, there was something deeply unsettling about knowing what was going to happen before the event.

With a nervous laugh Felix wondered whether, if he were to find himself hungover on his desk at some stage in the next five minutes, he would be relieved or disappointed. In the corner of his eye, he caught sight of a dozen more fur-clad marauders advancing through the ruins by the river. More were battling out of sight, iron chirping like winter birdsong. He brought his sword again into a tried and true guard, bringing the glint of gold from his finger to his face.

He wondered what Kat was doing at this moment.

The thought was sudden and unwelcome, coming in the middle of a battle and just hours after he had had his lips on another woman's. The mental rebuke hurt as it probably should. He shook his head to clear it of snow. Why did the romanticists always end their works once the hero had rescued his damsel and the *difficult* bit began? His thoughts of Kat shaped themselves into the scene of his deathbed as shown to him by Aekold Helbrass's prophetic fires. The very real likelihood that she would not, in fact, be with him at the end hurt him more than he would have thought.

Then he recalled something that he had not thought of at the time.

Kat had had a child in that vision.

He smiled, oddly elated despite his situation. Ulrika must have been mistaken.

Life went on after all.

He had a child.

A brute howl pulled his gaze outwards. There in the snow, a sanguinary blur of starmetal silver and ink-strapped muscle hacked through a score of barbarian northmen. Felix's heart beat with superstitious dread. The foreknowledge of who he was going to find here on the anonymous snowfield hadn't even begun to ready Felix for how hard in the chest the sight would hit him. He wanted to punch the air.

It was Gotrek.

Gotrek Gurnisson had found his own way to Praag!

The Slayer fought in a ring of bodies and human debris. Despite wearing nothing above his tattered trews but piercings and spiralling blue tattoos Gotrek gave no care to the cold as, with a roar like a collapsing cliff, he swung his axe and severed a northman's leg below the knee. The marauder, meeting the bone-hammer of Gotrek's knuckles, was dead with a snapped neck before his knees were fully bent.

Even having seen it twice, even with the charnel reek to give it the pungency of reality, Felix feared he was about to be woken up and have all of this taken away. He could almost have laughed at how sorry he suddenly was at the thought of having a pointless skirmish at the edge of the known world whisked out from under his feet.

And then he did laugh. He had to.

Gotrek roared for more and more came. At their head strode a champion in a ringmail hauberk with a white bear cloak and an antlered helm. The northman's bare arms were heavy with trophy rings. He spun his twinned axes in anticipation as he chanted some guttural gibberish about his deeds and his gods. One blade left a crimson trail of power through the air it cut.

Felix's first impulse was to charge to the Slayer's aid, but he had already seen how this fight panned out and didn't want to do anything that might interfere and unintentionally get Gotrek hurt or killed. The dwarf already looked close enough to death. He had lost his eye patch and gore bled from the gaping socket. Cuts and bruises coloured his tattooed flesh. Strips of it hung off the muscle in places. A pair of arrows stuck out of his breast.

Slipping the Slayer's guard, the champion dragged his blade across Gotrek's chest, adding a deep score to the tally and bringing a spurt of blood. The Slayer howled, throwing the Kurgan champion off and driving him back with a storm of blows. His starmetal blade slammed deep into the northman's gut. The not-so-favoured of the Chaos gods regurgitated blood, choking on that last mouthful as Gotrek flung him from his axe and into those that came roaring in behind.

Now!

With a yell, Felix cut down the last Kurgan between him and the Slayer, hurdled the northman's corpse and, turning mid-leap, slammed into Gotrek's back to beat down a northman axe that had been destined for his unguarded shoulders.

That thumping contact sent an electric thrill down Felix's spine.

In that moment his whole body seemed to fizz, as if a fire warmed his blood and filled his muscles with new strength. It was not unlike what he had felt when he had kissed Ulrika, but ten times more intense. It felt meaningful. It felt *right*. He might have laughed again, he wasn't sure any more, but he felt almost reborn, parrying another attack as Gotrek's massive shoulders ground over his. Felix ducked a swinging adze, parried a sabre.

The northmen were coming thick and fast from the river, drawn to the ring of steel and the Slayer's bellowed challenges. Felix sliced through a Kurgan's jack, then reversed his grip and sliced his blade back across the northman's throat in a red slash of arterial blood.

'I can't believe I actually missed this madness.'

'What do you... want?' Gotrek wheezed, parrying the stab of a knife, then punching the eye of his axe into its wielder's gut. The man doubled over, head parting company with his shoulders a moment later. 'Another... gold ring?' A hand-axe decorated with evil glyphs clanged off the flat of his blade. Gotrek elbowed the Kurgan in the face, kneecapped another, and sliced his axe through the belly of a third. 'Was Altdorf not exciting enough, manling?'

Felix blinked in confusion, feeling his earlier surge of energy fade into his muscles and almost missing the sword that thrust for his belly. He twisted sharply, parried, then sliced through the offending hand with an incisive counter.

That hadn't been what he'd expected to hear.

'Is that all you want to say to me after a year?'

'A year?' Gotrek grunted. 'Is that all?'

'Damn it, Gotrek!'

The Slayer hacked a northman in half, painting his gasping mouth with arterial spray. 'You went your own way, manling. And I went... mine.'

'That was the promise you made.' Felix blocked a flurry of blows and retreated back against Gotrek's broad shoulders. 'Keep Snorri alive until Karak Kadrin and you'd release me from my oath.'

'Release?' Gotrek growled. His expression somehow darkened still further. He pulled his axe from a Kurgan's shoulder and broke a man's elbow with the flat. Then he grunted, as if words were harder than bones. 'Aye. And I honoured it.'

Felix parried hard, dumbfounded and numb. Did Gotrek resent him for not choosing to stay with him once he'd had a say in the matter? Could he really hold that kind of a grudge for this long?

Stupid question.

'Kat is safe in Altdorf,' he yelled over his shoulder. He wasn't sure why he said that, except perhaps to extract some reaction from the Slayer besides that passive, incomprehensible rage. Gotrek had always been fond of Kat whom, right up to their wedding day, he'd persisted in calling 'little one'. 'She might be pregnant.'

'Then you're a fool. There's only one place you should be now.'

Felix shook snowflakes from his brow, turning his simmering anger into a riposte that beat an axe from a northman's grip and severed his fingers. The temptation to spin around and let the Slayer defend his own stubborn back was almost great enough for him to countenance the suicide-by-Kurgan that that would inevitably mean for him as well. Instead he snarled and parried a stinging neck-thrust.

'I had a daughter once,' Gotrek panted, speech completely almost eaten into by breath. 'I knew I shouldn't have left her behind but I was... talked into it by a friend.' There was a pause, split into two by the crack of a northman's spine. 'Pray you don't regret it like I did.'

'I–'

Hoofbeats rumbled through the blizzard. Damir and his riders. No!

Felix knew nothing of Gotrek's shame, and precious little about his life before becoming a Slayer. This was important, he knew. There was so much he wanted to say and ask before the opportunity was taken from them.

'*Gospodarinyi!*'

Swaddled in sheepskin and hemp, Damir galloped from the storm, standing high in the stirrups as he drew back on his recurved composite bow. Coloured tassels shivered from the tips as he loosed. The feathered shaft zipped through the falling snow, and smacked through the Y-shaped opening of a marauder's bull-horned barbute with a ferocious *clang* as the metal head exited the back of the man's skull and struck the inside back of his warhelm. The marauder spasmed backwards before being dashed off the breast of the careening pony.

A second horse-archer chivvied his horse through the shank-high snowdrift, screaming 'Yhah!' at the top of his lungs and drawing back on his own bowstring. The arrow flew over Gotrek's shoulder and took his assailant through the heart. Gotrek howled pure frustration and beheaded the dying northman. Another centaur-like shadow breezed in false-silence through the blizzard and charged into the disordered northmen.

The Kurgan broke, and Damir and his men yipped and urged their steeds to give chase.

Gotrek growled and sank to one knee. He caught himself on the haft of his axe and pushed himself back up. Felix offered no help. He could not have supported the Slayer's weight even if he thought his aid would be welcomed. The Slayer met his look and glowered.

'Itchy feet then, was it?'

'I'm sorry?'

'Marriage and children does something to human men, I've found. Oath and hearth just isn't enough for you.'

'For goodness' sake, Gotrek–'

Before Felix could say more he noticed the brightening glow of Gotrek's axe. The runes were red and hot and spitting in the snow. Chaos. With a glint in his one eye, Gotrek hefted his axe once again. He regarded Felix grudgingly.

'If my doom should happen while you're here...'

Felix sighed. If that was the warmest welcome he could expect then he'd take it. 'It is the end of the world, I suppose.'

Gotrek leered, running the pad of his thumb down the edge of his axe until it produced a bead of blood. It was one of the few parts of the Slayer's body not already bleeding. 'Good, isn't it.'

Both fighters readied their weapons, Gotrek's rune-axe turning the snowflakes into ruby droplets as a snow-white destrier bore Ulrika through that crimson haze.

She looked monstrous, and not in any way that could be explained away by the harsh glare of Gotrek's axe. She could not have got herself any bloodier had she physically crawled inside a Kurgan warrior and torn her way out. She tilted her chin arrogantly upwards as she regarded the Slayer, exposing her sharp fangs and the blood where it was thickest under her jaw. A skein of moaning spirits swirled over the shapely contours of her armour. They darkened her eyes and mouth with a penumbral gloom, deepening the hard, immortalised lines of her face. And unlike Felix and Gotrek, swathed in steamy breath, she sat without, a transient visitor to the cold.

Breathing like a bellows, the Slayer turned a black look on Felix.

Felix flinched under the intensity of it, feeling again the guilt of Ulrika's kiss. He tried to hide it from his face, but it seemed to blush from his cheeks as though written there in dwarfish runes. Gotrek gripped his axe and nodded like an executioner.

'Now I see.'

Ignoring the dwarf, Ulrika closed her eyes and looked away, transacting some steep personal cost of willpower in exchange for concealing her fangs and retracting her claws. She shook her head and then pointed to the collection of cottages sited beside the dark, ice-floed body of creaking slush ahead of them. The shapes of the riverside outpost were just about visible as humps in the ground. If Felix concentrated on it, he could still hear the rumble of hoofbeats, the wild yells of the Ungol horsemen, the occasional *crack* of an arquebus or a pistol, and what might have been a drunken dwarf's war cry.

'Come, Felix. We can pick up Snorri and hold out there while I work us a way into the city.'

Gotrek arched a blood-bristled eyebrow at the name of his old friend, but was too stubborn to ask. Felix decided that if he wanted to be that way, then Felix could be too stubborn to volunteer. The Slayer grunted and crossed his arms over his chest.

'We're here to get Max,' Felix muttered, feeling that the most pertinent – the most *innocent* – fact. He waved vaguely northward. 'He's in there.'

Again, a grunt.

Before Felix's temper could fray any further, there was a disturbing underfoot crunch of snow and human gristle from behind them.

A bowman with arrow nocked and drawn advanced over the bodies that Gotrek had left strewn. He was hard and thin, like a twist of salted meat, and garbed in a motley assortment of weather-beaten furs and hanging armour plates. The bow was a darkwood Kurgan recurve, the arrows fletched black like cousins of those in Gotrek's chest.

'Are you going to fight them then, *zabójka*?' asked the bowman, his Kislevite accent muffled by the layers wrapped over his mouth. 'Or must you live another day?'

Slowly, Felix eased his grip off his sword and glanced a question at Gotrek.

'No one told you to leave, manling,' was Gotrek's terse reply.

'What does zabójka mean?'

Ulrika smiled coldly. 'It is not affectionate.'

The bowman lowered his weapon, and nodded a curt greeting to the mounted boyarina. 'Kolya, my lady. Of what was once Dushyka.'

'Do not speak in haste,' said Ulrika. 'We are not beaten yet.'

Kolya shrugged as if he couldn't care and perhaps never truly had. 'No matter.'

That neat summation of Kislevite philosophy brought a rare smile to Ulrika's lips. She extended a hand to the north as if commanding the storm to part or the polar gates to open.

'Come,' said Ulrika again, her voice this time echoed by what sounded like hundreds of others.

Felix heard weeping, indistinct, as though he'd just entered a castle in which someone in a distant wing was crying. The spirits that swam over her began to accelerate and blur. Faces gnashed their teeth and blended with others that cursed or wept or raved, summoning a wind that moaned and smelled of the dankness within a forgotten crypt. Ulrika's eyes pulsed red in their sepia pools.

Felix backed away.

'There are too many of the northmen here,' said Ulrika, her voice echoing as though she called to him from across a gorge. Felix didn't think she had ever looked so beautiful. Or feral. This was Ulrika the vampire without the mask. She was an eagle glorying in flight, a lioness exulting in the power of her bite. 'Chaos warriors and daemons and monsters from beyond the mountains. Too many to fight. I can confound them long enough for respite.'

She spread her hands, a spider spinning her web with aethyric silk, threads of torment and pain spooling from her fingertips. Where the spirits she summoned flew, northmen gave shouts of confusion and horror and turned unwittingly back. As Felix watched, a fearful tightness compressing his chest, the spirit maze expanded around them, visible against the background night as an empyreal mesh of half-felt taps on shoulders, whispered fears, and childhood nightmares.

'The leech does magic now?' Gotrek observed, drawing his axe so close it opened a cut across his cheek. Blood trickled into his beard. One eye and a vacant orb glared at the vampiress in the throes of her necromancy.

'We should've killed her back in Drakenhof.'

TWELVE

Cruel Surprises

Nothing buried a corpse like snow.

A chilling northerly wind worked its shovel with the callousness of a serial killer, covering the northmen left by the Kislevites' charge under shallow mounds of white powder. The remnants of the riverside outpost they had sought to defend rose from the snow like the fingers of the unquiet dead. Spirits whispered though the dark. The cold smell of impermanence clung to every broken stone.

The largest structure was a burned, ice-blistered headstone with one side sunk into the icy waters of the Lynsk. Its walls were of thick red brick, its windows suspicious slits. Crenellations ran the perimeter of its roof that climbed into a tiered onion dome tiled with frosted lead. A customs house, Felix reasoned, likely doubling as a relay post for southbound riders and as a fort to guard against smugglers and poachers.

An iron chain clenched across the river. The passing ice caused it to clink and rustle. The stripped-down ribcage of an ice-breaker barque lay upturned on the bank beside it. The wood had been peeled away for fuel and for repairs to the surrounding structures and only the iron cladding remained. A Kurgan warrior hung from it, pinned by a pair of arrows through the chest.

The fortification's highest point was a circular bartizan with its foundations in the river itself. The circle was a prominent symbol in Kislevite philosophy as well as their architecture. It was the curve of the world, of the wide oblast sky. It was death and rebirth. A tattered banner fluttered from the bartizan's flagpole, a sore on the eye that seemed to rot even as Felix looked at it. A rhythmic *bang* echoed from the ramparts as a trio of Gustav's men, loaded with gorilka and dry tinder to burn the foul icon down, sought to break into the locked tower.

The Troll King might have denied the Kurgan and their allies Praag, but something had succeeded in making this place their home.

The surrounding buildings were a mix of semi-intact structures. They had been loosely repaired and refortified with scavengeable scraps and were filled with bedding furs and gear, all left behind when the Ungols had ridden through.

Rubble lay everywhere a man could put his foot. It made the snow cover lumpen. Here and there, red leached into those snowy lumps to mark a Kurgan grave. The uneven ground between ruins was taken by a haphazard maze of pickets and stockades that housed shaggy, broad-shouldered cattle. They were not cows such as an Averland farmer would recognise. They resembled the Norscan breed that his brother had at times grudgingly traded in with landowners of Nordland and the Middle Mountains. Adapted to cold and misery and the weird aspects of the Chaos-tainted north, they were gruff, lean, and permanently on the knife-edge of goring a warily passing soldier.

Gotrek studied the thumb he had sliced on his axe blade with a scowl. Some poison in the air stopped wounds from closing and kept the blood flowing. Even the Slayer wasn't impervious to the taint. He glanced sideways as a disoriented whisper echoed from the deep snow, one of Ulrika's unleashed spirits. He launched a gob of spit after it. Felix had no way of knowing if or what it hit.

'Your girlfriend has until this stops running.' He stuck the thumb between his lips and leered, sucking it dry as he then withdrew it. 'Then I'm off.'

'Ulrika asked us to wait,' said Felix.

'I'm here for the Troll King and the doom that was promised me,' said Gotrek. 'I'm not here for the wizard, and as sure as the treachery of elves I'm not here for her.' He jabbed his thumb, just again sheening with red, back towards the despatch-fort.

Ulrika stood there under the old fort's shattered main gate, wearing a cloak of aethyric shadow and a halo of weeping spirits. To look on her was to share the horror all prey feel for their predator. The blood of men painted her beautiful white armour. Gobbets of it matted her hair. Her face was more crimson now than white.

Around her, men worked to clear a section of the stockade of cattle to make space for a corral. Left pats of dung steamed. Ungol ponies and Ostermark horses shivered together under wool blankets and snorted vapour. Other men were prying wood from the pickets to erect what looked like a pentagram around the gatehouse under direction from Damir. The Ungol chieftain stood with his hands on his hips and his cheeks sucked in and shouted instructions from Ulrika's right hand. Wearing a beatific grin, Gustav stood behind her and to the left with his thumbs tucked into his belt. Occasionally a man looked up from his task as one of the warding spirits of Ulrika's ghost-maze moaned overhead and mouthed a prayer.

The tension was garrotte tight.

Felix felt it in the rising hairs on the back of his neck. He leant his crossed arms over the waist-high fence that separated him and about thirty head of cattle from the river and rapped his ring nervously upon the upright. With a perversion so subtle that Felix hadn't even consciously noticed it at first, the water was pushing ice *upriver*. He wondered how that was even possible. Was the Lynsk somehow sucking in seawater from Altwasser Bay and bearing it north to the Goromadny Mountains? He shuddered again.

So simple a thing, and yet so wrong.

Beside him, sat in the snow like a rock that had just dropped there out of the sky, Gotrek silently watched his thumb bleed by the rune-light of his axe.

'Kat is well,' Felix said, haltingly. He worked his lips. His mouth felt imponderably dry. He waited, but the dwarf said nothing. 'She is getting stronger.'

'Good.'

'Is that all you have to say? Is there nothing you want to ask?'

The dwarf's one eye was as hollow as the empty socket beside it and fixed on his thumb.

'We travelled together for twenty years, Gotrek. Have you forgotten all that?'

Gotrek glowered dangerously, the insult to his long dwarfish memory implicit.

Felix hung his head, gave it a sorry shake. He had always felt guilty about the decision he had made to leave the Slayer and return with Kat to the Empire. It had seemed like the right one at the time though and there was no more a man could do than that. Even now he wasn't sure that it was necessarily wrong. If he'd opted for friendship over family then Kat would have followed him for certain. And how long would Kat have survived in Kislev in her condition?

The speculation gave him a shiver. Again, he resolved to return home to her in one piece, something that having Gotrek and his axe alongside of him could only improve the chances of.

Felix glanced over his shoulder as Ulrika took Gustav, Damir and a handful of free company soldiers with her into the fort. He frowned. For some reason, Ulrika did not appear nearly as alluring as she had just hours before. It was more than just the blood on her. His feelings towards her were confused. She was unquestionably beautiful, had even become more so as he had aged and she had not, but it was beauty of an untouchable kind. She was a ritual blade, something to be admired but not without a shiver of something other at the forces locked within. Unexpectedly his thoughts turned to the jaded old poet who would drink himself to nostalgia in his office in Altdorf.

He wondered whether it was Ulrika or himself who had changed the least.

'Riders!'

The cry came from the sentries to the north-east. On a nervous flex, Felix's grip tensed around Karaghul.

A shattered bay gelding crunched over the loose ground on the river bank, led by one of Damir's colourfully garbed scouts. The poor animal made it almost as far as the fort, then whinnied in quiet distress and pitched its rider into the water. Snorri Nosebiter flailed drunkenly, then punched through the ice in a spume of water and sank like an anvil but for a train of bubbles.

Felix swore, pushing his sword back into its scabbard and ducking under the fence. He ran over the wharf's cracked flagstones for that perversely whispering river, half diving and half skidding onto heels and backside to plunge his arm in. The cold shocked him senseless. He grit his teeth to keep from screaming but, after hardly any time at all, the pain was replaced by a tingling numbness. That wasn't at all reassuring. He waved his arm under the water, pushing it as deep as he dared. Could Snorri swim? It seemed unlikely with that metal leg, and with the amount of vodka he must have put away. Then Felix felt a brush around his wrist, less a sensation than an awareness of pressure, and tried to impel his fingers to close. He cursed loudly as his body began to slide in.

'Hand him over, manling.'

Squatting down beside him, Gotrek plunged his own arm into the water.

'On the count of th–' Felix began as Gotrek heaved one-handed, dragging Snorri from the water and onto a bed of black ice.

'Snorri hates water,' Snorri managed between gasps that made his throat and chest judder, coughing up a pint of ice water onto his short red beard. 'It tastes like...' His eyes fluttered open and he rubbed a bicep over his lips. 'Well, it tastes like water.'

Gotrek crossed his arms sourly. 'Snorri Nosebiter, you are the greatest wattock I ever did know.'

Snorri gave a smile that grew increasingly watery as his eyes focused on the dwarf stood over him. Gotrek uncrossed his arms and extended one hand – low enough to be an offer, high enough so as not to make a big elven fuss about it. Snorri hesitated only long enough for one more sodden cough before clasping it and letting Gotrek haul him up.

Felix didn't know what passing madness had assumed that the ancient companions might reunite with a bear-hug embrace, or at least *some* physical intimation of mutual respect with an emotionally chiselled kind word. All Snorri got was an appraising grunt as he dripped off on his own two feet. Snorri didn't even go so far as to meet Gotrek's eye, applying all his – admittedly limited – faculties to shake off the punished old leather satchel that he had clutched under one arm and stamp residual water from his mace-leg.

Felix flexed his fingers and rolled life into the near-dislocated joint of his shoulder. As if Snorri hadn't already been heavy enough.

'I like the leg,' Gotrek grunted after a silence that humans would definitely have considered awkward. 'Good metal-work.'

'It's very popular with everyone,' said Snorri, avoiding Gotrek's eye. 'Except that horse. It's not as though Snorri kicked it on purpose.'

'What did you expect?' said Gotrek as the Ungol rider nodded wordlessly and led the tired animal to the corral. 'There's only one thing I despise more than horses.'

'Is it elves?' said Snorri with a weak smile. 'Snorri wagers all the vodka in Kislev that it's elves.'

Gotrek's glower softened marginally. 'Do you have any?'

Snorri hung his head.

'Typical.'

Snorri scratched negligently at one of the scabbed punctures in his scalp. If Felix didn't know dwarfs as he did, then he might have thought that Snorri wanted to talk about something deeply personal. But he did know dwarfs as well as any man could. They could talk for days about gold and clan honour and old grudges, but a matter of the heart would go unsaid with them to wherever it was dwarfs went after death. Snorri went on tiptoes to peer around Felix's shoulder to make sure the Ungol was gone. He glanced at Felix, picking uncertainly at the knot in his satchel. Gotrek nodded at the bag over his shoulder, showing the wonderfully dwarfish fascination in old things even over and above old friends.

'There's a name I've not seen in a long time.'

Snorri nodded. He looked awkward. He licked his lips slowly as if imagining good ale. 'Snorri has remembered a lot of things, but there is something he wants... something he needs...' Snorri tapped his mace-leg on the cobblestones and mumbled under his breath. Then he rubbed his hand down his beaten-up face and started again. 'It is about Snorri's shame.'

'Stop there!' Gotrek raised a hand sharply to forestall any further comment on Snorri's part. He took a step away. 'That is not something a Slayer ever speaks of.'

He glared at Felix, then spread the fingers of his raised hands and grinned harshly. He presented Felix his thumb. It had stopped bleeding.

'Time's up, manling. Come, stay, I no longer care. I'm going.'

Snorri's shoulders slumped as Gotrek strode off into the herd of burly cattle, disappearing from view but for a snow-capped orange crest bobbing fiercely towards the opposite side of the enclosure. Felix had never seen him looking so distraught. He wished there was something he could do, but it was clearly some dwarfish issue that, despite his unusual status in their society, Felix could never hope to understand. He couldn't even offer Snorri a drink.

Through the cloud of steam that rose from the lowing herd, Felix's gaze crossed Kolya's. The Kislevite sat bestride a stile conjoining their enclosure with another. In wrapped and mittened hands he worked a flat stone with a knife, carving what appeared to be a stick image of a horse. He acknowledged Felix's look with no gesture. He did not look up as Gotrek approached. Felix sighed.

He had the distinct impression he had been cuckolded for a younger and less talkative man.

'I didn't think it would be this way,' said Felix, to himself more than to anyone else. A year apart and it was as though they had all become strangers.

But he had *dreamt* about this. He had to believe they were all reunited for a purpose.

He watched Gotrek and Kolya make their way to the outpost's northern approach, in two minds about whether to follow them or whether to wait with Ulrika. There, a group of Ostermarkers were busy throwing up a rough wall of blocked ice and rubble. Beyond them, spectral figures twisted the night snow into eerie shapes. It made Felix's neck crawl just looking. 'Do you believe in fate, Snorri?'

'Fate believes in Snorri,' Snorri answered with uncharacteristic glumness.

'Is that the same thing?'

Snorri's jaw worked as if over a rotten tooth, and then he shrugged. Idly, he lugged a frozen cow-pat into the river. It smashed a floating block of ice and then slid under with a last gasp of night air. 'You were always the clever one, young Felix.'

Felix followed Snorri's stare across the river. A swirl in the snow became the gothic frontage of the Hergigbank on Otto's street. The dimples in the water where the flakes landed reminded him, inevitably, of Kat. A gust of wind turned the shapes into that of a running child.

'Did you know that Gotrek had a child?' he asked quietly.

'A little girl,' Snorri replied without looking up, voice coming from some distant place. 'She wanted to be an engineer.' Snorri shook his head, chuckling though Felix had the distinct impression the dwarf wanted to be crying. 'Snorri told her she was silly. Snorri would be an engineer before the guild let a woman learn their secrets.'

'You knew Gotrek that long ago?'

Snorri nodded.

'So what happened to her?'

'Goblins happened, young Felix. It was all done by the time Gotrek came home, so he took his grudge to the lord who should have protected them.'

Felix glanced over his shoulder as if expecting to see Gotrek glaring with disapproval. He and Kolya were traipsing over slushed ground towards the rising north barricade. He had a good idea how this story was going to end. 'Is this something you should be telling me? If Gotrek wanted me to know...'

'Gotrek is a kinslayer,' said Snorri, as simply as if he were explaining that Gotrek had once had brown hair. 'A dwarf lord and his house died that day. Secrets like that are harder to bury than... than...' Snorri scrunched up his face as though remembering something he had once heard. 'Than gold.'

Snorri's voice dropped to a hoarse whisper. His fingers ground into the leather satchel in his hands. 'If only someone had been sent to warn our home. If only someone had been there to fight when the goblins came.' Unclenching his fists, Snorri smoothed down the leather pack until the golden rune glittered in the false, eerie spiritlight that streamed under the sky. 'Snorri thinks... Snorri wasn't...'

Felix waited as Snorri struggled. He couldn't say he was surprised by the nature of Gotrek's supposed wrongdoing. Felix had little enough respect for the nobles of his own race and had the shortcomings of one of them led to the deaths of Kat and his own child then Felix would probably have done exactly the same thing. He smiled ruefully. He would have tried to.

Snorri appeared to have wrestled himself into a mental stalemate. Patiently, Felix prodded the bag. 'What's in the bag, Snorri?'

Blank-eyed, Snorri passed it over. The damp leather was rough in Felix's hand. The rune stitched in gold into the side glittered. It was heavier than it looked, and when he gave it an experimental shake something inside answered with a metallic rustle. His fingers hovered over the buckle.

'May I?'

Snorri nodded once. Felix offered a smile and opened it. He didn't know why, but he was excited to see what was inside. The rune on the front had clearly meant something to Gotrek so, he reasoned, it surely had to be something important. He coughed at the aroma of stale dwarf sweat that drifted up from inside. It was full of old clothes. Felix tried to hide his disappointment. Trust Snorri Nosebiter to carry a bag of soot-caked rags halfway across the Old World. He was about to hand the bag back when a blood-stained shirt slipped aside to reveal a heavy golden chain. Felix took it out for closer inspection and gave the bag back to Snorri.

'It's beautiful. Dwarf made?' Snorri shrugged so Felix returned his attention to the artefact.

Around the thick links dwarf runes had been engraved in an exquisite hand. Felix ran his finger around one of the links. He was no jeweller, but he recognised quality when he saw it. In fact the only time he'd seen gold this pure and well fashioned had been in Karak Kadrin when Gotrek had presented him and Kat with their rings. Slowly, his scrolling finger paused. The runes looked familiar. He held his breath. His heart seemed to grow heavy as he spread his fingers. His wedding band glinted in the light.

The runes were the same. This chain had belonged to Gotrek.

No.

It had been a gift from Gotrek.

Cold spreading through his chest, Felix tightened his grip on the chain. 'Who did this belong to, Snorri?'

'Snorri... doesn't remember.'

'Was it Gotrek's wife? It was, wasn't it? How did you get this? You said nobody was there when the goblins attacked.'

The old Trollslayer looked on the verge of tears. Frost prickled his squashed nose. 'Snorri... can't...'

With hands numbed by more than cold, Felix pushed the chain back into Snorri's keeping. He thought he understood. No wonder Snorri had tried so hard all these years to forget his shame. Snorri had been there that day.

'Oh Snorri,' he breathed. 'What did you do?'

* * *

The thick red stone muted the cries of the oblast dead. The air within the ruined despatch-fort was dank, musty and stale, and cold too if one felt it, but buffered against the wind it was a gelid kind of chill like the handshake of a ghoul. Arrow slits and ceiling tears let in light enough to glance off iron wall brackets where in less hopeless times there might once have been torches. The only illumination of note in fact derived from Ulrika herself.

In her charred, enamel-white plate, she stood in the centre of the chamber with legs braced and hands balled into fists by her side. Amethyst-coloured tracers of energy arced from her hands, probing up her vambraces and over her belly. Occasionally, the arcs crossed to produce a crackling burst of nightshade and the tang of ozone. She faced the door. Her eyes glittered like diamonds and her jaw was set. Concentration gleamed from fang and claw. It was etched into every supernatural sinew.

'Is there anything more I can do, general?'

Gustav Jaeger slumped back into one of the bowman's nooks, disturbing the snow that had blown in through the narrow embrasure and been allowed to build up there. Breathing shakily he began fumbling with the collar ties of his cloak, hiding the still-seeping punctures in his neck.

Ulrika permitted herself a smile of pleasure. So handsome. More men lay scattered across the floor with expressions of bliss on pale faces and blood staining the slashed shoulders of their doublets. They were not Kislevites. Their blood was hers to expend as she saw fit. She wondered if she had always thought in such terms, but then reasoned that she probably had. It was only pragmatic, and as the only child of a March Boyar Ulrika had never been anything but that.

'Thank you, Gustav. That is sufficient for now. If I require more power then I will summon more of your men.'

With a faint look of disappointment, Gustav lapsed into semi-consciousness. Ulrika watched his fluttering eyelids and silently moving lips in the same way that she had once watched her father's hunting dogs as they slept – she wondered what such a simple animal might dream of.

'And I, boyarina?'

Speaking his native Kislevarin, Damir stood amongst the splayed bodies of the southerners as though this was an utterly natural state of affairs. His hands were on his hips where they could be close to his hatchets. A man of the Troll Country, through and through. His yellow eyes flashed with amethyst discharge.

'I will be weakened while I perform the ritual. I will be relying on you to defend me from whatever may come.'

Damir nodded and turned back to the door. He would know what to do. The man had served her since the outbreak of the war. She had been in the Troll Country then, on Lahmian business, and had been overjoyed by the opportunity to spread her claws. She had seen more fighting then than at any other time in her new life, but the sheer number and power of the arch enemy had been too much. Even then she had been loathe to leave, and Damir and his people had objected bitterly to abandoning their tribal lands. Fortunately, her kiss had opened his mind to reason and to a whole new world of possibilities. To servitude. Perhaps one day to immortality.

She just couldn't understand why mortals were always so intransigent. Could they not see that she only wanted what was best for them? She knew that she should not blame them. They could not perceive the world as sharply as she could. Their minds could not process it with the same clarity and speed as one of the Arisen.

Felix, for instance, would undoubtedly object to her using his nephew this way. It was more than just jealousy. He honestly seemed to think it wrong. She pitied him that as she pitied poor

Katerina, trapped in a frail and failing mortal shell because of her lover's weakness of imagination. Trying to see things in the limited fashion of her companions, she reasoned that they would probably not appreciate what she was trying to achieve now either.

She was going to open a door.

Invasion after invasion had steeped Praag's bedrock with the stuff of Chaos. The means to ritually tap it was similar to the magic with which the Auric Bastion was erected. Deep in concentration, Ulrika bared her fangs. The very ritual that one of her own kind had delivered into the hands of Balthasar Gelt. Not that any man of the Empire now alive was going to offer their thanks to the sacrifices of the Arisen that had allowed their Supreme Patriarch to save them. Nor would they mourn the destruction of the nation that he had not seen fit to spare.

Borrowed blood boiled within her veins. And Gabriella had wondered why Ulrika had left her for Vlad von Carstein.

The Empire had let Kislev fall, had made a puppet of Boyar Syrgei Tannarov of Erengrad and claimed the stolen territory of 'North Ostermark' for its own. Even in the End Times, men were still men.

They needed the shepherding hand of the Arisen.

And with that hand she was going to drive a stake through the heart of Chaos and watch the rest of the world drown in its blood.

Max Schreiber's mind perused the corrupted aethyr of Praag. It was a web of life and of death that touched every creature currently contesting the city's walls. In an abstract sense, every natural scholar knew about the interconnectedness of life. Every creature had its place in that web, surrounded and connected by those it killed and those that killed it. What fewer scholars knew however was that what was true for life was also true for Chaos, only more so.

A portion of Max's mind stood now with the beastmen on the

city's ramparts. He felt their near-human soup of hatreds and fears as daemon-possessed munitions set the sky ablaze and the walls atremble. They bleated their battle cries as Chaos warriors stormed their position by the thousand. Max moved on.

A wyvern with two heads and poisonous spines roosted upon the hanging shell of the old wizard's tower. What had it been called? The memory rose up from another time and place. There it was. Fire Spire. The power of Chaos had twisted it into its current, misshapen form during the last Great War. Its history was irrelevant now. He saw it in flat monochrome through the wyvern's eyes, felt the latent magic beneath its claws as it peered through the blizzard for prey in the streets below. Again, Max's thoughts shifted.

A band of trolls lumbered against the thrust of the wind and snow down the Grand Parade towards the Gate of Gargoyles. Max shared the glacial quiet of their minds. They had a destination. The gate. They had a purpose. A vague imprint of a white-haired sorceress. Nothing Max would consider true thought, but there was seductiveness in simplicity. Calling on the same rote exercises that had served him as an acolyte of the Light order, Max differentiated his mind from theirs.

Warp lightning stabbed from the tormented sky, exploding with a thunderclap against the highest point of the city – the north-facing watchtower of its hilltop citadel. A flurry of wild magic rippled out from its pinnacle, obliterating the falling snow and haloing the dark presence within. For a moment Max felt their minds touch. It was a servant of the Troll King, an immortal monster so ancient and terrible that Max could not even begin to comprehend the nature of its thoughts. Its long extinct race had trod the earth with the Old Ones before even the coming of the Chaos Gods. Their own name for their kind was long forgotten. Now, men had a different name for those few that remained. There came a low growl that transcended both the physical and the aethyric realms and Max's spirit took flight.

He forced himself to focus.

It did not require the hyper-surreality of mage-sense to perceive the fan-like conductor array being assembled by the warlock in the cell opposite, or the mind-opening trance of the goblin shaman in the next one after that. Secrets were difficult to keep in confinement and one man's hunch could easily become another being's race to the finish. And no doubt that had been Throgg's intent. Nothing incentivised success like competition with a hated rival and the very visceral consequences of failure.

The Troll King was brutal, but he was smart. Max felt that his continuing survival was owed in large part to his willingness to concede that fact. That, however, was to do his captor's intelligence a disservice. It was neither hubris nor Chaos taint to acknowledge that he was a more adept wizard and a better researcher than any goblin, skaven, liche or ice witch that Throgg could acquire. It was just a fact.

And the research he had conducted under the patronage of the Troll King had led him to the inalienable conclusion that there was something wrong with the world.

The minds of men were not capable of controlling more than one of the eight derivations of High Magic. The lessons of Teclis to the first magisters on this subject could not have been clearer. To even attempt to circumvent this inviolate law of nature was to open one's mind to Chaos. And yet in his experimentations with eliciting higher thought in the troll in his cell, he had accidentally touched upon Azyr, the Celestial, the magic of abstract thinking and narrative order amongst seeming Chaos.

That was the reason for the self-splitting spell he now performed. It was the proof of his suspicions. Max's aethyric self could see in colours that he should not. He could draw connections that he previously could not. The world had indeed gone wrong. The winds of magic no longer flowed as they should. The legacy of Nagash's rise.

For all that however, for all he had seen and suffered, he was still a magister of the Light. He could not dismiss the possibility that these new abilities were a symptom of his own corruption rather than some global shift in the rules of magic. Even Max himself could see something amiss in his current pursuit. Scholarly curiosity could become obsession, self-preservation could mutate easily into willing determination. It was not every day that one was set the task of creating a new race of intelligent beings. He probed within himself but could find nothing overtly at fault. He had longstanding mental wards, all apparently still intact, to warn of and resist any incursion by Chaos but, of course, any taint deep enough to afflict his personality could circumvent or corrode even the best laid safeguards without his being aware.

A man could second-guess himself to oblivion once he started down that road. What he could say for certain was that what he sought to accomplish did not feel evil.

Which meant there was every chance of him doing some good.

By helping Throgg stand strong he would help the Empire. Yes, that much was obvious. His homeland needed its strongman in the north.

And now, his mind opening to the pure glory of the aethyr undivided, he saw how it would be done. Back in his cell, his body laughed. It was so beautiful, seductive even, in its simplicity. Max had told Throgg no lies. He was neither a Teclis nor a Nagash, but he did not think it too bold to count himself amongst the second tier of magicians below them. If what Throgg demanded could be done, then Max Schreiber could do it.

Conceptualising the ritual cant to return him to his bruised flesh and broken bones, Max felt a trembling in the web of Chaos. Focusing his divinations, he followed the source of the disturbance to a place beyond the moribund spell wards of Praag's walls and to the very periphery of his senses. It was another spellcaster. Outside! So unexpected was that he was almost ready to believe that his own senses were at fault, and with them everything else he had become prepared to accept. It was with good reason that even the most brazen daemon prince dared not deploy magic within reach of Throgg's gates.

For a moment longer his spirit lingered at the outermost limits of Praag's walls, hovering above the Gate of Gargoyles as it opened to disgorge a band of brutish trolls into the besieging horde. Max looked away. He had long ago ceased to wonder at the sound made by a warrior crushed inside his own Chaos armour. Instead, he looked outside.

The mage's signature resonance felt familiar and yet not, almost like an old acolyte who had matured into a magister, or a friend who had since fallen to Chaos. A reassuringly human sense of pity for the poor soul was marred only by a bleak curiosity.

Whoever it was, they were in for a cruel surprise.

THIRTEEN

King of Trolls

Felix knew more about trolls than most men.

One of his earliest adventures had brought him face to face with such a beast in the bowels of Karak Eight Peaks. With his own hand had he struggled to force steel through flesh as hard as rock, only to then watch his best effort regenerate before his eyes. He had seen men dissolved in the monster's infamously potent gastric juices and seen others crushed to jelly by its sheer massivity and physical strength. Later, he had sought out and studied the *Anatomicum Bestiarum*, which, despite coming complete with coloured illustrations of blank, lopsided heads and dissected intestinal tracts, was a treatise that had somehow passed him by during his studies at the University of Altdorf.

There was however one hitherto overlooked fact that Felix very much hoped he would survive long enough to see disseminated in the next volume of *My Travels with Gotrek*, or at least as a referenced appendix in the next edition of the *Anatomicum*.

Trolls were not afraid of ghosts.

Confusion and fear required a complexity of thought that a troll could not boast. The spirits shackled to Ulrika's maze coiled around the hulking frames that condensed out of the snow and darkness. They tugged, prodded, whispered in bullet-hole ears, but the dim brutes came on, leaving the screams of the northman horde behind them under an avalanche of walking stone.

With a cold and spreading dread whose evolved sophistication provided him no consolation, Felix drew his sword. Karaghul's former owner had after all met his end in the belly of that Karak Eight Peaks troll. Felix was still debating whether it was best to run or to fight as the men working on the northern barricade gave a wail and, weapons in their hands, did what came most naturally.

They opened fire.

Handguns popped, discharging flutes of black smoke and peppering the leading beast with solid iron shot. It was too dark and Felix was too far away to judge how much of the fire was simply wayward and how much of it ricocheted off the stone titan's grey hide. One moment more was all it took for the stone troll to hit the barricade.

The loose wall simply disintegrated around the stone troll's charge. More and more trolls crashed through after it in a storm of masonry aggregates and crushed men too slow to run.

The big stone troll glazed over in confusion upon finding itself in open space where its brain still believed there to be a wall. It was a granite colossus fifteen feet high, its body spined with arrows and axe blades and jagged with regeneration scars. Dull moon eyes blinked slowly over the men fleeing from it into the ruined outpost. Its mouth dropped open, then a pistol shot fired one-handed by a running man blasted a chunk off its lower jaw. Blood spurted sluggishly – once, twice – before the flesh began to close. The troll's tongue flopped out of its regrowing mouth as it focused on the red-crested warrior steaming towards it with an axe held high and a dwarfish war cry.

Still Felix hesistated. His grip tightened indecisively on his sword. His feet seemed to root deeper into the snow. Should he help Gotrek or warn Ulrika? Before he had a chance to arrive at a decision, Snorri Nosebiter issued a furious hoot of joy, flourished his axe and hammer, and charged. Felix swore with the vivid colour of the well travelled as Snorri tottered into the herd of Norse cattle towards the fence between them and the trolls.

The Trollslayer looked ridiculous.

Sweeping what the harpies of Kurzycko had left of his cloak over his left shoulder to free his sword arm, Felix hurried after him. Ulrika could take care of herself. Only a miracle could look after Snorri if Gotrek found out about his wife's chain without a ready explanation for how it came into Snorri's keeping. It could be innocent and probably was, but Gotrek was hardly known for his understanding. Felix was firmly of the mind that Snorri should absolutely *not* be left alone with Gotrek until Praag was a long way behind them all.

Snorri hobbled through the herd with Felix close behind. He held his sword upright and his arms tight to his chest, mindful of the hot-blooded belligerence that pressed perilously close on all sides. All it would take was one wrong step, one horn-swipe at an imagined itch, and Felix wouldn't have to worry about trolls. They emerged the other side into a bitter flurry of snow, Snorri scrambling under the fence while Felix swung a stile.

Still climbing fences, Felix thought ruefully. Oddly though, he didn't feel nearly so stiff this time.

While Snorri picked himself up out of the snow, Felix quickly surveyed the scene.

The Lynsk was to the left. The flood plain of southern Praag and Ulrika's ghost-maze were ahead and to the right. The trolls had smashed through the barricade and reduced a swathe of the northmen's stockade to splinters. Already, cattle were wandering aimlessly into the surrounding ruins and getting in the way of the soldiers desperately trying to run the other way. With cries of despair, some scattered into the buildings and returned fire. Relentless, the pursuing trolls stamped through the ineffectual scatter of handgun and pistol shot as blithely as they did through the buildings that their minds couldn't adjust to the presence of fast enough to avoid. How could men fight an army like that? What was stopping the Troll King from conquering the world? Felix watched open-mouthed as whole structures went down in geysers of red dust. The rumble of falling stonework couldn't obliterate the screams of those buried inside.

Men crawled through the snow to escape, fleeing towards the lanterns that shone from spears by the despatch-fort's gate. There, Felix could just about pick out Ulrika's Ungol guard assembling into ranks. Their bright wool coats fluttered gaily over hide armour. Tassels whipped from the heads of their spears. Chapka hats glittered under the lantern-light with frost.

Why were they just standing there?

Felix's initial annoyance faded when he realised they didn't need to go anywhere. The trolls were coming straight for them. Felix's lip twitched with the sudden realisation. Aekold Helbrass had claimed the Troll King was collecting sorcerers. He was after Ulrika! He stopped running and glanced back. The trolls were being slowed by gunfire, and distracted by the northmen's livestock and fences and the deep snow, but no force of men was going to stop them.

His blood ran cold. Gustav was with her.

'Snorri. Wait. We have to go back.'

No sooner had he said the words than Snorri bellowed an unintelligible stream of sounds and hurtled towards a river troll that, distracted by the cattle that surrounded it, had blundered off the main thrust of the assault and into Snorri's reach. It was hunched nearly double, flattened almost by the mass of its own shoulders. Its head was squashed and dripped with a shank of red algae. Trolls adopted the character of their habitat, Felix knew, and this one was the rugged white of the cliffs of Nordland. In one chalky fist it dragged a broken Chaos warrior like a club. The vinegar reek of its breath made the hair on Felix's face shrivel. Its bellow as it pushed aside a shaggy Norse bull and charged onto Snorri's weapons shook Felix to his insides.

Snorri's hammer smote splinters from the monster's kneecap while his axe chipped ineffectually at its belly. The dwarf dodged a sweep of the troll's club, then swung a mace-kick to its splintered kneecap to drive it down onto one knee. The troll smacked its lips dumbly as Snorri ducked under its arm and landed another kick into its side. Snorri laughed, skipping a single-legged tattoo around the kneeling troll, under its grasping claws, and then reached up for a fistful of the semi-mineral red mat that tufted from its chin. The monster roared as Snorri tightened his grip and used it to launch himself off the ground and land a shuddering head-butt between its eyes. A strange ochre fluid squirted from the troll's eyes and a crack fissured its nose.

Snorri staggered back, grinning like an idiot with a big chalky print covering his face. Felix winced. Even the troll seemed to have felt that.

With a roar, the troll swept its Chaos warrior over the dazed Slayer and at Felix's head like a morningstar. Felix ducked, dropping into a barrel roll that carried him under the hopeful stroke, and came up facing the troll's groin. Though lacking Snorri Nosebiter's wrestler's brawn and brute power, his magical blade carved open the troll's thigh like a roasted joint. Its passage halted with a jarring clang when it struck bone. The troll flailed its arms in confusion as

Felix circled behind, applying the precise pressure, angle and carving action to sever the troll's femoral artery on the blade's egress and spray his right side with blood.

It was remarkable, in hindsight, what could be learned from a colour illustration.

Losing blood faster than even the river troll's formidable metabolism could replenish it, the monster crashed face down into the snow. Snorri made loud and messy work of hewing its head from its shoulders.

Felix sagged, but was quickly pressed to move aside for a bull that had wandered across from one of the shattered pens to investigate. It snorted hotly and poked the downed troll with its horns. It wasn't dead. A troll could regenerate even a severed head. It would take fire to finally put it down and Felix had nothing of the sort.

'Come on,' Felix wheezed, turning back to Snorri. 'We can still get back to the fort to... Snorri?'

Wiping snow and troll blood from his face, Felix saw Snorri barrelling through the snow towards the wreck of the north barricade with an ululating outpouring of glee. For there, knee deep in rubble and held at bay by a frighteningly small-looking dwarf with an axe, was the largest troll Felix had ever seen. It had been the first to breach the barricade, but while the other trolls had been faced with Gustav's free company, this one had had the misfortune to run into Gotrek Gurnisson.

'Snorri! Get back here!'

Knowing it was a pointless waste of breath even before he opened his mouth, Felix shouldered his sword and ran after him.

Kolya crouched in the foxhole he had dug out of the snow and sighted the stone troll down a nocked and partially drawn shaft. It was taller than a mounted man and looked like something that had stepped out from the rocks of Urzebya where Ursun had taken a bite out of the world. Thinking of biting, he massaged a handful of snow into his gums. His mouth still throbbed where Gurnisson had kicked out his teeth. It was a wonder it had not broken his jaw. He tracked his aim to the dwarf.

Gurnisson was not a quarter the troll's mass. He was bleeding freely where his exertions had reopened unhealed wounds and was blowing hard. Somehow though, the dwarf found strength to brandish his axe and beckon the behemoth on. He was mad, he was infuriating and, Kolya was beginning to suspect, singularly blessed by his people's gods.

The troll reared up to its awesome height and punched down. Instead of diving clear as any sane man would, the dwarf gave a cholic roar and hammered his upswinging axe into the troll's knuckles. The rune weapon split the monster's hand up to the wrist bone and, impossibly, diverted the punch over his head. The troll roared as its fist ploughed through the snow. Kolya shook his head in wonder. The dwarf was astounding. Loose inside the beast's guard, Gurnisson unleashed everything in a brutal flurry. His starmetal blade cut the troll's belly to ribbons, freeing a ropey mass of steaming entrails that the dwarf ground underfoot with every appearance of satisfaction. The splattered juices produced a sharp hiss where they landed and, smelling the acid corrosion of his boots, even the dwarf withdrew with a grimace. He slid his boots under the snow until they stopped smoking. The troll's belly was already knitting back together.

'Are you going to help?' he called over his shoulder.

'No.'

The dwarf thought about that for a moment and started to laugh. 'I like you, manling.'

'Tor help me,' Kolya muttered under his breath. He had almost come to like the murdering Slayer himself.

Cackling, Gurnisson swept his axe through a rune-streaked blur of a figure-of-eight. From the expression on his face, Kolya wondered if dwarf hearing might be better than men's. 'Stand back then, and take word of this doom to that ghastly horse-loving afterlife of yours.'

Kolya lowered his bow. If he was resigned to watch, then there was no more fighting to be done here. It was not that he did not pity those oblast men in the fort, but they were already as dead as their boyarina and it was pointless to mourn a dead man. Their screams were tinny, separated from him now by the roar of the trolls and the crash of collapsing buildings. Blackpowder weapons crackled in the distance like a dying fire. Set against that expectation, the sound of another charging fighter actually caught him off guard.

The senile old dwarf with the metal leg careened through the loose rubble and snow waving an axe and a hammer above his bald head. A leather satchel slapped at his back like a riding crop.

'Snorri's turn!' the dwarf yelled, muscling Gurnisson aside just as the stone troll dispatched an open-handed punch that would have ripped Gurnisson's head off had he still been there to meet it. Gurnisson gave a shout as the body charge of the other dwarf threw him sideways and sent him plunging into a rocky snow heap. The newcomer wobbled drunkenly on the uneven ground, but somehow managed to bat the troll's punch aside on his hammer. The impact spun him around, but he kept his feet, coming dizzily about and raising his weapons.

'That horse kicked Snorri harder than that.'

All Kolya could do was gape. Was insanity a common trait in the dwarfs or had the End Times cracked their minds?

Gotrek pulled himself from the drift and shook snow from his crest. His entire body looked clenched and swollen with wrath. He strode towards Snorri, axe gripped in one massive fist. 'Of all the dooms in all the world, Snorri Nosebiter, you had to come and spoil mine. Again.'

'This one's Snorri's,' Snorri growled, fending Gurnisson off with his left arm while simultaneously hammering away at the troll's groin.

'That so?'

Gurnisson and Snorri tangled arms, each using the spare hand to strike a claim on the troll. Snorri's hammer bashed its hip. Gurnisson's axe severed its arm at the elbow. Gurnisson produced a triumphant leer that cracked under Snorri's elbow. The dwarfs shouted insults and manage to wrestle each other down under the troll's swinging fist.

'Damn it, Snorri!'

Snorri spluttered snow from his mouth and clambered on top of Gurnisson's back, wedging the struggling Slayer down beneath his thighs. 'If Snorri's rememberer hadn't pulled his crest out that would have got him.'

'I'll pull out more than that if you get in my way again.'

'This one isn't yours,' said Snorri patiently, as though training a horse. 'The spider lady told Snorri he would have his doom when all his friends were together again.'

With a tectonic rumble, the troll lumbered forwards, cracking Snorri's forehead with a stray knee and hurling him back. The troll stamped after him, missing Gurnisson's back by inches. Shivering with fury, the dwarf drew himself up. His one eye glittered hatefully. He grasped his axe two-handed, so tightly that the scabs of his biceps burst.

'I couldn't give a rabid rat's dribble what you think your human witch said. I've been here from the start. I was at the Tobol Crossing. I was in Kislev City.' The Slayer looked hot enough to melt the Frozen Sea. His words meant nothing to Snorri, but Kolya they hit like a charge of winged lancers. He and the dwarf had shared a battlefield! The Tobol Crossing had been a rout he had been lucky to survive and, though the Dushyka rota had long fled, the sack of Kislev City was by all garbled accounts nothing short of a massacre.

That the dwarf had survived both and more was further testament to his prowess.

'I've been searching since the fall. I need no one's help to fail again today.'

'Snorri's not been having a fun time either,' Snorri protested, hobbling out of the troll's path and then slamming a kick into the side of the troll's knee. He looked up as Gurnisson came up behind him. 'But you don't want to hear about it.'

Gurnisson moved so fast that his elbow blurred into his fist, smashing a haymaker through Snorri's jaw. The bigger dwarf hit the ground like a slab of meat. The power behind Gurnisson's arm sent him sliding a short way through the snow. Gurnisson shook out his knuckles and re-established his two-handed grip on his axe. He returned his attention to the troll. 'Because I don't care about it.'

Gurnisson's rune-axe hewed upwards into the troll's midriff. The monster bellowed, swaying back and forth as the dwarf levered his axe free in a spurt of acidic bile. His friend was already forgotten. Kolya shook his head. The dwarf really was a selfish zabójka. With a bittersweet shout, Gurnisson reversed his grip and thundered his axe into the troll's opposite hip, almost meeting his first strike in the middle and chopping the stone troll clean in two. As it was, the troll wavered back, tongues of regenerative tissue licking out from the open wounds.

'There is something Snorri has to ask,' Snorri shouted hoarsely, having rolled onto all fours. His metal leg stuck out sideways like a pissing dog, but his skull must have been similarly iron clad. 'It is about his shame.'

'Tell it to your priest.'

'He blew up.'

Gurnisson snorted. 'Lucky for some.'

Snorri heaved himself up. His scarred cheeks were flushed bright red as if with shame. 'Snorri was there.'

Kolya read Gurnisson's lips shaping the question 'where?' before the dwarf grit his teeth, shook his head and muttered, 'I still don't care.'

Angrily, Snorri shoved his weapons into his breeches and reached for the bag that he wore over his shoulder. 'If you won't listen and you won't let Snorri have his doom then he will show you.' He yanked at the strap, forgetting to unbuckle it in his haste, but before he could spot his oversight and do something about it, a rich voice shouted out from the direction of the river.

'Snorri, stop!'

It was the Empire man, Jaeger. He had an open palm raised, his cloak hanging from it like a scrag of red ribbons. The Norse bulls close around him snorted aggressively at the flapping strands. His mail was scratched and loose several links. He was older than Kolya's father would have been had a goblin raider's arrow not taken him early, but there was a steeliness about him that the grey in his hair and beard and the furrows in his brow seemed to enforce. In a strange way he reminded Kolya of Gurnisson.

Snorri looked at the man blankly. His hand clung to his satchel buckle as if he had forgotten what it was doing there.

'This isn't the time,' shouted Jaeger, out of breath from running. He stabbed his sword into the snow so that he could lean on it. Then he gazed pointedly at the troll. His eyes widened. 'Oh, blood of Sigmar.'

A yellowish plume was rising from between the troll's striated rows of teeth. Its gut rippled and began to bloat. Its throat swelled.

With the honed reflexes of a solitary hunter, Kolya drew back his bowstring, aimed right down the monster's opening mouth and loosed.

The shaft smacked through soft flesh and embedded in the stony tissue at the back of the troll's neck. The troll gagged, flailed in Kolya's direction despite his being a good hundred feet away, and then spewed a gush of steaming yellow vomit that missed the two dwarfs by the height of a Slayer's crest. Gurnisson's face screwed up at the smell of singed hair coming from the tip of his mohawk while, behind him, yellow vapour hissed into the air as snow and rock were dissolved.

Gargling its own stomach acids, the troll lumbered now towards Kolya, falling straight into the Kurgan-dug trench that Kolya had spotted by the darker coloured snow and used to position his own foxhole. Trolls were ruggedly built and powerful, but without a man's intellect they were just another animal to be hunted. He nocked another arrow to his bowstring.

'What did you do that for?' Gurnisson bellowed angrily, yellow-red steam rising from his crest as though his head were on fire.

Kolya shrugged, holding his aim as the monster struggled to dig its way out of the snow-filled ditch. 'You can die, zabójka, that is good. But I made no promise to these others.'

Gurnisson glowered at the other dwarf. Kolya had no idea what past lay between them, but it wasn't going to end well.

'You cheat me again, Snorri Nosebiter.'

Equally angry, Snorri brandished his two weapons. Held side to side, the stance could have been intended to emphasise the older Slayer's greater bulk. 'Last to get killed by a troll buys the beer.'

Ulrika blotted the riot of gunshots and screams from her mind. It felt as if she were being lifted up on a rising swell of blood magic.

It was an incredible out-of-body sensation, one that she could only wish she had more time to explore. A crash like a collapsing rockface impelled her to open one eye and divert a portion of her attention towards what was going on in the real world. Such compartmentalisation of thought and action was yet another of the gifts of the Arisen.

A brutally unequal melee raged in the doorway. Her loyal guard of Ungol warriors screamed as they battled to keep formation, warding off a glittering ice troll with their spears. As Ulrika watched, a spear shattered and the fierce nomad that wielded it broke under a punch from a crystalline fist. At a word from Ulrika, the man creaked upright on broken bones and continued to stab dumbly with the stub of his shaft. Behind them, arquebusiers in the mismatched colours of Gustav's free company knelt in ranks, primed matchcords and rattled into a firing line. The staccato bark of gunfire within the enclosed space was deafening and filled the chamber with smoke. The first rank knelt to reload while the second took aim and fired. Chips of stone-like flesh sprayed from bullet wounds, but the trolls kept on coming, crunching through the Ungols faster than Ulrika could reanimate them.

Soldiers in piecemeal plate mail assembled into formation with longswords and pikes. Their faces were wan, their eyes glassy. They were petrified, but they would die for their immortal mistress. Leading them, Gustav played weakly with his pistols.

'Hold by me,' Ulrika murmured. 'I will still need loyal men on the other side.' She would rather have retained her own Ungols, but Gustav's free company were too weak to fight at the moment and, in any case, it did not matter.

The bodies of Damir and his men would all still be here waiting for her when she returned with Max and her master's boon.

Distancing herself from the immediate danger, she opened her expanded senses to the black depths of the oblast's magic. Successive incursions by Chaos had made this a cursed place, cursed but powerful. As she drew that magic in, exploited it to mould before herself the outline of a shimmering portal, she became aware of the fact that she could no longer sense the beast she had been struggling with so long.

After a second's panic, she found it. It was calm, as if its own power and rage were placated as hers grew. In fact, she was no longer entirely sure where Ulrika ended and the monster began. It was this place. Not for the first time she wondered what had become of the Arisen of Praag.

'Damir,' she called. The Ungol chieftain pulled out from the fighting. He was still alive, but he was badly hurt. His patchwork coat was bloodied and ripped and he looked to be carrying a broken arm. Despite his injuries there was nothing in his face but love unconditional and the desire to serve. Ulrika could no longer imagine the time when she had found that displeasing. 'Bring me Felix.'

The man nodded and then, after a moment's thought, she added: 'Only Felix.'

An impulse flashed across the aethyr, a stab of will that originated in the dark citadel of Praag.

Shivering in his high tower as he enacted the final preparations for his own great ritual, Max Schreiber perceived it as a tremor in the all-connecting web of Chaos that lay over the city. Drowning in borrowed power and as raw to it as an open wound, Ulrika felt it pulse across her mind. Hacking at the stone troll's grasping arm as it floundered in the snow-filled trench, Felix saw it more immediately as a red glow condensing out of the air.

Of them all, it was only Max who recognised the signature for what it was. He gave it no further attention. He had been expecting no less.

Throgg, the Troll King, had entered the fray.

The troll began to glow, red light blazing from its eyes and bleeding from the fissures in its rocky flesh. Already on the backswing after hewing into the monster's elbow, Felix fell back before the explosive intensity of its gaze. He squinted into the glare. The troll's eyes seemed to be following him, studying him, a pair of burning rubies painting him red against the night dark. Heart in his mouth, he angled his sword unconsciously into a guard, firming a fighting stance into the snow. Watching him with what Felix could only call interest, the troll's ridgeline lips cracked upwards. Was it smiling? Could trolls smile? In the corner of his vision he saw Kolya draw back his bow but hold. On the other side of the ditch, even the two Slayers seemed momentarily taken aback by the change.

The troll's lips parted further, crunching experimentally through a range of motion like an orator preparing for the stage. Where previously the troll had been distracted by so many assailants on all sides, now its big hands dug into the snow at the lip of the trench and it hauled itself slowly up. Its eyes were fixed on Felix. A rush of noxious air came up from its gut, shaped by a fluke conformation of lips and tongue into what almost sounded like a word.

'*Hayger?*'

'Did it just... say my name?' said Felix, tightening his grip on Karaghul just a little more.

'Trolls don't talk,' said Gotrek.

'I don't know,' said Kolya cautiously. 'It seems brighter than the average troll.'

Gotrek gave a derisive snort. 'Snorri's brighter than the average troll.'

'And Snorri can talk,' Snorri stated proudly, then hobbled towards the edge of the trench and cracked his hammer against the back of the troll's skull.

More of that red light shone through the cracks that spidered out from the point of impact, but the troll didn't flinch. It wasn't just that the monster didn't feel it. Felix could see the thought behind the action. It knew that Snorri couldn't seriously hurt it with the weapons he had. Already those cracks were beginning to close over, and rather than waste effort retaliating against an assailant it did not seriously consider a threat, it was hauling itself out of its hole and coming after Felix.

Felix glanced at Karaghul. The magical blade shone dully against the snow that fell around it. He supposed he should probably feel honoured that a troll thought so highly of him.

Abandoning his stance, Felix hurriedly backed up. He tried to tell himself that this was nothing he had not faced before, but he wasn't terribly convincing about it. Before, this had been another troll but now it was something far worse. It was the eyes. There was something downright terrifying about the intelligent way the monster was looking at him. It knew who he was, what he could do, and was looking forward to the meagre test of putting an end to him.

It bellied out of the ditch, then drew its knees underneath it. A Kislevite expletive and a snap shot from a composite bow pulled Felix's glance right. Kolya's arrow snapped off the troll's lumpen shoulder. With a curse, Kolya crawled out of his foxhole, a fresh arrow already nocked and aimed, and sidestepped around to the monster's front. Wise to the threat, the troll kept its face and the soft parts it contained turned away from the frustrated archer. Snorri was hobbling hurriedly around the far side of the trench, yelling at Felix to leave his troll alone and scuffing snow and sending rubble flying in his haste, while Gotrek snarled across from the far side.

Felix swallowed and brought up his sword as the troll stretched itself out of its muscular hunch and to its full, appalling height. A sprinkling of frost cascaded from crevasses between muscles that had never previously been fully flexed. The troll tensed them all now, clenched its arms, its chest, its thighs, and balled its savage claws into fists. Its sheer bulk and power temporarily shadowed Felix against the wind and snow.

I'm being taunted by a troll, Felix thought. It might just have been the warmth that came from being out of the wind, but the idea left him feeling strangely hot. He had not journeyed all the way from his new life in Altdorf for this. He had not left Kat behind and brought Gustav to almost certain death *for this*.

'Do something then,' Felix shouted up, dipping his guard in a foolhardy moment of bravado. 'You're not the biggest thing I've ever killed.'

With a growl that sounded almost like it came from two beasts, the troll jabbed for the shoulder of Felix's sword hand. Felix drew in the arm and rolled his shoulder out of the way. It would have been enough, but the attack was a feint, the true attack coming with a backhand swipe to blindside Felix while his back was turned in the other direction.

It was Felix's hard-earned alley brawler's instincts that saved him, that and a shout from Kolya, and he managed to contort his shoulders enough for the massive, gnarled forearm to lunge over his head. Felix didn't even try to stay on his feet. Bent completely off-balance, he hit the ground and rolled, coming up again half a dozen feet back. He shook snow from his hair and brought up his sword. Another arrow cracked against the troll's ear.

Felix kicked himself for failing to recognise the feint. He was not some callow college duellist; he had matched swords with the best. In fairness however, he had never yet fenced with a troll. He had no idea how to pick up the cues in their body language. He doubted there was a man alive that could.

'Hold on, manling!'

A guttural howl roared across the trench as Gotrek took the gap at a run. The dwarf's steaming crest ruffled in the wind. The arrows still stuck in his chest quivered as if excited by the flight. Gotrek's strength continued to amaze. Even Felix with his longer legs would have thought twice about making that leap. The Slayer's axe was already a blur of motion as he thumped into the troll's deep footprint on the trench's near side and sent the blade cleaving through the monster's hamstrings with a sound like a snapping cable.

The troll gave a mangled cry and swung back, catching the Slayer a glancing blow to the temple that nevertheless flipped him head over heels and planted him on his back under a cloud of snow. Felix pressed the advantage his former companion had bought him, hewing madly into the troll's belly and sides. Stone chips and gruelish grey blood flying in all directions, the troll retreated. A stub of wall turned to dust under its feet. It was heading for the river. Another arrow ricocheted off the troll's chest.

In a crazed blur of weapons, Snorri appeared beside Felix. Felix was taken aback by the old dwarf's fury. Of course Snorri was a Slayer too, but Felix had never seen him quite so determined to die.

Its wounds healing apace, the troll continued to back off regardless. Felix followed it every step of the way with Snorri never more than a mad lunge behind.

Felix felt something brush his cheek and he quickly brought up his sword to guard as he glanced across to see what it was. There was nothing there, just a residual shape in the falling snow that might have hinted at a person. A whisper in the opposite ear snapped him back the other way. A cold hand knotted his guts. It was a voice he recognised. But he had fallen here in Praag a long time ago.

'Ulli?' Felix whispered.

He looked up, noticing the waspish shapes streaking through the snow overhead. Every so often, one swept down to tug back on Felix's cloak or whisper something of such dread import that Felix just could not make out the words. Behind him, Kolya had lowered his bow. The Kislevite kissed his carved stone and muttered a prayer. Snorri didn't seem to have noticed.

Tricked! The troll wasn't wounded at all; it had just lured them away from the fighting at the despatch-fort and out into Ulrika's ghost-maze. The realisation came too late as, a moment later, Felix looked north into the falling snow and the spirits cavorting through it to see a dark mass driving towards them.

It was men. Beastmen to be more precise.

It was lots and lots of beastmen.

The scattered Kurgan still camped out on the floodplain were being swept aside by the advance of a vast herd. Felix couldn't count their numbers in the dark, but he could hear the braying of what sounded like far too many. The ground trembled beneath their cloven hooves. The trumpeting cries and bloated silhouettes of larger beasts broke up the mass of what might otherwise have been boring. There were more trolls, at least one fearsomely mutated, four-armed minotaur with boneswords for hands and glowing tattoos crawling over its hairless flesh, and a bloated, toad-like behemoth that Felix could not even begin to describe and did not want to see any closer.

It was as if all the beasts of Chaos had rallied to the Troll King's call.

With a sick sense of realisation, Felix thought that in all likelihood they had.

'Snorri!' he shouted, waving to get the old Slayer's attention. 'We have to get back to the others. We have to warn Ulrika.'

But Snorri wasn't paying attention. The dwarf continued to hammer blows down onto the glowing stone troll, bellowing at it to hit back as he drove it steadily towards the river. Looking for help, he saw Gotrek pick himself out of the snow. The Slayer looked at the onrushing beastmen, knuckled gore from his one good eye, then smacked the side of his head to stop its ringing and looked again. He grinned.

'Not now, Gotrek. We have to go back.'

Before Gotrek could answer, Kolya took up his bow and pointed back in the direction of the fort. Felix swung that way and squinted into the dark. The snow rumbled as if carrying the shock of distant thunder. Felix's heart sank.

How could things get any worse?

He raised his sword, then gave an exultant shout as Damir galloped into view on his tough Ungol pony. The thick-skinned Ungol captain guided his mount solely with knees and stirrups. He looked to be carrying a broken arm, but his narrow yellow eyes were drawn with determination. His fur chapka was tied under his chin so it would not slip with the wind. Rings, charms, buckles and coloured ribbons fluttered angrily as he raised an axe in greeting. Or was it warning?

The thunder grew nearer, too loud to be down to just one rider, and the snow behind Damir's back had taken on a wavering darkness as though it hid an avalanche or a tidal wave. Felix backed away, heart drumming a warning of its own as a wall of snorting bulls stampeded through the snow on the Ungol's tail.

The troll's attack must have spooked them and now they were coming right for Felix and the others – trapped between the river and the beastman herd!

He almost dropped his sword and gave up then. What had he done to deserve this? For a moment he considered giving up, skipping the inevitable denouement to his life. But then he thought of Max, held in some dungeon just a few miles away. He thought of his nephew and Ulrika beset by trolls at his back.

He thought of Kat and the child she might not carry.

Gritting his teeth fiercely he shook his head. No. Dying now would be easy all right, but it wouldn't be right. He couldn't speak for Gotrek and Snorri, but he for one intended to return to Altdorf the hero, to see the world emerge from its current trials as it had been before.

Quickly, he assessed the situation. The beastmen were closing from the north and the stampede from the south. He could just now pick out the shape of the pair of trolls that were chasing the bulls down. The din of the two built like colliding stormfronts. There was no way out. One eye on both threats, Felix backed towards the river.

Wait…

Was that even escape or just death by another means?

'Into the river,' Felix shouted, sheathing Karaghul and turning to run.

'You're mad,' Kolya shot back. 'If you don't sink, you'll freeze.'

'I like my alternatives less,' Felix returned, still running, to which the Kislevite could only answer by joining him.

Together, they sprinted past the stone troll. Snorri looked up at their passing, puzzled, until Gotrek came up behind him and pushed him on after them.

'The Troll King is mine, Snorri Nosebiter, but mark this a lost doom repaid.'

Felix's awareness of his surroundings had shrunk to just the snow-covered pebbles between him and the Lynsk. He could smell the ice, could see the whorls that the snow made in the water's sickening uphill flow, could already feel his skin clench in preparation of the coming shock. He heard Damir rein in his pony behind him and shout something he couldn't make out over the blood pounding in his ears, just before a new and unfamiliar sound cut it off.

It was the sound of a man being thumped from horseback by a swinging boulder.

Felix jumped. In that split second he mourned. Damir had been a good man. He hadn't deserved what Ulrika had made of him.

There was an impact, a plunging darkness.

And then he felt nothing but ice.

The fort was coming down around Ulrika's ears. Fist-sized lumps of masonry and decorative gargoyles shattered against the back of her head and left dents in her pauldron plates. The effort of maintaining so many spells at once felt like a pack of dire wolves tearing her mind between them. There was the ghost-maze, the portal, the reanimations, the *danse macabre* that kept her puppets fighting on their strings. No mortal mind with the autonomic distractions of shivering or breathing could have worked so efficiently or so fast, but even for her it was proving too much. Something had to give.

She dispelled the ghost-maze. It was an irrelevancy now that her enemy was at the gates. Then she withdrew the necromantic vigour from her zombie thralls. The Ungols' motions grew torpid until their efforts at attack became slower even than the trolls that soon stamped the zombies into jelly. Ulrika did not bother attempting to reconstruct the mess. A terrific impact shook the entire fort from towers to foundations and the front wall caved in around the charging mass of an ice troll. The ceiling groaned as more of the wall crumbled. Masonry shattered against the troll's diamond-hard hide.

Her warriors were dropping like dolls. She could hear Gustav shouting for order. The young cocksure had discovered a knack for command just too late.

Ulrika focused only on the portal.

She could wait no longer. Damir had failed her and Felix was gone. Had she the time or energy to utter a word she would have cursed him on the names of Nagash and Neferata and every lord and lady of undeath she could recount. She should have made Felix a thrall as she had his nephew and forced her gift through Katerina's unwilling lips. Kin and lover between them would have kept the wayward mortal in line. It was only on Vlad von Carstein's advice that she had not.

A curse on them all!

The troll expanded to fill her view. To her enlightened perceptions it came on as slowly as a glacier, but with the same terrible aura of inevitability.

It came to this.

'Warriors, to me!' she shouted, drawing her sabre and stepping into the shimmering portal.

It was time the Troll King learned what he was dealing with.

FOURTEEN

City of Lost Souls

The Empty Bridge of Praag had been named with typical Kislevite irony. In times not that far removed, it had been the road by which the young poor of Praag had left behind the whitewashed walls and red-tiled manors of the Old Town to become soldiers. And the bridge was never empty. The city had seen too much horror for that, and it was a very brave or very drunk man who would cross it alone at night, for fear of dead warriors with a grudge against those who had not fought in their wars.

The End Times had changed many things. It had not changed that.

With a bleating scream that echoed between the struts of the bridge's frozen grey underbelly, a beastman flew over the side barrier. The fur of its chest was matted with blood as if it had just been hit by a mace. It flailed its arms and legs, wailing in the wish that its gods might suddenly mutate them into wings, until it punched through the ice in a column of black water.

The sounds of an ongoing fight spread thinly downriver – or up, as it might well be – as Felix sank numb fingers into the shingle that banked the river and dragged himself painfully ashore. His shivering sent pebbles skittering away but he didn't even feel it. The fashionable theory amongst the doctors of Altdorf was that a man's bones grew porous with age, explaining thus the fragility and sensitivity to cold airs of older men. Felix would like to have seen some of them try a winter's dip in the Lynsk at any side of forty. The breath in his mouth felt like dragonfire. His body felt as though it had been mummified in bandages that had first been dunked in ice water and frozen. With arms he could neither feel nor properly direct, he managed to flop himself onto his side and curl up into a ball.

Soft flecks of snow tickled his bearded face.

What a glorious way to die, Felix thought miserably. After everything he had been through to make it to Praag it would be just typical for it all to finally end in such ignominious fashion. Unsure why he even bothered, he blinked up into the driving snow.

Lightning sheeted across the black sky. Flashes of purple and green backlit the skyline of Praag's Old Town, the breaks in crumbling minarets and onion domes poorly infilled with snow. Felix's own rapid breathing slowed, enough to hear the river mock him with its susurrant uphill run. Hoots, barks and ululating shrieks echoed from the surrounding buildings.

Felix shuddered and fumbled for his sword, using one shaking hand to force the fingers of the other around its dragonhead hilt. He felt horribly like a prime piece of thawed meat tossed into the Imperial Zoo at feeding time. As he struggled to his feet, a monstrosity of fur and feather with the hindquarters of a mountain lion screeched overhead on eagle wings. Felix gawped up at it as it sailed past, turning to watch the griffon climb the steep spike of rock towards the monstrous citadel of Praag. There, it disappeared amongst the cloud of dark specks that flitted around the formidable-looking towers. Harpies or something worse, Felix thought, in no mind to sugar coat what he was seeing.

The citadel of Praag had always made for grim viewing. Its towers were topped with dragon heads and daemon horns. Grotesques in armour buttressed its walls. Its subjugation by Chaos and occupation by the legions of the Troll King had done little to diminish its mien of misery and neglect.

A shout from the top of the bridge pulled his attention back to the thing that had claimed it.

'Come to Snorri, you skinny beggars. He only has two hands!'

If Felix could feel his legs he could have kicked himself. In his selfish misery, he had completely forgotten about Snorri and the others. Raising a hand to shield his eyes from the snow, he followed the iron clamour of weapons and the bray of beasts to a knot of fighting on the near side. A crude timber and iron shelter had been erected there. Snow mounded high on its roof. A strange banner depicting the eight-pointed star of Chaos Undivided slashed by what looked like the claws of a beast clapped on a sagging pole. The light of a fire brought battling beastmen in and out of shadow.

It was the prospect of a fire more than any thought of running to the Slayers' rescue that coaxed enough strength out of Felix's muscles to move.

By the time Felix and his ice-stiffened limbs had made it onto the bridge it was all over bar the shouting.

'That was Snorri's doom,' said Snorri, standing possessively over the body of a wiry beastman with stubby brown horns and a face that was almost human but for a too-wide mouth filled with cow-like teeth. The near resemblance turned Felix's stomach more than any bull-headed horror ever could. It was as if the Dark Powers were showing just how far into what Felix considered humanity their powers of corruption could reach. To complete the picture it was clad in scrappy Praag wool, with gloves and a chapka hat. There was a hammer in its hand. Felix wished he could say for certain whether this beastman had simply raided the city's dead for its raiment or whether it had once been a man.

The axe wound splitting its chest in two didn't make it any prettier.

'You're mistaken,' Gotrek growled.

'Snorri doesn't think so. It was his head on the end of that hammer.'

'It was *my* doom,' said Gotrek. The firelight painted a threatening growl. 'It is naught but my luck that you should stick your thick skull in the way of it.'

The Slayer clapped blood deeper into his palms and then baked them dismissively over the beastman's hearth. The fire blazed from inside one half of a tin bath that would once have belonged to one of the wealthy lords and ladies of Praag. Felix saw curled scraps of book bindings and animal dung amongst the crackling wisps of wood shavings that had been built up inside. The unsteady blaze was sheltered from the worst of the snow under a wooden pallet that had been covered with a shopfront awning. The weight of snow caused it to sag in through the spacings between the pallet's slats.

Snorri scratched his head, then firmed the already tense grip on his axe and hammer. Veins popped up from his bald head and thickly muscled shoulders.

'You both followed,' said Felix, a shade too sharply and loud to be natural and he kicked himself for his great subtlety, but neither Snorri nor Gotrek appeared to notice the urgency in his tone. Snorri bit his lip, but didn't speak. So he hadn't yet told Gotrek what he'd told Felix. Good.

'Against my better judgement,' said Gotrek.

Snorri simply held Felix with an uncertain gaze, then shook his head and turned away. The dwarf stepped out of the shelter and into the blizzard and, for a moment, Felix thought he was going to carry on going right over to the other side of the bridge. He stopped about two paces out, turned his face into the wind and just stared into it. His eyes were red. Felix let out a relieved breath.

'What's that about?' said Gotrek.

Felix's heart lurched. 'What's what about?'

Gotrek shrugged as if he didn't care, which, on current form, he probably didn't. Felix sidled into the hearth's radius of warmth, a shiver running through his knotted muscles.

'Winters were colder over Karaz-a-Karak,' Gotrek grumbled, cracking his knuckles over the fire. Felix couldn't help but note that even they were criss-crossed with recent scar tissue. 'Would freeze the breath in a man's lungs.'

'Have you seen any sign of Gustav or Ulrika? Or anyone?'

With a brief tilt of the head, Gotrek indicated behind him. Kolya sat there on a three-legged stool, soaked through and shivering uncontrollably. Someone, though Felix could picture neither Gotrek nor Snorri ever doing such a thing, had draped a thick, blood-stained fleece over his shoulders. 'Snorri put that on him,' said Gotrek, as though discussing the mental descent of an elderly relative. 'He's got soft. And not just in the head.'

'Just you three?'

Gotrek grinned unpleasantly. 'You make four.'

Felix pinched his eyes shut. So that was it, then. Ulrika was gone, dead or captured, Gustav was gone, the mission here was as good as over: he had managed to fail everyone that still mattered. Even if he did survive this, how could he go home and look Otto and Annabella in the eye and tell them what happened to Gustav?

When he opened his eyes again Gotrek was still looking at him with that strangely animal detachment. The Slayer had become grimmer over the past year. He was not like Ulrika, but a mirror of her perhaps, one where both sides were in darkness. He scratched his knotted beard with a sigh. Perhaps there was still one person he could try to make amends with, if his former companion would let him.

'I'll not apologise for my decision to take Kat back to Altdorf.'

'Do you think I'd respect you if you tried?'

'Probably not.' Felix had never been particularly good at apologies. If he had been then perhaps he and Ulrika would not have become estranged in the manner that they had. It was too easy to look back on one's own younger self and judge their actions with the benefit of hindsight and regret. 'We both know it was my choice to make, and the right one for Kat.'

'Aye, maybe.'

'And I would have stayed with her,' Felix hastened to add. 'Sigmar knows I thought about taking it all up again and trying to track you down. I missed this, would you believe?' He sighed. 'I would have stayed. It was only because of Max that I came.'

'Rubbish,' said Gotrek, as short and ruthless with his words as he could be with an axe. 'You did it on the honeyed word of a fiend dressed up as a woman you once loved.'

'Ulrika has as much reason to want Max back as anyone.'

'You call her by that name, but that's not who she is any more. If she wants the wizard back at all then it's for her own reasons and I'd wager they differ from yours.' Gotrek grunted. His eyes glittered with malice. 'She drinks the blood of men and draws the dead from their graves before your eyes. What more will it take for you to open them and see?'

Felix took a deep breath, but couldn't argue. Ulrika had played his feelings for her like the strings of a lute. On a logical level he had accepted that from the very outset, but to be told it in no uncertain terms by another made him believe it in a way that he had not allowed himself to do before. Through everything, he had *wanted* to believe that it was still Ulrika underneath.

With one hand he massaged the ache in his heart. He had missed this, not the adventure, certainly not the peril, but this; the camaraderie around the fire, even in the limited, oft-brutally succinct manner in which Gotrek understood it. Just then, a part of him yearned to ask Gotrek about his wife, his daughter, and his shame, but he knew that he never could. Gotrek was still a dwarf and would not take lightly the knowledge of what Snorri had already told him.

'Ulrika was right about one thing, though.'

'She was, was she?'

Felix shrugged. 'It's better to be out here than not. What's the point staying at home, hunting rats and fighting the small battles when the ones that matter are out here?'

'Don't feed me the line, manling.'

'The line?'

'Aye,' said Gotrek, a sigh inflating his barrel chest. 'There's a greater doom around the corner, a bigger monster over the hill. Well I've climbed the hill, and I've killed the monster. The End Times are here and everyone wants me to be some kind of a hero.' The dwarf scowled, thumped his arrowed chest. 'All I want is to find my doom and be left alone.'

'A pity,' said Felix and meant it. Gotrek was worth a thousand men. More.

'Isn't it just,' said Gotrek sourly, then gestured out towards Snorri. He hadn't moved and snow was beginning to pile up around the old dwarf's ankles. 'Let him play the hero. It's what the idiot always wanted, after all. I'd say he's the hero this sorry world deserves.'

'That's bleak, even for you.'

'Those are the times.'

Depressed now as well as chilled to his marrow, Felix turned his back on Gotrek and his almost-rememberer and looked out over the ruins of Praag's Old Town. The city had always been haunted, this part of it in particular, but now it had been conquered too, and by something that had no intention of leaving it as a place in which men might again dwell. The path from the bridge curved past plundered shopfronts and through the rubble-strewn garrison district of the Old Town's east quarter. The Kislevite architecture was buried under a foot or more of snow, marked by the prints of hoof and paw of every manner of beast under the northern sun. There would have been taverns here, skin houses, dice dens, food halls catering to a permanent garrison of thousands. Felix did not need witch sight or the light of Geheimnisnacht to see the ghosts here.

The road wound upwards to a hill, so striking in the centre of a thousand leagues of open steppe, where the gargoyle-encrusted citadel of Praag perched. That was where the Troll King would be. Where Max was. Where Ulrika had wanted them to go. Lights burned from its windows, throwing long, wheeling shadows of the circling harpies over the surrounding districts.

'Do you think that Ulrika might still be alive?'

'No.'

Felix closed his eyes and took a deep breath. He rephrased the question. 'Do you think the Troll King staged the attack on the fort back there to get at Ulrika? He's collecting sorcerers after all and we both saw what Ulrika can do.'

'If so then she's right where she belongs in this nest of Chaos.'

'You're forgetting Max.'

'A dwarf forgets nothing. It simply doesn't matter.' The dwarf leaned forward until his whiskers were perilously close to the fire. 'Kislev has fallen. The Empire will fall next, then all the lands of men and elves one by one. The dwarfholds will fall last.' His face took on a black smile, as though taking this sore point of pride. 'But fall they will and there's nothing that you or I or anyone here can do about it.'

Felix shook his head, taken aback. He would never have believed that Gotrek Gurnisson would just give up, if that's what you could call this nihilistic quest into the enemy's stronghold.

'Snorri will fight the king of the trolls with you, young Felix.'

Gotrek and Felix both looked around as Snorri Nosebiter clattered back inside, his metal mace-leg striking a hollow *thunk* every time it hit stone. There would be no chance of stealth with Snorri with them, but Felix doubted the old Slayer would countenance such a stratagem in any case. Gotrek scowled, glaring at Felix as though suspecting he had been deliberately out-foxed, then bent to pick up his axe. Holding Felix's gaze throughout, he bolted the weapon's chain to his bracer.

'Well, Snorri can't,' said Gotrek.

Snorri looked about to argue but Felix shushed him with a wave. 'There'll be enough trolls for us all, I'm sure.'

'Snorri thinks the Troll King counts at least twice.'

'You can't count, Snorri,' said Gotrek harshly, sniffing the blood that clung to his axe's unwashed blade. He seemed alive again, driven, and Felix felt his skin prickle in response to it. It was as if there was a connection between the pair of them that he could neither see nor taste, but at times like this could almost touch. 'This doom is what *I* was promised.'

Snorri looked questioningly to Felix who could only shrug.

Gotrek started on the castle road. 'Let's kill some monsters.'

Ulrika awoke in darkness and pain. The dark was not an issue, not for one blessed to walk forever by night. Through every gradation of grey, she saw through the bars of her cage that she was in a large cellar. The walls were undecorated stone and curved upwards to form a ceiling. It was one of Duke Enrik's wine cellars. She had never been down here herself of course, she was a boyar's daughter, but the design was similar to one that had been installed at Fort Straghov by her grandfather. She could smell the sour odour of spoiled wine and a few chips of broken glass remained to attest to the chamber's original purpose. There were scores more cages like hers bolted to the walls where once there had been wine racks. All of them were empty bar hers.

Chained to the bars of the wall-facing side opposite her was an immense dirt-brown troll.

Ulrika's reflexive jerk brought a rattle from the manacles over her own wrists. Her hands had been cuffed through a wrought iron bar that appeared to have been bent into a figure of eight shape just for her. What looked like a naval chain fed through it and over her head. She looked up. The chain was thicker than her arm but had somehow been worked through a timber-hitch knot about one of the bars on the roof of the cage. Ulrika pulled down with all her inhuman strength but neither the bar nor the chain gave any quarter. She hissed at the darkness. The front-to-back orientation of the bars on the roof of the cage meant that she could move backwards and forwards if she should for some reason wish to get any closer to that troll, but could get no more than a step to either side without the chain yanking her wrists back.

It wasn't the subtlest dungeon she had ever been held in, nor the most deliberately torturous – that accolade surely belonged to the witch hunters of Altdorf – but it was definitely the sturdiest.

She dropped her knees so her full weight hung from the chain and pulled down until the pain of the iron bar digging through her wrists threatened to black her out. In frustration and spite, she rattled the chain and cursed in Kislevite. Her native tongue was made for such language. With a slowly spreading sense of fear, she looked at the bar around her wrists. Despite all her strength she hadn't even been able to make it groan.

What kind of a monster could shape something like this, and with enough control to not simply crush her hands inside of it? Some kind of machine, she told herself with certainty. She had witnessed wonders enough during her adventures with Felix and his dwarf friends to know that any marvel was possible.

These thoughts were distractions though, she knew, and brief ones at that. Captivity presented unique horrors to one with eternity to contemplate and a heightened capacity for thought with which to do it. The gifts of the Arisen could at times seem like curses. Bitterly, she tried to remember how she had got here. The last thing she remembered was the ice troll bearing down on her, and then...

Nothing.

She clutched her head. It felt like the memory had been beaten out of her, but that seemed unlikely. She knew from experience that it took an implausible amount of violence to do that kind of damage to one of her kind. She shook her head. It did not matter how she had got here, only that she got out and fulfilled her master's mission. She snarled.

She needed blood. She had almost exhausted herself trying to work so much magic during the trolls' attack and what little she had to spare had gone towards healing wounds she had no recollection of receiving. Her ribs and backbone both ached as though they had recently been broken and one of her legs was abominably sore, though Ulrika thought it was just bruising. Possibly the worst however was her left eye, which seemed to have been crushed and was now knitting itself together with such agonising slowness that had Ulrika's hands not been shackled she would have been tempted to tear it from her face to grow again once she had properly fed.

There were few mortals with the strength or the sadism to realise that there were degrees of pain that it took immortality to taste.

More hungrily than she liked, Ulrika eyed the troll on the other side of the cage. The mossy, worm-ridden monster regarded her placidly. Its pulse was so slow that its rhythm in her ears was almost hypnotic. Swaying in time to the beat, she licked her lips. Her fangs pricked her tongue. Was what she was contemplating even possible? The part of her that was still thinking clearly enough to be sick with herself sincerely hoped that it was not.

'So soon.'

The voice rumbled from the darkness immediately behind her. It was hard and inhuman and as deep as a grave. Ulrika did not think she had ever heard two words loaded with such derogation and loathing. Ulrika twisted through her hanging chains so that she was facing the front of the cage. On the other side of a rough floorspace was another row of empty cages. In the gloom in between, a pair of dull amber eyes glowed. A rush of sulphurous breath washed from a mouth crusted with jagged tusks as it split implausibly into a grin.

'Others of your race resisted longer. You are weak, vampire.'

Ulrika tried to shunt aside her hunger and focus. The speaker's heart was cold and slow, enough to make it difficult for Ulrika to make out its beat through the mountainous wall of his chest. Looking at him, it was an effort to disregard the monster before her eyes and see the speaker for what he was: a troll that spoke. He watched her, waiting for a reaction. His eyes were deep with hard cunning.

'Throgg,' said Ulrika. 'The Troll King.'

'Von Carstein sent you to my city,' said the Troll King, leaning in until his tusks were sawing into the bars. Ulrika rattled deeper into the cage and bared her fangs. 'Why?'

Ulrika glared up at the Troll King hatefully. She understood the stakes in play here, more than she had shared with Felix or even poor Damir. She was a Kislevite, after all, she had just spent the past months riding through the ashes of her country, but with every fibre of her unnatural being she wished that Count von Carstein could have found an ally in the north more stable than Throgg.

'Why do you think? The Auric Bastion prevents him from speaking with you by magical means.'

'Men are weak,' Throgg replied, looking over her buckled armour with a sneer. Ulrika returned the inspection. She still could not remember how she had got here, but the sight of the mineral-spiked and mace-like fists of her captor gave her a powerful suspicion. 'Von Carstein sends you here to speak for him? Then speak, pretty thing. Impress me with your clever words.'

The Troll King drew back from the bars, ceding the floor. He wrapped himself in a tattered red cloak, concealing the many mouths that silently opened and closed from his mutant torso. His head withdrew into the crystalline mane of warpstone that bulged from his shoulders. Ulrika licked thin blood over her dried lips.

'The war goes poorly for the Empire.'

'Of course it does,' Throgg cut in, his deep voice overpowering hers. 'You ask soft flesh to stand before the tide of Chaos.'

Ulrika bit her tongue, trying to ignore Throgg's goading and concentrate on the message that Vlad had risked her life to deliver. It was getting harder to think, harder just to speak without a snarl. The beast was out. It basked under the glow of the Chaos moon and it hungered.

'My master implores you to move against Archaon's forces before it is too late. You have strength enough.'

'Strength?' Throgg growled, raising his hands and looking down at them. He clenched them into fists. 'Yes, I have strength. Is that all you see here, vampire? Strength? Am I a dumb hammer waiting the guiding arm of Sylvania?'

What was the brute talking about? Ulrika tried to think, but her talents lay with swords rather than words.

'It is the hubris of men to see their own destiny in all things. Von

Carstein. The Everchosen. Dead men. Exalted men. In their skin they are all still men. This…' Throgg's eyes shone as he reached out to clasp the bars of Ulrika's cage. The iron groaned under his titan's grip. '…will be the Age of the Beast.'

'You are mad if you think you can stand against Archaon alone.'

'Perhaps,' said Throgg, stabbing the crown on his brow with a fingernail-like shard of dark crystal. 'Or perhaps I know more than you.' Then he chuckled, the warning cascade of rocks down a mountainside. 'But one day I will thank von Carstein for sending such a passable warrior to my side.'

'I would sooner take a walk in the sun than serve you.'

'All the beasts of Chaos are mine to rule. What are you, vampire, if not that? What do you think became of those other vampires of Praag?'

Ulrika did her utmost to stand straight, to look haughty despite the chains that lay draped across her shoulders and the fangs that burned like acid from her gums. She remembered well enough the petty, ineffectual Lahmian sisterhood of Praag, and falling under the yoke of a monster like Throgg was all that their near-sighted infighting had earned them. Ulrika was better than that. She was a warrior, a Kislevite, a Troll Country boyarina. Chaos was the source of her strength, but she was its master, not its puppet.

'I have friends that will come for me. Friends you would do well not to cross.'

'The poet and the…' Throgg gripped the cage in one hand and leaned closer. His voice dropped and his eyes grew wary. Ulrika caught an odd scent on the Troll King's breath. She knew too little of his race to be sure, but an instinctual understanding, some universal character, called it fear. '…the dwarf with the axe. Yes, I know them. There is not a monster in Praag that does not, in whatever way it is capable, fear the name "Gurnisson".'

'Then release me,' said Ulrika, the scent of weakness drawing her forwards. So Gotrek and Felix had both survived the attack. She could not imagine how they had achieved it, but she should not have been surprised. Her chain rattled as she drew herself straight and looked up into the towering horror of the Troll King. 'Let me go. And consider my master's request.'

'You overreach. I have marked your friends' approach and my most powerful beast awaits them. It is an immortal of pre-history, a relic of the Battle for Urszebya and the Year That No One Forgets.' The Troll King pulled away and swept his mauled old cloak over his shoulders. He banged his fist across the bars of the opposite cage and, in response, a door opened at the far end of the cellar and the heartbeats of a band of beastmen entered. He turned back with a grin. 'There are monsters here, Ulrika, that even Gurnisson has yet to face.'

'How–'

'Do I know your name? Even for a human, you exceed yourself with your sense of self-worth.'

The Troll King waited as the beastmen came to him. They were the scrawny, slightly more intelligent breed that called themselves ungors, the retinue of a larger beastman with the look of a shaman. His eyes were flat onyx disks in a hoary, tattooed face. Sweeping stag antlers bore eldritch runes made out in woad, scattered amongst symbols that looked like little more than cave art. The shaman and the Troll King held a whispered conference. Ulrika supposed it logical that Throgg would require lieutenants. It was not as if a troll could follow instructions.

Throgg returned his attention to Ulrika, a glimmer of amusement in his dull eyes. 'I have a riddle for you, Ulrika: king without a kingdom, general without an army, lover without a swain, warrior without a soul.' His expression became hard, the stone that it was. 'Do you not care to ask after those you brought with you into my city?'

Ulrika yanked at her chains, achieving nothing more than a metallic rattle and a smirk on the face of the Troll King.

'It has been a long time since my army has tasted untainted meat. You are with me now, Ulrika, and soon you and I will conquer an entire world that our future slaves will call *Troll Country*.'

'Release me,' Ulrika hissed, feeling her dark soul floating without an anchor on a rising sea of Chaos. She wrapped her chains around her wrists and glared at Throgg. 'And release Max to me.'

'He still speaks of you. He must have loved you greatly.'

'Bring him to me,' Ulrika demanded, to a rumble of laughter.

'He is mine, Ulrika, as you are,' said Throgg, turning at last to leave. 'Now feel a monster's true loneliness.'

The harpies that flocked the Square of Heroes were agitated. Hundreds of them gathered on the citadel's battlements to battle for roosts with the resident gargoyles. Excrement dashed the gothic stonework. The scrape of clawed feet on stone and the cries of their shrill proto-human voices echoed around the statue-lined square. From the window at the back of his cage, Max Schreiber counted a distorted face or a flap of fleshy wings every few seconds. It was as if every last one of the beasts in Praag had come here.

'Man-thing,' came the hiss from the cage opposite. Max tried to ignore it. 'Man-thing!'

'I do not converse with monsters like you.'

A nervous titter cut through the space between them. 'This that comes from you. You are the worst of us all.'

Wincing at the bruises that coloured his entire back and shoulders, Max pulled his gaze from the window. The skaven warlock stood pressed to the bars of its cage, the floor strewn with leftovers from the various mechanical apparatus hoarded away in the far corner. The headless torso of its 'specimen' lay slack in its chains. The head sat on a copper plate with a pair of tines connecting its cranium to a humming, wind-up device that delivered irregular electrical shocks. Watching its mouth chomp and its brow flicker with every pulse was far from the most disturbing thing that Max had been forced to witness of his neighbour's efforts.

'What do you mean by that?'

The warlock clapped its paws in a human parody of delight, but chose to ignore the question or perhaps save it for later use on its own twisted terms. It pointed towards the window. 'What happens out there, man-thing?'

'Nothing that concerns you, I'm sure.'

'Matters. Matters.' The ratman jittered sideways, looked over both shoulders, then clasped the bars of his cage in trembling paws. 'I smell more man-things. Yes-yes. Man-things being fed to the bird-beasts.'

Max closed his eyes. How many men had died when Praag fell, or Kislev city? How could Max be expected to grieve for a handful more?

Blowing hot air onto chapped and swollen fingers, Max returned his attention to his own subject. The hulking stone troll bolted to the wall of his cell returned his regard with dead eyes and the hollow murmur of a sigh. Trolls might have been slow but they were not impossible to train and this one had long ago learned that movement was impossible. With the remarkable adaptability of its race, its limbs were already beginning to atrophy. Its breathing was slow and rhythmic. It had no concept of what was about to happen to it.

'Man-thing!' the warlock hissed. 'The king will not thank you for this.'

'I am not listening,' said Max. 'You only hope to distract me because you know that tomorrow it will be you strung up for the harpies.'

The ratman fell silent, but even through the bitter cold Max's weak human nose could smell the sour odour of the warlock's fear. It spoke half-lies and nonsense as was the way of its kind. They both knew that it would be Max Schreiber who gave the Troll King his general.

It would be Max that got to return home.

'Did I mention that I'm getting far too old for this?' Felix muttered, peering out from behind the marble statue of an unnamed kossar at the outer ring of the Square of Heroes.

It was impossible to pick out a patch of snowy sky without a harpy shrieking through it. Hundreds of the creatures flocked over the battlements and the monstrously carved minarets of the citadel. At least twice as many were in flight, flapping, bawling and diving onto each other's perches to send others startled and screaming back into the air in sprays of disturbed snow. Despite the lumpen streaks of brown and white droppings that lashed their gargantuan frames, the trolls that squatted amongst the inner ring of more illustrious statues could not have been more unmoved by the pandemonium that swarmed above their heads. Felix counted ten of the heavy, brooding creatures. Fifteen. Twenty.

He stopped counting. There came a point where additional information became distinctly unhelpful and as far as Felix was concerned that point had been passed a few hundred harpies back.

Within the inner ring, a gibbet had been fashioned out of the statue of a hideously mutated warrior that Felix had to remind himself had once been the legendary war leader Tzar Alexis. A huge bonfire burned in a pit before it. A chain of beastmen passed what looked like books, paintings and wooden furnishings from as far away as Nippon and Araby to throw onto the blaze. The light and warmth brought low rumbles of contentment from the trolls. Occasionally, one would shuffle through the snow to be nearer to the fire. More of the beastmen worked around the monolithic monsters, swinging nooses over Tzar Alexis's many arms as more of their kin emerged through the snow shrouding the inner ring of statues leading a coffle of stripped and trussed human captives. The men were beaten and submissive. Their bare flesh was so blue that they no longer shivered. As they approached the fire, a group of beastmen with man-skin drums and bone horns tried to strike up a beat that could be heard over the harpy screech and failed.

'How old are you, young Felix?' said Snorri. Snow flecked the bristles of the old Slayer's head, giving him a thinning crop of wispy white hair. He stood with his back to the kossar statue and a determined grin on his face.

'Old enough that I think you should stop calling me *young Felix*.'

'Don't let that beard go to your head,' said Gotrek, looking across from his own hiding place behind the next statue along, placing him quite deliberately with Felix between him and Snorri. 'You're not a day over fifty.'

'And I don't expect to make it there either,' said Felix, offering a silent prayer to Sigmar to prove him wrong, then rolling against the stone at his back to take another peek into the square.

The captives were being led to the other side of the bonfire where Felix could no longer make them out. He squinted through the flames, watching as the beastmen fed wrists and ankles into nooses and hoisted bound men up into the air where they wriggled like caterpillars from Tzar Alexis's arms. The beastmen's spears discouraged the ever-circling mobs of harpies. From the picked bones that littered the square, Felix didn't think the beastmen's protection was going to be permanent.

Felix could still see more harpies flying in, beating hard against the snow, drawn by the excitement of what promised to be a feeding frenzy. Felix cursed his rotten luck. It looked like whatever slim hope they had had of making it to the citadel in one piece had just been whittled down to next to nothing.

'The Goromadny Heights swarm with these creatures,' said Kolya from what Felix still considered to be his customary position at Gotrek's left side. Barring the occasional uninduced shudder, he appeared largely recovered from his dunking in the Lynsk. 'They are scavengers and are never more wary than when there is food that another might steal. I think someone has set a trap for us.'

'Bring it,' Gotrek growled under his breath.

'Who even knows we're coming?' said Felix.

Kolya shrugged, a gesture that was strengthening Felix's urge to punch the man every time he saw it, then pointed around the outer square of statues. The route was steeped in shadows cast by the bonfire and circumvented the interior of the square altogether. 'I doubt we will make it.' The Kislevite glanced at Snorri who, watching harpies swoop overhead and miscounting aloud, was witlessly oblivious to the slight. 'But Lord Winter is on our side. If we go slowly and carefully then we might be able to make it around them.'

Felix peered as far into the blizzard as he could see, the point where the statues started to become ethereal and impossible to distinguish from whatever monster might lie in wait for them hidden out of sight. Fear churned in his gut. He kissed the hardness in his gloved finger where he wore his ring, a curious pre-battle jitter that he had never felt the need to indulge in before now, and then closed his fingers over Karaghul's dragonhead hilt. A hot glow prickled up his arm and pushed the fear aside. Without quite realising he was doing it, he probed the shades of the distant statues for a monster he did not even know was there. His heart was beating hard with anticipation, filling his veins with warmth and strength. Clearly Karaghul knew something that he didn't. Not for the first time, he wondered if the old Templar blade was more trouble than it was worth.

'All right,' said Felix, more eagerness in his voice than he liked the sound of, searching Gotrek's face for approval and getting it in a curt nod. 'We'll go around.'

Keeping low and his hands on the statue's back, Felix edged out into the open and tried to track the seething mass of harpies in order to watch for an opening. He was beginning to think that he would have as much luck just going for it and trusting to luck when a terrific lowing went up from the gathered beastmen. Felix flinched back into cover as the ominous cry resounded between the statues and the low ceiling of snow and the roosting harpies flapped noisily to flight.

Suddenly, the air was filled with screams and beating wings and Felix watched as the beastmen strung up the last of the captives. The man had been strung by his ankles so that his length of blond hair trailed through the thin snow underneath him. His naked skin was so white it was only the heavy bruising and interlocking mesh of blue veins that kept him from vanishing from sight into the swirl of falling snow. His hanging body pivoted around to reveal his face. The man's straight jaw was broken and his face was puffy, his blue eyes had been sunk into his face by black pits of bruising, but it was still a face that Felix always expected to see when he found himself in front of a mirror.

It was Gustav Jaeger.

Felix gripped the statue in front of him, edging further out, only realising how long he'd been staring when a painful shriek from directly above forced him to look away. He turned his face up into the snow and met the horribly distended, feminine features of a slavering harpy looking back down. On instinct, Felix stabbed his sword at it but it flapped out of reach across the statue's shoulders where it hopped and crowed like a warning bell with wings. Felix swore loudly, his stomach dropping at the onrushing rustle of hundreds of fleshy wings.

'Very careless, young Felix,' said Snorri happily.

FIFTEEN

Square of Heroes

Felix threw himself flat on the ground and rolled under the statue of the kossar. A harpy bombed through the air where he had just been standing and scratched the cobblestones with its claws. It turned to scream at him, hideous features twisted into a bestial mask of outrage, but didn't stop, sweeping past and joining the growing flock that filled the sky above Felix's position. Felix's shoulder struck the statue's heel and he drew himself under the protection of its legs. Struggling to bring up his sword in that half-hunched position, he looked back.

Gotrek and Snorri hadn't moved from where they had been standing. Thrashing black shapes enveloped them both with a screen of wings and talons, but despite the harpies' advantage of numbers, both Slayers were continuing to mow through anything that came close enough for them to hit. Gotrek's axe killed so many so fast the blade was almost invisible but for the ruin it caused to rain out of the sky. Snorri fought like a dervish with his axe and hammer, reducing flying monsters to pulped corpses and even letting fly with his mace-leg more out of raw enthusiasm than in any expectation of hitting the fast moving creatures. Felix couldn't spot Kolya, but as he searched an arrow shot out from one of the nearby statues to drop a harpy that had been about to attack Snorri from behind. A few of them, smelling the two humans hiding amongst the statuary, peeled off from the attack on the dwarfs in search of easier prey.

In the instant he had, Felix considered his position. Would it be best to stay where he was with the statue's legs guarding his flanks and eliminating the threat of an attack from above, or to meet them in the open where he at least had a chance of effectively wielding his sword? Unfortunately, the sheer speed of his assailants made his mind up for him. A black mass of them mobbed the kossar statue before Felix could even think about moving.

Felix couldn't even hear himself cry out as everything he had previously been able to see and hear devolved into a maelstrom of teeth and claws and furiously beating wings that flooded the cramped space of Felix's shelter with their unwashed animal stink. Felix shielded his face with his arm. Claws like fish knives raked through his mail. The armour absorbed the worst of what came his way, but there were enough of them that some, by pure chance, managed to rip at bare skin or tear weakened links from his mail. Felix stabbed back with his sword as he was tugged this way and that by whatever frenzied creature managed to get a grip on the sorry remnants of his cloak, but from his crouched position he could get neither the power nor the necessary speed to hurt his attackers. He cursed. The statue reverberated to the relentless storm of wingbeats. The harpies were practically fighting each other to flush him out.

Noticing that there were fewer of the creatures on the opposite side of the statue to the one he had entered from, Felix made the short crabwise shuffle that way. Leading with Karaghul like a lance, he impaled one harpy between the ribs and managed to send another squawking skywards after he pulled his sword free and returned its scream with a fraught one of his own into its misaligned face. Wincing at the bruises that reminded Felix all too graphically of the torn arteries and severed limbs that his armour had spared him from, Felix backed into the statue and brought his sword into a guard. He had a moment to catch his breath so he took it, too battle wise to let it pass. He kicked back with his heel at the marble behind him. This way at least, his back would be covered and he could give the harpies something in return.

He heard their screeches from the other side of the statue as they belatedly realised that he was gone and clawed at each other in a bid to climb. Through the snow, Felix saw the beastmen gathering. They had spears and halberds and their musicians were drumming them into a loose formation facing his way. Others were running around, apparently trying to goad the slumbering trolls into action. One of the monsters snarled, bit off the speartip thrust into its face with a splintering crunch, and started unsteadily to rise. A thickset beastman with a large set of stag-like antlers and russet robes that reached the snowy ground directed them from the foot of Tzar Alexis's statue. It leaned on a black wooden staff, trussed men hanging around it, Felix's nephew included, and pointed furiously towards Felix.

The rifling of freezing air through furious wings pulled Felix's attention back to the point of his sword. Harpies spilled around the statue at his back and over it and Felix was fighting for his life all over again.

'Gotrek,' he shouted, somehow finding the breath as his sword slashed and parried faster than he could think. Harpies thrashed for him just outside his guard and there was no way he could fend them all off forever. 'Do you see the beastmen, Gotrek?'

'Aye, I see them,' came Gotrek's voice from somewhere within the onslaught. 'They can wait their turn. This Chaos vermin can't quench my axe's thirst.'

'They have Gustav and the others.'

In a storm of panicked figures, Gotrek strode out from behind the ring of statues. His back looked like it had been mauled by a bear and a full hand of claws had scratched his scalp from front to back along the line of his crest. One of the arrows in his chest had been gouged out, leaving a pit of red-soaked gristle behind. Judging by the manner in which the Slayer's axe dismembered Felix's attackers, the injury had done little to diminish his strength.

'For the little one then,' said Gotrek. 'She always hated beastmen.'

'For Kat,' Felix agreed, feeling his ring dig into his finger as he tightened his grip on Karaghul.

Gotrek marched through the scattering harpies with a gleam in his one good eye. The loosely ranked beastmen in his path issued a mighty holler and thrust their spears into the air. 'Straight down the middle. I'll take the troll. Kill as many as we can.'

'That doesn't sound like something you spent a long time thinking about.'

With a dark scowl, Gotrek brandished his axe. 'It's got me this far.'

Felix fell into stride with him as the dwarf broke into a run. He picked out a lanky, goat-bearded beastman just off the centre of the front rank for his target and drew his blade back. Gotrek and his axe hit the beastman formation like a rolling boulder, arms and heads and bodies in shattered armour thrown out around him. Following in the wake of that force of destruction, it would have been hard for Felix to put a foot wrong. His sword sliced down the lanky beastman's chest. Felix felt flesh and muscle open and organs spill and then he was moving on, in amongst the madness of battle.

Blades and weapon butts lashed in from every side and Felix parried wildly. He could feel blood drying in his beard, and sweat poured down his face despite the snow. Every callus in his hands seemed to ring with the impact of his blade on others and if not for his gloves, doused with sweat though they were, Felix felt certain that he would have lost his sword some time ago.

Keeping his guard true and his eyes open, Felix tried to keep the statue of Tzar Alexis and Gustav in sight. It would be too easy otherwise to get lost in the melee and forget what he was aiming for. He saw that Gotrek, true to the dwarf's word, was carving open the beastmen's ranks to get at the troll. Felix shook his head in wonder. He had thought Ulrika to be Gotrek's equal in strength, but somehow the Slayer made the slaughter of dozens look easy. Whatever stood in his way died until, at the bleating insistence of their shaman beneath the statue, they fell back from him and left him to the troll. Elsewhere, Felix spotted Snorri Nosebiter in amongst the fray. Where Gotrek was a single-minded and brutally efficient bringer of death, Snorri scattered it around like a careless painter with an overfull brush. The dwarf bludgeoned his way gleefully into the already wavering beastmen with all the crushing zeal that had been so wasted on the swift-dodging harpies.

Felix caught the downward stroke of a beastman's halberd, pushed it past him using its own downward momentum, and then kneed the warrior in the gut. Its breath wheezed out from its lungs and Felix moved past. He was too hemmed in to think about finishing it. Another was on him before he made a step, but Felix could tell its animal heart wasn't in it. Felix could see in its eyes that it hadn't been expecting this when it had formed up with its brethren against two dwarfs and a man. A human regiment, suitably motivated and well led, might have held up even against the losses the Slayers had piled up, but beastmen were never soldiers. They were forest reavers and night terrors, opportunists, scavengers that followed in the wake of the Kurgan armies. They were little better than wolves and when Snorri cracked open the shaman's skull with his hammer they broke as a herd, cloven hooves clattering over the flagstones as they fled back into the sweeping snows towards the citadel.

Felix stifled a disbelieving smile. Against his own sound expectation he was still alive. The trolls were largely still sat around the fire where he had first spied them, the harpies were craven vultures, and the beastmen were a rabble that broke at the first hint of a stand-up fight. The Troll King had built his kingdom on shingle. For the first time since he had jumped into the Lynsk, Felix actually began to believe that they might prevail. In the moment it took him to recover his breath and mop the cold sweat from his brow, Gotrek beheaded the one moving troll and then kicked the severed head into the fire. It went up in a shooting geyser of sparks and then shot out the other side where it left a charred trail in the snow until it lost impetus, a crisped skull swiftly cooling as the snow buried it.

Snorri meanwhile limped furiously after the fleeing beastmen, shaking his weapons above his head and shouting insults until it became obvious that the beastmen weren't coming back.

'They'll be back once they've got their friends,' said Gotrek, straining through clenched teeth as he squatted underneath the dead troll's headless shoulders and heaved.

'Good,' said Snorri. 'Most of them never even got to fight Snorri, and Snorri doesn't think that's fair.'

Gotrek merely grunted as, in an inconceivable feat of raw strength, he somehow performed the work of a team of dwarfs with a pit pony and rollers and dragged the troll's torso up onto his shoulders. He panted for a second, swollen muscles quivering, then rolled the body into the bonfire. It burned with even more vigour than had its head, throwing out thick black smoke that stank of burned flesh.

Shooting a glance back and around in a hopeless bid to track the harpies circling in and out of the snow, Felix hurried around the bonfire to the foot of Tzar Alexis's statue where the men of Gustav's regiment had been left to hang. Just looking at their naked bodies, blue and goose-bumped in the snow, made his own skin want to shiver. The echoing shriek of a harpy watching from somewhere amidst the encircling statues came as a stark reminder of the fate that these men had been intended for. He felt sick just thinking about it and tried hard not to, his hatred of the Troll King and the beasts that served him growing with every scream, crunch and tear he could not quench with happier thoughts. From a different direction came a staccato screech. It was only a matter of time before hunger and short memories triumphed over their fear of Gotrek's axe.

Whatever respite they'd earned was going to be brief.

He made a line for Gustav. His nephew hung upside down from an arm of living marble that, even during the course of the fight, seemed to have clenched into a fist around the rope that noosed his ankles. Caught from the corner of Felix's eye, the look of hunger on the great Tzar's face was sufficiently lifelike to make Felix's guts clench. It was an effort to turn his back on it and wrap his arms around Gustav's naked chest.

Damn it, his nephew felt like ice! Setting himself to bear Gustav's weight, Felix tried to raise the young man up and tease his feet back through the noose. The young man groaned as Felix's arms tightened over ribs that were, at best, horribly bruised. The rope danced back and forth on the end of his foot. Felix felt his thighs begin to burn. Tzar Alexis seemed to be licking his lips.

'Gotrek. Help me.'

The Slayer stomped over.

'I've got him,' said Felix. 'Cut the rope.'

Felix tightened his hold as Gotrek's axe flashed past his face and

Gustav's unsupported weight dropped onto him. It took a few seconds for a combination of Felix's embrace and the bonfire to warm Gustav enough for him to start shivering and when it came it came as hard and sudden as a fit. Felix held onto him, fearful that if he let go now his nephew was going to tear something.

Gotrek tossed over the clothes and – trust Gotrek to think of it – the halberd of a dead beastman before heading off to cut down the rest of Gustav's men. Felix called thanks after him and quickly tried to get Gustav dressed. Tending Kat through some of her worse days had given him experience enough in how to clothe another, but holding his shivering nephew down at the same time wasn't making it easy. After what felt like an unbearable length of time with the volume of the harpy cries increasing by the second, Felix managed to pull a patchwork jerkin of colourful Ungol wool over Gustav's arms.

It was then that Felix noticed the bite on his nephew's neck. Two marks, a sore-looking red with recent scabs puncturing partially healed scars.

Felix thought the Lynsk had left him cold. What he felt now turned the blood in his veins to ice water and sent shivers through the back of his head.

What had Ulrika done?

He was being irrational, he told himself. He had known full well what Ulrika was and what she was forced to do to sustain her unlife, but seeing the evidence on Gustav's skin was something else. Felix's own kin. Felix's blood! Doubtless Ulrika would argue he had been a willing vessel for a noble cause and Felix had certainly fantasised about such surrender often enough over the past weeks to sympathise with that point of view, but how could any man or woman consent with their free will corroded by pleasure? Ulrika had herself told him that those from whom a vampire drank were little better than slaves. After the battle of Kurzycko and their conversation on the oblast he had assumed that meant she would feed only on the enemy. He'd been stupid and blind.

Gotrek was right. Ulrika was a monster.

But there wasn't time for an 'I told you so.'

'Come on, Gustav, get up.'

His nephew's teeth gave an urgent chatter as, leaning into Felix's chest, he managed to get himself upright and stay there. He was appallingly pale, anaemic even, cosseting his bruised ribs with a hunchback stance and leaning a large proportion of his weight onto his newfound halberd. Even the hang of long hair over his shoulders looked tired.

Turning to check on Gotrek and Snorri, Felix saw that all of Gustav's men were down now. Some were in an even worse way than their captain, but a few of the toughest looking were in amongst the beastmen with the two dwarfs gathering gear and weapons and – Felix couldn't help but notice – a few valuables for themselves and their mates. The men were gathering themselves into a block, for warmth as much as mutual protection, but even as Felix watched a harpy dived for the centre of the formation in a snap of clawed feet only to be warded off at the very last second by an upward-thrusting spear. One man lost an untied chapka hat rather than a head, and the harpy wheeled about for another pass with a frustrated shriek.

More of them were drawing in. Those still in the air were circling ever closer. The free company were dead men walking and the beasts could smell it.

'Everybody stay close. Keep your spears high.'

'Here comes the real thing!' Gotrek roared.

Emerging from the blizzard between the rank of statues like daemons from a portal came the beastmen, ominous black shapes with curling horns and spiked shields. They clutched their spears and snorted, fierce in numbers and with their castle at their back. The clap of their cloven feet on the flagstones became a dirge. With a curse, Felix made ready. Beastman armies, once broken, did not generally rally this quickly. He had thought they would have more time.

'Snorri thinks we should meet them halfway,' said Snorri.

'I think we're good enough where we are,' said Felix, with what felt like a glorious overstatement even to one accustomed to composing propaganda for the Reiksmarshal.

'I agree with the manling,' said Gotrek. Felix lowered his sword a fraction and turned to his former companion. Clearly certain death had affected his hearing in some way. Gotrek shrugged and jerked a finger back over his shoulder. 'Why move now that that lot are starting to pull themselves together?'

Before he could stop himself, Felix glanced in that direction, a trapdoor swinging open under his gut.

Sniffing heavily at cold air into which the reek of burned troll flesh had been effectively frozen in, a mammoth troll mantled in thick brown fur gave a tremorous sigh and opened eyes like agates. Felix backed away, a reflexive instinct, as the troll unfurled ape-like arms and then smashed its knuckles through the cobbles in front of where it was sitting with a sound like a brace of cannon misfiring in unison. Then, with frightening speed for something so massive and, mere moments ago, sedentary, the troll lurched upright. Felix swept his sword around with a cry, a sound weakly parroted by the free company as they too saw the unfolding monsters around the light of the bonfire.

Those gains that he had been so proud of – all they had achieved was to get himself surrounded!

Feeling a tug on his cloak, Felix glanced back over his shoulder.

Gustav let go the tattered wool strip and added the second hand to that which already leaned heavily into his halberd. He shivered in his coloured rags, pried open chattering teeth.

'Is General Straghov with you? We... failed her.'

'Don't worry about Ulrika,' said Felix with conviction, angling his sword to guard both Gustav and himself from the advancing beastmen as Gotrek and Snorri's arguments over the trolls grew increasingly ill-tempered. 'She's doing better than we are.'

Hunger cramped Ulrika's belly, hunched her double until the chains that shackled her wrists to the ceiling pulled taut. Snapping at the loop of naval chain that lay across her shoulder, she closed her mouth over the thick iron ring and sucked. Her fangs rooted uselessly over the surface, but the bitter iron taste and the sensation of feeding seemed to fool her stomach. Her pangs calmed, enough for her to realise what she was doing and pull away, spitting rust from her lips and pitching up against the bars of her cage with a clangour of metal.

Was this what she had been reduced to? She refused to give Throgg the satisfaction.

Dimly, she became conscious of the violence being done on the surface. Stone and starvation could not block out the terror of so many beating hearts. In fact the hunger only made her senses more acute, sharpened the huntress's instincts and heightened the already formidable vampiric drive to endure. It was Felix, she was certain. He had tried to save her before and, lost cause though he must have known it was, had been trying ever since. He would try again. He had always been a hopeless romantic.

Ulrika wondered whether it might be best to wait for him to rescue her – he *could* still save her – but dismissed it with a snarl that shook her entire frame with its fury. She was not some Bretonnian maiden who had to await her questing knight. She was a warrior queen of the undying oblast and she would not put herself at another's mercy: not Throgg, and not Gotrek or Felix either.

Her gut beginning to clench once again, she glanced up through the curtain of chains to the troll bound to the opposite wall of the cage. Her eyes shone in the pitch dark. She shuffled forward, chains shadowing her like crows over a seer of Morr. Its somnolent heartbeat seemed to draw her in. Her gaze locked onto its neck and she licked fangs so sensitive that it hurt.

She was hungry.

'Gustav, behind me!'

Felix backed into his nephew, pushing him bodily out of the path of a beastman spear and batting the weapon's shaft aside on the flat of his sword. He wove under a questing knife, kicked the wielder in the shins, and then rose up on Gustav's other side in time to block a strike intended for his nephew's back. The impact rang up Felix's arms. His shoulders felt like he'd just come off shift from a dwarf mine. His lungs burned. Had he really spent the past twenty years doing this? With a weary grunt, he flicked aside the beastman's blade and ran the creature through.

Beastmen flooded the square, filling it with breathy, braying cries, stamping hooves, and a smell whose only earthly analogue Felix could conjure was wet horse. Gustav's free company was already outnumbered at least five to one and more of the beastmen were charging in between the statues that stood between them and the castle.

The men were as weak and slow as Gustav himself and most had been left to defend themselves using weapons with which they had received little or no training. Only their discipline had prevented them being overrun in the first seconds, tightly blocked ranks serving them in lieu of shields and armour. They probably now wished they had spent as much time in Badenhof drilling as they had spent drinking Gustav's wine, but no free company in the world could have expected to end up in a situation like this. Arrows zipped through the fray from somewhere behind them, taking out beastmen and harpies faster than Felix would have thought possible for a single archer. Felix had forgotten about Kolya amidst the action. Clearly the Kislevite was still ensconced somewhere amidst the outer ring of statues. Still, men were dropping like an ice troll's winter scales, and the harpies, against whom the men had no defence with the beastmen at their front, were picking them off at will.

Felix parried another blow meant for one of him or Gustav, he had ceased trying to distinguish, and then ducked as a harpy dropped straight down out of the sky a few feet away before flinging out its wings and shooting towards his head like a bullet. The creature swept overhead, the clawed tip of its wing missing Gustav by the length of a close shave, and tore a free company man from his feet. His savaged corpse dropped to the ground a few seconds later on the opposite side of the company's formation. Licking gore from its stretched and fang-lined snout, the harpy glided higher and then swooped back around.

Desperately, Felix cast around for a glimpse of Gotrek or Snorri amidst the chaos. If any of them were to have even the slimmest chance of getting out of this then it undoubtedly lay with the two Trollslayers. He couldn't see them amongst the brutish beast shapes that surrounded them, but he could hear them somewhere off to the right where Felix had last seen them both charging towards the big woolly troll. From that direction came the shrill, overlapping tone of beastman screams, accompanied by the percussive basso of the troll, visible as shaggy head and shoulders above the horns and speartips that bristled from the surrounding combatants. It made the ground tremble and Felix's bowels with it.

'Come to my axe!'

'Come to Snorri's!'

Felix made out the chomp of starmetal on flesh and saw a beastman physically lifted into the air by a rising blow, but before he could consider a means to reach them he was again forced to defend himself. Gustav summoned a cry and struck his halberd into the leather gardbrace of a thick-necked bruiser of a beastman. Sapped of any strength behind it, the blade sucked into the cured leather and caught there. The boar-headed beastman snorted, driving a hot dragon-like breath of rancid steam into Gustav's face as it shrugged the halberd from its shoulder armour and brought up its own top-heavy falchion for the kill.

With a gargling yell, Felix shoulder-barged the beastman underneath its swinging weapon. The creature was heavy enough to keep its feet, but was too big to react before Karaghul slid under its ribcage and speared its heart. Gustav sagged into his halberd.

'You heroic... idiot.'

Felix grinned tiredly. This was what happened when young men didn't read the classics. Lazy language. The End Times themselves.

He withdrew his blade from the beastman's chest, an awkward procedure due to the angle of penetration and the way the big gor had fallen against him, and was exposed and off-guard when a shriek went off behind him like a matchlock round.

Felix twisted quickly, making it just halfway when a black shape hissing with fangs and tearing claws barrelled into his side and flung him through the air. Felix felt the breath slammed from him and the bruise sink between his ribs and spread. Claws designed for slicing bone and opening the scaled underbellies of dragons raked down his mail, sending metal ringlets flying. Felix's armour had held up as well as Felix himself, but they had both seen their share of wear and parts had weathered the years better than others. Some of the links held while those around them scattered, denting, twisting, edges daggering into Felix's sides in a dozen distinct sources of pain. Felix screamed as the harpy tried to pull away and lift off, only to find its claws snagged between two deformed mail links just above Felix's hip. The creature shrieked and beat its wings harder. Its breath struck Felix with its rotten meat foulness. The body-reek, pillowed over his face with every beat of its black-flesh wings, made him nauseous enough to black out for a second, long enough to miss the moment when his feet left the ground.

And left his stomach behind.

He swung for the harpy with his sword, but the creature had snared him just under his left arm and however well he timed his strokes he couldn't lay so much as a nick on the harpy's wing. He fought back with knees and elbows even as the creature stuttered higher and itself struggled to kick him off. The blizzard battered him fiercely as he rose over the heads of the trolls. Felix's sword licked out as one passed briefly within reach, taking off its ear and distracting it enough for Snorri Nosebiter to batter it back into the fire.

The eruption of heat under its wings shoved the keening harpy higher. Felix screamed as it yawed and rolled, seemingly out of its own control, over the inner ring of statues.

They could have been headed towards the castle, but Felix was so disoriented by now that he could no longer tell up and down from left or right. He could see Gustav flailing about with his halberd as arrows punched down the beastmen closing from all around. Gotrek's orange crest and blazing rune-axe were spinning across his vision, growing ever paler and more ethereal until with the cold finality of ice sealing a frozen lake, the snow swept it all aside.

Snorri's despondent curses sank into the storm. All he could hear now was the wind and the numb ringing it left behind in his ears. The castle rolled into view.

Felix thought he was going to be sick.

Little squares of light wheeled across his vision as he spun, like stars accelerated across a night sky. A voice of calm reason somewhere inside his head told him that they were windows in the castle's higher towers and indeed in some of the nearest he could make out iron bars, and faces pressed against them. He tried to spot whether Max was amongst them but his own speed of approach made it like picking a single image from a running flipbook.

A pressing force of wind caused the harpy's wings to ripple. Even Felix felt it in his belly, a sense of pressure closing from above. The harpy gave a keening cry as Felix looked up.

A monster with the body of a giant lion and wings like a dragon's arrowed through the obscuring snow. It had three heads. A proud lion's mane and long ram's beard were wizened by snow and fullered by the wind. A third, reptilian head gazed frostily down, ignoring Felix and the harpy as entirely and literally beneath its notice as it shot past. The chimera levelled out just at the liminal of Felix's ability to see and then ploughed the flagstones with fire.

That he did see. He felt the heat rise on the screams of friend and foe alike.

'Gustav!' Felix screamed, as a second downblast of air pummelled his cheeks.

The griffon that he had earlier seen from the river powered overhead with an almost negligent beat of its vast feathered wings. Felix could not believe his eyes. It had to demand an iron will to hold such powerful and independent-minded beasts in step. The death of the Troll King then would surely herald the break-up of his army. Whether that was necessarily a good thing and would not simply entail more griffons and chimerae flying south to attack the Empire was a question he was not even going to try and answer while he was spinning towards a granite wall.

With a panicked tirade of wingbeats and piercing screams, the harpy jerked its legs in a bid to kick Felix off. Strong as its wings were, and well suited to its cowardly method of killing, it was not accustomed to bearing a grown man's weight for so long without dropping it and they were losing altitude fast. The wind whistled up from the ground between them. His tattered cloak whipped around his eyes. He couldn't even see the ground for the snow all around. Quickly, everything around him spinning, he tried to decide whether having the harpy pinned to his side was a help or a hindrance to his chances at this point.

With a resigned snarl, he gave up trying to hit the creature with his blade and instead turned his fingers to prying the creature's talons from his mail. Its claws were ivory white against its inky flesh, but cankerous and crusted with excrement. Felix slid his fingers between the harpy's toes and tugged. It shrieked and thrashed against him harder, unable to comprehend that they each wanted the same thing. A viscous foulness seeped from the creased flesh above its knuckles. One claw came loose, tearing away another warped mail ring. Felix gave a cry of success as the remaining talons slid out. There was a moment of joyous weightlessness as the harpy's wings ballooned out and it shot up with a parting wail.

Felix almost laughed. Then his stomach shot up through his mouth and he fell.

He still couldn't see the ground, but he soon realised that that owed more to the thickness of the snow than to altitude when he struck a stone slab not long after opening his mouth to draw breath on a scream. There was a crunch of mail, an all-encompassing hit of pain as if he had just been punched by a fist the exact size and mass of his whole body, and then he felt the stone beneath him push back and he bounced.

The image of an open gateway arced down through his vision. He realised he had landed on the top step of the procession that led up from the Square of Heroes to the citadel. The doors were dark, treated oak, carved with glowering faces and crossed with thick bands of steel. The doors were open wide and something reptilian and monstrous stood between them with an axe.

That was as much as an instant could reveal, and the next thing Felix became aware of was his shoulder hitting the next step down. The step after that beat on the flapping mail of his hip. He was rolling, his understanding of what was occurring beyond the borders of his own skin reduced to a painful succession of body blows. His head spun. His mail shook like a sack of rice. Trying to stop himself he almost broke his elbow against one of the statues that spun past on both sides. Tucking his head under his forearms and pulling his legs in to his chest, he hoped simply to ride it out to the bottom in one piece.

When the last step finally threw Felix's shoulders back onto the Square of Heroes he lay there flat for a moment and groaned. Slowly his thoughts swam back into alignment with the physical location of his brain. It wasn't a pleasant reunion.

Sigmar, he hurt! Eyes scrunched tight, he levered himself off his back and onto his elbows. Snow swept across the dramatic frontage of Praag's citadel. From up close it was uniquely horrible. Gargoyles and gothically realised daemons leered down from the battlements. Towers rose higher than he could see. Distant windows winked behind the snow like lighthouses in fog.

Shaking snow from his face, Felix turned his attention to the castle's most immediate and crushingly familiar feature with a sinking feeling. Statues stood sentinel between steps on either side, the likenesses of Imperial soldiers. Greatswords stared sternly across at dismounted pistoliers. Halberdiers with puffed doublets and dated wargear stood guard in cracked and weathered mail. All of them were mantled in heavy snow. They were the liberators of Praag, the soldiers of Magnus the Pious, granted this extraordinary tribute by the fiercely proud men of Kislev. Stiffly, Felix picked his sword from the ground where it had fallen and stood. The thought of climbing up that stair having just descended it in such abrupt fashion brought spasms to his aching joints and pain from their adjoining muscles. If he survived to see it, then he was going to be stiff as a board in the morning.

He looked back. Could he really leave Gustav and the others to fight alone? Who would keep an eye on Snorri? Was Max or Ulrika worth all of their deaths? Felix tightened his grip on Karaghul. And if he was going to start being honest with himself now, what made him think he was capable of dealing with the Troll King's remaining guards by himself anyway?

Trapped in indecision, Felix was about to head back to the fight when he noticed that the flagstones beneath his feet were trembling, as if fearing the approach of something dreadful. Not wanting to, but unable to stop himself, Felix turned back to the stair and looked up.

Descending the steps was a monster of epic scale, its terrible bulk nevertheless indistinct, wreathed in a lightning-charged penumbra of storm-black clouds. It was four-legged, its lower body covered in dark dragon-like scales while its torso and head were akin to a man's, only proportioned like those of an ancient god of war. Its chest was carved with tattoos written in a dead language, and pierced with iron spikes and rings thicker than Karaghul. A mane of dark hair fell past the waist to those monstrous forelegs, thick and charged with the lightning that flickered around its head and shoulders. Huge tusks thrust from a plinth-like jaw. The air crackled and steamed with its approach, the brute power in its lower quarters causing its humanoid upper body to sway with every step. With both hands, it hefted an axe that made Gotrek's look like something with which a halfling chopped firewood.

Felix knew then that he must be getting close. Even the Troll King could not have commanded two such champions as this!

He backed out onto the Square of Heroes but, to his surprise, he was not afraid. This was the monster that Karaghul had sensed from the river and he could feel the vague sentience within the Templar blade stirring in response to it, easing the aches from his body and filling his heart with strength. It had been forged to fight dragons, but despite centuries of warfare and scores of crusading masters it had never tested its enchantments against one of the legendary ancients: a dragon ogre of the prehistoric world. It was excited and, because it was, so too was Felix.

That, however, frightened him a great deal.

'You have come a long way and suffered so much just to die in my castle, Felix Jaeger.'

The voice did not come from the dragon ogre – the monster emitting only a sonorous rumble – but from further up the steps. As hard as it was to look beyond the looming Old One, Felix forced himself to. There, crowned head towering over the larger than life-size statue of an artilleryman on the step above him, tattered red cloak sodden and streaming in the wind, stood the Troll King.

'You know me?' said Felix, but then of course, the Troll King had Ulrika, and had held Max for the better part of a year.

As if reading Felix's thoughts, the Troll King did not answer.

'I am Throgg, the King of Trolls, and I had been hoping to watch the Trollslayer die here at my feet. But his henchman will suffice. For starters.'

* * *

For a long moment, Max Schreiber stared at the window. Had he really just seen the face he had thought he had fly past his window? Impossible. Even if Felix had managed to pass the Auric Bastion, his chances of making it this far were infinitesimal. Throgg had picked apart Max's dreams of escape and rescue surgically enough for him to know that.

Reassured by this line of reasoning, Max ignored the phantasmagoria and turned back to his subject.

Then he spread his raw and swollen fingers, and began.

SIXTEEN

The Troll King's Champion

The holes in Snorri Nosebiter's head were tingling. He shook his head to clear it, stove a troll's ankle in with his hammer, then dropped onto his stiff metal knee as a boulder-like fist droned overhead and he stuck his axe into a second troll's thigh. Chips of stone flew out as Snorri yanked the blade loose with a joyous cry, tottering backwards and avoiding the clumsy kick from the first troll that instead hit the second's wounded leg and sent it crashing to the ground.

Snorri wobbled giddily on his feet and slapped the back of his hand against his forehead. The tingling wouldn't go away. It felt horribly like memories.

Everything around him was burning. Men were screaming. Smoke burned his eyes and dried his mouth. *The sweet smell of well roasted meat filled the air. It disturbed the ale sloshing in his otherwise empty belly and he threw up over the bloodstained flagstones. He dropped to his knees, crunching the charred ribcage of a goblin raider that had been hidden under the layer of soot.* Snorri ducked his head under a swinging axe. A beastman's axe, he reminded himself. Not goblins. His own axe gutted the beastman and he rose.

The scene around him resembled the stories of Grimnir's March, the first Slayer's doomed quest to do battle with the gods and their daemon legions. Smoke rose up from the ground to choke the driving snow, the wind blending them together into a choking grey pall that deadened sound and killed sight cold. The three-headed flying monster had gouged a trench of fire that had missed Snorri by inches and still flooded the square with heat. Tattered scraps of murk drifted across the beastmen's big fire while all around bits of burning troll glowed like brands. The lowing of beastmen and the shrieks of harpies echoed oddly and from every direction. Monstrous shadows loomed teasingly out of the dark.

Coughing, the air sticky with roasted blood, Snorri staggered after the standing troll, clashing his weapons above his head as much to block out the incessant tingling in his skull as to attract the troll's attention. The troll grunted, distracted, rapping its own head with its knuckles as if mimicking Snorri's behaviour, and slowly sank onto its haunches.

'Stand up and kill Snorri!' The troll's mouth hung open and Snorri noticed that its nose was bleeding, a sticky brownish paste oozing over a protruding upper lip. It issued a groan. It eyes flickered up into their sockets. Snorri lowered his weapons. 'Gotrek. Snorri's troll is acting funny.'

A tripled shriek echoed through the smog and Snorri squinted to glimpse Gotrek amidst the rubble of at least one large statue and surrounded on all sides by several more. His old friend was singed and savaged front and back with angry red slashes, and partially obscured under a haze of heat. A gout of flame belched over Gotrek's head and blasted another statue to smithereens. The dwarf brought up his axe, red-faced and furious as he laboured down a lungful of fiery air before a swipe of the three-headed monster's claws sent him piling through the statue of a Kislevite horse-archer in a shower of rubble.

Snorri probably shouldn't feel jealous. If his old friend were to meet his long-awaited doom then that would spare them all a lot of trouble, but he couldn't help but think about his own promised destiny. *And when you are whole again, when those you most love surround you again, then you shall have a death that brings you nothing but pain.* Somehow he knew that that meant Gotrek was not going to die here.

He had to be present for Snorri's.

The troll emitted a stuttering sigh, its head yawing back, and Snorri felt a sudden shock of *connection* in which he thought he saw himself through the monster's rolling eyes. Snorri lifted his hammer, getting the greyed image of an old and tired-looking dwarf with no hair and one leg mirroring the same action, and then sought to blink it off and turn the hammer. He gave it a shake.

That was strange.

It reminded Snorri of his journey with old Borek back through the Chaos Wastes when the sky had been fat with magic. That had felt like this.

The tingling in his skull continued to grow more intense, becoming a buzz that was starting to make his head hurt. Somewhere in the blizzard a harpy shrieked as it angled overhead towards the big statue where the humans fought, sounding in Snorri's one ear like the mocking laugh of a harsh old witch. Giving his head a vigorous shake, Snorri swept up his hammer with the intention of cracking it on the troll's out-thrust chin. The buzz became a whistle like a kettle in the pinhole scar of his other ear. Snorri grimaced. And then his eardrums bled.

There was a sharp pain as if he'd been cleanly skewered ear to ear and a rivulet of blood ran the gnarled course of his jaw. The troll in that same instant seized, every muscle in its monstrous body tensing and then falling suddenly slack as the light was snuffed from its eyes. It hung upright for a moment, blood pooling under now lifeless eyeballs before it slowly toppled backwards, sprawling over the body of the troll that it had earlier knocked down. That one was dead as well, although the wound in its thigh continued to regenerate. Blood streamed from its nose and eyes and thick clots of it plugged its ears.

Everywhere he could see, trolls were dropping like meat cut from a butcher's ceiling hooks. Snorri stuck a finger in his cauliflower ear and scraped out a crust of blood. He arched a crooked eyebrow up towards the sky as it exploded with the black wings of startled harpies.

Very strange.

Felix's sword felt like a lightning bolt in his hand. The blade glowed an intense blue-white, electrical bursts firing out from the tip with cracks that split the air and seared it with a burned, bitter taste. Though its fierce vibrations had numbed his arms to the elbow, Felix brought his sword into a guard and peered into the storm of arcing white light and deafening sound.

Silhouetted within its own aura stood the dragon ogre. Black, lightning-struck clouds leached from its muscular torso like sweat from the body of a man. The air around it trembled with perpetual thunder that crashed and crescendoed like an infernal chorus. A bolt of lightning whiplashed through the storm and earthed in his sword and Felix staggered back as if physically struck. The runes etched into his blade glowed so brightly he could see them with his eyes closed. He groaned as fresh strength restored tired muscles with old aches, nevertheless gripping to Karaghul as though it were the one secure hold in the midst of a storm. He felt in his fingers the sword's efforts to match the monster's power and counter it, but even its potent enchantments were being overwhelmed by the torrent of raw, elemental fury. And as more of the sword's protective magicks turned towards Felix's survival, the first chink of genuine horror at what Felix was actually facing seeped in through the cracks.

Here was a monster that had seen the first days of the world and survived the dawn of Chaos, or so some scholars had it. He was Felix Jaeger; a poet, a propagandist and a one-time sidekick to a Trollslayer. What claim could he have to best a monster like this?

Punch drunk, Felix brought up his sword again.

Hard laughter that bore a pain all its own reverberated through the thunder and lightning. Felix tried to pinpoint the Troll King, but he was lost in the squall of noise.

'What do you hope to achieve, Felix? You are not a hero. You are a hero's shadow.'

Breaking its own storm front, the dragon ogre swung up its massive axe in two hands, driving a downward arc towards a blow that would have cleft an anvil in two. Bellowing like a cornered bear, Felix brought Karaghul up to parry as if any man had a hope in the End Times of blocking that blow.

The impact hammered Felix down and sent arcs of lightning flaring over Felix's head from where steel had struck volcanic glass. A compression wave pulverised the flagstones beneath Felix's feet, throwing the dust up into the air before it was incinerated by the dragon ogre's lightning halo a second later. The air burned and Felix felt as though his lungs were filling with molten copper. But Karaghul had somehow kept Felix alive. With too little time to marvel at the fact, Felix felt the overbearing pressure force him to his knees. With every ounce of his own strength and that which the sword could loan him he pushed back, but his sword arm quavered:

it felt over-large and ached as if from days of exertion. The axe ground him under it, forcing his blade down until its white heat and static brilliance caused Felix's beard and eyebrows to stand erect and sizzle.

'When Shagga first came to me, he had just lost a war. Do you know how badly your kind had hurt him?'

Felix groaned, the dragon ogre pushing its advantage until he was almost bent backwards over the shattered ground. Desperately, he looked around for something to use, some tool, some trick, but there was not even a paving stone within reach that hadn't been obliterated. He lay in dust fit for the grave. Even the snow was vaporised by the lightning mesh before it could make it as far as Felix's exposed face. A tinnitus filled his ears, likely a consequence of thunderclaps going off every few minutes a foot from his head. He decided that if humouring the Troll King would buy him a few extra seconds to think of something then he would do it.

'Did you help him recover?'

'I did not have to. His kind is beyond your power to injure.'

Great, Felix thought, gritting his teeth and straining against the dragon ogre's strength while, seemingly unrelated in any way to the storms after all, the ringing in his ears had grown in pitch to a shrill whine. It was a pressure that seemed to be pushing outwards from inside his own head, like a particularly awful hangover although Felix had had worse, but most shocking was the effect that it had on the Troll King.

The monster gave a long bellow of agony.

Felix felt the ungodly strength bearing down on his sword arm relent as the dragon ogre turned away in concern for its master and Felix had to fight to keep his legs from jellying to the ground in relief. The tormented air became easier to breathe as the dragon ogre moved away, black clouds dissipating before the wind and unshrouding the figure of the Troll King. The troll was bent double, clutching at the statue of a halberdier on the first step up to the castle as if it were an anchor, the face crumbling round his claws.

'What is happening?' the Troll King growled, voice so sonorous that it shook Felix's innards with its fragile sanity and its rage, then threw his gaze up towards the distant slits of light that glimmered through the snow above the castle's battlements. 'Max.'

'Max Schreiber?' said Felix, getting stiffly to his feet. The dragon ogre regarded him stormily from its master's side but made no move. 'You're an intelligent creature. Will you bargain for him?'

The Troll King wiped a trickle of blood from his nose and stared at it as though attempting to extract meaning from a pattern that was not there.

Through the snow above, harpies flapped wildly for their eyries in, to all outward appearances, a blind panic. The blizzard echoed with the shouts of beastmen and peals of phantom thunder. Felix tightened at the weary sound of running feet approaching from behind but did not turn around. This was what he had come here for. And besides, unlike the cosseted fools and liars who boasted about such things in taverns, Felix had no great preference as to whether he faced death when it came or not. Despite aching muscles though, he almost jumped when a rough hand fell on his arm.

'I hope you weren't trying to keep this for yourself,' said Gotrek.

'Very selfish,' Snorri agreed with a nod that almost pitched him over he was so wearied.

Both dwarfs looked as though they'd fought across a road paved with hot coals to get this far. Snorri bled from both ears and swayed as though he had taken one blow to the head too many. Dried blood creaked with his movements like the joints of armour plate. Gotrek however was not just plated with blood, but layered in it: it encased his skin, soaked his breeches, clogged the top of his boots, dyed the roots of his crest. A wet smear covered his axe, a smattering of golden hairs stuck to it like flies in amber. Runes glowed diffusely from underneath. He noticed none of it. His gaze was locked on the dragon ogre.

'Mine.'

'Not if I get there first,' said Felix before he could bite his tongue. Silently, he cursed Karaghul and its single-minded drives. The sword was just metal: it had no concept of when it was overmatched.

'Is Snorri fighting the Troll King then?' said Snorri amiably. 'Because he really doesn't mind.'

'Witless animals and blind fools,' roared the Troll King, with his head clutched in one hand. 'Chaos itself holds at my walls and soon the world will follow where Kislev has shown the way.'

The monster glared over Felix's head with a look like thunder and withdrew a step towards the castle. Felix pulled his gaze from the smouldering ancient to see why: a group of exhausted but armed men trailed in the dwarfs' wake. Kolya was amongst them and – Felix's heart lifted – Gustav as well.

'Shagga,' said the Troll King, indicating Felix and the others with a pained wave of one dully luminescent rock of a wrist as he backed away. 'I have to see what has happened for myself. Kill them all.'

'Leave this to me, manling,' said Gotrek, brandishing his blood-smeared axe as the dragon ogre gave a thunderous flex of its muscles and charged.

Wishing very much that he could, Felix positioned himself at Gotrek's left side and slightly behind, angling his sword to guard the Slayer's blind side. Gotrek merely grunted and let it slide. If Felix didn't know better, he would have labelled the mausoleum grin on his former companion's face as almost pleased. Felix couldn't even tell any more if it was Karaghul or his own sense of duty to the miserable dwarf that compelled him to do this. Neither possibility was particularly reassuring so he didn't overly lament the too-brief second he had to consider it before seething storm clouds lashed the shaking flagstones with thunder and the dragon ogre swung its black axe.

At the last second Felix and Gotrek shared a look.

Gotrek bared his teeth and rolled right while Felix, just a fraction slower, tucked his shoulder and ducked left. In an awesome display of power and control, the dragon ogre checked its downstroke, monstrous biceps swelling as it turned it into a pendulum slash for Gotrek at the same time that Felix was forced to parry a stray lightning bolt that blasted him from his feet.

The Slayer swung his own axe to parry the blow as charged black clouds descended from the monster's torso to wash over him. Gotrek snarled in pain at the impact, backing up and tossing his axe to his left hand. He flexed his right hand, yanking out the wrist until the chain that bound axe haft to right bracer pulled taut.

Clothes steaming where the snow landed on him, Felix pulled himself up. His hands and feet were shaking like tuning forks. Discharging static clapped from the frayed ends of his wool cloak. His woollen undergarments delivered further painful shocks to various out of the way places as he bade his legs to carry him forwards.

'Uncle!'

Felix turned sharply at Gustav's voice. His nephew and the last handful of his free company had been made haggard by snow and battle and rendered smaller than men by terror. A couple of wavering spears pointed back into the snow-swept Square of Heroes and the raucous din that raged there, but most simply gaped in horror at the rampaging ancient.

'Stay back,' Felix commanded them and those still of sound enough mind to register human speech needed no second telling. Felix focused on Gustav who looked physically torn over whether to intervene. 'You too, Gustav. This is not for you.'

That said, Felix took a cold breath of air that tasted of scorched stone and charged into the storm-wracked umbra that now shrouded the dragon ogre's rear. His ears popped as he lunged through the monster's electrical corona, a tingling in his skin translating into a vibrant, violent light that suffused Karaghul's rune-etched length as he drew back and then rammed the blade deep into the creature's thigh.

The dragon ogre bellowed in unexpected pain as gromril-hard scales as old as the world parted before Karaghul's baneful enchantments and razor edge. A stamp of the ground with the monster's wounded leg sent Felix staggering and he only just avoided a swipe of its thick tail as it tried to swat him down again to pile its full power onto the Slayer.

Felix saw his former companion fighting axe-to-axe right under the tusks of the monster's front. Their dual was a blur of obsidian and starmetal, fearsome tattoos and brutal piercings, dispersed into a haze of static torture. By Felix's snap assessment, the Slayer was more than holding his own, but the flesh was being literally seared off his bones by a succession of lightning strikes. Gotrek staggered back before one dazzling thunderclap, shaking his head, dazed, and then presented his axe with a snarl.

That he was still alive was a miracle worthy of Sigmar.

Ducking low Felix slashed his blade across the dragon ogre's hamstrings, eliciting another roar and a swipe of tail, and then rolled between the monster's legs slicing into its tough green underbelly as he went. The monster shuddered and drew back, earning Gotrek a second to catch his breath as Felix came up beside him. The Slayer decided to waste it instead on a disparaging grunt.

'You could have just walked.'

Felix found himself grinning like a lunatic, but the respite was as short-lived as Felix imagined he was to be. The dragon ogre pounded forward, axe rising amidst a gathering pall of lightning and then hammering down on Gotrek's blade. Muscles knotted across the Slayer's back as he pushed back against the dragon ogre's strength and, impossibly, matched it. The two axes remained locked, wavering up and down within the span of an inch as both fighters strained. Lightning limned the boundary of the struggle, but rather than striking the Slayer those random discharges now converged on the lightning rod in the midst.

Cursing the Templar sword through clenched teeth, Felix tensed rigid with pain as jolt after jolt cracked against Karaghul's blade. The weapon's protective enchantments absorbed most of the energy from the impacts, but Felix wasn't feeling particularly grateful for that fact just now given that it was those same enchantments that were pulling the dragon ogre's power onto him in the first place. The blade glowed brighter with every strike. He couldn't have let go of the sword now if he'd wanted to. His body coursed with electricity and had the dragonhead hilt in a rictus grip.

Even if he could have dropped the sword and run, he knew he wouldn't have. This was Gotrek's only chance of slaying the beast.

Lightning flashing across his gaping eye socket, Gotrek inched one hand from his axe, grunting as the full strength of the dragon ogre bore down onto one shaking arm. Gotrek's bicep swelled and knotted with veins, but slowly the two axes ground inevitably down.

'What are you doing?' Felix managed to stutter as the Slayer used his free hand to loop the chain locking axe haft to bracer around the dragon ogre's wrists.

Baring his teeth in a lightning-flecked grin, Gotrek hauled the chain tight until blood trickled between the steel links where they bit into the monster's flesh. Thunder rumbled from the dragon ogre's throat, but the unexpected pain was a distraction and, moreover, the constriction around its wrists was fouling its grip on its axe. Gotrek pushed back.

Felix however could take no more. His sword was shining so brightly that its corona encompassed him entirely. He could barely see, could hear nothing but the crack of lightning and the occasional wild burst of charge that arced off from the tip of his blade to strike a flagstone or a statue and blow them apart in a ravaging storm of energy. Again Felix cursed the damned sword. Fighting the dragon had been easier than this.

'Gotrek!' he screamed, knowing that dwarf ears were better than men's and praying that his former companion could hear when even Felix himself could not. 'Let go of it. Now!'

With a howl, Felix lashed out with Karaghul as if striking a death-blow. Lightning flashed around the sword with an apocalyptic *crack* of godly thunder and a torrent of energy burst from the tip of the blade and struck the dragon ogre square in the chest. Gotrek had heard and pulled clear at the last minute and now watched as paralysing paroxysms overwhelmed the dragon ogre's nervous system. Given the stories Felix had read of dragon ogres feasting on warp storms and bathing in mountaintop seas of never-ending lightning he didn't expect the blow to prove fatal, but the moment was all that the Slayer needed.

Gotrek stepped in towards the shuddering beast and buried his rune-axe deep into the monster's abdomen, roughly transecting the line where the dragon ogre's monstrous half took on its human character. Blood and guts spat from the wound as Gotrek withdrew his axe and cut again. It took several more blows for the monster to fall and several seconds more for the last spasm of electricity to arc across its limp carcass.

Felix slumped onto one knee, leaning on the dragonhead hilt of Karaghul like a knight in prayer. His body felt like it had been torn up from the inside and now bits of himself that he had no name for flapped loose. But somehow he was all still here. Shakily, he kissed the ring on his finger. Perhaps it was good luck after all. He decided it was a ritual he was going to keep.

The approach of Gustav and the other men brought a crunch of snow and pebbled flagstones under their nervous feet. Kolya took up the rear, his swaddling furs thick with snow and a hood keeping the worst of it off his eyes. With bow loosely drawn, he eyed the blizzard at their backs. It was no longer just shapes that peopled the snow but animal shrieks and a clangour that seemed to be drawing in from every side.

Felix could only guess what was happening out there and from everything he had witnessed on his way in, none of it was good.

'Do we go inside, then?' said Kolya, with a nonchalant nod towards the citadel as if the corpse of a monstrous ancient did not lie across the bottom step. 'We can all die in the warm.'

Just what the party needs, thought Felix with a sideways glance at Gotrek, another optimist.

'You could have helped out,' said Felix.

The Kislevite offered another of his infuriating shrugs. 'He is a Slayer, Empire man. A man can take a horse to water...'

Felix waved down the platitude with a grimace and stood. His bones creaked. It felt as though more than a few muscles weren't pulling their weight.

'This is why you were a shoddy rememberer,' said Gotrek. 'You never did get the point.'

Felix felt something in his heart wrench. He regarded the Slayer, hoping for an indication that he joked, but of course he didn't. The moment of comradeship he had thought he'd sensed as they fought was nowhere to be seen now. 'Fine then. Let's get you killed, shall we? It shouldn't be too difficult.'

'I'll believe it when I see it.'

As cold inside as out, Felix turned to the men to offer at least a few reassuring words when he noticed something gravely amiss. He scanned the faces around him. One was missing.

'Where is Snorri?'

The entrance hall of Praag's gloomy citadel was a large and circular space made of dark stone blocks. Thick pillars rose past a succession of galleries before coming to a domed ceiling decorated with painted panels depicting a sweeping horse battle over an icy field. It was the only colour to be found in what was otherwise a desert of stone. The galleries looked like they should have been hung with tapestries. Embedded into the walls at intervals were hooks and bars that might have held portraits, weaponry, animal heads and skins. There were also indents where suits of armour would have once stood, but now they were empty. It looked as though the castle had been stripped of anything of beauty or value.

Snorri Nosebiter liked it better this way. It reminded him of home. His tuneless whistle echoed back at him from the distant ceiling.

Halfway down the hall a wide staircase climbed partway towards the next floor before splitting into two halves that spiralled up towards the upper storeys, crossing again somewhere above Snorri's head. Snorri took the left-hand stair to the next floor. It was a corridor, longer than the hall beneath and lined with plain wooden doors interspersed every few doorways with benched alcoves.

The other side of the passage opened out onto the entrance hall through a row of elaborately carved stone arches in the form of wrestling gargoyles. Through the symmetrical feature on the opposite side of the staircase, Snorri saw a single file of armoured beastmen hurry by before disappearing again. They ignored Snorri entirely and Snorri couldn't figure out how to get across without going back down to the hall and taking the other branch of the stair up, so he ignored them too. The beastmen's hard, bony feet and rattling mail echoed through the halls long after they were forgotten about and Snorri followed the corridor deeper into the castle.

Snorri knew he was no great mind – he was reminded of it often enough – but he was good at following. Even he couldn't miss the cratering in the stone floor where something big and very angry had recently walked or the occasional still-crumbling punch wound torn out of the side of the little wall nooks. He followed the trail until he came to a door that had been ripped clean off its hinges, snapped in two, and hurled down the corridor.

It led onto a staircase that wound upwards. A light flickered like a cat's eye in the distance and Snorri grinned determinedly. It was his turn to be the hero now. Images of Durin Drakkvarr and Skalf Hammertoes flashed through his mind. A lot of people had put a lot of faith and sacrifice in Snorri's supposed destiny and if there was a doom to be had here then it would be Snorri's.

The Spider Lady had promised him one.

And it would be the mightiest.

SEVENTEEN

True Selves

At the sheer granite face of the Mountain Gate overlooking the Goromadny Road and a white sea of snow-covered tents, thirty thousand northmen raised a raucous cheer as the immovable line of trolls upon the ramparts jerked and fell. The cry became a berserker roar on every man's lips as cold, hungry, frustrated men surged forwards as one. Chaos warriors already on the siege ladders suddenly found themselves opposed by nothing more than beastmen and a long overdue slaughter began in deadly earnest.

Five miles back from the East Gate and the killing fields littered with the bodies of Kurgan and Dolgan and other marauder tribes, Khorreg Hellworker watched with a grin as black as coal as a string of trolls pitched from artillery-scarred walls one by one into the Lynsk below. Snowmelt screaming from the glowing fissures in his flesh, the daemonsmith bade the host of Zharr-Naggrund to attack. The Dawi-Zharr were a patient and stubborn race, but the Troll King had defied them all for long enough. At his word, the sky whined with a sudden onslaught of rockets and shells. The walls of Praag shook to their foundation stones under the onslaught as block after block of remorseless heavy infantry marched on.

To the south, the Gate of Gargoyles was still to be re-sealed after the Troll King's sally and battles raged between beastmen and Kurgan across several miles of open plain. The block of massive stone trolls that anchored their rear within the open gate staggered and all at once stopped fighting, only their collected bulk holding them upright and plugging the gate until a charge of Kurgan cavalry and charioteers scythed them down and howling marauders spilled onto the Grand Parade.

Across Praag, trolls dropped dead in the street and beastmen fled in panic for the inner walls of the Old Town.

Fires sprang up out of nowhere in the cramped heart of the Novygrad and a huge, fiery-winged daemon began to take form out of the cinders as a cabal of Chaos sorcerers finally dared to let their powers be felt. A pair of giants wielding massive stone hammers bellowed Throgg's name as they strode through the ruins to do battle with the summoned being. On the wide body of the mighty Karlsbridge, a wild hydra with scales as grey as morning sleet sent torrents of flame rippling through the snow and incinerating any that dared attempt the crossing. Huge, armoured beastmen bellowed for order in its fiery shadow, rallying their routed forces to the prepared stockades there until volleys of precise Kurgan horse-archery brought the beast down and the bridge went the way of the gates.

Fire and bloodshed lapped at the Old Town walls, closing on the citadel of the hated Troll King like a rising flood of Chaos.

Dragging on a dry vein within the dark of a forsaken cellar, the beast that had been Ulrika felt herself drown. Dense, foul-tasting blood ran through her veins like oil in water, churning, churning, but never fully mingling with her own. She could feel the war going on between her own blood and the troll's. She felt sick. Through it and the strange magical connection that this troll seemed to possess with the others of its kind within the city, she experienced every death as a spasm in her mind. She too groaned at the tug that sought to draw her spirit from her cold flesh as it had from the now dead troll in her embrace.

Ulrika however still retained wit enough to fight back, just; but there was something in its siren nature that appealed directly to her, to Ulrika. There was a familiar taste, a scent that carried only on the winds of the aethyr and was thus unhindered by stone and undiluted by distance. It conjured memories of a wise man, a handsome man, a man whom she had once loved and whose goodness still existed somewhere within the monster she had become.

Pulling up from the troll's neck with a gasp of hunger despite the blood smeared across her face and chest, the beast shuddered. Chaos was rising on the tide of the End Times. The call was made in vain.

Ulrika did not live here any more.

A low growl started up in the belly of the Ice Tower, rising up its throat with such a shaking fury that the cages of its topmost level began to rattle. Their captives, already in a state of near hysteria following the sudden death of every last one of the trolls, found a second wind to wail like dying wolves and even the stub-horned ungor lamplighter whose sole purpose it was to keep the torches lit on the wizards' work trembled as the wall brackets rattled against their fittings.

It reached the floor below; a bellow of pure disbelieving outrage that shivered through the floorboards, followed by the crunch of a wooden door yielding before something that did not know what it felt like to be stopped. The crash of hurrying steps drew closer until, with a baleful roar and a scream of iron fixtures, the last door between that wrath and its most prized prisoners flew inwards and slammed into the side of the cage opposite. The occupant, a night goblin with a sharp green chin protruding from a hooded cloak, shrieked innocence and set the entire level to clamouring.

Head swimming with the effort of re-establishing his will within just one earthly host, Max struggled to absorb what was going on.

'I told you, man-thing,' hissed the skaven warlock, glaring at him through the two sets of bars between them. The troll chained to the skaven's wall was limp, a piece of mindlessly regenerating meat. The severed head that had been wired to the warlock's wind-up shock machine was equally slack, barring a periodically induced twitch as a current directly stimulated its dead brain. With a glance over his shoulder, the ratman hunched his shoulders and retreated into the far corner of his own cage. 'I told you the king would not be pleased.'

Max felt the floor beneath him shake and looked past the skulking ratman as the hulking figure of Throgg strode between the shuddering cages straight for Max's cell. The Troll King bristled with rage, the crystalline mane of warpstone that ran down his neck and shoulders pulsing like angry hearts. Max had never seen him this way, his monstrous nature laid bare past the limits of all his godly gifts to set him beyond.

It was terrifying to behold.

With a bestial growl, Throgg reached out for Max's cell and then with one throw of the shoulder tore the door clear from its housing and hurled it back across the chamber. Then the Troll King thrust mineral-spiked hands around the bars to either side of the opening and wrenched them apart sufficiently for him to enter.

'What did you do, Max?' he said, thrusting his huge head through the mangled door frame while the iron bars squealed in his grip like swine. 'How many of my people did you kill?'

'You said you did not care for one or for a hundred,' said Max, abuzz with achievement and the residual thrill of magic. Why was the Troll King angry? Could he not see for himself what Max had accomplished for him?

'You fool. You weak, *human*, broken-minded fool. There is an army outside these walls. There are ten armies. These are *my* walls.' Throgg shook the bars in his grip until one bent with a lingering scream and then tore off in his hand. He beat the iron rod against the remaining bars and roared: 'Mine!'

'But I have done it,' said Max, trying desperately to get his captor, his patron, to see. 'Every being within a race resonates similarly to the touch of Ghyran, the Jade Wind. It was simply a matter of gathering enough of that life force, using the Gold to catalyse the change with a spark of the Celestial. It was... elegant.'

'Elegant?' The furiously intelligent eyes of the Troll King passed from Max to his subject where he was chained to the wall. The newborn mind gawped up at the world around it, stony grey eyes wide with incomprehension and nascent wonder. Earthy saliva dribbled from its gaping mouth. Its breathing was vapid and uneven. Atrophied limbs jerked feebly after every cry or flicker of light. The Troll King gave a snarl. 'He is broken, Max. Like his father.'

'He is one mind from many. He is simplicity, a refutation of the inevitability of Chaos.' Max stumbled towards Throgg, hands pleading, voice rising as passion took over from good sense. The Troll King regarded him contemptuously. 'He is your child. I merely delivered him into the world. See him for what he is.'

The Troll King's mineralised brow furrowed, indecision cocking his golden crown: thinking – always, always thinking. His gaze lingered on the newborn, longing, and yet, faced now with the equal he had thought he craved, jealous of his own uniqueness. 'What I see is the end state of man – gaping and helpless as their doom closes.'

'No! He simply doesn't yet know how to control his thoughts. Your kind is adaptable. He will adapt.'

'No, Max, you were right before. A Teclis or a Nagash you are not, and thanks to your worthless efforts my city is lost.' With a dangerous growl he summoned the quivering ungor lamplighter.

'Fetch me the vampire and spread the word that we are soon to march south. Tell her I have reconsidered her alliance with the Empire.'

'I remember this place,' said Felix as the group padded into the castle's entrance hall, voice hushed by the high domed ceiling as if they had just entered a tomb. 'This is where Duke Enrik received Max and Ulrika and Ivan Petrovich and I for a victory feast. He pointed across the desolate hall to an empty pedestal that backed onto an alcove. 'There was a suit of armour there. A winged lancer of the Magnus Legion if I recall. It was large enough for Ulrika and I to sneak off during some of the longer speeches and–'

'Please uncle, spare us the sordid details.'

Gustav clutched his halberd as though he intended to throttle it and affected interest in the empty hooks that were spaced across the bare stone walls. Ulrika had drawn of him too deeply for him to blush, but Gustav wasn't nearly wily enough to hide the subtle cues from a man of Felix's experience.

There was fear for her, perhaps. Jealousy, almost certainly.

'It's not men doing the feasting now anyway,' said Gotrek with what might equally have been a deliberate attempt to further darken the mood as a reminder of where they all still were. A low murmur of activity reverberated through the castle's stones and, though the cold numbed Felix's nose effectively, the sweaty scent of beastman laced the air. The Slayer further stamped out the solemn air with the snow from his boots.

Felix looked up, past the overlooking galleries and the decorative bandings by which friezes of monsters such as wyverns and trolls being ridden down by Kislev's lancers separated the levels to the frescoed ceiling high above.

'It is the last ride of the Ungol,' said Kolya. 'When the Gospodar crushed them and took Praag for a united Kislev.' He gave an appreciative sigh. 'I never thought I would see it.'

'You've not been here before?'

'You have feasted with the *krug* of the duke. I would not even know him to see him.' His gaze lingered on the fresco and Felix saw not a laconic and slightly irritating northerner, but a man who would draw horses on stones between battles, a man who had lost it all but for some reason carried on. 'But I always thought... one day.'

Pushing deeper into the hall, it wasn't difficult to tell that the ducal palace was first and foremost a fortress. The galleries provided both cover and excellent angles for crossbowmen posted there and the staircase up ahead, though wide enough for a rank of ten to fight across, presented an open target to archers firing down from the flanks while the height between steps was unusually steep to confer a significant advantage to any defender fighting from above. There were no windows whatsoever. Felix glanced again to the ceiling, wondering how much more castle there was beyond that dome. Where did it sit in relation to the battlements? Where were the towers with the barred windows and lights inside?

'I think Max is being held up there somewhere,' he said, while Gotrek wandered further into the hall and looked intently around with his one good eye.

'Don't forget Ulrika,' said Gustav. A murmur of assent sounded from his men. 'We've given oaths of service and we're not leaving without her.'

That's not all you've given, Felix thought but chose not to say. He didn't know if Gotrek had noticed the marks on the men's necks or what the Slayer would do if he knew. Perhaps nothing. These men were innocent victims after all, but it never paid to assume that dwarfs – and Gotrek in particular – perceived innocence in the same frame as did humans.

'We should go that way,' Gotrek cut in with a nod towards the left-hand sweep of the staircase and the corridor it led to.

'What makes you say that?'

'The ground is wet where snow has been traipsed in from outside, and see those marks?' Felix and the others looked to the staircase where Gotrek pointed. There were indeed an array of tiny indents in the stone. Felix hadn't noticed them, and if he had he would have assumed them porous imperfections in the rock or simple wear and tear – this castle was hundreds of years old and had been overrun by Chaos on two separate occasions. Or three if one counted the Troll King's usurpation of Aekold Helbrass. 'That's from Snorri's leg. You can tell by the pattern.'

'When this is over you should hunt with me, zabójka,' said Kolya.

'He can't have got far on that leg,' said Felix, striding towards the staircase, determined to find the old Slayer before Gotrek did. 'We can catch him before he does something stupid.'

Gotrek's grunt said everything that a dwarf never would.

Snorri upped his pace, running with one hand scouring along the outside wall of the stairwell, bashing the lip of every step with his mace-leg in his haste. He burst through a splintered doorway and into a circular chamber filled with iron cages and wailing. He blinked against the harsh glare that came from braziers spaced regularly all around the room and tottered through the screaming voices and grasping hands and through the door onto the next flight of stairs up.

Every few turns of the stairwell, a broken door opened onto the same scene. The only difference was that the cages became slightly larger, probably so as to fit the increasingly impressive array of what Snorri unthinkingly characterised as 'stuff' that the better fed and less battered prisoners all seemed to have inside with them. Goblins and beastmen and orcs gave way to men and skaven and even an elf. The Troll King had been thorough. On one floor, Snorri spotted a greybeard dwarf in runesmith's robes, but he didn't pause, almost running down a skinny beastman that clattered through the opposite door and completely forgetting to try and hit it until it had skidded past him and sprinted off down the stairs.

Even after that near miss Snorri only slowed down a little. The constant spinning was starting to make him dizzy, threatening to dislodge a jumble of loosely stored memories, but the Troll King was so close he could almost smell his destiny.

Innate dwarf intuition told him that the next level would be the second from last. The air smelled like the alchemist's shop that Bjorni Bjornisson had made him go to after a hard night in the Red Rose. A cacophony of screams returned him to the present and he looked up to see a rectangle of bright light against the dark stone. Snorri gave an excited yip and spilled through into a brightly lit scene of destruction.

Snorri took it all in as quickly as he could. The layout of cages was similar to what had come before, but following the pattern, with larger and fewer cages. Another door, presumably the last, faced him through a pair of cluttered cages. It was intact but ajar and he could see more steps beyond it. The door he had just stumbled in through was in a bad way on the floor a few feet ahead of him where it had struck the most immediate cage. Snorri could see where the brass fixtures had chipped the iron. The hooded goblin within had its long strangler's fingers wrapped around the bars and was staring at some commotion that Snorri couldn't see for intervening cages, off towards the rear of the tower that overlooked the Square of Heroes.

'Snorri's looking for a Troll King,' said Snorri loudly. 'He's got a destiny.' The night goblin turned to stare at him agog. 'Snorri, that is. The Troll King can get his own destiny.'

As Snorri watched, a shudder passed through the bars and the goblin pulled away as if shocked, then turned back to where it had previously been looking and squealed. A low growl rumbled through the chamber and something detached itself from the far wall behind the blocking cages – Snorri had thought that it had *been* the wall – and stamped around into full view of the door.

A ratman in a tin hat whimpered as the Troll King set his hand upon the top corner of its eight-foot-tall cage. The monster's crown shone on all sides against the braziers that encircled it. His stony bulk glittered under a mantle of frost. Scores of tiny mouths over the Troll King's belly yammered breathlessly until he cut them off with a sweep of his tattered red cloak. Snorri clutched his axe excitedly and drew his hammer.

A mighty doom. When those he loved most surrounded him again.

'The half-wit,' growled the Troll King, pointing a massive claw to the door behind Snorri. 'I do not care enough to wish you harm. Take this one chance to leave. I have no patience left for fools.'

Snorri scowled. Sometimes he didn't realise that he'd been insulted until well after the event, but that one he got. Fortunately, Snorri wasn't in the habit of listening to trolls, even if they could talk, and instead strode under the Troll King's hands while he was still talking and cracked the teeth from a dozen gnashing mouths with a blow from his hammer. Snorri grinned at the Troll King's indignant roar and drew back his arm for another blow. Who was stupid now?

The Troll King's fist hit like a cannonball.

'We will return to Karak Kadrin,' said Borek firmly. 'I expect there is an oath there that you will wish to make.'

'After,' said Snorri, sadly. 'After Snorri tells Gotrek's family what he did.'

Snorri came to with arms and legs flapping, just a second before he slammed into the cage behind. The bars caved around him as though a big, clawed hand had just risen out of the floor and caught him. Snorri's mouth worked in pain he couldn't find the breath for. Bent metal trapped his limbs. Something screamed that wasn't him and Snorri shifted his head around to see a gaunt human in threadbare black robes holding out clasped hands and yammering while he backed further into his cage.

'My thoughts are gifts from the gods, you moronic, dirt-chewing oaf. They will not be broken by the likes of you.'

The Troll King readied a fist and this time Snorri saw it coming in good time. It was a club of overlapping crystal edges and was almost as large as Snorri was. He heaved on his mace-leg but couldn't free it in time, then turned his face aside as the blow landed.

Snorri let the body drop, then slumped down onto his backside beside it. Injured dwarfs groaning and whimpering all around, he took a sip from his liberated ale skin. What had that ranger been trying to say about towns and goblins?

Sharp, glittering debris tinkled from Snorri's shoulders as he wobbled upright. For a second his jumbled memories couldn't place where he was, but then the swirling in front of his eyes slotted together. It looked as though he'd been punched right through the bars and into the pale human's cage. The human lay unconscious amidst a pile of glass and metallic debris that lay between Snorri and the mangled remnants of the cage's front wall. The Troll King glared at him from the other side.

'Why are you smiling?'

'Was Snorri smiling?'

With a roar of fury, the Troll King wrenched the breach in the cage wider and pushed through a rugged shoulder. 'You are infuriating, dwarf. An insult to every beast that stares in stupidity at the stars and cannot wish to comprehend.'

Blinking away the last of his daze, Snorri kicked aside a sheet of corrugated metal and threw himself forward with axe and hammer held high. The Troll King blocked Snorri's hammer on the craggy crystalline stuff that covered its wrist in the same way an adult would fend off a child. Breathing hard, Snorri ducked under the return blow, bashing his mace-leg into the Troll King's shin in a hail of dark green shards, and then hammered his axe into the troll's waist where it stuck with an unsatisfactory flat *thump*. With a rumble of laughter, the Troll King brought his elbow crashing down on Snorri's bald head.

Smoke hung over the western hills and Snorri nearly choked with worry as he fumbled drunkenly for his hammer and ran the last miles home. The village burned. Dwarfs floated face up in the Skull River with goblin arrows in them. Their livestock lay butchered on hillsides that had since been torched.

Who? How?

Snorri tottered back minus his axe, metal leg stepping awkwardly on the uneven carpet of detritus. He looked up to see a knee the size of a black orc's spike-bossed shield driving towards his face. Oh yes, Snorri thought with a grin that hurt his neck, Snorri had forgotten.

Dwarfs floated face up in the Skull River with goblin arrows in them. Their livestock lay butchered on hillsides that had since been torched.

'Your skull has grown thick from too many beatings,' came a deep gravel-pit voice that jarred Snorri from his memories. He was still here, he concluded with disappointment, so probably couldn't have been out for more than a few seconds. The Troll King stood a few feet away, hunched like an ape under the cage's roof, arms spread so that they hung off the left and right walls. A joyous, self-hating, animal gleam shone from its eyes. 'Perhaps that is why your brain is so slow.'

'No. Snorri has always been this way.'

'Then for a dwarf you are very stupid.'

'You're pretty clever for a troll. Does that make Snorri more smart or less? He's confused.'

'You–'

Whatever the Troll King had intended to say sank into a volcanic pit of rage as, with a roar that caused stonework to shake and glassware to shatter, he hauled down on one shoulder without letting go of the bars. Pitted against the Troll King's strength, the entire cage wall bent inwards and came away from the bolts connecting it to the ceiling bar and the floor. The unsupported roof tipped down onto the Troll King's head, but he shrugged it off, ripping out the opposite wall as well and wielding both as improvised weapons. Snorri hefted his hammer.

The Spider Lady had been right. This would be a mighty–

The two squares of iron smacked together around Snorri like cymbals.

The sweet smell of well roasted meat filled the air. It disturbed the ale sloshing in his otherwise empty belly and he threw up over the bloodstained flagstones.

He swayed for a few seconds before a hand like a wall scooped him up and in the same motion thrust him into the stone wall at the back of the cage.

He dropped to his knees to vomit, crunching the charred ribcage of a goblin raider that had been hidden under the layer of soot. A high-pitched war cry stopped his heart and he turned to one of the burning buildings.

He was hauled back, bits of rock cascading over his shoulders. Crying an oath to Grimnir, he kicked out, chipped the troll's chin and bellowed as he was driven into the wall again.

A horribly burned fighter charged from the house towards Snorri. It was Gotrek's house, Snorri realised, fury souring the ale still in his belly as he rose, a blow from his hammer dropping the goblin in its tracks. The goblin fell onto its face and was still.

Snorri couldn't feel his hands. His eyes were going dark and it felt like some other dwarf being drawn out of the wall in the Troll King's tightening grip. This was what death felt like. Snorri was glad. There were times when he'd thought it would never happen and it wasn't nearly as terrible as the Spider Lady had said. He saw the old crone now over the Troll King's shoulder. She was smiling, pleased. Except it wasn't her at all, it was Ulrika. Only that made no sense. Ulrika would never stand by and watch even if Snorri had asked her, and he couldn't imagine her ever looking so hungry to watch someone die. Then it hit him with a blow to the heart.

It was surely the dwarf woman from his dreams!

The Troll King bellowed in annoyance at finding him still alive and Snorri felt himself flung forward again.

It was big for a goblin, and with long braids like a dwarf's. Snorri's anger turned cold.

What?

Snorri turned the body over. It was a dwarf woman with a golden chain.

No!

The old lady had promised Snorri that his doom would bring nothing but pain, and here it was. A new kind of determination welled up inside of him – for the first time in a hundred years he felt a powerful resolve to *live*. He had to confess. He had to make amends. Gotrek had to know who was responsible for his shame!

With every bone, tooth and nail that Snorri could lay onto the Troll King's fingers he fought, even as the blows kept coming and his struggles grew ever weaker.

The last impact he didn't even feel.

And then Snorri Nosebiter closed his eyes.

'No!' Felix's cry hung in the hollow space that had just been torn from his chest.

He staggered under the door frame and into the brightly lit cell chamber as though struck under the ribs with a knife. He couldn't breathe. He watched with a numb, distant kind of horror as Throgg withdrew his fist from the stone wall and let Snorri drop lifelessly from the gouge he had been driven into. A patter of loose mortar covered him like earth scattered over a grave.

Not Snorri, Felix found himself wishing, as if the gods ever heeded that kind of prayer from the likes of him. The old Slayer was cheerful and kind, as innocent as a child.

Why did it have to be Snorri that fell?

A shift in the rubble and the tangled bars warned of the movement of the Troll King and Felix gripped his sword with a hate so sudden and intense it crowded out every other sensation. He was aware only vaguely of the racket being raised by the creatures in the surrounding cages. Broken glass crunched underfoot as Felix strode towards the towering figure. Karaghul burned his eyes with the hateful glare of the surrounding torches, blinding him until the final second to the figure that slid out from behind the Troll King and blocked his path with a cold, hard hand on his shoulder.

She was clenched inside a battered suit of pearl-white plate armour like a crumpled ball of bloodstained paper. Her ash-blonde hair had been pulled ragged, as though raked by the inch-long claws that dripped blood from her fingertips. Her eyes were dominated by huge black pupils that stared out from some lightless place. The hunger in those empty pits was enough to startle Felix from his grief, but even then it required a conscious moment to recognise Ulrika behind that twitching, snarling visage.

'What did he do to you?'

Ulrika merely hissed and drooled.

Behind her, Throgg turned fully from the wall and drew himself as near to his full height as the ceiling allowed. His tattered red cloak fell back from his shoulders to reveal a chest riddled with regeneration scars, crossbow bolts, tumourous warpstone growths, and mouths that gasped in a constant fix of hunger or suffocation. At the sight of a familiar axe embedded in the troll's waist, Felix gave a strangled cry of loss and took an unconscious step back.

The Troll King lifted his gaze over Felix as the sound of huffing men finally rounded the last turn of the stairwell and Gustav, Kolya and the rest crunched out onto the carpet of broken glass, doing their best to shield their eyes from the sudden glare. Gotrek followed just behind, a consequence only of his shorter stride rather than any sign of his wounds catching up with his formidable stamina. His axe glowed red as though hot from the forge, bright even by the standards of the over-lit chamber. Ulrika slithered back from the touch of the rune-light on her skin.

Gotrek absorbed what had happened with a single sweep of his unblinking gaze. 'A good death. Well earned.'

Felix bit on the impulse to snap back with something sharp. It was easy to be magnanimous now, but where had Gotrek's compassion been when Snorri was alive and hurting? Whatever secrets

Snorri had wanted to tell his friend about his shame went with him to his afterlife now.

Watching Gotrek's axe warily, the Troll King edged backwards, iron bars and alchemical apparatus buckling underfoot as he moved towards another open door at the far side of the chamber. Felix started after him, but Ulrika's marble grip on his shoulder stopped him in his tracks with a gasp, forcing him to lower his sword as the effortless crush cut off the blood to his arm.

'These are the friends that abandoned you to this, Ulrika,' said Throgg, continuing to back away towards the door. The vampiress bared her fangs and snapped at the mention of her name, but some command in the Troll King's voice spoke directly to the beast that now owned her. 'There are things I cannot leave behind. Ensure that none pass and their blood is yours to feast on.'

That elicited a mindless grin and Felix groaned as the pressure on his shoulder intensified. Did Ulrika even realise her own strength any more?

'This isn't you Ulrika, I know it. Help us to stop him. Come back to the Empire with us.'

Ulrika met his eyes but if she comprehended a word of what he said there was no sign of it. Her fangs glistened with bloody saliva. She stared at his temple vein, lips twitching as a shudder of hunger passed through her body and elicited a gasp from Felix as it reached the hand gripping his shoulder. With only his free hand, Felix managed to lift the tip of his sword off the ground.

'I told you, manling,' said Gotrek as he strode forward with axe raised. 'Didn't I tell you?'

'Go after the troll!' Felix screamed. 'Ulrika is mine, do you hear me?'

Never in his career as Gotrek's henchman had Felix dared speak to the Slayer like that but, without a word spoken to convey his understanding, Gotrek lowered his axe and ran past. Ulrika hissed and looked up to watch the dwarf go, caught in animal indecision between satisfaction now and the command of a master who already seemed a foggy memory. It was all the opening that Felix could hope to expect.

With a cry that gave vent to all his pain and his grief, Felix lashed around with his sword. He knew that he had little chance of causing a being as powerful as Ulrika anything more than an inconvenience with a blow struck from his supine position at Ulrika's feet, but he did it anyway. The ornate dragon's-maw grip guard cracked her in the ear and the base of the blade scored a shallow cut across her scalp, and elicited a startled bark. In an agonising pulse of sensation, Felix felt blood rush back into his arm as Ulrika's grip loosened and then instinct took charge.

Pushing up through his buckled knees Felix rammed himself into Ulrika's chest. She might have had the strength of twenty men and powers beyond his ability to comprehend but in one sense at least she was still a rapier-thin woman, far lighter than he was, and they both fell to the ground. Ulrika reacted like a cat, flipping onto all fours and punching deep into the stone where Felix had fallen before rolling hurriedly away. Again, she turned to chase after Gotrek but Felix brought her attention back with a stabbing thrust for a gap in her back armour where buckling had caused the shoulder plates to push apart. Spotting the stroke at the last second, the vampiress spun away with frightening speed, drawing her sabre in the same blinding motion and parrying Felix's sword with an impact that ravaged through his still aching shoulder.

Lips twitching, transitioning between something not quite animal and something almost human, Ulrika smiled at something behind Felix's back. 'My loves. See how this man threatens me. Protect me.'

Felix's heart sank as he felt men close on him from behind.

No, Ulrika. Please, no.

'Put down the sword, uncle.'

Felix shifted to try and cover his side with the cage to his left, but what the men lacked in martial discipline they made up for in brawlers' instincts and that included knowing how to corner one man into a tight spot with five. Felix, though, didn't take his eyes off Ulrika – or whatever it was she had let herself become.

'You're not yourself, Gustav. If any of this makes any sense to you right now then I'd love to hear it.'

'Oh, it makes sense. You're jealous.'

Felix shook his head, eyes forward.

'Don't lie to me! I read that pathetic pfennig dreadful you call a biography. I know that you and General Straghov were together in the past. You had your chance and squandered her. You disgust me, you adulterous popinjay.'

Maybe it was that final barb that made him snap, but Felix spun around and threw a punch to the jaw that snapped back Gustav's head and knocked the man cold before Felix even knew what he was doing. Gustav flopped into the arms of his man behind.

'One small lapse, damn you.'

'*Doskonale*,' Kolya boomed approvingly. The Kislevite, apparently forgotten by everyone, observed proceedings from the doorway. He lifted a foot and drew a long hunting knife from his boot. 'A good hit for an Empire man.'

Ulrika snarled and lunged for Felix just a second after her thralls fell on Kolya. This time Felix was able to anticipate her speed even if he could never hope to match it, and got his sword in the way. The phenomenal application of strength smacked Felix's sword against his own mail and staggered him into the back of a grizzled soldier just as he was about to thrust at Kolya with a spear. The strike went wide. The Kislevite parried another with his knife, then clubbed his attacker senseless with an elbow between the eyes. The soldier crashed back against the bars of the cage behind him, leading to an upsurge of noise from the prisoners still held all around. A *boom* sounded overhead and dust rained from the ceiling, but Felix had no time to consider it. He pushed the spearman out from under him and returned his attention to Ulrika.

Why was she still here? Gustav's distraction had given her ample opportunity to escape.

The vampiress twitched, a ripple tracking the course of her jugular vein as if some pernicious corruption fought with her own vampiric blood for dominance. 'I dreamed of you after Krieger remade me. So many days. I dreamed of hunting you, catching you, tearing the blood from your heart and feasting until I drowned.'

Disgust crawling up his throat Felix angled his sword for a rising slash across Ulrika's chest, but before he could make the swing Ulrika extended a long claw and uttered what sounded like a lullaby and the strength in his limbs began to fade away. Felix gasped at the sudden paralysis and sought reflexively to bring his sword back up into a guard. His arms remained stubbornly where they were, not numb, not dead – just *stuck*.

The din from the surrounding cages had reached fever pitch and Ulrika smiled as if nothing could be more pleasing, watching the brawl being fought behind Felix's back. She reached out to stroke Felix's cheek with the back of her hand, knotting her claw in his beard.

'I lied to you, Felix. You left Katerina with child to be with me.'

Felix pulled back his head, but there was only so far he could defy her while she controlled his arms and legs.

'I suspected,' said Felix. 'Helbrass showed me a vision of a child and...' He trailed off as his mind ran back to an event that he had not since considered the ramifications of. 'You knew from the first moment. I thought you must have been mistaken but you knew and you intended to make Kat a vampire anyway.' Angrily, he tried to lunge at her but to no avail. 'You would have killed my child!'

Ulrika gave a hissing laugh, delighting in his futile struggles and his pain, and dragged the claw in his beard down to his throat. The hairs all over Felix's body tingled and he felt a pressure building on his ears. Powerful magic was being gathered somewhere nearby and, judging from the feral gleam currently occupying Ulrika's eyes, Felix doubted it was hers. His eyes rolled left to where a skaven hissed at him with unfettered malice through the bars of its cage.

Felix groaned. They were surrounded by sorcerers whose captor had just fled. No wonder he felt that he had walked right into the jaws of a trap.

'Let him go, Ulrika.'

The voice came from the direction of the doorway that had just taken Gotrek and the Troll King. The torches bracketed either side of it burned with an eerie absence of any light and the cages and floorspace around them were mired in blackness from which Felix could discern only the outline of a human figure. The voice was familiar, but etched with a deep pain that Felix would never have forgotten had he heard it before. It was the voice of a man who had seen how the world was to die.

At the sound of it, Ulrika cringed as if from an open flame and turned her face from Felix to see it.

'Max. This is for you.'

'I was not asking.'

Squinting into the gloom, Felix saw him. Captivity had changed him. He was gaunt, hunched and unwashed, apparently wearing the same ivory and gold battle magister's robes in which he had been taken captive half a year ago at Alderfen. The change that had come over him however went far beyond that. The whites had faded utterly from his eyes and his skin had bedimmed to a mealy grey. It was as though every pure glimmer of light had been drained from his body. There could be no mistake, though.

It was Max.

Ulrika flung Felix down as though he had been trying to force himself upon her and turned instead to Max. 'Help me, Max. Help me. I didn't want this. I thought I would be strong enough. I thought that Felix–' A shudder wracked her armoured body. Her head jerked as if to shake off some intrusion of her mind and she balled her clawed hands into fists. 'I was doing what had to be done. I'm just… so… *hungry.*'

'I see that,' said Max, sorrow in his bearing. 'And I can help you.'

The wizard extended a hand and, through a clear strain of will-power, the shadow that enveloped that portion of his body began to force out a sublimating white light. Ulrika shied away from it, meshing her claws before her eyes like a shield, and, in a sibilant tongue that hissed betrayal, spat a counter-spell of her own.

Felix felt his own open wounds shiver from the touch of Dark Magic, and then gasped as blood was drawn from them to thread through her hair like a lover's forget-me-nots. Strength returned to his limbs as her attention left him behind and he redoubled his grip on his sword.

She was so achingly beautiful. And she was right, of course – he would always love her.

He swung his sword for where her shoulder plates hung loose, decapitating her in one clean stroke.

A sob burst from him unexpectedly and he had to cover his face with his arm and take several heaving breaths before he dared look at her body. It was surprisingly bloodless and shockingly mundane. There was no cloud of dust or sudden onset of rot, but then Ulrika had been relatively young. There were mortal men still living who were the richer for sharing in her life.

'*Starovye*,' said Kolya with a gentle pat on the back. 'In Dushyka dead things go in the ground and we do not expect them to grow.'

Felix ground his eyes and held his tongue. There was just too much death.

'You did not have to do that, Felix,' said Max quietly. 'She was a child with those powers. She could not have harmed me.'

'You shouldn't have been the one to do it,' said Felix, pinching tears from his eyes and wiping his nose on his cloak. 'I think you loved her more than I ever really did. And you always were more deserving of her.'

'Maybe that was true once. Now?' The mage looked down at his shaded hands. 'Nagash's rise affected everyone with a close bond to the aethyr. Perhaps that is why Ulrika fell so far so fast.'

'No, she was always this way. She was always too in love with strength.' He took a settling breath and turned to Max, reaching out to take the wizard's arm. He had expected it to be cold but aside from being far too thin it felt more ordinary than it looked. 'Are you well enough to go?'

Max smiled. 'As opposed to being well enough to stay? Just give me a few minutes. It will take that long to heal these men in any case and doing something good with my magic will undoubtedly be a restorative for me as well.' He glanced back through the bars of the nearest cage, past the hissing ratman, to something beyond. 'Strange how being on this side of the bars changes one's perspective.' He sighed. 'At the time it all seemed so right, but I fear there is also a terrible mistake I need to rectify.'

Felix nodded and turned to Kolya. The rangy Kislevite was resheathing his knife in his boot.

'What are you doing?'

'I swore to see the zabójka die,' said Kolya, tapping the concealed blade. 'So I will not need this.'

EIGHTEEN

The Honesty of Death

Snow drove in through the high windows. It swirled and it cut and it froze the eyes if they stared too long into the churning white. Wherever there was an object large enough to stand against it the snow piled up in drifts, half buried treasure glittering on the surface like crystals in white stone.

The pinnacle of the Ice Tower was a trove, and one that had been collected by a most unfussy magpie. Rare books in filigreed leather bindings lay in stacks or in snow-covered heaps beside jewelled weapons, artefacts of Scythian silver or Ropsmenn amber and items of a scientific or magical nature so arcane in their value that only a handful of men left in the world would recognise them as precious. Against one wall, raised on a plinth of shields and chests and other artefacts all buried in snow, rested the ducal throne of Praag. It was a grim, imposing affair, as befitted the cursed city, carved from a single piece of rare Shirokij oak and embellished with cold stone. The strength or guile required to manoeuvre it to this high place was astounding. Incalculable wealth, troves of knowledge, and cultural beauty lay scattered like seed for the snow. Standing against one arm of the throne was a portrait of a raven-haired beauty with the eyes and cheekbones of the Sylvanian aristocracy before the coming of the vampire counts and garbed in the attire of that era. It looked to be a signature piece of the great portraitist, Kantor, one of the most influential to emerge from a city that had in his time been as famed for its culture as for its high walls and its kossars. It was worth a fortune.

And then Gotrek put his foot through it.

The backing board cracked under the Slayer's ironshod boot, ripping the canvas, while the frame, itself a minor work of art, snapped like a twig as the dwarf kicked the encumbrance off his ankle and ducked. The Troll King's massive stone hammer smashed the ducal throne to flying splinters. Gotrek covered his face with a massive arm and dived for the cover of a Gospodar tapestry, but too slow to prevent his arm and back from being stippled with slender wooden daggers. Throgg bellowed in horror at the irreplaceable beauty he had destroyed, goading himself to ever greater fury as he brought his hammer crashing down on that tapestry mere moments after Gotrek had got clear and hacked his axe across the monster's shins.

Felix wondered at the contradiction of a monster who would collect and treasure such things, when he was reminded of something he had read – it might have been a play by Tarradasch – which described a great work of art as 'loneliness's window'.

Then he thought he understood.

Throgg lifted his bleeding leg, the wound already clenching shut, and stamped the foot down where Gotrek had been. Snow flew back into the air to add to the swirl. Coins and jewels scattered like marbles. Felix debated whether or not to intervene, but this was Gotrek's fight as much as Ulrika had been his. It was Troll King against Trollslayer, but more than that it was about vengeance for fallen kin and the rememberers had no part in it.

Gotrek stood in knee-deep snow, his chest rising and falling like a bellows. The rune-light of his axe on the snow and his steaming breath gave him a red aura, deepening the dwarf's empty eye socket until it resembled a pool of blood and throwing short and lancing shadows from the arrow in his bare chest. His crest was singed by acid and fire but somehow, like the Slayer himself, it still stood.

The Troll King came in with his huge sledgehammer in a short grip, wielding the stone hammerhead almost as an extension of his own fists. Gotrek met the Troll King blow for blow, fighting with jaw clenched and teeth bared. Besides the rasp of his breath and the occasional grunt as his axe struck rock armour from Throgg's hide, the Slayer fought in bitter silence. After one brutal exchange that had Gotrek furiously ducking and parrying, the Troll King gave a bottomless howl of frustration and flung his hammer out to its full length. He caught it at the base of the haft and swung it over his head, a dipping and cresting figure-of-eight that ploughed through antique cabinets and projecting columns alike and filled the chamber with a withering haze of debris.

Felix swore.

The chamber was surprisingly large when devoid of cages, but not nearly big enough for his comfort just then. He flung himself back to the wall and pressed himself flat as the hammerhead shot around at head height with a *whump*. Displaced air thumped his face. The bellows of the Troll King filled the chamber. Out of the corner of his eye he saw Kolya stumble into a dresser and then drop into a foetal crouch as Throgg's hammer ripped through and buried him in kindling. Felix had a moment to think while the hammerhead shot around the room in an arc of destruction before whirring back at floor level.

At the last second, Felix clambered onto a gold-banded pinewood chest, took a breath, then screamed as it was smashed apart from under him.

The hammer's impetus threw him a short way and he landed on his feet in the snow by one of the gaping windows. The ground beneath him wobbled and he realised he must have landed on a buried plate or shield. His heart lurched as it pitched him towards the window. He flailed but there was nothing to grab that hadn't already been reduced to firewood and, for a second in which time slowed to a heartless crawl, it felt that the only thing holding him aloft was the icy wind pushing against his back. His fingers clawed through snow and air until a rag-bound hand caught them and pulled him back from the edge.

Kolya flinched and dragged Felix low as the Troll King's hammer whirred not far overhead. Felix nodded thanks and drew himself up against the wall beside the window, spreading his arms across it to reassure himself that it was not about to be taken away. Unable to help himself, he looked down. His stomach turned.

It was a long way down to the Square of Heroes.

The snow blinded what should have been a view across the entire city and beyond. Felix could see ghost glimmers of light within the snow. Occasionally another would flare brightly into existence before burning back. It could have been fires spreading through the city, some kind of artillery bombardment from the besiegers without or perhaps even some kind of magical assault. It was impossible to say for sure. The wind rushing through his hair brought thin and distant cries, like the sound of the sea heard through a shell.

'I do not recall the troll having that weapon before,' said Kolya.

Tearing his eyes from the view, Felix clasped his hands around his sword. It seemed likely that Throgg had stored a weapon here for this eventuality, planning the necessities of an escape that he had foreseen might one day be required. Felix found himself looking around the devastated chamber, wondering what treasure the Troll King could not leave Praag without. The thought saddened him. Here was Kislev and he was watching its destruction.

'Enough of this!' Felix yelled, long hair whipping about his face as he brought up his sword. 'I didn't come all this way to watch at the end.'

'Wait,' Kolya shouted back. 'Give the zabójka his chance.'

'Fulfil your oath your way. I'll do so in mine.'

A throaty roar pulled the men's attention back from the precipice in time to see Gotrek's axe slice through Snorri's embedded weapon and cut deep into the Troll King's abdomen. Thick blood spurted through the Slayer's crest and Throgg's bellows turned from anger and frustration to pain. Scything his hammer back across his path, Throgg stumbled back. Almost immediately the wound began to regenerate, but Gotrek's axe struck faster even than the Troll King's metabolism, carving up fresh wounds faster than the old ones could be healed. The Slayer was tearing the troll apart piece by piece.

'I can make you a rich dwarf, Trollslayer,' Throgg roared, making a desperate parry and losing a thick wedge of his hammerhead to Gotrek's starmetal blade. Gotrek's axe answered for him, turning the Troll King's hammer and slicing its blade through the mouths in the mutant troll's side, and tearing off a scrap of red cloak. Throgg clasped his hand to his bleeding hip and howled so loudly that the snow whipping around him was momentarily shaken to a standstill. 'There is wealth here beyond your imagining. A copy of the Karak Ungor Book of Grudges, perhaps, brought to Praag by its people after the hold's fall. Now it is here. There is more. It is yours.'

Gotrek ground his teeth and pressed the Troll King into full retreat with a storm of blows. He was being pushed towards the window, Felix realised, sliding out of the way and circling around the chamber wall with his sword raised in a guard.

Throgg caught the bright flutter of his shredded cloak and turned to face him. His huge body was framed within the opening by a rippling white canvas of snow. 'An alliance between my Troll Country and the counts of Sylvania, Felix – think of it. Max was wise enough to understand that I can save your Empire.'

Felix shook his head. He didn't consider himself especially wise, but he understood the Troll King's argument well enough. Maybe it was even true that alliances with acceptable monsters like Throgg were the only way that the Empire would survive the current strife. Ulrika had certainly thought that way, but she had been cozened by easy power, and all Felix saw when he tried to see things her way were the bodies of those he loved.

Snorri.

Ulrika.

Even poor Damir had deserved better than he'd got.

A cold fury simmered in his chest. How did this beast even dare look him in the eye and request a boon of him? He took a deep breath and returned the Troll King's gaze.

Felix lowered his sword tip to the ground and gave the Troll King nothing.

'I am surrounded by fools,' Throgg growled, sweeping up his hammer and sending Felix and Kolya scrambling for cover. Gotrek simply stood with a faint leer of condescension on his brutal features. Throgg held his hammer poised above his head with the Slayer in his sights, and roared with confounded intellect. 'There is not one here whose race deserves to survive more than mine.'

Gotrek stepped negligently to one side as Throgg's overarm stroke crashed through snow and flagstones alike with a force that shook the floor and had Felix hugging the wall for fear that it would collapse. Gotrek stamped his boot on the hammerhead as if to pin it down, then stepped fully onto it and brandished his axe above his head.

'My father fought the bloodsuckers at Hel Fenn. I'd sooner spend the rest of my days digging dwarfs' graves than lend my axe to them or you.'

A look of malignant cunning entered Throgg's eyes and in that second Felix saw what the troll meant to do. If the Slayer didn't move when Throgg pulled back on his hammer then Gotrek was going to be going right over the troll's shoulder and out the window for good measure.

'Fools all!' Throgg roared, drowning out Felix's warning shout as huge muscles bunched under the Troll King's arms and he pulled.

Gotrek swayed for balance as he rose off the ground, spreading his feet across the stone and bringing his axe streaking down to shear through the hammer's wooden haft. The Slayer rode his blockish stone mount for another few feet before it ran out of momentum and crashed back to the ground. The Troll King, however, found himself suddenly pulling against nothing. His arms flew back over his head and the mammoth beast stumbled. A foot trod in emptiness and Felix saw the comprehension in Throgg's bitterly intelligent eyes as the distant earth secured its grip.

The Troll King screamed as he fell.

Felix tried to track his fall, but the blizzard had swallowed him whole and soon blew over even his cries. It was as though the Troll King had fallen into a pit with no bottom. Shaking his head, Felix withdrew from the edge. He felt like he hadn't taken a breath in days.

It was done. They were probably all dead men, but it was done. Not for the first time, he found cause to pick fault with whatever so-called destiny had brought him to this sorry place and time.

'Troll thought it was cleverer than everyone,' said Gotrek, peering down with his one good eye before spitting after Throgg to add a salty dose of insult to his injuries, and then stabbed a reversed thumb into his chest beside the arrow that was still stuck there. 'Well, this dwarf was an engineer.'

'Are you sure he is dead?' said Kolya. 'It is a big fall, but he is a troll.'

With a grunt, Gotrek turned his back on the ledge and leant his axe against his shoulder. 'I'm not walking all the way down there to find out.' The Slayer deflated and shook his head glumly. He turned to Kolya. 'That old woman promised me a doom.'

'And one for your companion,' added Kolya with a pointed nod towards Felix.

Felix looked at them both blankly. This was, unsurprisingly enough, news to him. No one explained themselves, but he found he couldn't rid his mind of the image of a headless body in bloody white plate.

Ulrika.

'She also promised one for Snorri.'

Snorri Nosebiter stood under the doorway at the top of the stairs and Felix doubted he had looked as hale on the day he departed Karak Kadrin for the north. The injuries he had suffered in the battles leading up to the citadel had been closed. Even the ugly and infected wounds that the removal of his crest of nails had left in his head had shrunk to pinpricks of scar tissue. If not for the blood that no one had yet found time to clean from his massive torso and the rips in his breeches, Felix would have assumed he was looking at a ghost.

Felix would have kicked himself if he wasn't laughing so hard.

Snorri wasn't dead at all!

Max Schrieber followed the old dwarf up looking tired and drawn, but his efforts healing Snorri and the others seemed to have proven the purgative to the system that the wizard had thought it would be. That eerie shadow still clung to him, but he seemed more himself, even finding the spirit to express dismay at the ruined treasures around him. Looking troubled and confused as though just woken from an unsettling dream, Gustav and his men filled the stairwell behind the old Slayer's broad shoulders.

They might all have been just portraits of men borne on Snorri's back for all the attention they received from Gotrek. Even Max, with all the strangeness of his appearance, garnered little more than a raised eyebrow.

'Snorri has to talk to you,' said Snorri, staring fixedly at Gotrek. Felix had never seen the simple-minded dwarf so focused, so intense.

'If it's about your shame then I still don't want to hear it,' said Gotrek.

Felix shook his head. For a race so infamously resistant to altered circumstances, Gotrek had taken his friend's near-resurrection in his stride.

'Snorri,' said Felix in his most conciliatory tone, sliding between the old Slayer and Gotrek. 'Perhaps this isn't the best t–'

'No!' Snorri roared, striding forward and pointing an angry finger past Felix at Gotrek. 'No. You will listen to Snorri now.'

Felix held up his hands in an appeal for calm but he might as well have been invisible. Gotrek stuck out his chin and squared his shoulders.

'I'm listening.'

That seemed to take Snorri aback and his upper lip started to tremble. Felix noticed that he was carrying something golden in his hand.

Sigmar, no, Felix prayed. He had already lost Snorri once.

As if Felix were a child, Snorri pushed him out of the way and tossed the golden chain towards Gotrek who snatched it out of the air without looking. His one-eyed gaze held Snorri's for a moment before lowering to his open palm. His breath caught and for a moment Felix thought that both dwarfs were going to weep, but then Gotrek's expression darkened as if the sun had just passed away.

'The Spider Lady told Snorri that when all his friends were together again he would have his doom. She told him it would bring nothing but pain.'

Gotrek held out the hanging chain. 'You tell me where you found this, Snorri Nosebiter, and pray that it's a good tale.'

Snorri's eyes were puffed red as he shook his head but, though there was a tremor in his voice, his words were clear, as if recited from rote. 'Snorri was there that day. He went home after he and old Borek lost you in the Wastes. It is his fault nobody warned them of the goblins. It is his fault–' The threatened crack appeared at last, but Snorri managed to pass it and continue. 'That you murdered that thane and had to become a Trollslayer. It is all Snorri's fault!'

Gotrek hadn't moved a muscle, but his eye glittered.

'I'm sure that's not true,' said Felix. A tension hung over the chamber as if the wind no longer blew and the temperature of the snow had dropped to somewhere far below the point at which human marrow froze. Gustav looked between the dwarfs as if they had to be mad and Felix didn't blame him. Max simply wore the stunned look of one too wearied by horror to reasonably process any more.

Kolya, however, had the fearful look of a man watching prophecy unfold.

Instinct caused Felix's fingers to tighten around his sword's grip. With a conscious effort he forced them to relax. What exactly did he plan on doing with it? Would he fight Snorri? For that matter, would he fight Gotrek?

'It's *not* your fault that you couldn't save Gotrek's family,' said Felix more firmly. However stubborn the two dwarfs wanted to be, this foolishness was *not* going to end in violence if Felix had any sway at all over either of them.

'Helga was still alive,' said Snorri.

There was a faint rattling sound that Felix realised was Gotrek's axe chain. The dwarf held his weapon so tightly that it shook. 'And the little one?' One of the pieces of Felix's heart broke a little more. *Little one.* That was what Gotrek called Kat. Shallya's tears, that had been what Gotrek called his daughter. 'What of Gurna, Snorri?'

Snorri shook his head. His eyes were wet, his cheeks red, and it looked like opening his mouth now would be the breaking of the dam.

'Tell me what happened to my wife, you clod-witted *zaki*.'

Tears streaking unchecked down his face, Snorri held out his hammer. 'It wasn't...' He paused, corrected himself. 'It was Snorri's fault. She was burned. It was smoky. Snorri thought it was a goblin. But it was Snorri's fault.'

Felix felt the death knell in his heart as Snorri uttered his next words.

'It is Snorri's fault you are a Slayer now. Snorri killed Helga.'

One muscle at a time, Gotrek's face tightened into an image of such primal fury that Felix found himself backing out of the way of it lest he unintentionally make himself a target. Gotrek glared at the hammer that Snorri held before him. 'I'd take that back if I were you.'

Nodding acceptance of what he had to have known must come next, Snorri did as he was bid, settling into what passed as a ready stance. Gotrek bared his teeth and brandished his rune-axe.

'It was an accident,' Felix screamed at the top of his lungs. 'Tell him it was an accident, Snorri. And Gotrek, I can't believe you have a better friend in this world.'

'I've killed better friends than Snorri Nosebiter,' said Gotrek.

Felix watched in anguish as the two old friends circled each other. There were no more words to be spoken.

Gotrek feinted left, then struck a short blow for Snorri's right shoulder. Half blind with tears, Snorri saw it late, parrying on his hammer with a sombre *clang* and replying with a punch across Gotrek's jaw. Gotrek took a step back to steady himself, then thumped out with the butt of his axe and cracked something under Snorri's armpit. The old Slayer took it with barely a grunt, swinging out with hammer and mace while Gotrek parried with a cold-simmering wrath.

'Stop this,' Felix croaked, realising that it was no longer just Snorri with tears in his eyes.

This could not be happening! Felix pinched the skin of his wrists between glove and sleeve. Surely this must be another dream.

The two dwarfs fought through the raging snow in bitter silence, barely even moving from the spot in which they'd started, their efforts punctuated only by the crunch of muscle and bone and Snorri's wracking sobs. It appeared even. Snorri had the clear advantage in brawn and the benefits of Max's healing, but Gotrek's axe balanced those odds considerably. Felix gave his head a violent shake. He couldn't believe he was even thinking about this, but nor did he dare to intervene. Snorri swung his hammer for Gotrek's temple with a shuddering sob only to see it blocked, then followed through with a kick of his mace that Gotrek turned aside by a deft interception with his knee. Snorri's metal leg was pushed behind him and landed in the snow amidst a loose pile of coins. He flung out his arms for balance, presenting Gotrek with as clear an opportunity for a killing blow as he was ever likely to see, but it was as if the Slayer didn't even see the opening, instead knocking Snorri back onto his feet with a jab from his axe butt.

Gotrek was holding back, Felix realised. Kolya and the others might not even have noticed, but Felix had known the Slayer too long. Had it been otherwise then Snorri Nosebiter would never had stood a chance.

'Fight Snorri properly,' said Snorri. 'Let him die like a Slayer. Let him walk in the Ancestors' Hall. Let him do something *right*.'

Felix watched with his hand over his mouth. He must have misheard. Surely even Snorri could not think of this as some act of kindness.

With his one eye scrunched tight, Gotrek unleashed a strangled roar and struck low. Snorri parried it, but Gotrek came again. Again Snorri blocked but there was no chance for him to counter now before Gotrek's axe came for him again and he was forced to give ground under a torrent of blows. Snorri fought furiously with tears running down his cheeks and blocking his squashed nose. Gotrek pressed him back with his eye still closed. Both wanted to die although neither wanted to kill, but they were both still Slayers.

To the end.

Gotrek's starmetal blade clove through Snorri's metal leg just below the attachment to his thigh. Snorri wobbled, an idiot smile on his tear-stricken face as Gotrek then cracked the flat across his mouth and knocked him down. The old dwarf looked up with a full face, wet eyes meeting Gotrek's one and seeing peace.

No, thought Felix. No, no, no–

He looked away.

There was a wet *crack*. Then a thump.

Felix buried his eyes in his hand and wept. Tears blurred the gaps between his fingers, but beneath him he saw blood seeping through the snow around his feet.

There was a moment's silence and then a voice at his side.

'We're done here, manling. I should never have let him talk me into that journey to Karag Dum. I knew I would regret it.'

Pulling his hand from his face and wiping tears into his beard in the process, Felix looked up. The Slayer's one eye was dead, his face a funerary mask of someone Felix no longer recognised. His

voice, however, was rune-hard and deadly clear.
And it brooked no argument.
'On my oath, you're going back to the little one where you belong.'

EPILOGUE

Early Spring 2525

Talisznia burned. The tirsa's stubborn earth huts glowed a fitful bronze, choking in smoke whilst yielding the barest flicker of flame. These were the last weeks of winter: the snow over the Eastern Oblast had become heavy as it turned slowly to ice and the tirsa's wood stores were all but exhausted. Tables and chairs had been used for cooking or whittled into arrow shafts. Even the precious stocks of dried grass and animal feed had been consumed weeks ago while the animals' dung, normally reserved over the deep winter as a fuel in case raspotitsa did not relinquish the roads before the wood stores ran low, had been turned to shoring up the stockade. There was not a single drop of kvass.

In short, there remained precious little in Talisznia of fit state to burn, but the Kurgan were determined to make a pyre of it just the same.

The wise woman did not know why, but the smoke billowed up into the endless blue expanse of the Ledevremya sky. It would have been visible for hundreds of miles, a tribute pole two miles high erected in blood and ash by the destroyers of Talisznia. Perhaps that was the reason, but she suspected that gave too much credit to their intelligence.

Watching from horseback half a mile out from the sputtering south stockade, she saw marauder horsemen race circuits of the conquered tirsa, brandishing the severed heads of its people and yelling at the top of their lungs. In a temporary encampment of rippling skin tents just out of bow range of the stockade, large bearded men with arms decked in silver rings fought over what meagre loot the vanquished of Talisznia had not already eaten or burned.

It was all precisely as she had foreseen it. The wise woman had shown these events and others to the dreams of so many. That was her gift, to cast dreams of portent into the aethyr that they might find a home in the unconscious of one to whom her prophecies bore special resonance. Through dreams had she foretold the Troll King's fall, the Auric Bastion's collapse, the sack of Rackspire and Badenhof and Bechafen and scores of other towns and forts that she knew only by the image of them aflame.

Sometimes she wondered how it would feel to have a dream of her own.

'You share your dreams with all, Morzanna, or whatever name you now go by, visions that could make an empire – or break one.'

The wise woman pursed her lips, studying the black eddies in the rising smoke. For a passing moment they formed sweeping black wings, a crown.

'Perhaps,' she answered, although she was alone but for the horse and the cutting oblast wind. 'No one I have forewarned has cheated my fate yet.'

'Is that regret I hear?'

'This is not the first time I have watched my home burn.' An ululating cry carried from the Kurgan encampment and she watched the zar and his chosen champions parade out from the slow-collapsing stockade in the glittering wargear of Stefan Taczak and the Dushyka rota. 'These were brave men. I gave you my soul but I still have a heart.'

'*Your pain soothes me in my oblivion, my daughter. I will taste of it more in the coming days.*'

Morzanna bared her sharp teeth in a reluctant smile. She knew. She had seen it. Why else would she be here?

'The daemon-slayer and his companion will try to stop you.'

The wind passed cold laughter over her ears. '*They will try, but they are destined to fail.*'

'How many times have I watched others make such a claim about those two?'

'*This time is different. The world is different. You have foreseen their demise and through you have I willed it so.*'

Morzanna shivered as the air around her cooled. A darkness bled into the sheer blue sky and the smoke of Talisznia rose like a horned black head to regard her – small in her evil, insignificant in her power, and but transient in her immortality. She nodded obediently and turned her horse around. It was a long way to the Empire.

'Yes, Dark Master.'

The saga of Gotrek and Felix will conclude in *Slayer*
March 2015

ABOUT THE AUTHOR

David Guymer is the author of the Gotrek & Felix novels *Kinslayer* and *City of the Damned,* along with the novel *Headtaker* and novella *Thorgrim,* and a plethora of short stories set in both the Warhammer World and the 41st millennium. He is a freelance writer and occasional scientist based in the East Riding.